Saddam's Horses

By Patricia A. Chenoweth

Debbie,

Enjoy

Jack

1

Dedication

This book is dedicated to my mom, Mary,

who believed I could do anything.

Editing by Colette Tozer

Cover art by Rodney Tozer

First Published by Tozer Publishing
2016

www.TozerPublishing.com

Acknowledgements

Anna – I think it is safe to say that without you this book would never have happened. You were the first reader and all you had to say was no, and the book would have forever been hidden in a file. Thank you so much for your encouragement and belief in my vision.

Connie- Thanks for being my cheerleader. You supported my ideas and my vision for the book. I know it got tiring night after night discussing plot lines but it helped immensely.

Cheri- You are aware I have the black thumb of technology. Thank you for your technical help and support throughout the book. I know what a thumb drive is now. We were there when Oprah said not to let this trip define us, well we have both went on to better ourselves and our community.

The Friday Night Crowd - Dee, Linda, and Susan- Thanks for your encouragement and ideas over many glasses of wine.

My niece Sarah and nephew Erik– You gave me the courage to put this book in print and were my role model to gracefully accept criticism.

Judy, BettyJo, and Libby- Thanks for all your encouragement and some great ideas.

Gail – When I wrote about Ree riding, you were my model. Thanks also for your technical riding advice.

To the Outlandish fellow travelers- Although you won't see much of our Scottish adventure in this book, look in the second book. I was inspired by the trip. To Marti, the best guide in Scotland - Let's storm a castle! And to Joe, the best driver in Scotland – thanks for the fairy glen.

To all my friends and family – You have always been there for me in the good times and bad. Thank you from the bottom of my heart.

Guinness – My rescue puppy. You were so patient as I was writing this book. You had the ball between your paws waiting to go out and play, while I was saying, "Just one more chapter."

Mike Begley – Thanks for the great pictures of Xeena. She is my Syn.

To the great horses in my life who taught me that it is the journey in life that is important everything else is just window dressing.

Finally, to Tozer Publishing, Colette and Rodney- You made my dream come true. I never believed I would hold my book in my hands. Thank you.

Table of Contents

Chapter 1

Eight months into the Iraqi War:

She could feel the horse's muscles ripple beneath her legs as she urged him faster. He flew, hooves barely touching the ground. She grabbed a tighter hold of his mane. Man and beast became one, as they galloped across the plain; the moon shining the way. Suddenly, the moon went behind the clouds, total darkness. Fear. She cried out.

An arm snaked around her waist.

"Be quiet."

She turned abruptly, pulling on the reins. The horse reared. She slid off and landed on her shoulder. Pain assaulted her body. She tried to sit up and saw hooves coming her way.

Her head exploded. Nothing...

Ree woke with a groan. The dream again. How many times this week? She lost count. She turned over and looked at the clock. Eight am. Feeling more like sixty-nine than her twenty-nine years, Ree crawled out from under the covers. She sat on the edge of the bed, rubbed her shoulder, and took a deep breath, trying to break up the brain fog caused by her dream.

After her head cleared, she made her way to the bathroom and splashed water on her face. As the droplets ran down her cheek she studied her reflection in the mirror. The same brown hair from last year, a bit longer.

The same blue eyes, a bit sadder; even the same dreaded freckles, everything the same but somehow different.

For some reason, she remembered her favorite car. She had gotten a job at Princeton University and to celebrate, she bought the car of her dreams, a red BMW. She had the car two weeks, when on her way home from school one evening, a deer ran into the side of her car. The deer flipped onto the roof down the windshield, onto the hood, and finally, to the ground. She was devastated, her new car, ruined.

Two weeks later the car was fixed. The first time she drove it, she knew something was not right. The auto shop assured her the car was like brand new. Ree disagreed. The car was not the same. After a month of back and forth, she traded the car in for another.

Ree felt like that car, fixed on the outside but still broken on the inside.

Unfortunately, she could not trade herself in.

She threw more cold water on her face to stop the inner musing. She brushed her hair and put on her riding clothes. As she made her way down the two-hundred-year-old staircase, each step creaked and squeaked protesting the added weight. They were comforting sounds, though, the sounds of home.

Ree put the kettle on for a strong cup of English Breakfast tea, her favorite. As she waited for the water to boil, she checked her agenda for today no appointments, just her and the horses. She poured her tea and stood by the old farm sink, looking out the window, towards the pastures.

It was a typical September morning in New Jersey. The fields were covered in a thick mist, the rays of the sun, fighting to break through. The horses walked in and out of the mist, giving them an ethereal look.

It was peaceful.

She glanced over to the barn and noticed that the workers had fed the horses their breakfast, her cue to get to work and begin her day. Ree started to walk out the door and saw her Mom's note on the table.

One word: Eat.

She grabbed a power bar and was off.

As she walked out the door she was hit with crisp air of fall. She took a deep breath and hoped this would clear her mind, in order to help her focus on work. On the path to the barn, Ree noticed that the ground spiders were busy last night. There had to be a hundred webs all over the grass and stones. The webs had the morning dew on them, so when the sun hit them, they shimmered like pieces of jewelry. The webs were beautiful in their complexity, but still deadly. She stopped and looked down at one of nature's feat of engineering. She sympathized with the trapped bug. Was she like the bug?

Ree went into her office; checked the schedule and went to work, answering calls and correspondence.

After a while, she got into the rhythm of work and was finally ready to concentrate on riding. One of the first lessons her Mom taught her about being a successful rider, no distractions. The rider always had to remain in the present.

"Leave your troubles on the ground when you mount your horse", her Mom would say.

Today, that rule was especially important.

Her first training session of the day was with Morgan, a black Friesian.

He was a dream to ride, very light and responsive. He reminded her of the horse in her dream, but she knew he wasn't.

She knew exactly who the horse in her dream was, a horse she could only dream about but never see, never ride again.

Before the past completely took over, she refocused and finished the workout.

As she walked Morgan to cool him down, Francisco, one of the ranch hands, approached her to tell her that someone was up at the house looking for her. Ree asked him to escort the man to the barn. She didn't have any scheduled appointments but it was not unusual for people to stop in to inquire about lessons or training.

She put the horse in the cross ties and started to unsaddle him when a shadow fell across the back of the horse. It was somewhat familiar.

"Hi Ree, it's good to see you. Did your Mom tell you I called a few times, asking about you?"

Ree tensed, the horse reacted. She put a hand on his neck to calm him and whispered to him.

She didn't know if it was more for him or for her. Was her nightmare coming true? This man, who was the architect of some of the best and worst times of her life, was back.

Jim Peterson, Assistant Director of the State Department. Why?

Ree did not know how to respond.

So, she simply looked at him.

Jim cleared his throat, "I didn't see your Mom up at the house. Is she home?"

She turned away from him and concentrated on the horse. "Mom went to Florida with a client to look at some new horses. She'll be home Sunday."

Jim let out a sigh of relief.

At least she's talking to me.

"How's she doing?"

Ree picked up the brush and started to groom the horse. "Mom's doing great. She certainly keeps me busy here at the farm. She's always coming up with a new project. It's good, though. How's Sarah and the kids?"

His shoulders relaxed and he took step towards her. "The girls are doing great. In fact, that's why I'm in the area. We took Jim Jr. for a tour of Princeton. He loves the school. I think it will be his top choice. He would be our last one to be sent off to college. I don't think Sarah is ready for the empty nest yet. Are you still teaching there?"

Ree stopped in mid-stroke.

After a few seconds, she finally said, "No, Dean Tomes gave me an indefinite leave of absence. They have been very understanding. My therapist told me I would know when I was ready, and I'm not ready yet."

"Your Mom told me about the counseling. How's it going?"

"I love my Therapist, Dr. Brown, she's great. At first, they wanted to give me medication, but I couldn't take it. It made me feel --- blah. When I first started the counseling, the dreams stopped altogether. Lately, though, I guess because the news of the Iraqi war is everywhere, they started up again."

Ree turned and looked him square in the face. "Why are you here?"

Jim looked down, a little unnerved by her stare. "Ree, I'm sorry. I'm here because I have to ask you something, something that's very important to the State Department, but I also think it's important for you."

"I don't understand."

"Have you been watching the news coming out of Iraq?"

"How can I avoid it; it's everywhere. I try but..." She whispered and sat down on the closest storage box.

He shook his head.

"I get it Ree, but there have been some positive changes with the surge. The military has doubled its efforts and things are finally quieting down. Order is being restored."

17

She took a deep breath.

"Maybe if you listened to me, there wouldn't be any need for a surge because there would not be any need for a war."

Jim moved closer to her and placed his hand on her shoulder. She winced.

"I appreciate your feelings, but you have to understand it was out of your hands. It was out of my hands. What happened, happened, and now we have to make the best of it."

She got up and started to pace. Finally, she threw her hands in the air.

"Make the best of it? Tell me, Jim, just how are we going to do that? Most of Baghdad has been bombed to kingdom come. People I loved are probably dead. The horses, oh God, the horses!" She took a deep breath and sat down again. "You asked if I watched the news. The last time I watched, they were showing people looting the Palace and the stables. They were leading the horses, those beautiful innocent horses, out into the street. Do you know what the newscaster said?"

Jim shook his head no.

Ree tried to control her emotions.

"He said that these horses were some of the most valuable in the world and would probably be butchered and end up on an Iraqi dinner plate."

He put arms around her.

"It's okay. I understand. You have to believe things are not as bad as they show on TV. Look, the surge is working; law and order is being restored in Baghdad. We want to show the people that life can return to normal."

"How are you going to do that? Turn back time?"

Jim could not help but smile at her last comment. The fire was still there.

"The government wants to restore successful programs that we had before the war."

Realization dawned of what he was asking; quietly at first then increasing in volume. "No, no, no! You cannot ask me to start up the school again."

"I'm sorry, but your school was very successful. The State Department wants to reopen it. We need you. It can work again and this time it will continue. We have Iraqi and Iraqi-American women willing to teach the classes. The people love you; if they see you there, we hope that they will have more trust in the program."

"But how? Most of Baghdad was bombed. I'm sure there is nothing left."

"Believe it or not, that neighborhood was hardly touched by the bombs. I've had my people check it out. The school and your apartment are still standing. Here's the best part. The neighbors loved the program so much, that when the war started they went to the school, and took all the computers, books, and supplies, and hid them. They are waiting for you to come back."

"Are you kidding me? Really?"

"Yes, really. I was told the effort was led by a Mrs. Hadine, the next-door neighbor. She told everyone you would be back. What do you say, Ree? Are you willing to give it another try?"

At any other time, she might have said no, but she read something the other day that gave her a new perspective. She had her therapist's appointment a week ago.

While she was in the waiting room, she picked up PEOPLE magazine. There was an article with pictures of celebrities attending charity events. On page twenty-three was the star of her nightmares. If Jim was the architect, then this man was the star. He was posing with a young Hollywood starlet.

They looked like the perfect couple.

Obviously, he had gotten back to his life; maybe it was time for her to get back to her life. He was in Texas. There was no way she would run into him in Baghdad.

"I am willing to give it some thought." Her eyes softened at the idea.

Jim hugged her. "I'm thrilled. I'll leave you a packet of information of what to bring. Also,

I'll send you directions on where to meet and the time of the flight. Sorry, this time it's military transport."

"I haven't said yes yet, but if I do, I have one condition."

"Name it."

"I don't need a handler this time; I don't want to be anyone's assignment; I can take care of myself."

"Don't worry Ree. I'll be going with you so more than likely you'll have to take care of me."

After Jim left, Ree retreated to her office, put her head down on her desk, and cried. She cried for all she lost. She cried for what could have been. She cried because she felt so broken. Maybe this was just what she needed to make her life whole again. How did everything go so wrong?

That night she dreamed again.

Chapter 2

Early September 2003:

Eight months before the war

Reanna Malloy

Princeton 106

Ree's heart pounded as she pulled into her parking space. Its' been two weeks since her new appointment and she still could not control her emotions when she saw her name on the placard. She wanted to jump on the roof of her car and do the Snoopy happy dance.

She longed to yell to the world, "I made it, a professor at Princeton University."

It was a true accomplishment, a professor at twenty-eight and the youngest in the Mideastern Studies Department.

Ree got out of her car and began the long walk to Woodrow Wilson Hall, where her classes were conducted. It was a beautiful September morning; the air was crisp, the leaves just starting to change colors. She took a deep breath, the chill energized her. Everyone thought she was crazy, but she loved Monday mornings. It was a new day, a new week, filled with endless possibilities.

Her lecture today was *Myths about the Burka.*

Ree expected the class to be overflowing, due to the topic. She had to give her students credit; they craved information about this region, which was so foreign to their own. It was challenging for her to present these sensitive topics in a fair and unbiased way. It was Ree's experience that so many people had the wrong idea about women and Islam. Most Americans believed that Moslem women were oppressed and forced to wear restrictive clothing like the burqa.

Although, it was true that in some cases the women were oppressed but in other cases, Moslem women opted to wear the burka, as a proclamation of their faith.

At the end of the lecture, she noticed the back door opened; Dean Tomes and another man entered. They stood in the back for the last few minutes of the lecture. When the last student left, the men approached the podium.

Dean Tomes shook her hand and congratulated her on her promotion.

"Professor Malloy, I would like you to meet James Peterson, a personal friend of mine and also, Assistant Director to the Secretary of State."

Ree was speechless.

Why would the Assistant Director be interested in her class?

She quickly regained her composure and shook his hand.

Jim was dressed impeccably in a black suit with a crisp, white shirt and red tie. He was tall and a good looking older man, probably in his mid-fifties.

"Professor Malloy, Jim would like to speak to you about a tremendous opportunity for you and your department. I will leave you two to your discussion, but Professor, I want you to know that whatever you decide, you will have the full backing of the university."

Jim motioned for Ree to sit at a small table by the podium, pulled out a manila folder, and handed it to her. "Ree, if I may call you that?"

She smiled and nodded, yes.

"Okay, Ree. A wealthy donor has given the State Department a very generous grant to open a school for women in the Mideast. The school will offer courses in English, computer, and business skills, as well as art and literature. We would like to open this school in Baghdad and would like you to get the school up and running, hire teachers, oversee curriculum, and maybe teach a class. What do you say?"

Ree was overwhelmed. She sat up straight in her chair and held the manila envelope like a piece of fine china.

"Mr. Peterson," She said breathlessly.

"Jim, please."

"Alright, Jim. What you are asking is a tremendous opportunity, but I have a commitment here." Ree wiggled in her chair, not sure if she wanted to bolt from the room or if she was impatient to hear more.

"I understand your concerns, but as Dean Tomes said, the university will support you if you decide to do this, and besides, I will guarantee that your position will remain open until you decide to come back. In reality, the

Dean knows this is a tremendous opportunity for you, the university and especially for your department. This grant will bring a lot of positive publicity to you and the school."

"But..." Ree could not process what was happening.

"I know it's a lot to take in, so I'm going to leave a packet of information for you to go through, along with my card with my direct number. Call me if you have any questions. Please read through the grant with an open mind. Dean Tomes told me you don't have classes on Friday, so let's say...today is Monday, that we set up an appointment for Friday, eleven am, at my office, in Washington, DC. While you are there, you can meet some of the people you would be working with. That is if you decide to accept."

Ree looked up at him and smiled. "You know, you remind me of someone I was very close to. Once he got something in his head, there was no stopping him. I haven't even said yes, yet!"

Jim's body language relaxed as he sat back in the chair. "Are you comparing me to your Dad?"

Ree looked momentarily surprised, but, after all, her father had been a part of the State Department for twenty-seven years.

"I didn't realize you knew my Dad."

"I knew and respected your Dad. I worked with him for a few years over in Baghdad. I remember the picture of you and your mom he had on his desk. In fact, one of the reasons we picked you is because of the experience you had with your Dad."

She raised her eyebrows questioning. "I don't understand?"

"According to what your Dad told me and what is on your resume, at age six, you spoke Farsi better than English. By the time you were ten, you were going on archeological digs with your Dad. He also had the picture of you and him with that piece of pottery he found. Let's face it, Ree, you practically grew up in Iraq. You're comfortable there. You know the people, the culture, the language."

She smiled at the memory. "He did love that piece of pottery. I still don't understand, why me?"

"How many summers did you spend in Iraq?"

"I started spending the summers there with my Dad when I turned six. I spent every summer and extended holiday there with him. I'm twenty-eight, so, twenty-two summers."

"Exactly and I understand you were a willing pupil of all things Mideastern. Your Dad was a great teacher and role model."

"Yes, he was. It is definitely where I get my love of the area. He was so enthusiastic about the region. He believed that one person or one program could have a tremendous impact on the area".

"Yes, and we at the State Department believe that this program, one of many we are planning, will do just that. Please, think about it. What do you think your Dad would say?"

This put a new spin on things. What would her Dad say about this opportunity? Should she 'go for it'? She was very tempted.

"Yes, I will definitely give it serious consideration. I'll be there. I'll see you Friday at eleven, but I haven't agreed, yet."

"All I can ask is that you give it serious consideration. By the way, how is your Mom? I never had the pleasure to meet her, but your Dad spoke of her often."

"She's doing great. Always busy at the farm. There are always new riding students and new horses to train. She loves it; the busier the better."

"I'm glad all is good with her. I'll tell you Reanna, I don't know how you did it: expert in Mideastern culture and nationally ranked Dressage rider. My hat's off to you."

"I had the two best mentors in the world, both the top of their field. I owe them everything."

Jim stood up and put on his coat. He told her his secretary would email her the time and directions to his office.

Ree watched him walk out the door. She got the sudden feeling that somehow her whole life was about to change.

Chapter 3

Reanna canceled her last class Thursday afternoon so she could get an early train to Washington. She knew she could drive or even take the bus, but to honor her Dad's memory, the only option was the train.

When Ree was a child, her Dad would come back from Iraq in early June. He spent time in Washington, then took some vacation and waited until Reanna was released from school for the summer. When she was young, he would meet her in New Jersey and they would take the train together. As she got older, she was able to take the train by herself and meet him at the train station in DC. Ree could easily pick him out of the crowd. He was the one that held a stuffed animal, when she was younger, and later, a bouquet of flowers. The reunion was always joyous.

When she arrived at the station, an empty feeling overwhelmed her. He would not be there to greet her; she held back the tears, got her suitcase, and went in search of a cab. She was off to the Washington Hilton where she had stayed with her Dad.

The Hilton was as she remembered, grand and stately. After a quick dinner, Reanna retired to her room and continued to study the packet of information Jim had given her. The more she read, the more uneasy she felt about the program. She could not put her finger on what was bothering her but something just didn't add up.

The next morning, during the cab ride to the State Department, Ree could not shake the uneasy feeling she had about this project.

She kept wondering, *why me?*

Was she doing the right thing?

She straightened her shoulders. After a lot of mental back and forth she decided, definitively; *Yes, I am. After all, I have been groomed my whole life for this opportunity.*

She checked her watch; it was only ten-thirty. She got there early, for some time to reminisce. When her Dad took her to work, they would often sit on the benches in front of the steps and watch the people coming and going. Her Dad told her they were regular people, but many had the power to change the world through their recommendations for foreign policy.

He would pick out the most ordinary looking person and make up a story about how this person would stop nuclear proliferation or an older grandmother-type would step up the war on terrorism. She would choose people with the same outrageous stories to share with her Dad. They would both laugh, as one tried to outdo the other. It was a great game but a game that got her to realize just how much a single person could influence world events. She wondered what impact if any, her little school would have on Mideastern relations.

She checked her watch, ten-fifty; time to go.

She picked up her briefcase turned and looked up the steps just as one of the doors opened.

Out walked a very handsome, no beautiful man. She could not help but stare at him. He was very tall with broad shoulders, trim waist, and long, strong legs. He had chestnut colored hair and when the sun hit it, it sparkled with red highlights. He had a strong jaw and a straight nose. She wondered what color his eyes were.

There was no doubt in her mind, he would put the statue of David to shame.

What story would she make up for him? He could be military but his hair was too long; maybe he's undercover.

She smiled; what a yummy idea, undercover with him.

Ree snapped back to reality.

Her best friend, Epee, was a bad influence on her.

If Epee was here, she would probably go over to him, introduce herself, and get herself invited for a drink.

Ree got herself together, entered the building, got her ID badge and located Jim's office.

"One moment, Miss Malloy, I'll tell Mr. Peterson you're here," The receptionist told her.

She tried to gain her composure after her imagined encounter with that good-looking man. She knew he was definitely out of her league, but she could dream.

She sighed, lost in her thoughts.

"Reanna, are you okay?" Jim said, a little worried.

"No, I'm fine. Thanks, just a little overwhelmed."

"I'm sure that this trip must have been a little hard for you. When was the last time you came to Washington?"

"About a year ago, right before my Dad died."

"Just so you know Reanna, I had the utmost respect for your Dad. He made a tremendous contribution to our understanding of Mideastern culture. He was very influential in shaping the policies that we have today. Come into my office; let's discuss how the next generation of Malloys will affect Iraq."

The office had a familiar feel to it. It was very similar to the one her dad occupied when he was in Washington.

She took a seat across from Jim, looked him in the eye, and took a deep breath.

"I read the grant and it's a wonderful opportunity. It should help US and Iraq relations, as well as being beneficial to women. It's a fabulous idea, whose time has definitely come."

Jim tented his finger in front of his mouth. "Somehow, I feel a but in there."

"It's not a but about the program; it's a but about me. Why me?"

"You are extremely qualified. You know the city, the people, the language, and the culture. Why not you?"

"And so, do at least a dozen other people I know, who are even more qualified, more knowledgeable, and more experienced than me," She said firmly.

Jim looked down and attempted to shuffle some papers. He sighed.

"You are so much like your Dad. He could see through any smoke screen almost immediately."

Reanna's heart started beating hard against her chest. What smoke screen was he talking about?

"Jim, all I ask is that you are honest with me and I have the WHOLE story to allow me to make a decision."

"Okay, Reanna here goes. You're right. We could have picked any number of people more qualified than you, but you have a particular talent that the others don't have."

"Talent? What kind of talent?"

He raised his eyebrows, twirling the pencil in his hand.

"Riding horses."

Reanna could not hide her incredulous look.

"Are you serious? How is my riding ability connected to this grant or this job?"

Jim put his fingers up to his temple and massaged it a bit before he continued.

"Reanna, I don't have to tell you about the serious problems between the US and Iraq, especially since the Gulf war."

"Go on."

"Well, we need someone on the inside."

"On the inside of what? I'm not a spy, nor do I want to be one."

"No," he chuckled," not a spy. I'm not asking you to break into palaces or steal government secrets."

"Then, what are you asking?" Reanna was still confused. "How are horses connected to this?"

Jim pulled out another folder and handed it to her.

"Uday, Saddam's son, is the head of security. If there are weapons of mass destruction in Iraq, he would be the one in charge. Uday has many passions and, other than women, horses are at the top. He loves to ride, train, and race. The Palace has a state of the art training facility for some of the top horses in the world."

"But, I still don't understand. Where do I come in? "

"I sent your dossier to Saddam's people, knowing it would be checked by Uday. We are hoping that he will invite you to the barn and maybe give you riding privileges, occasionally."

"Jim, I get that part, but what am I supposed to do when I get there? Take pictures? Record conversations? Come on. I'm not trained for that."

Jim chuckled.

"No, I just want you to look around. In your weekly reports, innocently tell us what you see. If you are given access to the stables, you will be inside a part of the palace that no one, and I repeat no one is allowed, other than Uday's workers, guards, and special guests. This will give us valuable insight into what's there. Look for anything suspicious. Are a lot of soldiers using particular doors? Does there appear to be an underground level? Just keep alert to anomalies."

With lifted eyebrows Reanna replied, "How do I report to you on these weekly reports?"

Jim seemed to relax a bit and took a deep breath.

At least she's still listening, he thought.

"I will have someone working with you for a few days on what to do and how to write up the reports. Honestly, someone with your ability will not have a problem. Also, I will have people covering your back while you're there. If there is any danger, no matter how small, you will be taken out of there immediately. You have my word on that."

Reanna pursed her lips and squirmed a bit in her seat.

"You have given me even more to think about. How soon do you need my answer?"

"How about Monday," he said with a smile.

Ree stood up and shook his hand.

"Okay, I'll call you Monday with my answer."

She left with a lot more on her mind than when she went in.

Chapter 4

"Hi, Commandeer McLeod. Right on time, go right in he's expecting you," the receptionist said with stars in her eyes.

No matter where he went Colin McLeod had the same effect on women and even some men.

The fact that he was three inches over six-foot, with dark brown hair, green eyes, and built like a Highland warrior, might be the cause.

Colin was used to it and found the reaction, at times, amusing, but mostly annoying.

When Jim saw the door open, he stood and offered his hand to Colin.

"Commander, good to see you. So, glad you could meet with me. How's your Mom and Connie?"

They both sat down.

"They're doing better but it's still hard for them. Connie brings the grandkids over a lot. That really perks my Mom up, but recovery has been slow."

"I know, I can't believe it's been almost two years since the crash. Did they ever find out the cause?"

"No, not really. The FAA thinks it was instrument failure, but with the crazy weather in Alaska, anything is possible. I still can't believe it at times. My Dad and brother, at the same time. They never traveled together and one of the few times..."

"How are you handling the transition from SEAL to CEO? I imagine it must be hard. I know it's not something you aspired to."

Colin laughed.

"There's no comparison. I loved the Navy and being a SEAL was the epitome. But, even if I could stay active, I'm thirty-two so my career would be coming to end anyway. At least you keep me busy with assignments every now and then. Now, I have the added cover of being CEO of one of the US's biggest oil companies. This call was great timing, my Mom has been on my case to marry and have kids. I am more than happy to get out of Dallas."

Jim laughed.

"Well, then this latest favor will be right up your alley. It will get you out of Dallas for a few months. Are you interested?"

Colin raised his eyebrows.

"What's the assignment?"

"Do you remember Thomas Malloy?"

Colin wrinkled his brow.

"Wasn't he assigned to the Iraq embassy?"

"Yes, that's him."

"I heard he passed away last year."

"Yes, that's right; he was a good man, leaving behind a wonderful family."

"Come on, Jim. Don't be cryptic. What's the assignment?"

Jim pulled out a folder and handed it to Colin.

"The assignment is Jim's daughter, Reanna. She's opening a school in Bagdad with a US grant. I need someone to look after her."

"You're kidding, right? You want a babysitter? There must be any number of operatives that you could use. Why me?" Colin, usually cool, could feel his temper rising. One thing Colin could not tolerate was his time being wasted and he was coming to believe that this entire trip was going to do just that.

"Now, Colin, calm down. You have two things that the other operatives don't have."

"Don't bullshit me, Jim. What's the magical something I have?"

"For Thomas Malloy's daughter, I want the best and you are the best."

Colin sighed.

"Don't patronize me, Jim. The second reason?"

Jim grinned. "You know horses and you ride horses."

With the last comment, Colin raised both eyebrows and massaged the back of his neck.

"What the hell do horses have to do with this?"

"Just take some time to read through the folder. I'll give you some time, but Colin, I really need you on board for this. I would consider it a personal favor. I'll get us some coffee."

Jim stepped out of the office and left Colin reading the information.

Colin opened the folder. The first thing he saw was a picture of Reanna Malloy. She was an attractive, all-American girl, average height, brown hair, blue eyes. He finished reading through the dossier and came away with a lot of respect for Ms. Malloy, but she was the opposite of everything Colin looked for in a woman.

He liked tall women; Reanna was average only 5'4".

He preferred blonds; Reanna had brown hair with hints of gold.

An important requirement for Colin was that a woman's breast size should equal her IQ.

If any of those pesky questions came up like, "what are you thinking," or, "where is this relationship going," all he would have to do is dangle something shiny in front of them and he would be safe for a few more weeks.

He knew it sounded shallow, but it worked for him. He had a feeling, based on Ms. Malloy's accomplishments, that she did not fit into this category either.

Jim came back into the office just as Colin was finishing up the dossier.

"So, what do you think?"

Colin smiled.

"I'll ask again. Why me?"

Jim shook his head.

"You're getting soft, sitting behind a desk. I could have picked any number of experts. Why Reanna?"

Colin scratched his head.

"Yeah, I was wondering that. Why her? I mean she seems competent enough, but I'm sure there are plenty of other choices, who are more qualified."

"Horses," Jim replied.

"Horses. What the hell does that mean?"

"Yes, Horses." Jim smiled as he watched the light bulb moment for Colin.

Colin snickered.

"You son of a bitch! You think she's going to get an invitation to the Palace stables?"

"Yes, and I'm hoping that you will be invited right along with her."

He crossed his arms over his chest.

"How am I going to accomplish that feat?"

"Get close to her, have her invite you to Uday's Gala at the Palace."

"Jim, come on. I'm sure she's a nice woman but..."

Exasperated, Jim sighed.

"Colin, I'm not asking you to marry her, not even date her, just get an invite to the Gala. If she can get into the stables, go with her and report back. I know, she's not your usual taste. Look, Reanna is a really nice, smart, talented woman. Give it a shot."

"Okay, as a favor to you and Thomas Malloy. I respected him, so yes, I'll do it."

"Good, here's your ticket. You fly out of Newark next Friday, direct to London, then on to Bagdad."

"Why Newark?" Colin questioned.

"Reanna lives with her Mom on a horse farm outside of Princeton, NJ. It's the closest for her. You will be sitting right next to her, so you'll have time to get to know her."

Colin glanced at the ticket.

"The seats are in coach. How am I going to fit in a coach seat?"

Jim laughed.

"With all government cutbacks, no business class. Sorry."

They both stood and shook hands. Jim patted Colin on the shoulder and wished him well.

Colin knew his first phone call would be to his PA, to change both his and Ms. Malloy's tickets to first class.

Colin didn't care much for creature comforts but flying first class was a necessity with his height.

He walked out of the building. He felt the sun on his face and stopped for a moment. It was nice to be outside. One thing Colin hated about his new job as CEO was being shut inside. He craved the outside.

As he soaked up the sun, the hairs on the back of his neck started to prickle; His, "Spidey Sense," as his SEAL team called it.

Colin felt like someone was watching him. He looked around. He didn't see anything out of place. All the usual people were on the steps of the building and nothing looked suspicious.

He started to walk away, when he noticed a young woman with a briefcase, walking up the steps.

She had on a white, silk blouse, with a black, pencil skirt. She had a grace about her when she walked. Her back was to him so he could not see her face.

Nice legs, he thought in passing, before continuing on his way.

Chapter 5

Reanna sank into the backseat of the town car, on the way to the airport. Her head was still spinning from the events of the last two weeks.

One meeting with Jim Peterson and her whole life changed. The question was, would it be for the better?

The driver pulled up to the curb, for departures at Newark.

She grabbed her hand luggage and turned to give the driver a tip, when a large man, carrying a tray of four coffees, plowed into her sending Ree and the coffees flying.

She was not hurt, but the same could not be said for her outfit.

The man was extremely apologetic.

Ree controlled her anger and just nodded.

The driver and a skycap got her up from the sidewalk, helped her in with her luggage and made sure she checked in; at least she could be thankful for their help.

She looked a mess.

Coffee was spilled down her blouse and pants.

Now what? She thought.

All her clothes were in her suitcases and were on the way to the plane. Her only option was the bathroom.

Ree went into the ladies' room and did the best she could to wash out the coffee from her clothes.

She got enough out that she didn't smell like Starbucks...much. The blouse was silk so the stain was horrendous.

She thought, if she kept her briefcase in front of her, it would not be so noticeable.

As Ree left the ladies room, she heard her name being paged to report to the ticket counter.

"Please," She prayed. "I don't want to be bumped."

Ree identified herself to the airline agent.

He smiled and told her there was a change to her seating. She was upgraded to first class and was welcomed to proceed to the first-class lounge if she wanted.

Great, she thought. *My luck, I get upgraded and I look like a slob.*

She thanked the agent, took her new ticket and settled in on one of the chairs, regretfully letting the first-class lounge go this time.

****

Colin was in the first-class lounge, drinking his second beer. He tried to look calm but felt his anxiety level rise every time the door opened.

"Where the fuck is she?" He steamed.

He could not decide on the best approach to talk to her.

Hell, he felt like an untried schoolboy on a first date. He heard the call for first class passengers to board. Still no Reanna Malloy.

Colin pulled out his phone and called Jim.

He answered on the first ring.

"Do you know where the fuck she is?" Colin growled.

"By she, I guess you mean Reanna," There was a smile in his voice, "I'm assuming she should be boarding the plane about now, but from the tone of your voice, I have to guess she's not there yet."

"You're right, she's not here," Colin growled, "Did she change her plans?"

"Calm down. I'm sure she will be there. She did not call me with any change of plans, so my guess is, she will be there. Maybe she's just running late. Relax, I'm positive she will show up."

"I'm boarding now," He growled, "If she's not on the plane, I'll get off and call you back." Colin slammed his phone shut and proceeded to board the plane. He checked out the rest of the first-class passengers, Reanna wasn't among them. He settled into his aisle seat and watched everyone as they boarded.

****

Reanna was so engrossed in her reading, that she almost missed the call for first class boarding. She grabbed her hand luggage and went down the walkway, into the plane.

The airline started to board other passengers so Colin had turned to the back to watch the passengers get on in the second part of the plane. He wondered if somehow Reanna's ticket never got changed to first class when he felt a light tap on his shoulder.

"Excuse me, I think my seat is next to you," Ree said, shyly.

Colin looked up into the bluest eyes he'd ever seen. They looked like the ocean in the Caribbean. He smiled up at her.

So, this was Reanna Malloy! She really was an attractive woman, he decided instantly.

Ree started to climb over him to get to her seat when she felt strong hands span her waist to stop her. Colin gently pushed her back. He got up and allowed her full access to her seat.

"Thank you," She blushed.

Colin grinned. He was totally mesmerized by her blush. It had been years since he saw a woman blush. It was nice; really nice.

It made him feel protective.

Ree was a mess. If she could crawl into a hole she would. This man is so handsome and she felt like she looked like a Jackson Pollack painting and smelt like Starbucks.

Please God... She prayed, *just zap me up to heaven now because if I have to sit next to this man for seven hours it will be hell. I won't be able to think. I won't be able to speak.*

As Ree got settled, she kept her briefcase in front of her, trying to hide the stain. She somehow deluded herself into believing that she could stay like this for the whole flight and no one would notice.

Colin looked over at her and smiled.

"Are you okay?"

She nodded yes and continued to look straight ahead.

"Are you going to hold your briefcase up like that the entire flight? I mean, if there are state secrets in there, I understand, but I can guarantee you, I am very trustworthy."

She turned to look at him and tried to stop her intake of breath.

God, he's gorgeous, she thought.

The man was tall with brown hair, wide shoulders, and massive arms. He reminded her of someone but she could not place him. It was his eyes, though, that had her mesmerized.

Ree's favorite necklace was one her father gave her, made of jade, that he got on a trip to China. His eyes reminded her of that beautiful jade necklace. Eyes that were green, but so much more, a hundred different shades of green, with gold specks.

I could get lost in them, she thought.

She was just about to set down her briefcase and try to explain her unfortunate run-in with four coffee containers when...

"Reanna, Reanna Malloy is that you?"

Colin looked up to see an elderly woman, trying to work a leg cast down the aisle.

"Oh my God, Mrs. Fitz! What are you doing here?" Reanna exclaimed.

"Well, I guess your mom didn't tell you, but my youngest is getting married and I'm going to London for the wedding."

Reanna looked at her leg, Mrs. Fitzgerald laughed.

"I know, I know, my daughter was so mad at me, I thought she would break my other leg. I fell, changing a light bulb; just sprained, thankfully, not broken. I'll be fine to dance at the wedding!"

Reanna started to gather her things.

Confused, Colin asked, "What are you doing?"

"Mrs. Fitz, you sit here. You will be so much more comfortable. My good fortune just became yours."

Mrs. Fitzgerald looked concerned.

"Are you sure, dear?"

"Absolutely! You have a comfortable flight," She said, as she vacated the seat.

Ree called a flight attendant over and asked if the seat change would be okay.

The attendant assured her it would be fine as they exchanged tickets. The attendant walked

Ree down to her new seat and patted her on the back.

"That was a really nice thing you did for that older woman. If you are having any drinks they will be covered by the airline".

"Thank you, that's very nice." The reality was, Mrs. Fitzgerald was an answer to her prayers.

Fate just stepped in and stopped her from making a fool of herself.

"It will be our pleasure. Thank you, again, Ms. Malloy."

Colin helped Mrs. Fitzgerald get settled in her seat. He sat back, closed his eyes and mentally said *fuck*, his favorite word for situations like this.

After he got over it, he remembered his uncle saying, "Use every opportunity to your advantage."

So, he did.

Chapter 6

The six-hour flight to London was uneventful. It could have been six hours of hell, but for Colin it turned out to be very enjoyable, talking and laughing with Mrs. Molly Fitzgerald. She reminded Colin a lot of his mom and aunts; very direct, witty and smart.

Colin had thirty-two years of experience dealing with the McAlister women, so it was easy to direct the conversation to Reanna.

In fact, all he said was, "That was a nice thing that woman did for you," and Mrs. Fitzgerald was off on the life and loves of Reanna Malloy.

He learned things about her that could not be found in a dossier and, begrudgingly, came to admire and respect her.

In Colin's experience, daughters of diplomats or State Department executives were selfish and shallow.

They would dine at the latest places in Washington, trolling for rich and influential husbands. Colin was a target for these women. As a SEAL, the women wanted the danger. As a CEO, the women wanted the money. He wondered if Reanna was like these women, but according to Mrs. Fitzgerald, Reanna was the exception to the rule.

"You know," Mrs. Fitz told him, "Ree is a nice, caring young woman. I have known her since she was born. I even remember her Dad. Thomas was a nice man. It was too bad that he and Mary Margaret couldn't make the marriage work."

"How did Ree take the break up?"

"Ree is a strong girl. She loved her Dad and was with him as often as she could be. He just passed. Such a shame. He was a young man...only fifty-five. She loves her Mom and works very hard on the farm. You know, they rescue racehorses?"

"No, I didn't know. That is very commendable."

"Yes, both her Mom and Ree are accomplished riders and trainers. My granddaughter takes lessons at their farm. Ree is an excellent teacher; my Ryleigh adores her."

"They must have lots of workers there. I'm sure they don't do all the work."

"Oh my, yes. They have helpers, but let me tell you, Ree is the first one to pick up a shovel and clean. She's a whirlwind, for sure."

"Does Ree have a boyfriend?"

She smiled up at him with a twinkle in her eye, the one his Mom would get when she was going to say something wicked.

"Are you interested in the position?"

Colin coughed.

She was so like his Mom.

"No, just curious; she's a very attractive woman."

"I know Ree had a few boyfriends. I remember the professor, but I don't know what happened there. Epee, on the other hand, had a new boyfriend every week up until she got married."

"Who's Epee?"

"Oh, that's right, you don't know them. Epee, or Epona, has been Ree's best friend since they were seven or eight. They are different as night and day, but as close as sisters. Funny, both Ree and Epee were named for the Celtic Goddess of horses. When they were kids, Epee would tell everyone they were goddesses. Believe it or not, Epee had most of the kids in the neighborhood convinced, especially with Ree's gift of training horses. It is a gift from God. She does talk to them and they listen."

The conversation continued through dinner, with more stories about Ree and her friend Epee.

After dinner, the cabin lights lowered, lulling the passengers to sleep. Colin put his headphones on, turned to the Oldie's station and fell into fitful sleep while listening to Phil Collins' *Invisible Touch*. His dreams centered around woman with a tiny waist and blue eyes, riding a horse across the Scottish Highlands.

At the end of the flight, Colin helped Mrs. Fitzgerald off the plane and into a waiting wheelchair. An attendant was already there to take her through customs.

As they parted, Mrs. Fitzgerald reminded him of his promise to take care of Reanna and make sure she got to her hotel safely. It was a promise he was more than willing to fulfill.

Colin went to the carousel to retrieve his luggage.

How was he going to approach Reanna and offer her a ride to the hotel?

He spied the same piece of luggage, continuously circling the carousel. A check of the tags indicated that they belonged to Reanna. He secured the luggage and waited.

The flight for Reanna was hell.

She was away from that handsome man, but her seat was in the middle of the last row, between two men, who insisted on invading her small amount of real estate.

She got no work done and longingly thought about the hot towels being distributed in first class, as she used another wet one.

Finally, the flight came to an end; she deplaned and went in search of her luggage. She was so tired and groggy she regretted her decision not to get a ride to the hotel.

Instead, she had planned on taking the underground.

She was one of the last people to walk over to the carousel to pick up her luggage when she spotted the green-eyed god.

He waved at her.

She looked around. *Maybe it's someone behind me.* She thought, moments before she heard him call her name.

How does he know my name? She wondered suspiciously as the light dawned. Mrs. Fitz. *I'm going to kill her.*

Colin looked rested, refreshed, and very handsome. At that moment, Reanna hated him. He greeted her with a big smile.

"Mrs. Fitzgerald made me promise that I would look after you and get you to your hotel safely. I got your luggage and I have a car waiting." He explained as his expression morphed into a wicked grin.

"Thanks so much, but it's okay. I'm taking the underground. Thanks for getting my luggage," She managed pleasantly, "Besides I don't even know your name."

Colin put out his hand.

"Colin McLeod from Dallas, Texas. Pleased to meet you, Ms. Malloy."

As she took his hand, she shivered.

Even his speech had a bit of a Scottish burr.

Could this man get any hotter? She wondered, hoping the thought didn't show through on her expression.

"Nice to meet you, Mr. McLeod. Please, call me Ree."

"And I'm Colin. Mr. McLeod was my Dad. Now that we are properly introduced, how about that ride?"

"I don't know!"

It was so tempting.

Colin noticed she started to waiver. He pushed the luggage cart towards the door, put his hand on her lower back, and led her out the doors.

"Oh no, you are not getting away that easy, I have burning questions that need to be answered."

She raised her eyebrow.

"Questions?"

"Yes, like, why didn't you go to the prom with Stanley Taylor and what happened to that nice professor you were dating. He seemed so perfect for you?" Colin said with a devilish grin.

She turned every shade of red, but couldn't help but laugh.

"Got an earful from Mrs. Fitzgerald? I think you probably know all of my deep, dark secrets, some probably only my best friend knows."

"You mean, Epee," Colin said with a smirk on his face.

Reanna groaned.

"Another hour on the plane and you would probably know my bra size and the type of toothpaste I use."

"How do you know I don't, Ms. 34C?" Colin said with a wicked grin.

Ree turned a shade of red unknown to man. She was so embarrassed, she wanted to crawl into a hole.

"I'm sorry," He said. "That was out of line, but seriously, will you accept my offer of a ride? I assure you my intentions are honorable. I'm staying at the London Hilton. Where are you staying?"

"I'm staying there also." Reanna was too tired, too groggy, and the offer was too good to turn down, so she graciously accepted.

They settled in the car and soon fell into an easy conversation about London. Ree showed him her disaster at the airport.

"I was so embarrassed. Here I am, sitting next to you and I'm wearing a Jackson Pollock painting stained with coffee smelling like Starbucks."

Colin could not help himself and burst out laughing. Ree turned bright red again. Sensing her distress, he took her hand and squeezed.

"I was heading into an important meeting when my assistant spilled a pitcher of water on me that landed right on my lap. I had no time to change, so I went into the meeting."

Ree was mesmerized. She could not believe something like that could happen to this man.

"What happened?"

"No one said anything. I thought maybe they didn't notice. We ended the meeting. The next day, I went into my office and there sitting on my desk is a box of Depends."

They both laughed this time. The story broke the tension and they were both able to relax.

The conversation flowed after that. Reanna told him about her trips with her dad. He told her about his trips to London with the Uncles. Ree found out Colin was also on his way to Iraq on business, so they talked about mutual places of interest in Baghdad. Colin realized that it had been a long time since he enjoyed a woman's company as much as he did Reanna's.

Reanna realized that Colin wasn't a god, but just a man, a very nice, very handsome man.

At the hotel, Colin helped her check in and got her luggage sorted out. He walked her over to the lifts. He turned to look at her.

"One of my favorite places for drinks in London is the upstairs bar. I would hate to be alone while enjoying such a spectacular view. Would you do me the honor of having drinks with me, say six?"

It was one of her favorite places also. The hotel bar was spectacular; it was at the very top of the building with a beautiful view of London at night. What could it hurt? Besides Epee would kill her if she didn't go.

As the elevator doors closed, he said, "Six then?"

She nodded.

When Reanna got into her hotel room, all she saw was the big bed. She knew the best way to beat jet lag was to stay up and get as much sunshine as possible. It had always worked in the past, but the lure of the bed seemed to be overwhelming. Maybe after a hot shower, clean clothes, some tea, and of course, scones, she would get her second wind.

With a plan in mind, she set out her things and went into the bath.

The shower gave her a bit more energy after the flight from hell. She decided she would take a walk, and maybe do a little window shopping, before she got ready to meet Colin for drinks.

She also wanted to call her Mom and Epee to let them know she arrived safely.

Ree checked the time. It was ten am so about three in the afternoon at home. Epee was probably home with the kids. She placed the call and waited for it to go through.

Epee picked the phone up on the second ring. She sounded out of breath.

"Ree, is that you? Is everything okay?"

"Yes, Epee everything's fine. Just checking in to let you know all went okay. Are you okay? You sound out of breath?"

"I'm fine. The baby just woke from her nap and she's clinging to me like flypaper. I can't get her fingers out of my hair."

Evidently, Cody has the same fascination with Epee's hair as she did.

She remembered the first time they met; they were seven.

Ree was brushing her pony in his stall when this little girl opened it and said, "Hi..."

Ree turned and there was this girl with a halo of blond hair surrounding her. Ree thought she was a fey child, like the ones her Mom told stories about.

They became best friends and Ree quickly found out Epee was more of a lovable devil, in a fey body.

"When is Kevin coming home?"

"Have you forgotten it's football season. He'll be at practice until seven or later. I'll tell you, Ree, that man and football when he's "in season" he's worse than some of your stallions in spring. All he thinks about is football. I swear when we make love at night he pictures me as a football."

Ree laughed.

"TMI Epee; way too much information. How are the kids?"

"You know I love them, but I already miss you. I need adult conversation. When I talk to Kevin if it doesn't have an x or an o in it, he doesn't listen. The kids don't listen at all. Believe it or not, I can't wait to get back to teaching. So enough about me how was the flight?"

"It went okay."

"Just okay. What aren't you telling me? Come on, spill. You can't hide things from me, Ree."

"Okay, okay. Which disaster do you want to hear first?" She sighed.

"Oh, no! Ree, what happened?"

Ree proceeded to tell Epee all about the coffee incident, getting upgraded to first class, giving up her seat to Mrs. Fitzgerald, the ride to the hotel with Colin, and his invitation for drinks.

"So, what's this Colin like?" Epee asked.

"Oh, Epee he is so handsome and nice he could be my Jamie. He's perfect, but I know I'm out of his league".

Epee shrieked so loud Ree was sure that most of New Jersey heard her.

"Oh my God, Ree, your Jamie?"

Jamie was the code name for the man of their dreams, "the one."

"Reanna Marie Malloy. Do I have to get on a plane right now to slap some sense into you? Are you nuts? Out of your league! Where do you come up with this stuff? He's lucky you agreed to have drinks with him. He should be kissing your feet. You're a catch, girlfriend, when are you going to realize that?"

"But Epee..."

"But nothing. What are you going to wear? The black dress or the red one? I'm thinking the black one. It says sexy and sophisticated and you have, I mean have to the wear the shoes. In fact, when you're dressed, you are to take a picture and email it to me. Do you hear me?"

"Yes, Epee, I hear you, but I was thinking maybe the black pants with the white silk blouse, with my flats. My feet hurt."

"Ree, do I have to get on that plane? You will wear the black dress with the Jimmy Choo shoes; they are soooo sexy. Please, Ree, just do it. Have I ever let you down?"

"Okay, okay. I'll wear them."

"Do you promise?"

"Yes, Epee, I promise...Aand I'll send you a picture."

"Good, because my only excitement anymore is living vicariously through you. Kevin thinks me wearing the school's football jersey is a turn on so I'm in big trouble. Let me have this fantasy. Will you have time to get the girls the Paddington Bears?"

"Yes, I'm going out now to get a little sunshine and do some shopping. I probably won't be able to call you tomorrow. My flight is early but as soon as I can I'll call from Baghdad. Can you call my Mom and tell her everything is fine and I'll call her as soon as I can?"

"Will do. Do you have any idea when you will be home?"

"I'm still hoping for Christmas. Why?"

"Remember we were going to go to the alumni dinner at Rutgers. Do you think you will make it?"

"I sent my registration in so I'm going to try. I want to be home by Christmas".

"Ree, I miss you like crazy. I love you."

"I miss you too Epee. Love you, talk to you soon."

Ree hung up the phone and sighed. She took out the black dress and the outrageously high heels and looked at them.

"Okay for you, Epee. I'll wear them." She said out loud, holding the dress against her as she turned toward the mirror. "I hope Colin appreciates it."

Chapter 7

Fayed and his friend Ari were at the Hilton's bar, discussing how they were going to arrange a meeting with Dr. Malloy.

Their contact gave them a picture of her and confirmed that she checked into the hotel at nine-thirty am.

Ari was discussing a possible plan to get Dr. Malloy out of her room when Fayed nudged him with his elbow to look towards the door.

In walked a vision of beauty, Reanna Malloy. She looked around the bar apparently looking for someone, then settled in the empty barstool near Ari.

****

If Ree had a penny for all the times she changed her mind about coming, about wearing the dress, about the shoes, she probably would be able to cure world hunger.

Yet, Epee's words were still ringing in her ears:

"Wear the dress."

She took a deep breath and decided to channel a little of her friend; be brave, see where the evening took her.

Ree was ready at five-thirty. She took her shoes off and on. She paced, tried to do some work then walked around the room again. Only a few minutes went by. Rather than drive herself crazy she decided to leave early and get a good place at the bar, hoping a glass a wine would help calm her nerves. She left her room took the lift up to the bar. When she entered the first thing she noticed was the view. It was getting dark and the lights of London were just coming on. It looked like a sparkling Christmas tree with white lights. The view was as lovely as she remembered.

The bar was busy, but there were some empty seats. Ree looked for Colin, but he wasn't there yet. She checked her watch, five-fifty. Good time for that drink.

For her eighteenth birthday, her Dad took her here for her first legal drink.

He ordered a bottle of champagne.

Lost in that memory, she looked up and saw a man staring at her. She looked away and blushed. The man cleared his throat to get her attention.

"I am so sorry, Mademoiselle, for being so rude, but you remind me so much of my brother's wife, I almost thought for a minute it was she. I was wondering what she was doing here without her husband. Again, please forgive my rudeness."

Ree smiled at him and told him it was no problem. The bartender came over and took her order. Ree was fumbling with her money to get the correct amount to pay...

"Please, allow me, Mademoiselle." He handed the bartender money for her drink.

"Thank you, but that was not necessary."

He smiled at her.

"Please, allow me, for being so rude before. I am a little jet-lagged. You see, my family and I just arrived from Baghdad. We are here to celebrate my cousin's wedding."

Ree thanked him for the drink and asked what part of Baghdad he was from. They started a conversation about different areas in and around Bagdad, the pros, and cons of each. Fayed ordered a wine for himself and toasted Ree.

"To a beautiful and smart woman named?"

She smiled back at him.

"Reanna, my name is Reanna."

"To Reanna, the most beautiful woman in London," He announced.

While they were talking, another man approached them.

"Ah," Fayed said, "Ari, my friend, please meet the most beautiful woman in London, Reanna."

Reanna blushed.

"Are you here for the wedding also?"

Ari seemed a little confused. Fayed slapped him on the shoulder. "My cousin's wedding or have you forgotten already?"

"No, no, I remember." He said confidently.

The three of them fell into an easy conversation about Iraq and Baghdad. Ree told them about the school and how thrilled she was to have this opportunity. Fayed seemed very interested in the school. He told Ree he had a ten-year-old sister and asked if she would be a candidate for the school. Ree assured him she would be and gave him the phone number of the person to contact in Baghdad to get the registration papers.

Ree checked her watch, six-ten. It looked like Colin stood her up. She tried to hide her disappointment.

Both Ari and Fayed ordered a drink and insisted on getting another for Ree. She was ready to refuse and go back to her room, but changed her mind and decided to stay.

Ree was a little surprised when Fayed and Ari ordered a drink but then remembered that many Moslems drank when they were outside of their country. Many drank inside the country but kept it very quiet. One of her Dad's Iraqi friends loved Scotch, so every time he went back to Iraq, he always brought his friend a bottle.

****

Colin was cursing the slow elevator. He was beginning to believe that it was some type of universal law that when you are in a hurry the rest of the world moves at a snail's pace.

He lost track of the time while on a business call to Texas. When he got off the phone, he checked the time and realized that he was already ten minutes late. He hoped that Ree was like all the other women he knew who were always late.

Although, something told him she was totally different from any woman he met before.

He entered the bar and scanned the tables, but didn't see her. He checked the bar. Colin saw a woman at the bar with long, wavy, brown hair, falling down her back and shapely legs. She wore the type of shoes he loved, high and sexy.

He groaned. He had to stop himself from staring and reminded himself he was on an assignment. He wanted to see her face.

She turned.

Oh fuck, he thought, it's *Reanna.*

The last time he saw her she was dressed conservatively, with her hair up.

Now, that dress, those shoes...

Damn, that is one fine looking woman.

Colin was about ready to approach her when his cellphone rang; it was Jim Peterson. Colin decided to take the call. He moved to the back of the bar where he would have more privacy, but keep the Reanna in view.

One of the things Colin liked about government work was having access to the newest gadgets.

Jim had given him the latest Motorola phone, the V3, not to be released until next year. It was compact, had a great camera and global capability. He answered the phone and was amazed at the clarity of the connection.

Landline connections were never this clear and certainly not this convenient. Jim called just to check in and make sure all was going according to plan. Colin assured him that everything was fine.

He ended the call but decided to try out the camera in the phone. He focused in on Reanna in the black dress and sexy shoes. As he was lining up the shot, he noticed she was talking to two Mid-Eastern men. Something did not seem right; his Spidey Sense never let him down. He snapped the shot and made his way over to Reanna.

As he approached her, he noticed the two men getting nervous. He stood next to her put his arm around her shoulder; she looked up him.

She could not focus.

"Hi babe, sorry I'm late." He leaned down and gave her a kiss on the cheek. "Who are your friends?"

Ree didn't know what was wrong with her. Maybe she was getting sick. She only had one glass of wine and just started the second when the dizziness started. She wanted to get up and go to her room, but her feet would not follow the commands of her brain.

She tried to say something, but the words seemed to come out all garbled.

A man put his arm around her and said something to her, but she could not respond. She recognized the man. It was the hot guy from the plane. He showed up. Her heart leaped.

When Ari and Fayed saw Colin approach Reanna, they collected their money and made their way to the lift.

Now, Colin knew something was wrong, something was very, very wrong.

Colin sat next to Ree, he took her hand in his.

"Ree, how do you feel? Do you know who I am?"

She nodded yes and croaked out, "You're the hot guy from the plane; I don't feel good, must be getting sick, think I'm going to pass out."

Colin held onto her and stood her up.

"Ree, are you still with me? Can you at least walk to the lift?"

She shook her head yes again. He helped her up and as an afterthought grabbed the empty wine glass and put it in his pocket.

He held Ree up and guided her to the lift. When they got inside, she collapsed. He picked her up, pushed the button for his suite and carried her rest of way.

Chapter 8

Colin got Ree into the room and laid her on the bed.

She groaned.

"Ree, are you okay? What do you need?"

Ree groaned again and tried to sit up.

"No, sweetheart, lay back down. You'll feel better."

She opened her eyes and tried to focus on Colin.

"Oh God, Jamie, I think I'm going to be sick."

Colin picked her up and brought her into the bathroom. He placed her next to the toilet and held her hair back while she vomited.

After a while, she laid back down on the floor.

"Ree, can you hear me?" He checked her pulse and breathing.

She groaned again and mumbled something that sounded like Jamie. Colin picked her up and brought her back to bed. He kept his eye on her while he called his contact at the embassy.

He explained the situation. The embassy agreed to send a doctor over to check Ree. They assured Colin the doctor would be there in about a half-hour.

Colin removed Ree's clothes and braided her hair, a skill he learned while living in Scotland with his Uncles. He tried to be clinical but he had to admit, she had a great body, perfectly formed. He left her bra and panties on and pulled the covers up.

He got a towel from the bathroom and placed it next to her in case she felt sick again. She appeared to be sleeping soundly.

Once Ree was settled, Colin called London headquarter and spoke to the Bureau Chief about what occurred. He asked Colin to email a full report to him ASAP.

He also requested that he forward a copy to Jim in Washington.

It seemed like hours but a short time later, a very attractive blond woman knocked on the door and identified herself as Dr. Kindon, the Bureau doctor. After he checked her credentials, Colin let her in and escorted her to Ree.

While the doctor examined Ree, Colin told her about the wine glass with the remaining wine.

The doctor did a complete exam, checking blood pressure, pulse, and all vital signs. She let out a sigh and looked at Colin.

"I'll take the glass back to the lab, but based on what you told me about her physical symptoms I'm positive that's it Rohypnol, a date rape drug."

His Spidey Sense never let him down. This was the worst possible scenario.

"Will she be okay? Will there be any aftereffects?"

"The drug makes the user very compliant and completely unaware of what went on around them for about five hours.

The good and bad news for Reanna is it appears that she was given either way too much of the drug, or she was allergic, which caused the vomiting and the semi-conscious state."

"Is there something we can do? Should we bring her to the hospital to have her stomach pumped? Can you give her an antidote?"

The Doctor shook her head.

"Unfortunately, no. This drug is very fast acting. There is nothing we can do except watch over her to make sure if she vomits again, she doesn't choke. The most important thing is to make sure she is in a safe environment. The way this drug works is, it takes a person's free will away. They are unaware of their surroundings and what is happening to them. To compound the problem, the victim will not remember anything of the incident after the drug wears off."

The doctor also informed him that flying out tomorrow was out of the question. She needed at least twenty-four hours to make sure there were no further complications. Colin thanked the doctor and showed her to the door.

The doctor again assured him that when the test results came in, she would call him immediately to see if any follow-up was necessary.

She gave Colin her private number in case he needed anything. She told Colin to call her if Ree's condition worsened.

Colin got his laptop and phone, before he settled in bed next to Ree.

He watched her sleep.

She really was a beautiful woman. He could not believe he did not recognize her when he entered the bar. He would never make that mistake again.

There was something about her, so different from any other woman he had ever been with; she was sweet and real.

He vowed he would do everything in his power to protect her.

When he thought about what could have happened, he wanted to punch something.

He fantasized about finding those two fucks and administering some Navy SEAL justice.

In the middle of his musing, thought, his cell rang.

At the other end of the line was a very angry Jim Peterson.

"What the hell happened? Damn, this could have been a disaster! Do you have any idea who they were?"

"Jim, whoa, one at a time. I was on the phone with you when it happened. I was late getting to the bar. When I went in, I didn't see her right away." He ran a hand through his hair in utter frustration. "You called me, we were talking. I had my eye on her. I saw the two Mideastern guys talking to her at the bar. Her back was to me, she didn't see me. Then, I don't know, something just didn't feel right. I hung up with you and went right over to her."

"Sorry, Colin, I'm just upset. Ree is like a daughter to me. It wasn't your fault: it's those idiots. How is she?"

Colin explained what the doctor said about her condition. They would also test the wine glass, but the doctor was very sure it was Rohypnol. The good news was there were no long-term effects. The bad news, they could not fly out of London tomorrow.

"So, Colin, do you think this was planned, or do you think it was just a random act?"

"I think it was planned," Colin said grimly, "We will know for sure in a few hours. I was able to get a picture of the two guys with that new phone you gave me. I sent the picture over to the embassy. The tech people are checking into it now. My gut feeling is that it was planned and Ree was the target. I think they planned on taking her to their room, raping her and taking very compromising pictures of her. They would blackmail her by showing her the pictures. Then, she would have to decide to let the pictures go public or give up on the program completely. They could even force her to pass information to them. The picture isn't pretty."

"Damn, Colin. Just the thought of that makes me sick. Do you still think I sent you on just a babysitting mission?"

"No," Colin smirked. "I'm glad I was there. Ree doesn't deserve what happened or, worse, what could have happened."

"Ree, is it now? I told you that is a wonderful girl. I figured it wouldn't take long for her to weave her spell around you."

"Yes, she is a wonderful woman but there is no spell." Even as Colin said it, he knew it was a lie.

There was something very, very special about Reanna Malloy.

Colin told Jim he had sent a message to his company. They would have the private jet available to fly them to Baghdad the following day. He felt it would be safer. Colin promised Jim that Ree would not leave his side.

Before he hung up Jim asked, "Are you going to tell Ree what happened?"

Colin covered his face with his hand out of frustration. He took a deep breath.

"I don't know I've been wondering that myself for the past hour. What do you think?"

"No," Jim said firmly, "Let her think she got some kind of bug or food poisoning, but let's not tell her, at least not yet."

"I agree. Okay, I'll give you a call tomorrow and let you know how things are going. Oh, one last thing. Do you know who Jamie is in Ree's life?"

"No, you read her dossier. No significant others. No brothers. No, no idea. Why?"

"No reason. It's just that every now and again in her sleep she calls me Jamie and thanks, this Jamie for rescuing her. I'll ask her in the morning. Thanks again. Talk to tomorrow."

Colin settled back onto the bed next to Ree. He e-mailed instructions for the company jet, then answered some correspondence. He closed his laptop, checked his phone for messages and looked over at Ree. He couldn't help himself, he pulled her to him. He tried to tell himself he was only doing this so if she stirred during the night it would wake him, but knew he only kidded himself. He was totally intrigued by this woman.

Chapter 9

When Colin woke up, he looked over to check on Ree. She was still asleep and did not appear to be in any distress. He, on the other hand, had gotten one of the worst night's sleep of his life.

He hoped a shower would help, the colder the better. A night with Ree in his arms, imagining all he wanted to do to her and not being able to do anything, pushed his self-control to the limit.

While in the shower, he tried to determine why this small slip of a woman was having such an effect on him. Every time he was near her, he had to fight to control himself. All he wanted to do was take her in his arms and kiss her senseless. He put his two fingers on the bridge of his nose and squeezed. He had to get control of his emotions. She was a job, someone, he needed to protect.

The question was, to protect her from whom?

After the shower, Colin called for room service. He checked the time. If Ree didn't get up soon he would wake her. The doctor wanted a report on her condition this morning.

In accordance with the doctor's orders, he placed a big glass of water next to the bed with two Advil.

The doctor said she would probably wake up dehydrated and with a splitting headache; the water and Advil would help.

He checked his watch; time to give Jim a call.

Jim answered on the first ring. "What the hell is going on? Is she okay?"

"The doctor said she would be fine, but needed to rest today."

"I got the doctor's report a few hours ago, and it was Rohypnol. Damn, Colin, if you hadn't been there I can't even imagine how bad this could have gone down. I got the pictures you sent of the two guys. We couldn't ID the one, his face was too covered, but we got the guy on his left. It's as you thought. He works for Iraqi secret police under the direct command of Uday, Saddam's oldest son. I can't believe it. I can't believe he would go this far. He is a sneaky, underhanded bastard."

"Do you agree with me that they were going to blackmail her?"

"Absolutely! Think about it, Colin, he shows her these pictures and either she is forced to abandon the project altogether or she starts feeding him information. Either way, he wins. That son of a bitch."

Colin agreed. "So, what do we do now? Do you want me to bring her home? Do you want me to tell her what almost happened?"

Jim was quiet for a while.

"I don't know, Colin. This project is really important to us. Believe it or not, it could avert a war, but I hate having her in such a vulnerable position. She's like my own daughter. Thomas's ghost would haunt me for the rest of my life and probably beyond if anything happened to her."

"Don't you think you should have thought about that before you got her involved in this?" Colin quipped.

"I know, I know, but we are involved now. The question is, do you want to go on? Can you keep her safe?"

"Fuck, yes, I can keep her safe, but does the end justify putting her in harm's way?"

"I hate to say this Colin, but yes, yes it does. This is a very important project, not just to the state department but even higher up. I'm putting this in your lap. If you think you can keep her safe,

then continue with the assignment, but if not, come home. If you continue, I don't think you should tell her what happened, just as we agreed yesterday. Tell her it was food poisoning or the flu. So, what do you think?"

"Sometimes, Jim, I really fucking hate you. Yes, I can keep her safe and yes, I will continue the assignment...God help me."

****

Ree tried to open her eyes. A flash of pain splintered through her head. She groaned. The groan caused a burn in her throat. Her mouth tasted like something died in it and her teeth felt like they had little sweaters on them.

Other than all that, she was perfect. She chuckled, realizing even that hurt.

What hit her? A horse or truck? Whichever it was it was big. She did a mental inventory and tried to come up with her last conscious memory. What was the last thing she remembered? Blank. Wait she was at the bar then...blank.

Who was the last person she remembered talking to? Seeing? Blank.

Wait. Jamie Frazer?   What? Who? She thought.

Ree sat up a little too fast and the room started to spin. She put a pillow behind her back and looked around the room. It didn't look familiar. She moved her legs and tried to get out of bed.

Oh my God, I'm in my panties and bra. What happened to my clothes? Who took my clothes off? She slowly turned to the other side of the

101

bed and it was obvious that someone slept right next to her. *Holy shit, I slept with Jamie Frazer!*

Her rational mind told her that her last thought was crazy. Jamie was a fictional character.

Then, why did she remember that Jamie saved her? No, couldn't be. He carried her? Not likely. He slept with her? A beautiful thought, but again, impossible.

She looked over at the side table and noticed a big glass of water with what looked like two Advil tablets next to it.

She smelled the water. It smelt like water. She tasted a bit. It tasted like water. So, she drank the glass dry.

It tasted heavenly.

She checked the pills. Yes, they were indeed Advil, so she took them.

After a few minutes, Ree got out of bed she was a little shaky at first but managed to sit up and put her feet on the ground. Her ears started to buzz; she felt dizzy.

Finally, her head stopped spinning and she could focus. She heard a man's voice talking to someone in the next room.

Colin heard a noise from the other room. He told Jim he would call him later. He headed for the bedroom.

Maybe now, he could find out who the fuck Jamie is.

When Colin entered the bedroom, Ree was standing and stretching. Colin was struck speechless. He saw her body last night when he removed her clothes but now, he could appreciate an almost perfect female form.

She had the perfect size breasts, round and firm; a small waist; rounded hips; a taut, firm ass; and for a small woman, very long legs. All he could picture at this moment was his hands around those breasts and her legs, wrapped around him.

She was an equestrian; she could ride him all night.

He cleared his throat to get her attention. Ree jumped, squeaked and reached for the blanket.

"Where the hell am I and what the hell happened to me?"

Colin noticed she had drunk the water and took the pills, a good sign that there was some trust. He dragged his hand through his hair and looked away.

"Ree, why don't you get dressed." He handed her a t-shirt. "Come out to the sitting room. Breakfast will be here soon and I'll tell you everything."

"Okay, sounds fair. But just so you know, you are on notice. You have a lot of explaining to do." She walked into the bathroom and slammed the door.

Chapter 10

Reanna almost felt human again after her shower. There's something about hot water and soap that's good for the body, as well as the soul.

She found the hair dryer and went to work on her hair. It was always a chore; her hair was so thick and wavy.

The hotel shampoo and conditioner, as well as the body cream, were great; in fact, they were nicer than hers, but she would kill for a toothbrush and toothpaste. All her toiletries were still in her room. She noticed Colin's black bag on the counter and, jackpot, inside was his toothbrush and paste.

Should she? The little devil on her shoulder said yes. Did she want to go through the day feeling like she had little sweaters on her teeth?

What Colin doesn't know won't hurt him, right?

With her final task completed, she felt like a new woman, ready to take on the world; or, in this case, Colin McLeod.

While Ree was busy in the shower, Collin made some phone calls to plan for the day. He arranged room service for breakfast, called headquarters to have an agent to pack up Ree's things and check for any bugs. He also arranged for her things to be brought to his room.

He knew he was being paranoid, but he swore he would not let his guard down.

Obviously, the Husseins were playing hardball, so he could play that way also.

How he was going to explain the new sleeping arrangement with Ree was another story.

Colin called the doctor and reported Ree's condition.

He was assured by the doctor that she could do most anything today but to make sure she wasn't dizzy or nauseous.

If any of these symptoms occurred, call her immediately.

Colin's final call was to his PA to check on business details.

While he was on the phone, someone knocked on the door and announced room service.

Colin let the waiter in and told him where to set up for breakfast.

Ree walked into the other room and was hit with the wonderful smell of bacon. Her stomach growled.

Colin looked up and smiled.

"You know you looked absolutely beautiful in that black dress last night but, well, you do the Navy proud in that t-shirt."

Ree tried not to grin.

"Stop trying to distract me with compliments. Is that bacon I smell?"

Ree sat down and tried not to look at Colin. He had gray sweatpants on, lying low on his hips. Her eyes followed up his back, to very broad shoulders that made a perfect V down to his waist. As he removed the silver covers from the breakfast, she could see the muscles moving under his black tee.

She was suddenly filled with the urge to run her nails down his back and feel each, individual muscle respond. His brown hair was a little longer than she expected and it curled down the nape of his neck. She wanted to grab those curls and try to wrap them around her fingers.

Ree was definitely lost in this fantasy when he looked at her. She could get lost in those green eyes. There was no way humanly possible, that she could disguise the lust in her eyes.

She blushed.

Colin was taken aback by the look in Ree's eyes and his body's response to it.

He grinned at her.

"Ms. Malloy, if you keep looking at me like that then I can't be responsible for my actions."

She got herself under control and ignored his last comment. Ree crossed her arms over her chest.

"Okay, Mr. McLeod, spill. What happened last night and don't leave anything out."

He handed her a cup of tea.

"What's the last you remember?"

She thought for a minute.

"I remember getting dressed in my room and thought about changing my dress, but at the last-minute, I decided not to."

"Good choice," He smiled.

"I took the elevator up to the lobby." Ree continued, "The bar was busy, but there was a seat at the bar. I was really early; you weren't there yet. I sat at the bar and ordered a glass of wine. I talked to the bartender for a little while and I remember thinking that you stood me up. I had decided to finish the drink and go back to my room, order room service and go to bed early. I remember talking to some guy, or did I dream that? He said his name was Fayed and he wanted to enroll in the school, but the school is for women. I don't know where that came from, then I remember..."

"Then, what happened?" Colin urged.

"I don't know, dreams...really bad dreams. The next thing I remember was waking up in your bedroom, feeling really sick. What happened to me?"

"We really don't know," Colin replied seriously.

"The doctor thinks that a combination of jet-lag, not enough rest and food poisoning. You just passed out."

"Doctor? You got a doctor for me?"

"Yes, the hotel sent one up. She wasn't concerned but said you had to rest today. Ree, I'm really sorry I was late getting to the bar. I had to make some business calls and before I realized it, it was after six so I dashed up to the bar. I saw you talking to someone. So, you remember any more about him? Was his name Jamie?"

Before she could stop herself, she looked up at him with wide, scared eyes. She got control and looked down into her plate.

"No nothing more. Why do you think his name was Jamie?"

He knew she was holding something back, but decided to let it slide.

"Not important. Anyway, I approached you at the bar, you turned to look at me and just passed out. I got you to the room and at this point, you started vomiting".

"Oh God, I'm so embarrassed."

"Stop it, Ree you were sick. No reason to be embarrassed. Your clothes were stained so I sent them to the dry cleaner. By the way, you looked beautiful in that dress. I'm looking forward to seeing you in it again."

If Ree wasn't bright red before, she was now. Colin watched her reaction. He loved that she was so real, no pretense.

He shook his head, unable to understand where these ideas were coming from.

"One more question," She asked shyly.

"Ask me anything."

"Why did you sleep in bed next to me?" Ree could not even look at him when she asked the question.

The devil got Colin for a minute and he was going to say something smart, but when he looked at her bright red face, he decided to go easy on her.

"Ree, honey, the doctor said you might start to vomit again during the night. I was there simply to take care of you if that happened. I did not want you to choke. Believe me, nothing happened."

Colin could see the relief wash over her face.

She smiled up at him.

"I feel good now, but I'm starving. That breakfast looks amazing. Do you mind if I dig in? My flight isn't until two pm, so I have plenty of time to get ready."

As Ree filled up her plate, Colin thought this would be the perfect time to tell her about the delay.

"Ree, there is something else the doctor said."

He looked her in the eye. "The doctor said that traveling today was out of the question. You will have to postpone your trip twenty-four hours. She was worried about dehydration and dizziness."

She put her fork down.

"Oh, okay. Well, that changes things. I'll have to change my flight and contact the State Department." Her mind was working at lightspeed trying to determine what to do first.

Colin pulled up the chair next to her and took her hand in his. "Ree, don't worry. I have everything under control. Unfortunately, the next commercial flight to Baghdad isn't for three days."

She put her cup down and sat up in the chair.

"No, I can't wait that long. I have meetings. I have so much to do I can't possibly wait three more days."

He smiled.

"Could you wait one more day?"

"I guess."

"Good. My company's corporate jet just happens to be in London, so I arranged for it to take us to Iraq tomorrow. That is, after the doctor gives the okay. Will that work for you?"

"My God, Colin. I can't ask you to do that. Besides, you have done so much already. Won't your boss be angry for using the corporate jet for something like this?"

He shook his head and grinned. "I have a feeling that the boss will be fine with me using the jet to help a damsel in distress. Besides, Ree, I have to get to Iraq too and I'm not leaving without you. So, it works for both of us. Sorry, sweetheart, you are stuck with me. Let's have our breakfast and then we will decide what we want to do for the day. I didn't know what you like for breakfast so I ordered a variety of things; I thought that there would be at least one thing here that you like."

Ree looked up with mischief in her eyes.

"What, Mrs. Fitzgerald neglected to tell you my favorite breakfast? She must be slipping. I'll have to reprimand her next time I see her. Everything here looks great. I'm not fussy when it comes to food. If someone else makes it, I'll eat it. Is there more tea?"

"Of course," Collin said, "We're in England. You have to drink tea because the coffee is terrible."

"That's what my Dad used to say, but I'm not a coffee drinker. I love tea."

They sat quietly lost in their own thoughts.

Colin was trying to figure a way to approach her about the name Jamie.

"So, Ree, is there anyone you need to call about your change of plans?"

Ree thought for a moment.

"No, other than the State Department and I'm sure they will contact the people in Baghdad. If I tell my mother she will just worry and probably send me some herbal remedy for food poisoning. My friend, Epee. Well, she would she come over here and try to fire the whole kitchen staff. No, I'll call them later and tell them there was a flight delay."

He pushed her a little.

"Are you sure there's no one else? No significant other?"

"Why, Mr. McLeod, are you trying to find out if I have a boyfriend?" Ree said, in-between bites.

He looked a little sheepish.

"Yes, you see last night you kept calling me by another man's name. So, yes, Ms. Malloy. I am calling you out. Do you have a boyfriend?"

Ree could not look at him. She thought that was all part of her dream.

"What name did I call you?"

"Jamie."

She said nothing, just stared straight ahead.

"Do you want to tell me about him?"

"No, not really," She said with no emotion.

"But we are friends and friends tell each other everything." Colin knew the argument was lame, but his curiosity was getting the better of him

"We're friends?" Ree asked, a little bewildered

"I would like to think so," Colin replied smugly. "After all, we slept together, didn't we?"

Ree narrowed her eyes slightly as her lips pursed with annoyance, but other than that, she gave him no response.

"Look, Ree," Colin said firmly, after a moment of enduring her slight, but distinct glower, "If you don't want to tell me, you don't have to. I was only teasing you."

"You were teasing me about being friends?" She looked at him, crestfallen.

"No. Of course, we're friends, I meant about the sleeping together and about Jamie."

"Okay," She sighed, "I'll tell you but you have to promise me two things."

Curiosity got the better of him; he agreed.

"One, you cannot laugh. Laughing is not permitted, ever."

"Agreed," He said, straight-faced.

"Number two, you must never tell anyone. Do you agree?"

"Absolutely."

She took a deep breath.

"When Epee and I were about fourteen, she heard her older sister talk about a book; how hot it was and how much sex was in it. We were two curious teenage girls, especially about sex. So, when I spent the night at her house, Epee would steal the book, and we would both take turns reading it out loud. It took almost two months to get through the whole book. We learned a lot about sex. You have to understand; both our mothers are Irish and they don't talk about sex. I still think today that they want us to believe the fairies brought us. We both fell in love with the main character."

Colin had to stop himself from laughing.

"Let me guess. The main character's name was Jamie."

She shook her finger at him.

"Remember, rule one, no laughing. Anyway, we agreed that we were going to marry him someday. As we got older, we realized it was just a teenage fantasy, but we did agree that we would look for someone with his characteristics."

He smirked.

"And what were these wonderful character traits?"

"Well, he was a brave Highland warrior who was always saving his wife from some terrible situation. He was very handsome, brave, loyal and..."

Sounds like a dog, Colin thought as he released a big sigh of relief. He could not believe he was jealous of a fictitious guy.

Don't worry Ree, he thought, *I will never tell anyone because if my SEAL team knew I was ready to put a nine mm into this guy's head or the Uncles knew I was ready to run this guy through with a sword, I would never hear the end of it.* Colin was certain they would laugh for days. *No, we will just keep this very quiet.*

Ree looked very contrite.

"I'm sorry, Colin, truly, for everything. You have been more than wonderful. Taking care of me, arranging everything for me, caring for me, I am very grateful. Can we never mention this again?"

He got up from his chair and hugged her. "Ree there is nothing to be sorry for; your story was cute. I'm just very happy I was there to help you."

God, help you if I wasn't there, he thought.

"Can we pinky swear that we never mention this again?"

Touching pinkies, they both said together, "Pinky swear."

"Now, I'm starved. Let's finish eating breakfast."

Chapter 11

It took a lot to impress Colin.

He lived and worked with Navy SEALs for over seven years. He watched the amount of food they ate and yet, he quickly decided that this petite woman could give them all a run for their money.

He sat back and watched Ree relish her food. It was refreshing.

She bit into the scone with clotted cream, closed her eyes and moaned.

He groaned.

However, when she stabbed the sausage with the fork and put her lips around it and announced, "English sausages are so much better than American sausages," He wanted to be an English sausage.

He could not take any more food torture.

Colin cleared his throat.

"Now that just about every plate is cleared, what should we do today?"

Ree blushed.

"Oh, I'm so sorry. I guess I made a real pig of myself."

"No worries. It's refreshing to see a woman enjoy her food as much as you do. I'm glad you enjoyed breakfast."

"I try to control myself when I'm around people I don't know. My friends always kid me about my appetite."

"Someone you don't know? I thought we were friends. After all, we slept together, remember?"

She grinned at him.

"That's right, how could I forget that? My mom's the same way and she's thinner than I am. My Dad told me he hoped I got my mom's metabolism because he swore if he looked at a piece of cake, he gained five pounds. I guess I'm just lucky. I love food. I should make no apologies."

"No, you shouldn't," Colin replied, seriously, "I guess that's another thing we share. I also love food."

She arched her eyebrows.

"What else do we share?"

He could not help himself.

"We slept together!" He replied.

Ree laughed.

"So, what would you like to do today?"

"You don't have to babysit me. If I don't feel well, if I'm dizzy or nauseous, I'll sit down and call you. In fact, what's your number?"

"I already programmed it into your phone. I have nothing else to do today. Would you deprive me of spending the day in London with a beautiful woman? Besides, I come to London all the time and I cannot remember the last time I enjoyed the city."

"What do you say, Ree. We will do anything you want. Is it a yes?"

"Anything?" She said wickedly.

"Anything." He replied, but groaned. He knew women and what women liked to do in London. He was in for a day of shopping, his least favorite activity in the world. He would rather have his fingernails plucked out, one by one, than shop, but a promise is a promise. "Anything. Like I said, I get to come to London all the time, so the day is yours."

"Great, what time is it?"

He checked his watch.

"Nine-thirty, stores don't open until ten."

"Who cares about stores; the British museum opens at ten. If we leave now, we can get there when it opens. Is that okay with you?"

Shocked, he cleared his throat.

"That's fine with me. I have a car on standby. I will let them know when to pick us up."

She shook her head.

"A car? Are you crazy? We have to take the underground. There is nothing like coming up the steps from the underground and there in front of you is the worlds' greatest repository for culture, art, and civilization."

He had not been on the underground since he was a boy. His Uncles would take him to London every occasionally, and they would take the underground to get around London. He remembered his first experience; he loved it.

"Fine, we will pick up a map from the concierge and find the closest station."

"I know exactly where it is. I would take it with my Dad when we were in London. The British Museum was a 'must stop'. We would spend hours there."

****

The underground was crowded with the tail end of morning rush hour, but they were able to get seats.

Colin noticed Ree was tense; he leaned over.

"Are you okay?"

"Fine," She replied, "I am just so excited about this. I didn't think I would have time to visit the museum this trip. I spent so much of my childhood here. I can't wait to get there."

What seemed like hours to her was, in reality, a little less than fifteen minutes.

They emerged from the underground and Ree's eyes widened with excitement.

"Look at it, Colin. Isn't it beautiful? If the walls could talk, imagine the stories they would tell."

They walked to the building. "I would dream about my father forgetting about me when we visited, and I would get to spend the whole night here."

"Wouldn't you be afraid? What would you do all night?"

"No," She said confidently. "Anything I wanted. I'd sit at Churchill's desk; I'd lie in a mummy's sarcophagus; I'd touch everything you were not allowed to touch."

They got to the top steps as the doors were opening. Colin followed as she led the way.

They walked down the corridor and there on the right was one of Ree's favorite exhibits.

"Colin, look, it's still here."

There was a sheet of plexiglass on top of it. The last time she was here, she was able to touch it.

A little sad, she still ran her finger across the top.

"The Rosetta Stone," Colin said, a little awed himself.

He nodded.

"When I touch it," He put his hand over hers as they caressed the stone together, "I think that Napoleon touched this. He recognized its value and kept it safe. The history this stone opened up is unimaginable."

She looked up and locked eyes with him, feeling an electric connection she never felt with anyone else.

He squeezed her hand.

The guard hurried them along.

The moment was broken.

"Where to now, my lovely tour director?"

"Of course, the Mesopotamia section."

"Of course."

They meandered through the maze of corridors and entered an area entitled "The Cradle of Civilization." This section contained artifacts from all over Mesopotamia, some dating back as far as 2000 B.C. Some, were recorded as being created even earlier.

As they entered, she nodded to the guard in the corner and pulled Colin over to one of the cases.

"Oh, I hope it's still here. Wouldn't it be wonderful if it was? Come, hurry!"

"What's still there?"

They reached one of the cases, Ree looked down and squealed.

"Oh, my, Colin, look! It's still here."

"What am I looking at?"

"See that piece of pottery? Look at the card next to it."

"Malloy 1984." He read, "I don't understand."

"Malloy is my Dad. He found that little piece of pottery on an archeological dig. It's still here. I am so psyched. When my Dad was working in Iraq in the early 80's he was an undersecretary, in charge of history and artifacts. He became friends with a Scientist who was doing a lot of archeological research in one of the valleys. His name was Samir al Waheed. On his days off, my Dad would join Samir at the dig site, helping him to look for artifacts. My Dad fancied himself an amateur archeologist. It paid off. He found quite a few things but this was the best. It was the oldest piece of pottery they found in that area. When Samir got the job at the British Museum he told my Dad he would display the piece. We came the following the year and there was his find. My Dad was so proud. It was like he won the Academy award for archeology."

As they peered over the case, a booming voice bellowed, "Of course, it is Americans who are putting fingerprints on my nice clean cases."

Colin looked up and tensed.

Ree grabbed his arm and let out a squeal.

"Samir, oh my god." She ran into his open embrace.

They hugged for a minute, then he grabbed her shoulders and pushed her away.

"Let me look at you. Allah be praised, you look just like your beautiful mother and nothing like that ugly father of yours."

Ree laughed.

"How are you, Reanna? I cannot tell you how sorry I was to hear of your fathers passing. He was like a brother to me. I miss him still."

"I know," She sighed, "I miss him also, but I'm doing well, keeping busy. I know my mother answered your letter. She was so touched by what you said, especially all your stories about my Dad. You brought back a lot of happy memories for her."

Samir looked up and for the first time, noticed Colin.

"And who is this young man? Do I have to take your father's place and make sure he is worthy of you?"

Ree took Colin by the arm and led him over to Samir.

"I'm sorry. How rude of me. Samir, this is my friend, Colin McLeod. Colin, this is a very dear family friend, Samir."

After introductions were made, Samir invited them both back to his office for some tea and scones.

"You remembered. I always said the British museum had the best scones."

"Yes," He returned her smile, "I also remember a little girl of seven eating four of them. Your father and I were amazed. We could never figure where you put all that food."

She blushed.

"I still wonder." Colin had to tease.

Ree and Samir talked for a while, reminiscing of the times spent together.

Ree told him about the State Department project and her assignment in Iraq.

Samir was not pleased.

"Reanna, I must try to talk you out of this. The Iraq today is very different from the Iraq you remember as a little girl. It is very dangerous. Can I not try to change your mind?"

Ree reached for his hand and looked up into his eyes.

"Samir, I know you are only thinking about my safety. I know that Iraq has changed, but I believe in this project. I believe it can make a difference, maybe even help prevent a war."

He sighed.

"You may not look like your Dad but you have his stubborn streak. The only thing I can say is, go with God and may He protect you."

They hugged.

Colin shook his hand, but Samir pulled him to him and whispered in his ear, "Take care of her, please. She is very precious to me and many others."

Colin nodded and said, "To me also."

When they left Samir's office, Ree asked Colin if he wanted to visit any area.

"Yes, if you don't mind, the Medieval weapons."

Ree looked up at him and smirked.

"Of course. Men and their swords."

He reached for her hand and they traveled together, hand-in-hand through the corridors of the British Museum.

As they entered the medieval weapons section, Ree noticed Colin's face light up.

He went over to a Scottish broadsword. Ree watched him and for a second the museum faded and in front of her, was a Highland warrior, wielding the sword. He had a kilt, low slung on his hips; his chest bare and sweating; his long brown hair tied in the back.

It took her breath away.

Colin took Ree's wrist and brought her to him.

"See this sword? My Uncles wanted this sword so badly for their collection they were actually planning on ways to steal it from the museum."

"You are kidding me, aren't you?"

He shook his head and looked very serious.

"I wish I were. My Uncles are, shall we say, a bit unorthodox. They did not like the fact that an English institution held such a fine example of Scottish weaponry. Thankfully, I was able to talk them out of their plan. The museum agreed to lend them the sword on special occasions."

"Wow, they must be very special to earn that privilege."

"I don't know if 'special' accurately describes the Uncles, but they are unique. They were able to make some type of deal with the Medieval specialist. My Uncles have one of the largest private collections of Medieval Scottish weapons in the world, so I'm sure that gave them some leverage."

Ree was impressed. "I'm guessing you got to see this collection?"

"Not only see it but use the weapons; it was a fantastic experience."

"I noticed that you mentioned your Uncles often. Did you live with them?"

"It's a long story, but yes, I lived with them for about three years, three of the happiest years of my life. It's when I discovered who I was and what I really wanted to do in my life. I owe them everything. So, if they wanted me to steal a sword, I would somehow figure it out. Thankfully, they changed their mind."

She smiled up at him.

"I would really love to hear more about your Uncles. They sound like great guys."

He took her hand in his and brought it up to his lips.

"Another day, my fair lady. Where to next?"

"The underground, to Harrods," She said firmly.

"Harrods, it is," Colin said, inwardly groaning

at the thought of a shopper's paradise to the world, which, subsequently, was shopping hell to him.

Chapter 12

The trip on the underground was uneventful. The station was a few blocks away from Harrods so they walked along the sidewalk admiring the sights and sounds of London.

As they crossed the street Ree spied Fortnum and Mason.

"Colin, do you mind if I make a quick trip inside? I have to order some things for my mom and friend?"

Colin nodded.

They went inside.

She went to the food section and picked out some tea, a few jams, some cookies, and honey. She took her cache to the desk and arranged for them to be shipped home, separating the ones for her mom and the ones for Epee.

"Okay," She said. "Thank God that's done. I hate shopping."

"If you hate shopping," He quipped, "Why are we going to Harrods? It's a shopper's paradise."

"You'll see," She said with a wicked grin on her face.

They went in through the main doors with the magnificent statues and elevators. She avoided the elevators.

Colin stopped her.

"Don't you want to go upstairs? That's where the clothes and shoes are located."

"Boring. Why would I want to go there? The food halls are this way."

They entered the food halls, Ree's face beamed.

"Isn't this just amazing!"

Colin laughed.

"Don't tell me you dreamed of your father leaving you here all night."

"No," She smiled, "But what a great dream. Now, you did say anything I wanted, right?"

"Right." Should he be regretting what he said?

"Good, it's lunch time, so I think maybe we should get some cheese, a bottle of wine, maybe some olives and some cookies. It's such a beautiful day out; maybe we could do a picnic across the way at the park. What do you think?"

He was relieved, thrilled and happy.

"Sounds like a great plan. You pick out the cheese and I'll see to the wine."

They went their separate ways and agreed to meet by the cakes in fifteen minutes.

Before Colin got to the wine section, he flagged down a concierge and asked him to arrange something for him. He told him to follow that woman, pointed to Ree, take her purchases and pack them away. He went and picked out a nice bottle of Sancerre.

Ree was right on time, talking to the young man Colin asked to collect her purchases. Ree smiled at him. He felt his heart jump.

I am falling hard for this woman, he thought.

Ree laughed and pointed to the young worker.

"This young man keeps taking my food. He said

some real big guy told him to do it. I am assuming you would be that big guy."

"Guilty as charged, Ms. Malloy." Colin handed the wine to the young man and asked him to put it with the other purchases. "I thought we needed something to carry all the food in, so I arranged to have it packed for us."

"You are so thoughtful; thank you very much," She said as she started to pull out her credit card but Colin held her hand.

"Please Ree, let this be my treat. My thank you for such an enjoyable day."

"Okay," She said, "But I buy dinner."

He agreed.

Of course, he knew that was never going to happen.

"Why don't you meet me by the entrance we came in, while I arrange everything?"

She waited on the street in front of Harrods; it was a surreal experience. The last time she was here was with her Dad. She could not believe so much had changed. This new venture was a dream come true. She looked back into the store and thought about Colin. He was everything she wanted in a man. She conceded that Jamie Frazer was fiction but her Jamie, aka Colin, was alive and well. She could only dream that he felt the same way.

Ree was shy and self-conscious around men. She always felt they were never interested in her. She was too smart, her hair too wavy, her eyes too blue.

In the past, she didn't' care, but now she did, deeply.

Oh no, she was in trouble. She looked up and saw Colin coming out the doors carrying something.

As he got closer she whispered, "I can't believe you got a picnic hamper...I can't believe you got a picnic hamper," and started tearing up.

"I am so sorry. I'll take it back. I didn't know it would upset you."

"I'm not upset you, big lug, I'm happy! I'm so unbelievably happy. How did you know I always wanted one of those first-class picnic baskets?

He smiled.

"Lucky guess."

Colin picked up the picnic basket and they walked hand-in-hand to Hyde Park.

Chapter 13

It was a beautiful sunny day in London. The park was crowded, for this time of year, with people enjoying the unusually warm weather.

Colin and Ree found a secluded place under some trees, overlooking a pond.

Colin was fussing with the blanket as Ree started to unpack the hamper.

She had always longed for one of these picnic baskets with silverware and fine china; this was truly a first-class picnic.

Colin sat down next to her and opened the bottle of wine.

"I hope you like white." He handed her a glass.

She smiled.

"If it has a grape in it, I'll love it, I'm sure."

He poured the wine as she passed him a plate with some cheese, grapes, salami, and fresh baked bread.

They ate in silence, enjoying the beautiful day, the good food, and the spectacular scenery.

Colin especially enjoyed watching Ree; she was so graceful in everything she did.

She tried not to be too obvious, but Ree watched Colin out of the corner of her eye. He was a handsome man, perfectly formed.

But who was this man, this man who has been so kind to her? She realized as she observed him, that she knew very little about him.

"Ree, the way you are looking at me...Should I be worried that I'm going to be your next meal?"

She blushed.

"I don't know anything about you. Your family? Where do you live?" He could be married, she decided and paled at the thought.

"Are you okay? I assure you I'm not a serial killer or rapist. I'm an upstanding guy; don't be upset."

"It's not that, it's just I don't know anything about you, like family, friends, children?"

"Why, Ree, are you asking if I have a girlfriend?" He chuckled.

She narrowed her eyes at him.

"Well, do you?"

"No, I do not have a girlfriend. I am not, nor have I ever been married. Anything else?"

She breathed a sigh of relief.

"Tell me everything about Colin McLeod."

"Everything? I'm sure it will put you to sleep," He said as he took another bite of the crusty bread.

"I doubt that. Come on, spill." She grinned and inched closer to him, as though she expected him to divulge some deep, laden secret.

He took a big sip of his wine and started his story.

"My family home is in Texas. How the McLeod family ended up in Texas is a long story, so I'll give you the abridged version. My great grandfather was born in Scotland. The

146

economic and political situation in Scotland was not good, so he packed up his wife and migrated to the US. A boyhood friend of his left Scotland years before and wrote him about the opportunities in America. He begged him to join him in Texas. He made it there and met up with his friend. They pooled their money, bought property, and started raising, breeding and selling cattle. The partner died without an heir, so he left his portion of the ranch to my great-grandfather. He ended up with one of the biggest spreads in Texas. They had one child a son, my grandfather and he inherited it all. He was going to continue the cattle business when oil exploration became all the rage in Texas. As a laugh, he decided to check the property. Lo and behold, the property had one of the biggest oil reserves in Texas. Thus, Thistle Oil was born."

Colin did not want to tell this story but realized that she would find out sooner or later. Ree only knew him as some nice guy who helped her; it was refreshing.

Obviously, Ree did not read the tabloids. Otherwise, she would have recognized him.

If they put him in PEOPLE magazine one more time as one of American's most eligible bachelors, he swore he was going to move. His

SEAL team still ribbed him about the tabloid attention.

Ree could not contain her shock. "I thought you worked for Thistle Oil?"

"Technically, I'm the boss, but I do have to answer to my mom and sister- in- law," he said sheepishly.

"But that's one of the largest oil companies in the US, maybe even the world."

"Yes, your point?" He looked away from her.

"That's all you have to say, is yes?"

Colin released a sigh and turned to look at her.

"Ree, what can I tell you? Yes, I'm rich, very rich. Does it make a difference?"

"No, not at all. I'm sorry, but you are just a regular guy."

"I am a regular guy; I love that's what you see."

"Okay, go on, I can't believe you thought I would think this story boring. This could be a reality TV show."

Colin laughed. "Well, not much to tell after that. My grandfather, followed by my Dad, turned Thistle Oil into the thriving business that you see today."

"Do you have any brothers or sisters?"

"Yes, I have, I mean had, one brother."

"Had?" She said quietly.

He looked away for a minute.

Ree reached for his hand.

"If you don't want to talk about it, I understand."

"No." Clearing his throat he continued, "My brother's name was Duncan, after my great-grandfather, grandfather, and father. He was two years older than I. I idolized him. He could do no wrong and the thing is, he never did anything wrong. He was the perfect son. He was great at sports, all A's in high school, graduated summa cum laude from Harvard Business school. He married his college sweetheart and immediately had two kids, a boy, and girl, my niece and nephew, whom I adore. He never gave my parents one ounce of trouble. Living up to perfection was difficult. I'm sure a psychologist would have a field day with my issues. Unconsciously, I decided that if I couldn't be him, I would become the opposite."

He looked out into the distance.

Ree put his hand on his shoulder.

"It's okay, Colin, if you don't want to talk about it."

He took a deep breath.

"No, it's good to talk about it. You know, I never did. Going the other route I was always in trouble, drinking in ninth grade, fighting all the time. By tenth grade, I was out of control. One night, a guy from town came to the house. I kind of knew him, his daughter who was wilder than me, hung with the group I did. He told my mom and dad that I sexually assaulted his daughter and got her pregnant. If they paid him $20,000 he would not report it to the police. My parents listened to the man. When he was finished, my dad picked him up and threw him out of the house. He told him if he or his daughter ever came on the property, he would have them arrested. When he came back into the house he grabbed me by the collar, dragged me into the study and sat me down on the chair in front of his desk. I was never so scared in my life. I didn't know what he was going to do, but I was afraid that he would believe the lies. I swear, Ree, on everything that's holy, I never touched that girl. It was an early introduction in how some women use men for money. It's probably where my mistrust of the fairer sex began."

After what seemed like an eternity, my dad said, "Now, do you understand why your actions can affect not only you but everyone around you?"

I looked up at him and said. "Aren't you going to ask me if I did it?"

"Son," He said, "You may be wild and undisciplined, but you are a good, moral boy.

151

Your mother and I never for one minute believed you did it, but you have to understand what your wild ways will do to this family."

"I let out a breath. For the first time in my life, I cried. My mom came over and held me. She told me that they loved, me but I needed to have my thinking and behavior realigned. I was just so grateful that they believed me, even though I knew I didn't deserve it."

"Things got better after that?" Ree asked.

"Well, they didn't get better, but my life changed dramatically. My parents shipped me off to Scotland." At this point, Ree was sitting with her back up against the tree, so Colin stretched out and put his head on her lap. She stroked his hair as he continued.

"Why did they send you to Scotland? Did you have relatives there?"

"Yes. My Uncles live there. I have to go back a little to explain the relationship. When my Dad was a young man, he and his Dad would travel back to Scotland every couple of years. On one of the visits, my dad became interested in the

Scottish games. I don't know if you ever heard of them?"

She shook her head yes.

"My dad loved the competition. Every year, my Dad and Grandfather would go over to the Scotland and they would compete. One year, he was up against some very strong competition in the way of the McKenna brothers. My Dad ended up losing to them, but they struck up a friendship. The McKennas' invited my Dad and Grandfather back to their home. Well, you should have heard my dad tell this story," He said, "He and his dad drove through the gates and about a mile down the road, hell I can still hear my dad's voice, 'there stood a bloody fucking castle.' No matter how many times he told that story, we always laughed. While they were there for dinner, he was introduced to their sister, Mary, and the rest, shall we say, is history. My Dad and Mum got married in Scotland, came back to Texas, and had two sons; my brother and me."

"I don't understand. How did this change your life in tenth grade?"

He closed his eyes and relished the feel of Ree's fingers caressing his hair.

"It wasn't what but who. You see, the McKenna brothers, my uncles, continued to live in the ancestral castle. In fact, the oldest brother Colin, who I am named after, was the laird of the McKenna clan in that area. He married a few years after my dad and mum but unfortunately, his wife and child died in childbirth. He was devastated and never remarried. His brother, my uncle George, was a confirmed bachelor who never married. Their passion was history, in particular, military history, battle planning, and tactics. They also loved Medieval weapons. I told you about their collection at the British Museum."

Ree smiled at the memory.

"Okay, so how do the uncles fit into the picture with you in tenth grade?"

Lying on Ree's lap, he felt total contentment. He wanted this feeling to go on forever. He closed his eyes and tried to understand this new emotion. Ree shook him a little and giggled.

"Come on, no falling asleep, I want to know the rest of the story of Colin McKenna McLeod."

He opened his eyes and gazed into the bluest, kindest eyes.

He could get lost in them; but maybe not lost, rather, finally found. At this moment, he felt like he was home.

He cleared his throat and sat up, next to her. Colin took her hand in his.

"Enough about me. Lets' save the next chapter for another time. I want to know about Reanna Malloy. What about her life, her family, her friends?"

"Compared to you, it's really boring."

"I doubt that but go on. In your words, spill."

"I already told you, I don't have a significant other. I told you about my best friend, Epee. I'm sure Mrs. Fitz filled you in on most everything about my life."

"I want to hear it from you; maybe I just like the sound of your beautiful voice."

She gave him a playful slap.

"Oh, you flatterer, you. My story, like yours, starts with my parents. Believe it or not my parents met at a horse show. They felt an immediate connection. My Mom called it Irish Lightning. Anyway, they met, married, and had me all within a year."

"Irish lightening." Colin repeated. "Never heard of it."

"Yes, according to my mom, at the beginning of time the Tuatha De' Danann or fairies created all people as whole, but the Fairies were a bit mischievous. They were bored one day and split all the souls in two, male and female, mixed them up and put them into 'well the souls'. According to the myth, the souls go on a journey through many lifetimes searching for their other half or their 'soul mate'. When the two halves meet, it's like lightning or electricity, the bonding or joining of the souls.

Once they find each other, they will live together in eternity as a whole, never to be separated again. When my mom met my dad, she said it was like that. They were meant to be together."

"That sounds like my mom; she talks about stuff like that all the time. Were your parents happy?"

Looking down on the ground she said, "Unfortunately no. Their souls might have been matched but their careers were not. My mom owns a big horse farm where she trains young riders. She also re-trains race horses and gives them a chance for a new career. In fact, the farm's name is SECOND CHANCE FARM. My mom is an accomplished rider and as much as she loved my dad, she was not willing to give up her career."

"My dad, on the other hand, loved the history and culture of the Mideast, especially the area in and around Iraq and Iran. When he got his doctorate in Mideastern studies the state department offered him a job in the Mideast division. It was his dream job. He was not willing to give it up. My parents tried to make it work and tried even harder when I was born,

157

but it soon became apparent that absence does not make the heart grow fonder. They separated and just followed their own career paths. They never divorced and never had any other serious relationships. At least, none that I'm aware of. They did truly love each other, but couldn't live together."

"So where does this leave Ree? A rider? A historian?" Colin inquired.

"Both, actually. I guess I'm like your older brother. I wanted to please both of them. I worked hard. I wanted to be the best rider and help my mom with the farm. I also worked hard at school and became the best historian and expert on Mideastern language and culture. My specialty is Iraq, hence my job starting the school for women."

"How did you keep these two lives separate?"

"I would spend the academic year going to school, riding and training. Every summer I would be with my dad in Iraq. I know it sounds confusing, but somehow, we made it work. My parents never pushed me to do anything I didn't want to do. All they wanted for me was to be happy and to make a difference. I was blessed. I had two loving parents who taught me so much. Some people would see it as pressure, but I saw it as an opportunity. Ultimately, that's why I'm going to Iraq; I'm an expert in the field. I believe I can make a difference."

They held hands and were both quiet.

Eventually, Colin sat up and went over to the picnic hamper and declared, "Time for dessert."

Colin was a disciplined focused military-business man, but he had one big weakness. He absolutely loved sweets.

When his mom discovered his addiction to sweets, she used it to control him. It usually worked. He would do anything for a cookie or piece of candy.

When he went on missions with the team, he always had at least four or five candy bars. The team caught on to his need for sugar. They tried to nickname him "Sugar" but he stopped that right away.

Even today, he could not pass up anything that contains sugar.

That was the reason he had Ree meet him by the pastries, so he could buy his favorite cake; a spice cake wrapped in marzipan, covered in fondant icing. To Colin, that was what Heaven must taste like.

After he bared his soul, he was ready for something sweet.

Ree took the cake out of the box and cut it into pieces. She ran her finger down the side of the knife with her finger collected the icing. She sucked the icing off her finger. Some of the frosting ended up on the side of her lip. Before she could lick it off, Colin used his finger to remove the icing and put the dollop in his mouth. Ree's reaction to the simple gesture was pure lust. She looked over at him and felt a shiver run through her body.

He couldn't help himself any longer and leaned over and kissed her, tentatively at first and then more insistent. She melted in his arms.

She let out a little moan; he was lost. She was the sweetest thing he ever tasted.

He craved more, needed more. He moved her down on the blanket and covered her with his body, never breaking the kiss. His hands were in her hair, on her neck, holding her shoulders down; he couldn't get enough. His kiss was all-consuming.

She was the sweetest piece of candy ever. When Ree opened her mouth, he took full advantage and tasted her. She tasted of wine, honey, and home. He knew when he was around her he would have no control. She was hastily becoming his addiction.

Ree was shocked when Colin leaned over to kiss her.

It was something she had dreamed of, but could not believe it was really happening.

However, she abruptly forced herself to stop thinking and analyzing, so that she could just enjoy the kiss.

It was spectacular.

Before she knew it, she was on her back, covered by this sexy man. She never felt so safe, so sensual in her life.

Then, suddenly, he was gone.

What the hell? She thought.

Colin realized he lost all self-control. He picked himself up, walked away from the tree and started talking on his phone.

Ree lay there, dazed and confused, wondering what she did wrong.

Colin shut his phone and came up to her.

"Come on, Ree. Let's pick up all the stuff and get going." He said more gruffly than intended. "No, we are not taking the underground. I called for the car. It will meet us at this corner."

He helped her pack everything up without saying a word.

Ree held back her tears.

Colin picked up the picnic hamper and took Ree by the arm. He just about dragged her to the waiting car. He opened her door, made sure she was buckled in and got in the other side. He looked out the window the entire trip. He did not look at her once. She wanted to say something but decided against it.

As time went on, she became angrier and angrier.

When they arrived at the hotel, she jumped out of the car and ran to the elevator.

Colin grabbed the hamper and ran after her. He got to the elevator just as the doors were closing, but stepped in just in time. He put the hamper down and pressed the floor for his suite.

He turned to Ree and saw tears in her eyes.

"Ah, hell," He said.

Using his thumb, he wiped the tears, grabbed her around the waist and kissed her like a man dying of thirst and she was the oasis. She pushed against him in the beginning, but soon realized he was an unmovable object.

So, she just relaxed into him.

When the elevator doors opened to the suite, he broke the kiss, grabbed the hamper and Ree, entering the suite in one swift motion.

He put the hamper down, put his arms around her and looked at her with lust-filled eyes.

"Do you have any idea how much I want you?"

"You have a funny way of showing it. I thought I did something wrong. You pushed me away, Colin. I'm confused." Ree was trying desperately to maintain her emotions.

"If I didn't stop, we would have been arrested for lewd and indecent behavior in a public place. The English take that very seriously. I lost all control. Ree, I DON'T LOSE CONTROL. The only way I was able to keep even the smallest amount was not to touch you or look at you. I'm so sorry you thought otherwise, but I want you like I have wanted no other. Do you feel the same?"

She nodded.

That's all the encouragement Colin needed. He picked her up and brought her into the bedroom, where he not too gently started to remove her clothes. Ree tried to cover herself, Colin stopped her.

"Don't, let me look at you." He stepped back and got his fill. "God, you are beautiful." He picked her up and laid her on the bed, her hair spread out on the pillow, her lips parted. He was momentarily taken back by the perfection of what he saw.

She shivered not from cold, but from need.

"Please," She begged, "I want you."

He opened the drawer by the bed table and pulled out a condom. His clothes seemed to fall off his body as he joined her on the bed.

He kissed her, gently at first, but the kiss quickly grew in passion. He left her mouth and started kissing and licking his way down her body. She tasted like the finest icing: smooth, soft, and sweet. His hands covered her breasts caressing. He took her nipple between his fingers and gently squeezed. She moaned.

He looked down, the nipple, hardened into a perfect, cherry jellybean; red and ripe, he couldn't wait to taste it.

He licked and sucked; this was Heaven, so sweet.

Colin made his way down her stomach, savoring each part of skin; licking, and nipping.

When he reached her apex, Ree opened her legs in invitation, begging him to fill her.

His hands were on her thighs, teasing.

"Please..." She implored.

His fingers unwrapped her and exposed the center of her femininity; he blew gently and bent down to take a taste; ambrosia, he nectar of the gods.

Like the bear, he could not wait to dip his finger into the honey jar. He was welcomed with warmth and the perfume of need. He added another finger and started to move it gently.

Ree groaned.

"Colin, please...I need you. I can't take anymore."

He moved up to her ear.

"What do you need, mo duinne?"

"I need you, Colin. Only you."

Colin put on the condom and entered her slowly. She was wet and warm, a perfect greeting.

She was tight, so he went slowly at first, but her panting made him lose all control.

They reached nirvana together.

After he caught his breath, he moved to her side and pulled her to him. Her heartbeat matched his, erratic.

He realized he could never get enough of this woman. She was the answer to his sweet tooth. She became his new addiction.

Ree was blown away by what happened. She knew she didn't dream it; it was the most earth-shattering experience of her life.

He called her mo duinne, Gaelic for *my love*.

Is this what her mom meant by Irish Lightening?

Chapter 14

The first thing Colin noticed when he opened his eyes was a beautiful woman draped over his body, keeping him warm. He needed to get up; he had to make some phone calls before she woke up.

Cautiously, he disentangled himself from Ree and covered her with the blanket; she made a small noise of protest but fell back to sleep.

When Ree woke up, it was like déjà vu.

Where was she? Memories started pouring in from the night of sweet passion. She blushed, just remembering; she got all tingly just thinking about it. She was so lost in her thoughts of last night of what Colin did to her but more unbelievable what she did to Colin, she did not hear him enter the room. When he cleared his throat, she looked over at him with eyes filled with passion and lust from the night before.

"If you continue to look at me that way you won't get to the surprise I have planned for you this morning." He answered, a little unnerved, by her sensual expression.

"Surprise?" She squealed.

He nodded.

"Yes, surprise. I've laid out some clothes you are going to need. So, get up and get dressed. I've ordered a light breakfast before we take off."

"My clothes are in my room. Did you get them?"

"I forgot to tell you that the hotel needed your room so I had guest services pack up your stuff and bring it to my room. Good thing we slept together again last night otherwise you would have had nowhere to go."

"Well, I guess that means we are really friends now that we slept together two nights in a row," Ree said smugly.

Colin smiled back.

If I have anything to do with it, this is just the beginning. He thought. *I can't wait to taste that sweetness again.*

Ree got up, showered, and noticed a pile of clothes in the dressing room. She was more confused when she realized they were her riding clothes. She did not want to disappoint Colin, so she changed into her breeches, jacket, and boots, then went to greet him.

Colin was on the phone when Ree entered. He ended the conversation and hung up. He let out a whistle.

"Ree, you would look good in a paper bag, but in those clothes. Wow."

"Where are we going?" She grinned.

"If you haven't figured that out yet, then I am disappointed by your IQ and education."

She gave him a playful smack.

"Are we really going riding?"

"Ouch, you pack quite a punch, Ms. Malloy, and yes we are going riding in Hyde Park. I remembered you told me that you planned on doing as many of the things you and your dad did in London. You mentioned riding was one of them. As our outing was cut short yesterday, I thought we had a little time to at least get that in."

She grinned from ear to ear, went up to him, put her arms around his neck and kissed him. The kiss rapidly turned from a thank you to something more sensual.

Briskly, Colin pulled her away.

"Now, now. If we don't stop, there will be no riding and maybe no plane later." He smacked her on the bum. "Come on, let's go."

They got a cab to the mews, where the stable was located and were introduced to their mounts. Ree was given a leggy Warmblood gelding named Poncho.

Because of his size, Colin got a draft cross gelding named Galahad. They walked down the drive when Ree turned to look at Colin, his profile on the horse took her breath away.

In another time, another place, he was a knight, a warrior; tall and proud in the saddle.

It was another beautiful day in London the morning air crisp and cold. The ride was awesome. They passed by the area where they picnicked. Ree could not help the blush as she remembered the heated kiss they shared.

They trotted a bit and ended the ride with a canter that left them breathless.

When they got back to the stable, Colin dismounted first and went up to Ree, put his hands around her waist and helped her dismount. She slid down his body, keeping eye-contact, watching the dark storm of lust swirl in his eyes. When her feet hit the ground, she took his hand and looked in his eyes.

"Thank you. Truly, thank you. You have no idea how much that meant to me. I will treasure that memory always.

At that moment, Colin decided he would spend the rest of his life trying to make this woman happy.

"I hope this is only the beginning of memories we will share together."

One of the grooms approached them and told them their car was there. They thanked everyone and gave out the last piece of sugar to the two horses.

They walked out hand-in-hand.

Aware of Ree's appetite, Colin stopped at a small restaurant for a full English breakfast.

Ree was famished.

Colin was amazed, again, at her hearty appetite.

He decided that when he introduced Ree to his Navy SEAL team, he would challenge Ree vs big John to an eating contest. His team would bet on anything and there was no doubt Ree was his ringer.

By the time they got back to the hotel, it was time to shower, pack and get ready to leave. Colin wanted to ask Ree to shower with him, but he didn't want to push her too far out of her comfort zone. He suggested that he should shower first, while she packed.

Ree was a little disappointed that Colin didn't invite her to shower with him.

Maybe he's shy. Ree thought. No, that thought went out the window quickly. *Maybe he...* Before another negative thought entered her head, she replaced the thought with, *what would Epee do?*

Invite herself into the shower, of course.

Colin was rinsing off when he heard a tentative knock on the shower door. Surprise could not accurately describe the feeling that cascaded through him when he saw Ree, standing there nude.

She looked up at him shyly.

"I thought you could use someone to wash your back."

Without saying a word Colin pulled her into the shower.

She washed his back, his front, his arms, and legs. He reciprocated. When she got on her knees and took him in her mouth he thought he would explode. She licked, sucked, kissed and fondled him until he couldn't take it any longer. He grabbed her shoulders, tried to pull her up but she wouldn't let him.

"Please, let me finish."

He smiled.

"Anything the lady wishes."

When he finally climaxed, he thought his heart was going to go through his chest.

She looked up at him with her blue eyes; he went down on his knees and kissed her the water encapsulating them in their own world.

When the kiss was broken, he whispered, "Jesus, Ree, what you do to me."

****

On the way to the airport, Colin asked, "Have to ever been on a private jet before?"

"Colin, I'm a teacher. What do you think?"

"I thought, maybe with your dad?"

"No, he was a public servant. No private jets for us. The closest I've ever gotten was pictures."

"Good." He smiled. "I think you are really going to enjoy it."

Ree felt like a kid at her first horse show when they got inside the jet; she couldn't stop saying, "Wow!"

Colin had been on private jets his whole life. It was no big deal to him, but seeing it through Ree's eyes brought a whole new level of appreciation.

In fact, he decided that seeing the world through Ree's eyes was a pretty damn good thing.

After the plane took off, Colin opened a bottle of Sancerre and poured them a glass. They both sat back on the club chairs and relaxed. After a few minutes of silence, Ree smiled at him.

"Okay, Colin. Spill. I want to hear how your life changed dramatically in tenth grade."

He put his glass down and smirked at her. "You don't forget anything, do you?"

"You have no idea." She smirked back.

"Okay, where was I?"

"You told me about your mom telling you that you needed your behavior changed and then you jumped to the story of your uncles."

He nodded.

"Well, mom said," Using his best Scottish accent, "You need your thinking and behavior realigned and I know just the men to do it.

176

Even before this happened with the girl, your father and I were talking and we decided that you need to spend some quality time with your uncles in Scotland." Colin shook his head from the memory. "Now, I admit, if they told me this at any other time, I honestly don't know what I would have done; run away or worse, but I was so contrite after what happened, I would have agreed to anything. So, within one week, I was packed up, lock, stock and barrel, and sent to live in Scotland at the McKenna castle with my two uncles. I remember like it was yesterday; getting off the plane in Edinburgh and being greeted by Uncle George in full highland dress. He looked me over, said I was a bit scrawny, but I would do. 'Don't you worry, laddie, we'll put some muscle on ye.' Little did I know how right that statement was."

"I had been to the castle before, so it was no surprise to see it. We visited as a family a few times, but usually only stayed a week or so. I loved my uncles, even though they were a bit eccentric. I loved Scotland, but I had a feeling this was going to be a completely different visit."

"How was it different?"

Colin took another sip of the wine and continued with his story.

"When we got to the castle, Uncle George immediately took me up to the solar or the Laird's office where Uncle Duncan was waiting for me. I went into the room. Uncle Duncan looked up from his desk and smiled. I thought maybe things won't be so bad. Boy, was I wrong."

"He then proceeded to list all things I had done wrong: cursing, fighting, getting drunk, smoking pot, vandalism, taking my brother's car...the list was endless. Then, he asked if I did all those things. Timidly, I shook my head yes. Well, he said, at least you're honest. He went on to say 'Your mum and da think somehow George and I can straighten you out and turn you into a man. Well, I'm not quite sure how to do that, but what I can do is turn that scrawny body of yours into a man's body and hope that your brain follows along with it. George and I believe in scripture. Idleness is the devil's workshop, so from this point on lad, you will be busy, so busy you will beg me to go to bed. Right, on with you, now. George will show you to your room. We will have dinner and we will go over your responsibilities."

"Colin, you must have been so scared." Ree said.

"No, believe it or not, I wasn't scared. I think my head was still spinning from all that happened to me in less than a week. At dinner, Uncle Duncan informed me that I only had two jobs: one was to go to school and do all my school work, the second job was to keep the castle in firewood. Well, I thought neither job sounded too difficult. Anyway, after dinner, Uncle Colin said with a smile. 'Get a good night's sleep laddie, you'll need it' and then both of them laughed. 'Oh, and Colin, breakfast is promptly at seven.' I nodded and went off to bed."

"As a teenager, I was not an early rise,r so it was a miracle that I got even near seven on my own. I dressed and went down to breakfast. I was only about ten minutes late. Both the uncles were seated and already eating. They barely looked up from the paper when I sat down. I looked around at the platters and bowls and noticed that most of the food was gone. I asked Uncle George if I could ask the cook for more."

Colin stood up and squared his shoulders and scrunched up his face. Imitating his Uncle George using a Scottish accent he said, 'Laddie, my brother and I had a disagreement. He said that you are an idieet and have no idea what prompt means. I, on the other hand, gave you the benefit of doubt. Knowing the American education system, maybe you have not come across the word yet. Do you lad, do you know what prompt means?"

Colin sat back down smiling remembering the incident. He continued.

"I said, 'Of course I know what prompt is, it means on time.'

Uncle George said, 'Good, let's see if your reasoning is as quick. What time is it now?'

I checked my watch and told him seven-twenty.

Uncle George smiled, 'Good, see Colin, I told you he could probably tell time. Okay, boy, now let's put it together.' He looked at me expectedly.

I smiled weakly and said, 'You said breakfast was at seven promptly and I was late therefore I get no breakfast.'

Both Uncles smiled and shook their head. For the first time, Uncle Colin spoke up and said, 'Laddie there is hope for you. You have a brain and you are capable of using it. We did save you some breakfast, help yourself to finish up. Be quick about it, I want to show you your job. Also, I talked to the schoolmaster and you won't start school until Monday. So, you have today, Friday and the weekend to get a good start on the wood.'

"When they gave me a time I was never late again. In fact, even today I take pride in the fact that I am rarely late for anything.

After breakfast, Uncle Colin took me out to the wood pile. 'Have you ever chopped wood before, boy?' I shook my head no. 'I'll show you,' He said. He put a block of wood on the chopping block and proceeded to split it in one stroke. 'Like that, yes? You try it.'

I picked up a piece of wood put it on the block and swung the ax, but it got stuck. I tried a few more times and finally split it.

Uncle Colin patted me on the back and told me it wasn't bad for my first try.

He then pointed at a stack of wood. 'See this pile of wood? It all needs splitting and when you are done, you pile it up on that wall. Once you get the wall covered lengthwise start stacking, it should be piled to about your height. Once you do that we have enough wood for about a week. Every morning, before breakfast, come out and grab enough wood to stock the bedrooms and all the rooms that we use regularly. Even though we have heat, this old castle is drafty so we need the fireplaces to supplement the furnace. Understand?'

Again, I nodded.

'One more thing. On Saturdays, you'll fill the back of that truck with wood and bring it to widow Cross. I'll give you directions. When it's time, you will unload the wood and stack it for her. It would be nice to bring some wood into the house for her too. Understand?' I nodded again. 'Okay then laddie, get to work...' He told me..."

At that point, the stewardess came in and addressed Colin.

"Mr. McLeod, would you like dinner served?"

He looked over at Ree, she nodded.

"Yes, thanks, Cathy. You can set it up on the dining table."

Ree asked where the bathroom and Colin showed her.

Once Ree had disappeared, he opened his laptop to see if there were any pressing problems he needed to deal with.

Chapter 15

Ree and Colin sat down to a five-star dinner.

Not your regular airline food, Ree thought.

They ate in silence for a while, Colin still lost in the past, when Ree asked, "How long did you have to stack wood?"

He laughed.

"It felt like a lifetime. I split, I stacked and I delivered wood until every bone in my body ached. I begged for mercy. I started noticing that by the second month it was getting easier, I was getting stronger. The uncles started to notice also. I was doing great in school because if I wasn't doing schoolwork, I had to do more manual labor; school work was preferable. I even became interested in some of my classes. I loved history, math, and science, not so much English literature, especially poetry.

One Saturday I got up early to get a jump on cutting wood. I saw Uncle George talking to an older gentlemen. He was introduced to me as Jim the grounds keeper. Uncle George said he was in America visiting his son and he just came back. I was told I was no longer needed to chop wood that Jim would carry on. I felt bad for this old guy and told Uncle George I would stay and help him. My uncle laughed and walked away. Then I saw Jim go in the back of the barn and uncover a state of the art log splitter. It took him three hours to do what it took me all weekend. I was later told that they gave Jim a two-month paid vacation to visit his family in America. I have to admit, they got me good."

Ree could not stop laughing.

"I would love to meet them someday. They sound wonderfully devious."

"That's putting it mildly," Colin said dryly.

"So how long did you stay with the Uncles?"

"Until I graduated."

"Wow, I guess you came to like it there."

"Yes," He nodded, "In some ways, it was the best time of my life. I discovered who I was and what I wanted out of life."

"How so?"

"It wasn't just the wood they were devious with but other things as well. The headmaster kept the uncles informed what I was studying and when he told them we were on the unit of the Jacobites and the battle of Culloden, they started their next plan. One night at dinner, Uncle George asked what I was studying in history. I made the mistake of saying, 'I don't know some stupid battle.' They were quiet for the rest of the dinner. I had no idea what I said, so I wasn't even contrite.

Usually, after dinner, I went up to my room to study, but this night Uncle Colin said, 'Colin come with us we would like to show you something.'

We went to the second floor, to a room I had never gone into before. Uncle George opened the door and turned on the light and in the room, were big tables with metal soldiers in various positions all over. On the walls, there were all sorts of weapons, from Medieval to modern, some very nasty looking. They brought me over to one of the tables and told me to study it. My first reaction was to say that it's just a bunch of toy soldiers, but I had learned my lesson and kept my mouth closed.

I looked at the board and realized that there were English soldiers in the red coats and what looked like Scottish warriors with plaids and swords. As I looked closer and closer, I heard the voice of my history teacher in my head talking about the battle of Culloden and I realized that what I was looking at was a recreation of the battle.

I was amazed, shocked, impressed; the detail was incredible.

I started asking questions about the battle. They were extremely knowledgeable, almost like they were there. We talked and argued battle strategy until well after midnight.

The next morning, instead of being tired I was strangely energized. I couldn't wait until that night to go into the "battle room" as the Uncles called it and talk military strategy.

After that, whatever battle I studied in school we recreated in the battle room. I couldn't get enough information about battles, military tactics and such. Uncle Colin had me read Caesar's *Gallic Wars*, but he insisted I had to read it in Latin, so my Latin improved dramatically. I had to read Homer's *Iliad and Odyssey* in Greek, so my Greek improved. The only one I was allowed to read in translation was Sut Tzu *The Art of War*. Even Uncle Colin agreed Chinese was a bit much."

"So, they guided you to find what you loved, not what your brother loved or what your father expected of you. They were devious and wise."

"I don't know how wise. They told me that I had Scottish blood, so therefore, I had to love fighting and battles, and they were right."

"The only subject I still could not get a handle on was English literature. A thirteen-year-old boy reading romantic poetry and Bronte, it was the one thing keeping me off the honor roll. I tried, even the Uncles understood. Then, one day I came home early from the village. Uncle Colin had asked me to do some errands. I was going up to his solar and heard voices coming from the room but honestly, I didn't give it any notice and barged right in. This image is forever burned in my brain. There was Uncle Colin with his kilt up and Mrs. McGillvery, my English teacher, bent over his desk. There was no doubt what they were doing. I quietly closed the door and caught my Uncle's eye. Later at dinner, I was very quiet. Finally, Uncle Colin said, 'You'll thank me, boy, when reports come out in a few weeks. What is it you American's say? Take one for the team.' He was right. I got an A and made the honor roll."

"Why didn't you go home?"

"The family came to visit regularly and the truth is I didn't want to. There I was just Colin McLeod, not Duncan's brother or son or heir to Thistle Oil. I was just Colin. I could discover just what Colin liked, not what he was expected to like. By senior year, my parents wanted me to come home. I wanted no part of it. I had already decided on another life path."

"Which was?"

"Remember I told you about delivering wood to Mrs. Cross?"

She nodded.

"Every time I delivered wood, she would invite me in for tea. I always refused, until one day in December, it was bitterly cold. I wanted to get warm for a few minutes, so I accepted her invitation. I sat down and she poured me a cup of tea. I took a sip and almost spit it out. It was one part tea and three parts whiskey. I sat and drank tea with her every Saturday after that. She would talk about her family and all their accomplishments."

"One day, she showed me a picture of her grandson. He was in the RAF. The picture showed him in full military dress. When she talked about him, she beamed with pride. It was then and there that I decided that I would enter the military. I wanted my mother to be proud of me the way Mrs. Cross was of her grandson. I went home and told the Uncles my plan. They totally supported me. I looked into all of the branches and decided on the Navy, mainly because I wanted to become a Navy SEAL. Uncle George sent away for all the applications and information I needed to go to Annapolis. The three of us made a rare trip to London, where Uncle Colin called in some political favors and got an interview with the US ambassador. We met with him. The uncles told him of my desire to go to Annapolis and we needed a recommendation. He looked at my transcript and agreed to give me a glowing recommendation. My acceptance was almost a guarantee."

"But what about your Dad? How did he feel about it?"

"Ah, very perceptive, Ms. Malloy. That was the proverbial fly in the ointment."

"The summer before my senior year, my parents came for a visit, expecting me to come back with them. One night, at dinner, my Dad told me that he had brought the applications for Harvard. Maybe I could work on them and send them in. I was quiet and looked at my Uncles. They nodded, so it gave me the courage to go on. I explained to my dad I didn't want to go, Harvard, I didn't want to major in business and I didn't want to help run the business.

My dad glared at me.

'So, then what, Sonny, do you intend to do with your life? Live in the highlands with these two crazy old fools?'

It took every ounce of patience I had not to punch him right there and the funny thing was, I realized I could. With all the wood chopping, fence mending and sword wielding, I became stronger than my dad, even my brother, at only seventeen. I took a few deep breaths. I told him quietly that I was planning on joining the military. I had my application into Annapolis and was awaiting a reply.

My dad had a Scottish temper. His face turned bright red and instead of venting his anger at me he looked at my Uncles.

'This is all your fault! You and your fake battles and weapons. What have you done to my son?'

Uncle George started to get up. I think he was going to punch my dad, but Uncle Colin grabbed his arm and he sat back down. 'Duncan, he said quietly, we only did what you asked, we turned him into a man, a man capable of making his own decisions, not influenced by anyone, including us.'

My dad started to yell again, my mom took his hand and said very firmly, 'Duncan, I think it's time we retire.' She looked at us, thanked her brothers for dinner and pushed my very angry dad out of the room. In a few minutes, we heard yelling coming from their room. After about fifteen minutes, all was quiet. A few minutes later, my dad came back into the dining room apologized to the uncles, hugged me and told me he was proud of me. He then went on to say that he would support whatever career path I wanted.

The rest is history. I got accepted to Annapolis, graduated, became a Navy SEAL and enjoyed it immensely."

"Wow, Colin! You're a Navy SEAL?" Ree could not believe the talents and range of this man.

"Yes, I am. It was the most fulfilling time of my life. My team is my family."

"Are you still with the team?"

"Yes and no. Since I had to take the reins of the company, I don't do many assignments anymore."

"Why did you leave the SEALs and take up with the business?" Ree asked curiously.

Colin looked down at his hands.

"Two years ago, my dad and brother went to Alaska to look at a new drilling technique. When they left, they hit a freak storm and their plane hit the side of a mountain. There were no survivors".

Ree was shocked but regained her composure quickly. She walked over to Colin, sat on his lap, put her arms around him. Tears started falling. He looked up at her and sobbed. She held him and soothed him until there was nothing left.

Finally, he looked up at her.

"This is the first time I cried for them. I miss them every fucking day but I could never cry."

Filled with emotion, Ree could not say anything but continued to hold him.

They stayed like that until they both fell asleep.

Chapter 16

With Ree snug in his arms, Colin fell deep into thought.

How did this little slip of a woman come to mean so much to him in such a short period of time?

She became as important to him as breathing.

He picked her up, headed towards the sofa, carefully laid her down and took a blanket to cover her.

He sat next to her, grabbed his laptop, and worked on some neglected emails and correspondence.

After a while, he felt his eyes getting heavy so he closed the laptop and shut his eyes.

It took less than a minute for him to fall into a dreamless sleep.

The stewardess came in, saw them both sleeping, lowered the lights and left them to their dreams.

Colin was awakened by some turbulence. Disorientated, he quickly remembered where he was. After a quick check of time, he could not believe that he had been asleep for over two hours. He rubbed the ache in his neck and decided he needed to move them to a much more comfortable location, namely the bed. Should he be a nice guy and just pick her up and put her to bed or wake her? The devil won out; he shook her a little.

At first, Ree moaned and pushed him away, but as he started kissing and stroking her, she opened her lust-filled eyes and smiled.

"Just what are you up to, Mr. McLeod? Are you trying to take advantage of me when I'm sleeping?"

He chuckled and gently squeezed her breast.

"Now, would I do that?" He asked innocently.

"I'd be disappointed if you didn't."

"I am never one to disappoint a lady; actually, I woke you to give you an opportunity to join a very exclusive club."

She raised her eyebrows questioning.

"What club?"

He gave her a wicked grin.

"The Mile-High Club, of course."

She smiled at him smugly.

"How do you know I'm not already a member?"

He opened his mouth, closed it, opened it, like a fish out of water. She took pity on him.

"No, I'm not a member, but I would love for you to be the one to initiate me into it. What if someone comes in? Will we have to be quiet?"

"Don't worry, love." He picked her up and carried her to the far end of the plane and opened the door to the bedroom. He set her down on her feet by the bed.

Ree was in awe. She twirled around, taking in everything.

"This plane has a bedroom too? This is awesome." She turned and looked at the look of desire in Colin's eyes. She shivered but was somehow emboldened by the power she had over him. She gave him a devilish grin. "So, Mr. McLeod, what exactly are the requirements for joining this club?"

Colin sat on the edge of the bed and licked his lips.

So, she wants to play, he thought.

"The first requirement is, you have to get naked."

Ree blushed, but slowly started to pull her white silk blouse out from her skirt.

As if fell around her hips, she started to unbutton the shirt, slowly, looking up at Colin, occasionally and biting her lip.

When the shirt was unbuttoned, she parted it slightly so Colin got a glance at the white lace bra underneath.

She could hear his groan.

Next, she put her hands behind her back and unzipped her black pencil skirt. She wiggled her hips, leaning forward, giving Colin another glance at her breasts. The skirt pooled around her ankles. She stepped out of it.

The shirt still covered most of her body, giving Colin only an occasional glance at her breasts.

He started to get up but Ree put her hand up, indicating he needed to stay there.

He let out a low growl.

Ree looked up at him and wiggled her shoulder, the shirt floated down to the ground.

Ree was standing there with only her heels, thong and bra on.

Colin could not contain himself. He needed her and needed her now. This was torture.

He got up and ignored Ree's warning this time.

He stood in front of her, looking down into her eyes.

His hands, barely touching her, made their way up and down her arms.

Electricity. She shivered.

He pulled the pin out holding her hair up.

Her long hair cascaded down her back. He put his finger through her hair and when he reached her bra, he deftly unhooked it.

The bra fell to the ground. He placed his hands on her breasts, squeezing and caressing.

She moaned.

"What other requirement is there?" She whispered.

He smiled, picked her up and brought her to the bed.

In seconds his clothes were off and lay next to her.

He started to kiss her, first sweetly. Then, it became more heated. His hands moved along her body, not staying too long in any area.

Ree groaned in frustration. She tried to grab his hand and place it where her greatest need was.

He just chuckled, drew his hand back and continued to tease her.

Finally, though, his own need overcame him and he moved on top of her. He rubbed his body over hers.

"Colin, please...please make me a member of this club."

"Yes, darling, anything you want." He whispered in her ear.

He put a condom on and finished the initiation.

Afterward, they fell asleep but they both were awakened when the pilot came on the speaker and told them they had about an hour before they landed.

They got up.

Ree showered first.

Although, she wanted to shower together, Colin convinced her that the shower was way too small.

As Ree got dressed, in her business suit, Colin showered.

He came out of the shower with a towel wrapped around his waist, his wet hair clinging to the back of his neck.

Watching him do the simplest things left her with a dry mouth and a feeling of longing throughout her body.

What this man does to me... She mused.

As he bent down to pick up his clothes, she admired the way his muscles rippled along his back. When he stood, she saw the happy trail leading under the towel. Knowing intimately what was beneath the towel, she started to blush.

Lost in her lustful thoughts, she didn't see Colin grinning at her.

"You appear to like what you see. If you continue to look at me like that, I'll have to have the pilot circle the Baghdad airport for a few hours."

Blushing, Ree said, "I'm sorry."

He sat down next to her took her hand and squeezed it.

"Sweetheart, don't be sorry for desiring me. I'm flattered; Hell, I'm ecstatic because I look at you the same way."

"You do?" She so wanted to believe it but wasn't sure.

"I do," He nodded, "Now, come on. Finish getting dressed. There are some things I want to go over. Anna has some tea, coffee, and snacks waiting for us outside."

"Yum! I'll meet you out there."

"I guessed you would." He gave her a playful smack on the ass.

Colin sat down next to Ree and they dug into the cake and coffee that was laid out for them.

Ree was already finished with her first piece, going for a second.

With her mouth full, she managed to say, "What did you have to tell me?"

He crossed his fingers that this would go well.

"I hope you don't mind but I contacted the embassy here to let them know you were delayed and that I would be bringing you on this flight."

"Oh my God, Colin I never thought of that. Thank you so much."

"Anything for my lady. They are going to have a car for you at the airport when we land. From there they are going to take you to the embassy where they have a brunch set up as a welcome. It's also a way for you to meet some of the people you will be working with on a regular basis. After the brunch, they are going to take you to your apartment and then to the school for you to see what they have accomplished up to this point."

"Wow, that sounds great; will you be coming with me?" Ree said hopefully.

He took her hand.

"No, Ree, I think it best we try to keep this part of our relationship secret for a while. I don't want to do anything that would jeopardize your program. I think at this point, let them think I did you a favor and we are acquaintances. You have my phone number programmed into your phone. If you go to my name, you'll see I also put in my private business number. That number goes to my PA in Texas; if you can't reach me on my cell, call that number. Susan, my PA, usually knows where I am. Also, I programmed a third number and that is for my second in command here, Brian. If you can't reach me or Susan, call Brian. He is here in Iraq and if you need anything, anything at all, he should be able to help you."

She looked at him with awe.

"Colin, I can't begin to thank you for all you have done. I honestly don't know what I would have done without you in London. You turned a terrible situation into one of the best memories of my life. I honestly don't know what to say."

He squeezed her hand again.

"Then, don't say anything. It has been my pleasure; it was a wonderfully memorable day for me also. Besides, that's what we warriors do; we save damsels in distress. And don't think you are getting rid of me that easily. I'll be in Iraq until December, maybe even January, so I have full intentions of filling up all your available time."

"Then, I'm looking forward to all my available time."

He gave her a piece of paper.

"Here, put this in a safe place. It's the name of the hotel I'll be staying at, the Baghdad Hilton. Our company has two suites there. I'll be in the top one. I wrote the room number down. I understand you will be busy today with the school and getting settled in your apartment, but I thought that maybe tomorrow night, Friday, you could come over for dinner."

The pilot came on and told them that they would be landing in about ten minutes, to buckle up, and get ready.

The plane landed without incident. While they set up the stairs, Colin pulled her to him and kissed her; she melted into his arms and responded to his kiss. He broke the kiss and smiled at her.

"Hell, I'm going to miss you." He hugged her one last time and picked up her briefcase just as the cabin door opened.

Ree walked down the steps first and was greeted by a man who introduced himself as Keith, an aide to the Ambassador, Ryan Brooks.

They shook hands and as Colin joined the group, Ree introduced him as her savior.

She thanked him again. They shook hands and each went into their own waiting cars.

Chapter 17

When Ree stepped out of the car in front of the embassy, she was flooded with so many memories she appeared to falter. Keith was standing beside her and grabbed her arm to steady her.

"Ms. Malloy, are you okay?"

"Yes, I'm a bit jet-lagged. I haven't got my land legs yet."

They entered the embassy. She was led to Ambassador Brooks' office and could not believe how everything looked the same, but different.

How was that possible?

Ambassador Brooks approached her and took her hand.

"Ms. Malloy, it is pleasure to meet you and an even greater pleasure to be working with you on this very worthwhile project."

"Please. Mr. Ambassador, call me Reanna or Ree, whichever you prefer."

"Thank you. You must call me Ryan. After all, we will be working closely together on this project. I understand you had some trouble in London?"

She looked a bit confused.

"No, no trouble. I got food poisoning. If it wasn't for Colin, I mean Mr. McLeod, I don't know what would have happened. He got me to my room, called the doctor, checked on me the next day and even arranged for me to fly here on his company's jet. It will be a while before I eat stewed tomatoes. I think that's what did it."

Ryan agreed that it was good timing that Mr. McLeod was there and was able to help. The ambassador also realized that Reanna had no idea that Colin was her protection. He thought if Jim wanted to keep it quiet, then that was his call.

"Good, everything worked out. You're here, safe and sound. That is what's important. Come into the dining room. We have a little brunch set up for you. I'd like you to meet some of your co-workers."

They entered the massive dining room, where Ree was greeted by a wonderful group of people. Ryan introduced her to each one and told her a little about their job descriptions. After introductions were made they sat down, ate and discussed the upcoming school term. Ree was so impressed with the knowledge and dedication of her co-workers. If she had any trepidation about this program before, it was quickly put to rest.

She was particularly impressed by her administrative assistant, Sadira Gudgeon. Her father worked with Ree's father. He married an Iraqi woman and she was their daughter. Sadira was educated both in Iraq and at Columbia University in the US. She was savvy, smart and very attractive. Ree knew that she would be a valuable asset to the program.

When the brunch was over, Keith ordered the car to take Ree to her apartment, leaving her alone with Ambassador Brooks.

He took both her hands.

"Reanna, I can't tell you how happy we are to have you here. I didn't know your father very long, but I know that when he died, he left a big void here to fill. He showed me pictures of you from a young girl to a grown woman. He was so proud of you. I packed up everything in his office and sent it to your mom. Did you get to see any of it?"

"Yes, thank you so much for that. I know my mom sent you a card to thank you."

"I got it. It was the least I could do, and now you are continuing his legacy. How proud he would have been. We were talking about a program like this before he died; he was fully behind it. Your Dad was a strong proponent of women's education and you are the perfect role model. Also, before I forget, Saddam's son Uday, is having a gala Saturday night. I'm invited and he asked me to invite you. Do you think you are up to it?"

She nodded.

"Absolutely, I look forward to it, what time should I be ready?"

"Good, great! I'll come pick you up around seven."

Ree started to turn to walk out the door when she stopped, turned back to the Ambassador.

"May I ask a favor?" She said, shyly.

"Certainly. If it's in my power, anything."

"Mr. McLeod has been so kind to me, would it be a problem if I invited him?

He shook his head yes.

"Why didn't I think of that? It's a splendid idea.

Yes, please invite him."

There was a knock on the door. Keith stuck his head into the room and announced that the car was here to take Ree to her apartment and the school.

The Ambassador took Ree's hand in his.

"Reanna if you need anything, just call. In the packet of info Keith gave you, there is my private number as well as all the office numbers. Please don't hesitate to call me if you need something or if you just want to talk."

She gave him a big smile. Ree thanked him again and left with Keith.

The ride to the apartment was about fifteen minutes from the embassy in a very nice residential part of Baghdad. When Jim first told her where her apartment and school were located, she was excited.

Ree knew the area well.

When she stayed here with her dad she would walk this area and visit many of the local shops. She also liked the idea that her apartment was attached to the school. It would save valuable commuting time and if any students needed extra help at any time, she would be there for them.

When they arrived at the apartment, Keith took her bag and gave her keys to both the apartment and the school. They climbed up to the second floor. She used the key for the first time. It was mind boggling, almost prophetic, like opening a door to a new life.

The apartment was clean and neat. She noticed that all the things she had shipped earlier were neatly stacked near the sofa. It was only a one bedroom apartment, with a small kitchen and smaller sitting room but it was enough room, for her. Besides, she would spend most of her time either at the desk or at the school anyway, so she wasn't the least bit concerned.

After she put her things down, Keith took her out a door into a short hallway.

At the end was a door. He opened the door and they went down a staircase, through another door that opened into the school.

"See, isn't this great," Keith said, "If the weather is bad, you don't even have to get wet to go to work."

Ree walked around the school. She was impressed by the number of books and laptops that would be available to the women. The place was clean and well organized; she was so lucky. Ree realized she had a dedicated staff that wanted to make this work as much as she did.

****

As good a day as Ree was having, Colin was having just the opposite. It was definitely what could go wrong went wrong and anything that could go right got really messed up. It was truly a cluster fuck but he would figure it out. He could work on some of these issues, now that he didn't have Ree to distract him.

By the time he got to the hotel, he had one issue solved and was hoping that his PA, Susan,

213

would be working on other issues back in Texas. When the time difference was right, he would give her a call and try to work out some other problems.

The most pressing issue was Ree's security, especially after what happened in London.

Jim Peterson sent Colin an email with the info they had on the two guys from the bar. They positively identified one as one of the top guards assigned to Uday, Saddam's oldest son.

There wasn't enough of the other's man face in the picture to positively identify him, but the guess was that he also worked for Uday as a guard.

This was not good news.

Jim had told him Uday was very much against the school. Colin felt he would try to do anything to undermine the project. It was Colin's job to make sure he didn't and most importantly, keep Ree safe in the process.

Colin had arranged for security people to work around the school. This proved to be a challenge because it was a school for women and with the cultural mandates, men were not allowed in the school when the Iraqi women were there. It took Colin some time, but it was worth it. He found a woman operative that was both educated and lethal. Her name is Sadira Gudgeon.

Colin was impressed as soon as he met her; he was sure nothing would get by her.

Jim, as well as Ambassador Ryan, agreed to place her in a prominent position in the school. He just prayed that Ree liked her.

At some point, he wanted to visit her apartment and school to get the lay of the land. If there was an issue and he had to get people out of there quickly, he needed to know all the entrances and exits. He was sure Ree would invite him to both the apartment and school in the near future, so that should not be a problem.

With that thought, a wave of guilt washed over him that almost made him sick to his stomach. He had thought about this since he and Ree became intimate. She had become much more than an assignment. Should he tell her? It was on the tip of his tongue a few times but he choked; he lost his nerve. He never felt fear like this.

The most dangerous SEAL assignment didn't cause this mind-bending fear. He was so afraid that he would lose her and that was something he just could not handle.

Chapter 18

Ree was thrilled with the school. A lot of work went into organizing and setting up a workable learning space. She told Keith that she wanted to stay at the school and get acclimated.

He agreed, but as he started to walk out the door, he stopped.

"Oh, before I forget, I want to show you your office."

They walked down the hall. On the right, facing the street was a door with the name plate: REANNA MALLOY DIRECTOR.

She stopped at the sign and gently caressed the letters, then opened the door.

The room was small, clean and organized. She noticed that all the files and books she sent over were stacked by one of the bookshelves. Ree found her first job. She thanked Keith again and got to work.

As she was putting books on shelves, her mind drifted to Colin. She wondered what he was doing and how his day was going.

It was unbelievable. She had only known this man for a few days and he had already become one of the most important people in her life.

She wondered what Epee would think of him.

She laughed to herself.

She knew Epee was one to voice her opinion loudly and often. Her last boyfriend: wow, what a disaster.

She had to admit that Epee tried to warn her.

"I don't know; there is something sleazy about him." She had told her on more than one occasion and she was right.

Ree had met him at a conference for college professors in New York City. He was a chemistry professor at the University of Pennsylvania. He was smart, funny and good looking.

They hooked up at the conference and tried to get together as often as possible after that, which turned out, wasn't often. He seemed to show up only when something good was playing at McCarter Theater.

About six months into the relationship, she attended a conference at his University. She decided to surprise him, so she didn't tell him that she was coming.

Ree got to the university, registered for the conference and, with her visitor's badge, she was able to go just about anywhere. She found her way to the chemistry department, located an aide, and identified herself as a colleague of Jason Adams. He saw her badge, assumed Professor Adams was expecting her and brought her to his office. He explained the Professor was in class, but she could wait here.

She went into his office. It was warm and inviting, unlike what she expected from a chemistry nerd, as he referred to himself.

Ree couldn't help but detect the essence of a woman's touch.

Trying to ignore the feeling, she ventured over to the desk. There were lots of framed pictures.

She picked one up. She was stunned.

There, in living color, was Jason, with a beautiful woman next to him and three small children surrounding them. She looked at the other pictures; they were all the same; pictures of the perfect family that Jason never mentioned.

Just as Ree started to digest what was in front of her, the door opened and Jason came in, panicked.

"Ree, honey," He pleaded, "I can explain."

She picked up one of the pictures and walked over to him. She handed him the picture and then slapped him across the face.

"You can explain why you forgot to tell me you were a husband and father? The picture explains everything, Jason. Just one thing, why didn't you tell me?"

"You didn't ask, I thought you didn't want to know," He offered contritely.

She opened the door and walked out. She was there but not there; ensnared within an almost, out of body experience.

Somehow, she made it out of the building, found her car and went home.

She called Epee and over a bottle of wine, they remade their pact that only Jamie was worthy of their love.

She had to give Epee credit, she never said, 'I told you so.'

Ree also realized, that never again, could she ever, ever trust a man who lied to her or withheld important information from her.

She was so glad that Colin was different; they had an honest relationship. It started out that way and she was certain it would continue.

Therefore, she knew that Epee would approve of Colin McLeod.

Lost in some good and bad memories alike, it took a moment for her to realize that someone was knocking on the front door of the school.

She opened the door and there stood a tiny, older woman with a covered dish.

In very bad English she said, "You the female that teach my granddaughter?"

Ree switched to Farsi, introduced herself and invited her into the school. The woman told Ree she was Mrs. Hadine, her neighbor. She was happy that her granddaughter would learn English and possibly make contacts, so someday, she might be able to go to a western school.

She handed Ree the covered dish with a small bag. She explained that she made her harissa, a traditional dish of welcome, made of stewed chicken and coarsely ground, soaked wheat.

In the bag, was Kleicha, the national cookie of Iraq. It was dough molded into a half-moon and filled with nuts and sugar.

Ree was familiar with both the dishes and especially loved the cookies. She thanked Mrs. Hadine and told her she looked forward to meeting her granddaughter.

As she went out the door, Mrs. Hadine turned and grabbed Ree's hand.

"Thank you, lady, thank you so much." She turned and walked away.

Ree was touched by Mrs. Hadine's thoughtfulness.

Her stomach rumbled.

She checked the time; it was already past dinner.

Ree closed everything and headed up the stairs to her apartment. Heating the Kleicha in the microwave, she poured herself a glass of juice. She missed her glass of wine.

Maybe Colin had wine connections for her cabernet fix. She sat down and looked around the apartment. She thought back on her day and reveled in her good fortune.

She dug into the food – she was happy.

As she cleaned up, her cell rang; it was Colin.

"Hello, how is my big handsome warrior doing tonight?"

"Wow, someone's in a good mood. Have a good day?"

"Oh, Colin it was great, fantastic, awesome I can't believe how good everything went today. I was a little nervous about meeting the Ambassador. I heard some not nice things about him, but he was really nice and very supportive. The staff! You can't believe it. They are wonderful, especially my assistant, Sadira. She is amazing, smart, and savvy and seems to have the same vision for the school as I do."

He breathed a sigh of relief. He had hoped Sadira would be a good choice. She was his main contact and the first line of defense for Ree.

"Ree, that's great. I'm happy for you. How's the apartment?"

"It's small, probably not up to your standards, but it's clean; it has all I need." She sat down and ate another cookie. She was reminded of Mrs. Hadine.

"Oh, and Colin you can't believe this, I was organizing some stuff at the school when someone knocked on the door. I didn't hear it at first, but then I answered it and there was my neighbor, Mrs. Hadine. She gave me Harissa. Do you know..."

He cut her off rather gruffly.

"I know what it is; Ree, wasn't anyone there with you? Why did you open the door?"

"Colin, stop it. Just because I'm Director doesn't mean I'm not capable of answering the door. Besides, I gave everyone the rest of the day off after the brunch. I wanted to spend some time here alone, you know, to get acclimated, feel comfortable, don't be paranoid."

"Sorry Ree, I just had a bad day." It had just gotten worse. "And besides, how do you know your apartment wouldn't be up to my standards. When I was with the SEALs, I would be happy to find a dry spot to sit or thrilled to find a place with a roof on it. Remember, I spent part of my life growing up in a cold, damp castle, so your apartment sounds very cozy. I can't wait to see it."

"I can't wait to show you. I'm sorry you had a bad day...and here I'm going on and on about how great my day was. Is there anything I can help with?"

"Yes, you can tell me how much you miss me, you can tell me what you're wearing, that you're hot for me and you miss my tongue, my..."

"Colin, do you want to have phone sex?"

"No, not really. I want to have real sex, but there is no other choice."

She sat down with her glass of juice.

"No way, buddy. I'm not getting all hot and bothered. Then, I won't be able to get to sleep. I have a big day tomorrow."

"What's tomorrow?" He asked as he scratched his head.

"Did you forget so soon? You invited me for dinner. Is the invite still open?"

"Of course. In fact, that was the main reason I was calling you; you never answered me about dinner. I was just checking to make sure I wouldn't be stood up."

"I can't imagine any woman standing you up; if she did, she's either blind or stupid."

"Either way, I'm glad you're coming."

"Oh, I'm sure that I'll be coming. In fact, if I know you, probably a few times."

"Ree, Ree Ree, what have I done to you? I've corrupted you in just a few short days."

"Is that a problem?"

"Not at all; In fact, I love it. So, tell me, what else happened? What are you eating?"

"Mrs. Hadine also brought over Kleicha cookies. Have you ever had them?"

"Yes, I love them."

"Uh, oh."

"What happened? Did you just eat them all?"

"How did you know? I'm sorry. I promise when I have time I'll make you some."

"I didn't know you could cook, I'm impressed."

"Well, I can't really, but I could learn. For you, I would learn."

"I'm touched. Well, one of us will have to learn because I'm not really a great cook either. When we get home, we will be eating out a lot or ordering in. Doesn't matter, as long as you're there."

"Does that mean what I think it means?"

"What's that, sweetheart?"

"Are we going to see each other when we get home?"

"Damn straight! I've found you, my lost soul. Do you think I'll ever let you go?"

She tried to control her emotions. Ree was quiet.

"Ree, is everything okay? Did I go too far?"

She was breathless.

"No, Colin not at all. In fact, I thought my day could not get any better, but what you just said made everything else pale in comparison. I've found my lost soul too."

He cleared his throat.

Colin really didn't want to continue this line of conversation over the phone. This was a conversation he wanted with her in his bed or on his lap so he could kiss her and caress her anytime he wanted.

He changed the subject. He asked for more information about her meeting with the ambassador.

"He really is a nice man. He knew my dad and had nothing but good things to say about him. He even showed me my Dad's old office. He really wants to make the school work. He is very supportive. Oh, and before I forget, he told me that Saturday night, Uday, Saddam's oldest son, is hosting a gala at the palace. The ambassador is invited and Uday specifically asked for me to attend. He wants to meet me and ask questions about the school. Isn't that cool? Wouldn't it be great if I had his support?

The ambassador is picking me up at seven. Here's the best part. I asked if I could bring you as my date, you know, as a thank you for all you did. I hope you don't mind. I don't know if you like events like that."

"Honestly, I hate them, but I'll be with you so I'll love it. Thank you for inviting me. Now, Ree, this is important. If anyone knocks on the door, don't answer it; act like you are not home. Only answer the door if someone is there with you. Will you promise me that?"

"I don't understand why you are being so paranoid about this. After all, I'm in a good neighborhood and the people in the area seem to be very supportive of the school."

He dragged his fingers through his hair.

"Ree, please do this for me? It will make me feel more comfortable. Please, sweetheart, for me?"

"Okay, for you, but I still think you are being unreasonable."

"Thank you. I have to go; I have to work on some problems of my day. Unfortunately, my day was not as perfect as yours. I'll pick you up tomorrow about six. Is that good? It will give you some time to show me around the school and your apartment."

She was disappointed; she was looking forward to a little phone sex.

Ree told him she understood and couldn't wait to see him tomorrow. She hung up, took some reports to read and snuggled up in bed, alone.

After he got off the phone with Ree, Colin's first phone call was to Sadira.

"What the hell happened today?" He growled.

She was baffled.

"Commander, what do you mean? Everything went great. I was just going to call you. I love Reanna; she's smart, upbeat, and a hard worker. I really think we will do fine together. I think she likes me."

"I know you two have a mutual fucking admiration society. I mean about her being alone in the school. Do you know someone knocked on the door and gave her a gift? Damn, Sid, it could have been a bomb or poison. What were you thinking? Someone should have gone with her. If you can't handle this, just let me know."

"Are you done, Commander?"

Silence on the other end.

"Okay, Sir, now listen. First of all, she insisted no one come back to the school. She wanted time alone. I understand that. She needed to touch things, laugh, cry over this great project. Besides, she wasn't alone. John was in front of the school doing street work."

Colin took a deep breath and rubbed his forehead.

"Then how did that woman get over there?"

"That woman," She said sternly, "Is Mrs. Hadine; her granddaughter is attending the school. She has been checked out. She told us she wanted to bring Ree a welcome meal and we agreed. Remember, Commander, besides a school, this is a project designed to help win the hearts and minds of the Iraqis. Community relations are a big part. Believe me, Sir, the only threat is in your head. We had it covered."

He took a deep breath. "You're right, Sid, I over reacted. After what happened in London, I'm a little jumpy."

"Commander, are you going to be able to handle this? Are you getting too close? Because if you are, I need to know, Jim needs to know."

"No, I'm absolutely fine. Just a hard day. I definitely have things in perspective. Thanks, Sid. Really, you're doing a great job. Again, I'm sorry; it's just been a long day."

What started out as a disastrous day turned out a little better. Maybe he would get some sleep tonight and dream of a soft, sweet body, wrapped around him.

Chapter 19

Ree tossed and turned all night. She finally got up at five and made tea, a bowl of cereal and sat down to read the reports she didn't finish from last night. She wanted to go down to the school but didn't want to appear too anxious so she waited until 6:30 dressed and headed down.

As she entered the school, a few of the teachers were coming in, including Sadira.

With a big smile on her face, she greeted everyone.

Ree was overjoyed to find out Sadira brought some Iraqi pastries. Yum.

By seven, everyone was there. They started with a meeting and went over the most pressing problems.

Ree was thrilled. It seemed everyone was on the same page with the school and had the same vision for its future. The staff pitched in to set up books, laptops, and smart boards. Ree spent most of the time in her office getting paperwork organized.

Sadira brought her lunch; otherwise, she would have forgotten to eat.

Imagine that, Reanna Malloy missing a meal.

She would have to remember to tell Colin. Her mind began to wander.

What is he doing now? She wondered and almost as if she willed it, her cell rang.

"Hey, beautiful, still having a great time or are you ready to go home yet?"

"It's going so great. You can't believe it! I am so happy, but I'll be happier if you tell me we are still having dinner tonight."

"Would not miss it for the world. Can I come by about five to pick you up? I would love to see the school and your apartment."

"Absolutely perfect. I'll see you then."

After the phone call, time stood still. Every time she looked at the clock, she thought an hour went by and it was only fifteen minutes.

Finally, at four she couldn't take it any longer, told everyone if they wanted to go home, no problem, but she was going up to the apartment. Most left, but Sadira asked if she could stay for a while. She still had some things to do. Ree realized how lucky she was to have such a dedicated worker.

In her apartment, Ree washed up, before changing into a pair of jeans and t-shirt.

She was just going into Colin's car and then, into the hotel, which was American/European, so her choice of clothes would be fine.

At about four-fifty, she heard people talking downstairs.

Curious, she grabbed her purse and sweater and headed into the school.

She found Sadira and Colin, deep in conversation in the foyer and were headed into one of the classrooms.

Ree had the strangest feeling that they knew one another.

How ridiculous, she thought.

"Ah, I see you two have met," She said, smiling at them both.

Momentarily confused, Sadira responded.

"What do you mean? This is the first time we've met."

"Yes, I know, I'm glad you introduced yourselves." Ree felt that Sadira reaction was strange, but decided to ignore it.

Ree went up to Colin and put her hand out in greeting.

He grabbed her hand, growled and pulled her into an embrace. He hugged her and smelled her hair.

"You smell good. I missed you."

She grinned from ear to ear.

"I missed you too. Would you like to see the school?"

Ree took him on a tour of the school. Colin had to admit, he was impressed with what this small group put together in such a short amount of time.

Although, he knew that a lot of their progress was a direct reflection of Ree's work ethic and dedication to the project.

He arrived at the school a little early, hoping to have some time alone with Sid. He was able to ask Sid to distract Ree while he checked out a tunnel in the basement he found on the schematics.

They were almost done with the tour when Sadira called Ree over to one of the classrooms and told her there was a problem with one of the computers.

Ree excused herself, which left Colin alone to snoop. His first stop was the basement. According to the schematics, the opening to the tunnel should be on the south wall.

On that wall, he saw a big wooden wardrobe, right where the tunnel should be. He remembered to bring a flashlight, but could he move the wardrobe? Thankfully, it was not as heavy as it looked.

Was that done on purpose? He wondered.

He was able to move it enough to get a light behind it and sure enough, there was the tunnel. He would have to get John or Mark down here on the pretense of an electrical problem and check out exactly where the tunnel comes out if it's blocked, and most important if it's safe.

Colin shut off the flashlight and made his way up the stairs. Ree caught him coming out through the door.

"What in the world were you doing down in the basement? I've checked out every inch of this place and even I won't go into that basement, it smells awful."

Sadira smiled at Ree.

"Now, Ree, he's a guy and you know how guys like guy things like dirty basements, pumps, and furnaces."

She looked at Colin with her eyebrows up as if asking if this was true.

"Well, to be honest, Ree, I got turned around and thought this might be the door to your apartment. When I realized it was the basement, I couldn't help myself; I went down. I guess Sadira is right; it's a guy thing."

"Inquiring minds want to know. Is there anything interesting down there?"

"Nothing, absolutely nothing," He said firmly, "Come on, let's have a look at this cozy apartment."

Colin loved the idea of her apartment being attached to the school, not just for her convenience, but for her safety. He was already planning ways to get her out in a hurry.

Inside, the apartment was warm and cozy. He could see that Ree already made the apartment her own, with pictures of family, friends, and animals on every table and some walls. She showed him around, which took all of thirty seconds.

Colin's eyes rested on a picture of an older man, holding up an old piece of pottery. He picked up the picture and looked closely at the piece of pottery.

"Do you recognize the piece of pottery?" Ree asked him.

"Is it the piece we saw at the British Museum?"

"Yes, it was taken right after he found it. He was so proud. He sent that picture to me with a letter explaining every detail of his find. I take it with me wherever I go."

"Tell me about the other pictures."

They went around the room, either Ree or Colin picking up a picture, and Ree identified who they were and what they were doing.

He stopped at a picture of two young girls standing next to their ponies.

"Is this you and your friend Epee?"

"Yes, our first of many horse shows. We really bonded that day as lifelong friends. I don't know what I would do without her. She is my sister of the heart."

"Show me a picture of your mom."

"There are tons, but this is my favorite. We decided one year to do a Christmas card with the horses, dogs, cats and my mom and I in the picture. Epee came over to take the picture. The idea sounded good in theory, but it was a disaster: dogs not facing the camera, cats clawing dogs, horses biting dogs and my mom yelling at everyone. We finally got this picture. It's one of my favorite."

Colin could not get over how much Ree looked like her mother. Same petite figure; same auburn colored hair; her mom's, with a little gray in it; same classic face and lovely smile.

"She looks like a great woman."

"She is. I miss her, but I know she's happy at the farm, taking care of all the critters. Okay, enough of this. I'm hungry. I hope you have lots of food."

"Of course, Ms. Malloy. I wouldn't want you to go hungry. Come, let's go. The car is out front."

It was a ten-minute trip to the hotel.

Colin's suite was on the top floor so the view of Bagdad was spectacular. She could not stop her ohs and ahs over the view, the size of the bed and the beautiful table set up with candles and flowers. Colin opened a bottled of Sancerre and handed her a glass.

"Oh, thank you. You know, I didn't think I would miss my wine as much as I do. I was hoping that you had a bottle."

"No problem, sweetheart. I'll have a case sent over to you."

She went up to him and put her arms around his neck.

"You spoil me."

"Yes, I do. You can spoil me later."

"Which means?"

"I'll tell you later. Come on. Let's eat."

They sat down to a fabulous dinner. After they finished the appetizers, someone knocked on the door and brought in hot entrees with dessert. Ree was in heaven.

They ate in silence for a bit, both lost in their thoughts. Colin broke the mood when he reminded her of the gala Saturday night. He told her he would meet her there since she was going with the Ambassador.

"Okay, sounds great, and while we are on the subject, I have never really been to anything like this. What do you think is acceptable to wear? I brought a black, long, conservative dress that I've worn for faculty parties; do you think that would be okay? I always judge by my friend Epee. If she says it's boring, then I know it's okay for Princeton. Epee said this dress is a major bore; in fact, a snorer."

Colin laughed.

"I can't wait to meet Epee; she sounds like a lot of fun. Now you don't have to answer if you don't want, but did she pick out the dress you wore to the bar in London."

"Yes, how did you know?"

"That was anything but a snorer. In fact, when I saw you in it, the last thing I thought of was sleeping."

She lowered her voice; her eyes glazed over.

"What did you think of?"

He grabbed her shoulders and lifted her up.

"Let me show you what I was thinking..." He growled as he led her over to the bedroom.

They had dessert much later that night.

Chapter 20

Ree worked most of the morning at the school then turned her attention to unpacking her apartment.

Later, a quick glance at the clock told her it was time to get ready for the gala.

She pulled her black dress out. She felt more confident about it after Colin assured her it would be perfect.

The ambassador's car pulled up in front of the apartment promptly at seven. She walked out and greeted him.

"Ree, you look beautiful. I'm a lucky man tonight. I'll be escorting the most beautiful woman there."

She blushed.

"You flatter me, Mr. Ambassador and I love it."

Ambassador Brooks followed her into the car.

"Please, Ree, call me Ryan; This is a social occasion."

Ree wondered how much the Ambassador knew about her assignment. Did he know about trying to get into the stable? Should she ask him? She decided that discretion was the better part of valor; she didn't say anything.

If Jim wanted Ryan to know, then Jim would have told him.

The drive to the palace took about a half hour in traffic. They spent the time making small talk about the weather and the latest information about sports teams in the US. They discovered that they were both Yankee baseball fans.

Ree was in absolute awe when they pulled up to the Palace. She had never been inside but her dad had been a few times. He told her about how opulent and almost decadent the inside was; she couldn't wait.

When they stopped in front, Ryan got out and held the door open for her. They entered the foyer where they had to go through a metal detector. She was surprised, but she thought it's just a sign of the time.

From that point, they proceeded through the entryway to the ballroom.

Ryan gave the gentleman his invitation and their names were read.

At the mention of the Ambassador's name, quite a few heads turned. Some men started to walk towards them.

Ree looked around for Colin but kept getting distracted by everything that was around.

Ree agreed with her Dad's assessment: opulent and decadent, definitely over the top.

Ambassador Ryan introduced her to some of the people who approached them.

One gentleman, in particular, seemed very knowledgeable about the school, so the conversation was relaxed from that point.

Ree felt an arm go around her waist and felt a light butterfly kiss on her cheek. She turned and there was Colin, in a tuxedo.

Does this guy look bad in anything?

If she thought he looked good in jeans, he was positively gorgeous in a tux.

James Bond, meet Colin McLeod.

Colin leaned over and whispered in her ear, "There goes that look again and if you don't stop I'll embarrass us right here. Ree, you look stunning. I disagree with Epee; it's not boring at all; you look very elegant."

Ree did a short curtsy and said, "Why thank you, kind Sir."

Ambassador Ryan looked over and shook his hand.

"Colin, great to see you. I'm glad you could attend. As I recall, you usually don't like these affairs."

"I was very motivated this time." He looked down at Ree.

"Are you trying to steal my date?"

"No, Sir. I wouldn't dream of it."

They bantered back and forth for a while until the crowd parted and up walked Uday Hussein, dressed in all his military glory.

He approached the ambassador and nodded his head.

"Ambassador Brooks, you do this simple soldier an honor by attending my party."

"No, it is my honor to be here. Let me introduce you to my friends. I think you know Colin McLeod."

They shook hands and nodded at each other.

"Yes, we have had the pleasure to meet on several occasions. How are you and what brings you to my gala?"

Colin smiled at him but never broke eye contact.

"I am in Bagdad on business and was given this wonderful invitation. How could I refuse?"

"How could you, indeed." He turned to Ree. "Who is this lovely young woman?"

Ambassador Brooks introduced Ree as the director of the new school for women.

He smirked at her and said in Farsi, *I don't support this school. I think it's another example of Americans trying to dominate the world by forcing western ideas and beliefs down our throats, in this case, impressionable, naïve women. I don't know how my father was talked into this, but if it was my choice, I would close it down immediately.* "He gave her a fake smile. *"And send you, Ms. Malloy, back to America."*

Colin knew a smattering of Farsi and he knew enough to know that the conversation was not going well.

He nodded to Ryan, who shook his head in a negative.

He wanted to punch Uday in the face and knock that smug look off his face but that would accomplish nothing.

The only thing he could do was to be to be there for Ree.

Ree paled as Uday's tirade went on, but the more he insulted her, the more she dug in her heels.

Remember, you're a Jersey Girl. She told herself and decided to fight the only way she knew how, and that was with words.

Ree smiled up at him and responded in Farsi,

"Sir, I am sorry that you feel the way you do, but you are speaking in ignorance. The school is not meant to spread western ideas. It is meant to empower women with an education to be able to live self-sufficient lives and to help support their families. These are not western ideas, but universal ideas."

Ambassador Brooks could see that the discussion was getting heated and injected himself into it in English.

"Everyone lets calm down and discuss this another time. Uday, would like to come to the school someday and see some of the work the teachers are doing. I'm sure you will agree it's not the propaganda palace that you think it is."

Uday harrumphed, but at least, he didn't say no.

Colin spoke up.

"How is that two-year-old thoroughbred coming along? Are you still planning on shipping him over to the US to compete?"

Uday's whole face changed from scowl to a smile.

"Yes, yes," He said, "The trainers are working with him now. We are expecting great things from him. You know, he is descended from Secretariat's line."

"I've heard that. My family is also working on a two-year-old, hoping to compete in this year's trials. We have great hopes for him also."

He looked perplexed.

"I thought the McLeods were oil people. I didn't know you were also interested in horses."

"I live in Texas; Oil, cattle, and horses are part of the blood. We love them all."

Ambassador Brooks added," I don't know if you know, but Ms. Malloy is a nationally ranked equestrian. Her mother was internationally ranked as a show jumper."

Uday lit up and looked at her again, this time with interest, not disdain.

"No, I did not know that. Well, Ms. Malloy, I'm impressed. What riding discipline?"

"I ride dressage. I was nationally ranked, two years ago. My mom, on the other hand, was a hunter, jumper, rider and was internationally ranked. She has since retired from showing; she trains horses and riders now."

"Again, Ms. Malloy, I am impressed. Why dressage and not hunter jumper like your mother?"

"I guess because I'm also an academic. I like the discipline and focus of dressage vs. jumping. Sir, if I may, I understand that you have a relative of Gifted in your barn. I was a big fan of that horse. Is this horse showing promise? Gifted was one of the greatest Dressage horses in the world."

Ree did her homework, not only for the school but for her other project. She knew all there was to know about Uday Hussein and his horses.

"Yes, I do have Gifted's full brother. He is doing very well," He beamed with pride.

"Are you training him for dressage or jumping?"

"My trainers are just doing the basics with him. We will let him choose his path."

She nodded her head.

"Very wise, Sir. If it ever becomes possible, I would be honored to meet a relative of Gifted. I would love to watch him work."

"How could I refuse such a request from a beautiful woman. Obviously one so talented, who speaks Farsi and rides horses? I would be honored." He took her arm and started to walk away. As an afterthought, he turned to Colin. "You come too, Colin, and meet the next Kentucky Derby Winner and you too, Brooks."

All Colin could think of was; *Yes, she did it!*

Chapter 21

Uday led Colin, Ree, and Ambassador Brooks out of the gala, into the night. It was humid, with the air hanging heavy. They walked down a path that led to an iron gate. Uday opened the gate, bowed and swept his arm, allowing Ree to enter first. Ree walked into the walled garden and stopped in her tracks.

"Oh my God! It looks just like the..."

"Alhambra." Uday finished her thought. "When my father was a young man he visited Spain and the Alhambra. He was so impressed by it, especially the gardens, that when he became the leader in Iraq, he built the Palace and patterned the gardens after the Alhambra."

Ree closed her eyes for a minute remembering her trip to Spain with her Dad. When they traveled to Iraq for the summer, they usually stopped in London for a few days, visiting museums and shops but one year instead of London they went to Spain. It was a beautiful country. She remembered the great food and the friendly people but the Alhambra was the highlight of the trip.

The Alhambra was a Royal Palace, built in 1333 by the Sultan of Granada when the Moors occupied that part of Spain.

It is located in Granada, Spain.

Ree read a description of it from a Morrish poet as, "A pearl set in emeralds."

Ree felt even that description of the Palace paled in comparison to its beauty.

Her favorite part of the complex was the gardens and she had to give the elder Hussein credit, he copied them to perfection.

They walked through what Ree remembered as the Court of Myrtles. It was an open courtyard with a large, rectangle pool in the center, set in marble pavement, full of goldfish and surrounded by myrtles.

The sound of the water, along with the heady scent of the myrtle and orange trees was mesmerizing.

They continued walking into the next area that Uday called the Court of the Eagles.

Ree turned to him, questioning the name.

He laughed.

"Yes, I'm sure you remember it as the Court of the Lions, but my father's insignia was an eagle, so he had the fountain designed with eagles rather than lions. It is beautiful, yes?"

Ree remembered the original as an oblong courtyard with white marble columns and a sprawling, matching floor.

In the center was a fountain with an alabaster basin, supported by twelve lions, memorialized in white marble.

In this case, it was twelve eagles, but all of the other details were mirrored perfectly.

Ree turned to Uday.

"It is beautiful, just like the original. It takes my breath away."

"Come, we are taking too much time here. Let us get to the stables." He said abruptly.

The group made their way through the rest of gardens, walked down another path and there, situated down a hill, were the stables. The barn was a combination of classic and modern. The group passed the main riding arena.

Ree stopped and admired the footing; it looked like sand but it wasn't pure. She realized right away that there was something mixed into it. Uday turned, looked back and noticed her studying the footing. He walked back to her.

As he approached, she had to ask.

"What type of footing is this? It looks marvelous. Springy but solid."

That question dispelled any doubts Uday had about Reanna being a professional horsewoman. From his experience, only serious riders and trainers would even think to ask about footing.

"It is something new; they coat each grain of sand with plastic so the sand is lighter and creates almost no dust. It is mixed in with shredded leather to make it more, 'springy' as you say."

Ree bent down and picked some up.

"It's wonderful. I would love to have something like this in my riding arena at home."

Uday studied her for a moment.

"I will give you the information where we got it; I actually think it is a company based in your country."

He put his hand in the middle of her back and guided her towards Colin and the Ambassador. They entered the barn and again, Ree was awed; the place was spotless. There were stone and marble pillars, housing solid oak stalls, embellished with polished brass fixtures.

Ree was sure that even the biggest barns in Kentucky didn't look like this.

As she looked around, an older man approached the group. Uday introduced him as Shavo, the barn manager. He took them over to Present, the offspring of Gifted.

Ree did a quick assessment. He was a dressage riders' dream. He was big, about 17 hands, a beautiful blood-bay, with kind eyes. He had strong legs and a confirmation that assured difficult dressage moves, like piaffe and passage would be a snap for this horse.

As she admired him, Uday detailed his pedigree and training to-date.

Ree asked some follow-up questions about his training and then thanked Uday for the opportunity to see such a magnificent horse.

Shavo then ushered them over to the descendant of Secretariat.

Wow, was the first thing Ree thought, *he is big*.

Colin must have thought the same thing because the first thing he asked was how many hands.

"Eighteen, one. Is he not magnificent?" Uday answered proudly.

All nodded.

Uday and Colin discussed the finer points of training racehorses and even Ambassador Ryan, an avid fan of horse racing, added to the conversation.

Bored with the racing conversation, Ree looked around the barn and noticed, at the far end, a pile of rags in front of one of the stalls. She was startled when she noticed that a hand came out from underneath the rags with what appeared to be a carrot. The hand moved the carrot towards the stall door. She saw a black fuzzy nose of a horse poke his head through the barely opened stall door and bite off a piece of the carrot.

This happened a few times until there was only the small piece left. The little hand held up the small piece and the nose gently took it. After a short while, another carrot appeared.

Ree was intrigued.

What was going on? She thought, feeling compelled to investigate.

She walked over and looked into the stall.

She heard someone yell and was about to turn around when an angry horse, ears back, teeth bared, eyes flaming, bolted from the stall, after her.

She tried to take a step back but her heel got caught in the back of her dress.

Thankfully, Colin was behind her and caught her.

Shavo, right behind Colin, slammed the stall door shut, successfully keeping the horse inside. The pile of rags, which appeared to be a young boy, ran off.

Uday took Ree's hand.

"Reanna, are you harmed? I am so sorry that that horse frightened you, but he is the spawn of the devil."

She recovered quickly.

"What happened? What's wrong with that horse?"

"That horse was given to me by the Saudi prince as a gift, but I think it was an underhanded way to try to kill me. The horse's name is Rasyn and he is a descendant of Gamen, one of the finest racing Arabians in the world. So far, he has seriously injured two of my grooms. When I tried to tame him, he threw me into the far wall of the arena, nearly breaking my back. I cannot have the horse shot, though, it would be an insult to our Saudi friends. So, he is just used for stud."

Ree was intrigued. Something did not add up. How was it possible for the horse to be so gentle with the boy and yet be the killer Uday claimed? She decided to go with her gut.

"Sir, if I may, my mother and my specialty is re-training difficult horses. We get horses off the racetrack and rehab them to new lives in different professions. Some of the horses we train are much more violent than that one."

He raised his eyebrows.

"Are you telling me you can train this horse, a tiny person like you, a woman no less?"

She tried not to let his last remark fluster her. She dug her heals in.

"Yes, that's exactly what I'm saying. I can rehab this horse in one week. Give me a second week and I will be able to do a simple dressage pattern with him. The pattern will consist of a walk, trot, and canter; nothing fancy."

"Ridiculous," He spat," There is no way. The whole idea is absurd."

Colin held her arm and squeezed just a bit. Ree understood his message, but she refused to look at him. This was her fight and she would see it to the end.

"No disrespect intended, Sir, but are you afraid that this small woman cannot do it?"

He looked her right in the eye.

"Of course, not. Ridiculous."

"Then, what is the harm in letting me try? We can even make it interesting."

"What do you have in mind?"

"You are a betting man. How about, if I do what I say I can do, you will endorse the school."

Uday thought for a moment and smiled.

"Miss Reanna, if you do what you say you can do, I will not only endorse the school but I will send my second wife to your school."

She beamed.

"I agree."

Colin squeezed her arm so hard she was sure she would be black and blue.

Uday smiled.

"What do I get if you cannot do as you say? What if you fail?"

Unconcerned, she shrugged her shoulder.

"I won't fail, but what do you want?"

With a smile that made her blood run cold, he said, "What I wanted from the beginning; the school closes."

Ambassador Brooks blanched and Colin groaned.

With a nod of her head and a smile on her face, she said, "Deal."

"Can I start working the horse tomorrow, Sunday? The riding exhibition will be two weeks from Sunday. Will you be able to be there?"

"Miss Reanna, I would not miss it for the world. In the meantime, I will grant you unlimited access to the barn and riding areas only. I will tell the guards to let you into those areas only. Shavo will be here to help you with anything you need."

"One more thing, Sir, if you don't mind. Could Mr. McLeod accompany me at least for tomorrow? I need something built and I am sure he will be a big help."

"Of course. Colin will be welcomed but he will have the same limited access as you do."

Both nodded their agreement.

"Let us get back to the celebration." He led them out of the barn and back to the palace.

Uday left them as soon as they entered the ballroom.

Ryan turned to say something to Ree when Colin who still had a hold on her arm said through clenched teeth, "Ryan I hope you don't mind but Ms. Malloy told me on the way back that she is not feeling well and would like to get back to her apartment. I know you would like to stay, so please, allow me to accompany her back?"

Ryan saw the steely determination in Colin's eyes and agreed to the plan. He was hopeful that maybe Colin could talk some sense into her and somehow recover from this crazy plan.

"Ree," He said," I'll talk to you tomorrow."

Ree was perplexed by what Colin said.

She was not tired and did not have a headache. Maybe he wasn't feeling well and wanted to leave.

She agreed to leave with him.

Colin called for the car. When they were alone, Ree tried to ask him why he wanted to leave so fast.

Colin ignored her.

She tugged at his jacket.

"Colin, I didn't want to leave. There were people that knew my dad and I wanted to talk to them."

Again, Colin ignored her.

She was about to kick him when the car arrived. He opened her car door and helped her inside. He talked to the driver for a minute and then got into the car.

They drove in silence for a while.

Finally, Ree could not take it anymore.

"I guess you're angry with me, but if you just let me explain."

He did not look at her but saw her reflection in the window. He put his hand up and simply said between clenched teeth, "Not. Right. Now."

They were not headed either to her apartment or his hotel; they appeared to be headed into the industrial area.

Ree stopped herself from asking where they were going when the car started to slow as they entered a driveway with the sign, "Thistle Oil Refinery" on the gate.

Colin opened his window. The guard immediately recognized him and waved them through.

She thought they would go into the building, but the car continued onto a picnic area with tables and benches.

The driver came over the speaker.

"Is this okay, Sir?"

Colin said yes.

The car stopped at one of the tables. Colin got out and walked over to Ree's side, opened the car door and said: "Get out."

She looked straight ahead.

"No, you are obviously angry with me and it looks like you are going to kill me and leave my body in one of the oil tanks."

"Don't tempt me, Ree; just get out of the fucking car."

"No!"

He leaned in, grabbed her and threw her over his shoulder. She screamed and started to squirm.

Colin smacked her on the ass and told her to behave.

"Anything else, Sir?" The driver called out.

Colin said no and told him he would call when he needed him back.

Ree shivered as she watched the car pull away.

Colin carried her over to the picnic table and placed her in a sitting position, on top of the table. He walked away from her and alternated between pacing, running his hands through his hair and rubbing his face, all the while cursing offensively.

Ree was impressed, she never heard cursing with such creativity.

A few times, she tried to say something but he just put his hand up and Ree was certain that it was in her best interest to allow him the curtesy of continued quiet.

Eventually, he seemed to calm.

"Ree, I need to get control because right now the only thing I want to do is take you over my knee and spank your ass until its' red, not pink, red. I don't want you to sit down for a week."

"That's a little barbaric, don't you think?"

"Not according to my Scottish Uncles. I use to think that they were a little barbaric in their ways, but after that stunt, you pulled, I'm rethinking their ideas. Don't test me." He continued to pace.

While Colin was having his temper tantrum, as Ree saw it, she watched him. When he got upset, he would run his right hand through his hair. If his frustration got worse, he would take his left hand and rub his face and if the anger was really bad, he would pace. If that was Colin's anger barometer, then he was very, very angry.

Ree wasn't stupid.

Obviously, his anger and frustration was about the deal she made with Uday but damn it, she knew she could do it.

She never would have jeopardized the school if she wasn't one-hundred percent sure of her abilities. He needed to have more faith in her.

The more she thought about it, the angrier she became. Just when she was about to explode...

"I can't decide Ree, are you that fucking stupid?

Or naïve? Or are you that arrogant? Stupid, I can fix. I can explain to you how dangerous that horse is, how difficult it will be for you to try to ride that beast from Hell. I could try to reason with you and maybe if we put our heads together, we can try to fix this, maybe get Uday to change his mind. But if its arrogance, other than a hard spanking, I don't know how to fix it. So, which is it, Reanna?"

"None of the above." She answered quietly.

"None of the above? Fuck, Ree, do you have any idea of the danger you are putting yourself in? The school, that you so loudly profess to love so much might be destroyed because of your arrogance?"

He walked up to her and put his hands on either side of her on the table and looked deep into her eyes.

"Jesus Ree, if anything happened to you, I don't know what I would do, besides kill the damn horse. You can't do this. I won't let you do this. I fucking love you and I can't let anything happen to you. It would destroy me."

Ree looked up into his eyes, smiling.

"You love me?"

He put both hands through his hair walked away. "That's what you got from all I said, only that? Jesus, Ree, you're killing me!"

"Colin, come sit here. What do you know of my equestrian ability?"

He knew he could not mention anything from her file, but he did remember what Mrs. Fitz told him.

"I know that you are one hell of a rider and that you work with your mom rehabing race horses. But Ree, working with a horse like that is not like getting on a trained horse and putting it through its paces."

She raised her eyebrows.

"And who, Mr. McLeod, do you think trains those horses?"

"You do?"

"Exactly, Colin. I don't know if you have ever seen some horses come off the track. They are so crazed from drugs, mainly steroids, that sometimes they are homicidal. They are no different than Uday's horse. My mom and I use some training techniques that have proven very successful. We have saved a lot of horses through these methods. They have gone on to successful careers in dressage, jumping or just companion horses."

"Okay, Ree I get it, but this horse is different. You saw him, he tried to kill you."

"No, this horse is no different than any other horse I've trained," She said firmly, "He's just like many of the horses I worked with. Colin, I should be insulted. Do you really think that I would put my safety, the horse's safety and the school's future in jeopardy, if I wasn't one-hundred percent sure I could do this?"

"One hundred percent?" He questioned, with rueful sarcasm staining his tone.

"Well, at least 99.9999. Besides, I have an ace in the hole."

"What are you talking about?"

"Did you notice that pile of rags by the horse's stall?"

He shook his head.

"No, I did not."

"While you and Uday were talking racing, I noticed that every now and then a little hand came out of the rags and fed the horse a carrot. The horse ate all the carrot until the last small piece, when he gently took the piece from the child's hand. That's why the stall door was open; the child was feeding him. When I walked over, the horse reacted as he usually does, probably because of fear, or he's been conditioned to act like that. But, think about it, Colin. If that horse was so bad, so evil, the beast from Hell, as you called him, do you really think a small child would be able to feed him?"

He let out his breath that he didn't think he was holding. He had to admit, she was right.

"Why didn't you tell me?"

"I tried, but you didn't give me chance. Look, Colin, all you really know about me is my Dad's part; the teacher, the expert in mid-eastern studies, and, well, maybe it is arrogance, but

I'm also a damn good rider and trainer. I know I can save this horse."

He walked over to her and smiled. He reached for both of her hands and kissed each of her fingers. He looked into her eyes.

"I believe you, sweetheart, but I will be there every second, making sure you are safe. I am not going to lose you." With that, he bent down and kissed her sweetly.

The kiss quickly turned into something more heated. He picked her up and threw her over his shoulder again and walked towards the building.

Ree let out a little scream.

"Colin, put me down! You can't keep hauling me around like this."

"Why not, Reanna? At least I know where you are. I think it's the only way to keep you out of trouble." He chuckled and, using his ID card, he opened the door and headed down the hall to the last office on the right.

He was sure his site manager would not mind him using his office.

He set Ree down on top of the desk and moved between her legs.

Surrounding her with his body he whispered, "I think there's something you need to tell me."

She looked up at him, questioning.

Soon enough, though, the light dawned.

"Yes, I love you too."

She leaned in to kiss him.

With that, Colin took possession of her mouth, her body and her soul.

His kiss started out sweet but hastily turned more heated.

Ree groaned as Colin took possession of her mouth.

His tongue explored every part of the inside of her mouth, dueling with her tongue, promising what other parts of his body wanted to do to her.

Colin broke the kiss to nibble and caress is way down her neck.

His hand on her back found the zipper from the dress and pulled it down. The front part of her dress opened and her breasts were exposed. His hand covered them.

Ree was so sensitive that even the cooler air caused her nipples to harden, but when Colin's hands covered her, she gasped.

His hands were rough and calloused, resulting in a scratching sensation that caused her to, at one moment move away and the next, move deeper into his touch.

Colin lifted the hem of her dress up to her waist, exposing her.

He leaned into her center. She could feel his desire for her.

He was hard.

She rubbed herself against him.

When Ree did this, Colin lost all control.

He quickly undid his pants and lowered his briefs.

Ree leaned over him and her hands covered his manhood.

She gasped, almost afraid of the size of his need.

She could feel the moisture on the tip and used it to lubricate her hand moving up and down. Colin stopped her.

"Don't, or it will be over way too soon."

Colin pushed her legs further apart and ripped her thong away.

His hand found the center of her femininity. She was wet, wanting. He could not wait anymore, he had to have her.

"I'm sorry, love, I can't be gentle. This can't be slow. I need you so bad."

Ree called out his name as a finger entered her.

"Colin, now. I want you."

Colin removed his finger and entered her in one movement.

Ree grabbed his shoulders, breathing heavy in his ear.

"Oh God, I need you. I need you, fast. Don't be gentle."

Colin took hold of her hips and held her in place.

He could not stop.

He needed her like he needed his next breath.

Her scent was intoxicating, which egged him on, faster, harder. He felt her muscles clinch around him as she found her release.

He quickly followed.

He leaned her back down on the desk and lay on his side, next to her. He picked up her hand and kissed her wrist. He could feel her shiver.

"Don't every leave me."

Chapter 22

Ree was ready.

When Colin dropped her off at her apartment the night before, they had made arrangements to meet at nine to have breakfast together and discuss the plans for the day.

Ree wanted to get an early start, so they could construct what they needed in the morning, when it wasn't hot and then break for a few hours.

They would come back at about four to start the first session with the horse.

Wow, Colin thought when he saw her.

Ree looked great in her riding clothes. They definitely showed off her figure advantageously.

Mindful of the culture, Ree covered herself with a large robe, which she would keep on until they got to the stable.

They stopped for breakfast at a British-influenced café.

It was a treat to have a typical English breakfast in Iraq.

At breakfast, Ree explained to Colin the method of training she planned on using with Syn, her nickname for him.

She did not believe he was a sin, but it was a sin for what was done to him.

"So, tell me more about this round pen you want me to build."

"It's a method of training that has been around for a long time. Some people believe that Alexander the Great used it to train his horse, Buceliphis. But in modern time, it's been around since the 1950's. Some of the cowboys out west got tired of using techniques that didn't work with the wild mustangs. They found out that when they broke a horse, it did just that; it destroyed their spirit. So, they watched how horses behave in the wild and adapted their natural behavior into a series of leaning techniques. They watched to see how they reacted and interacted with each other, how they disciplined each other and what made them content. They used this information and put together a training program with the knowledge that they learned from studying their behavior."

"What is this program?" Now, he was intrigued.

"There are all different names, depending on the trainer, but the most common is called round pen reasoning. What we have to do is construct a round pen, about sixty feet in diameter. It has to be round, no corners, so the horse cannot hide, and it has to be horse proof, that is, the horse can't jump or climb out. Do you think you can do that?"

"Yes, with Shavo's help, I'm sure we can find the right material to build what you need. What do you use at home?"

"We have a permanent one built with solid fencing built into the side of a hill but many times they are portable. People use metal panels about six feet long and six feet high. They are usually chained or pegged together."

"I think I saw something like that on the side of the building all stacked up."

"Wow! That would be great if they had the panels. It would save a lot of time."

"Ree, I still don't get it. How does putting a horse in a round pen influence his behavior? I would think that a horse in an enclosed space like that would freak and nothing would get accomplished."

"That's a great question. It's basically a training program that uses the language of the horse. It's good for starting a horse or for a horse that needs remedial work and Syn definitely fits in that category; the round pen provides a place for the trainer," Pointing to herself, "To establish control and start a dialogue or relationship with a horse".

"How do you do that?"

She smiled at him.

"You and I have a relationship, would you agree?

"Absolutely."

"How did we develop that relationship?"

He thought for a minute.

"Well, we talked, we shared things we have in common, we ate..." With an evil grin he continued, "We..."

"Okay, okay! You perv. To establish our relationship, we had to communicate and we had to understand each other. Obviously, humans are much more complicated, but it's the same basic idea with a horse. You and I speak the same language and sometimes we still misunderstand each other. With a horse, we don't speak the same language, so we have to learn their language and they begin to understand ours."

"How do horses communicate then?"

"Through body language and body cues. First, you have to understand that horses are prey and have a fight or flight response to stimuli. We are predators. We have to be able to rein in our instincts at times or else we appear too aggressive. So, we have to know when to apply pressure to the horse, the prey and when to back off. You have to read the horse's response to determine what to do...You still look confused."

He nodded.

"I understand, because most of it is body language; something we use all the time, but something we are not aware of. It is best to see how it works in action and then you will understand. Let's go build that round pen now and I'll explain the steps later."

They got to the barn and true to his word, Uday had them escorted right to the paddocks.

They were met by Shavo who told them he was there to help with anything then needed.

Colin and Ree walked to where Colin thought he saw the panels and sure enough, there they were.

Ree was thrilled; they were perfect.

Shavo explained that they used the panels for temporary stalls, if they had guest horses at the barn, either for breeding or exhibition. He directed some of the grooms and even some of the guards to start carrying the panels into the arena.

While the men were carrying the panels, Ree looked around the barn for the little boy from the other night. She found him in the tack room, cleaning some leather. She quietly entered the room and cleared her throat. The child looked up, panicked, then smiled.

In Farsi Ree said, *"Hi, my name is Reanne, but you can call me Ree. What is your name?"*

"Missy Ree," The child said, in very bad English, "Please, to speak English. I want to practice. My name is Najee."

"Do you work here at the stables?"

"Yes, I help my grandfather."

"Who is your grandfather?"

"Shavo; He is the barn boss. He takes care of all the horses. Someday, I will be just like him," The child announced, proudly.

"That's wonderful, Najee, but I saw yesterday that you take care of a horse here, all on your own."

"Please missy, don't tell anyone what you saw yesterday. It would get my grandfather in much trouble. That horse is my friend. We both have no friends, so now, we are friends."

"I'm so glad you made him your friend. You understand that I'm here to help your friend, right?"

"You promise you will not hurt him? Some of the grooms, they try to hurt him; they poke him with sticks or throw things at him. If it wasn't for my grandfather, no one would feed him. Please, missy, do not hurt him."

She took the child's hand.

"I promise, Najee. I will not hurt him. I'm going to try to help him so people will stop trying to hurt him. He will be able to run outside with the other horses. You believe me, yes?"

After some consideration, the child nodded yes.

The door to the tack room opened up. Shavo came in, saw his grandchild, and asked if he was bothering Miss Ree. The child shook his head back and forth.

"No, grandfather. Missy Ree just promised me she would help my friend."

"Yes, that's what we hope. Now, run along and go into my office and find your meal."

After the child left, Shavo said, "I hope my grandchild will not be a bother to you. You see, both his parents and my wife are dead. Najee lives with me here. The child loves the horses and is very good with them, a trait I guess he got from his grandfather."

"No, please. Najee has been a big help and in fact, if it wasn't for him, I don't know if I would have undertaken this project."

He looked confused so Ree explained how she watched Najee feed the horse.

"Ah, now I understand why you were so sure you could tame this horse. But, can you really accomplish all you say in just two weeks?"

"Watch," Ree said confidently.

Colin entered the tack room.

"Good, I found you. We have the panels in place. Could you come out and tell us where and how you want them set up?"

The panels were laid out in a circle.

They decided the best way to secure them was to put the pegs into the welded slots on the panels. She insisted that that part of the panel with the pegs had to be facing outward. There were to be no sharp edges on the inside of the panels, lessening any chance of injury to her or the horse.

She also had to make sure that the pen was situated at the end of the walkway of the barn. Her plan was the horse would come directly from the barn, down a very short path and right into the pen.

The aisle in the barn was a straight run, so nothing had to be done there. They set panels up from the doorway of the barn to the opening of the round pen so when they coaxed the horse from the stall his only option would be to enter the round pen.

After a few hours of work, they were ready.

They all broke for lunch and agreed to meet at four for the horse's first session.

Chapter 23

Ree and Colin went back to her apartment for lunch.

She was so excited the night before, she did not get a lot of sleep and therefore, she yawned throughout the meal.

Colin convinced her to lie down for a short nap; she agreed but only if he would lie next to her.

He raised his eyebrows.

"If I do that, you know we won't get any sleep."

"Sure, we will," Ree insisted.

They went off to bed and actually did manage to nap.

Colin woke Ree up about three-thirty. He told her to hustle if they wanted to get to the barn on time.

Ree was ready in five minutes.

Colin was amazed.

Most of the women he knew would take hours to get ready.

Ree was definitely a cut above the rest.

On the way to the barn, Ree asked Colin to stop at a grocery store.

"Are you still so hungry that you need a snack before dinner?"

She gave him a playful slap.

"No, you'll see Mr. McLeod. You will be amazed at just how clever I am."

Somehow, Colin knew she was serious.

A few minutes later, Ree came out of the store with a large bag that had greens sporuting out the top.

"Oh, carrots. I should have known."

They got to the barn and were waved through.

The first thing Ree noticed, was that the amount of people there seemed to have tripled from the morning.

She would have to talk to Shavo about that. If her plan was going to work, they would all have to stay out of sight.

Shavo met them at the door and told them everything was ready.

Immediately, Ree pulled him aside.

"Look, Shavo, I understand if you don't want to do this, but would it be possible to put your grandson on the outside of the pen, near the path. I give you my word, he will not be in any danger. As a backup, I'll have Colin there to watch over him."

"Yes Ms. Ree, that would be fine but why?"

"I want all people out of sight when we first let Syn out, but if he could smell Najee, that might calm him a bit."

"Yes. Yes, I understand. I will explain it to Najee. I am sure he will be so happy to be part of helping his friend. Anything else?"

"Yes, please make sure that the guards move all the people away from the viewing area. They can watch. I don't have a problem with that, but I don't want the horse to see them."

"Consider it done."

He left to carry out Ree's instructions.

Colin walked over to her and told her that he rechecked the pen; all seemed secure.

Ree thanked him and started to get things ready. She removed the carrots from the bag as well as a few sugar cubes.

She placed pieces of carrots at intervals along the aisle, which she prayed would move the horse along, toward the pen.

She interspaced the carrots with sugar cubes.

She put the carrots and sugar cubes down the path and placed a small pile of carrots and sugar in the middle of the pen.

Once she was finished, Ree took a deep breath.

"Okay everyone, everything is

ready!" She called. "Let's get into position."

Ree had Shavo take the horse out of the stall next to Syn's, so Ree could hide in there once she opened his door. It would also allow her to view the aisle until he made his way towards the path.

She remembered her mother's warning, to always leave a way of escape in case things don't go as planned.

She would stay in the stall until the horse was outside.

When the horse was outside, she would go to the side of the path. This would enable her to move out of his way if necessary.

Colin whistled, signaling that they were all ready.

She crouched down in front of Syn's stall, so he would not see her.

Her heart was pounding.

She took a couple of deep breaths to calm down and slowly slid the bolt from the stall door.

She opened the door.

Once the door was open, she made her way back to the other stall, closed the door and waited.

Shavo told her they could have gotten the horse out of the stall with the help of a few grooms and much intimidation.

However, that was the exact opposite of what Ree was trying to achieve.

From this point on, she wanted the horse to think he was making the decisions, thus lessening his stress and therefore becoming more trusting of humans.

It took a few minutes, but eventually, Ree heard the unmistakable sound of hooves on concrete, followed by crunch, crunch, crunch!

She smiled and let out the breath she was holding. She heard the horse progress forward. She took a chance and peeked out; he was half way down the aisle, gobbling up everything in his path.

She heard a whistle, the signal that he was out of the barn and in the middle of the path.

Ree left the stall and very quietly, made her way to the back of the barn, close to the path.

As she approached, Syn raised his head and snorted. He started to turn around, so Ree crouched down, out of sight and Syn continued his progress towards the pen.

Najee was positioned on the outside of the pen, near the opening.

When Syn got close, he nudged Najee and from under the boy's clothes, emerged a carrot.

Ree wanted to hug that kid right then and there. He pulled his hand away and pointed to the inside of the pen for more carrots.

A little nervous, Syn continued forward, into the pen and towards the final reward; a pile of carrots and sugar.

Colin, very quietly, slid the door closed and backed out of the way.

Ree waited a few minutes for the horse to realize what happened to him and just as she expected, he exploded. He ran in one direction and turned to go in the other direction. When he realized he could not get out, he started banging himself up against the panels but the panels held fast. He did this for a short time. He gradually calmed and slowly accepted his fate.

Colin's heart was in his throat when the horse banged against the panels, but they held.

While they were having lunch, he asked her again what would happen when the horse entered the round pen. She explained all that she hoped would happen in a variety of steps.

Damn, if she wasn't right about the first thing he would do; explode and run around like a wild horse for a short time.

Eventually though, exactly as Ree said, he calmed down and looked around.

Now, came the part that had Colin in a panic; Ree would go into the round pen.

He had confidence in her. He believed she was good at what she did, but he still could not stop the fear. He would have preferred going into the pen, rather than Ree; at least then, he would be in control.

He felt so helpless.

Ree slowly approached the pen and stood at the door allowing the horse to get acclimated to her presence. She shooed Najee away and asked him to stand to the side and watch. She noticed Colin was right there, ready to jump in, if needed.

She wondered, *what good thing in life did I do to deserve such a great guy?*

Syn snorted and pawed at the ground when he saw her but didn't run. Ree was happy with his reaction; now she had to take the next step and enter the pen. The only thing she brought with her was a lunge whip, which is a long whip, used merely as an extension of one's arm; never to hurt, only to remind.

She smiled when she remembered that Colin wanted her to take a twenty-two into the pen.

Colin saw all was going according to plan; Ree was ready to enter the pen. She had the lunge whip pointed down; she explained this was a non-dominant move.

If she wanted to put pressure on the horse, she would raise the whip in proportion to the amount of pressure she wanted to exert on the horse.

The horse started to come at her with his ears back; she raised the whip and wagged it at him.

Between the whip and her body language, she appeared to be bigger.

The horse quickly turned and started to canter around the pen. Ree took up her position in the middle.

Ree was right on when she told him what the horse would do and how she would respond.

Now, he watched as she just stood in the center, with the whip down.

Her head was slightly down, but she watched the horse's every move.

The horse tried to ignore her at first but was getting curious about this thing in the pen.

For Syn, Ree was not acting like any human he dealt with before, so he started watching.

At first, Colin missed the first cue then noticed the horse's inside eye on her. He watched closely.

Yes! He thought.

Then his inside ear twitched towards her, indicating that he wasn't only watching her, he was also listening to her, just as Ree said he would.

Every now and then, Ree would raise the whip and walk toward the outside of the pen. When she did this, the horse would change direction.

When he did, she went back to her place and put the whip down.

Ree told Colin that when she had the horse's attention, she would ask him to do certain moves, like change directions. She never asked for a pace, the horse chose it, but he had to move forward.

The only time she would encourage him to move, would be if he stopped completely.

Once they established some basic communication, Colin noticed that Ree smiled.

He looked at the horse; he was making chewing motions.

Ree had explained that this was a horse's way of communicating: I want to be with you, let me stand next to you, I want to be your friend.

Ree continued moving him forward for a while.

Things seemed to be going well, until suddenly, he stopped, turned and looked directly at her.

Colin tensed. Was he going to charge her? He was ready but remembered Ree expected this behavior.

Ree made a kissing sound at the horse and to Colin's astonishment the horse put his head down and slowly started to walk towards her. Keeping her head slightly down but keenly aware of the horse's approach, Ree was ready, sure enough, the horse turned and kicked his back leg out at her just missing her face.

Colin had his hand on the gate ready to go in there and drag her out when he heard the most amazing thing.

She was laughing, laughing!

I'm in love with a crazy woman. A horse almost smashes her face and she laughs! Colin thought, astonished by his own disbelief, as well as Ree's response.

Although, after Colin regained his wits, he did remember that Ree told him this might happen.

In fact, she hoped it would occur.

She had explained that it meant the horse was being honest, whatever the hell that was supposed to mean.

They went through this dance again, between beauty and the beast, and for the first time, Colin really looked at the horse.

He was magnificent, totally black and very athletic. When he trotted, he seemed to float above the sand. With his tail up, a trait of the Arabians, he was breathtaking.

Ree was awe inspiring; She was cool and confident in directing this horse, knowing when to exert pressure and when to back off.

True to her name, Ree was a goddess of horses.

Finally, the horse stopped again and put his head down. Ree kissed at him and he slowly, tentatively made his way towards her.

When he got close, Colin held his breath, but this time, Syn kept his head down and almost meekly walked up to Ree.

Ree let him stand next to her for a while and then she gently stroked his neck.

Throughout the entirety of their movements, Ree talked and cooed to him.

When he got tense, she backed off. When he relaxed, she started to stroke another part of his body.

When she touched just about all of him, without taking her eyes off him, she called to Najee and asked him to bring her his halter and lead line.

Najee returned and placed it on the inside of the pen.

Ree turned, so she looked in the same direction as the horse. She matched her shoulder up with his ear.

She took a step back, the horse followed. She took a step forward, the horse followed. Each time, she praised him.

She walked into him and he moved away. She moved away and he moved to mirror her. It was the perfect dance, mirroring each other's movements precisely.

She walked behind him and he immediately turned to look at her.

She walked forward, toward the halter and lead. The horse meekly followed.

She picked up the halter and walked back to the center with him. She took it and let him smell the halter. After he had a chance to get its scent, Ree started to, very gently, rub it over his body.

He tensed, at first, but then got used to it.

When he relaxed, she slipped the halter on his head. She clipped it in place and gave him a lot of praise and treats. She attached the lead line, put her hand out to him for the last sugar cube and led him to the gate.

She found Colin in the crowd and smiled the biggest, happiest grin he'd ever seen.

He let out a breath he didn't realize he was holding for most of the session.

He looked at the time; it was the longest twenty minutes of his life.

He returned her smile and as he did, he realized he had to wipe away a little tear.

Damn, she has me eating out of her hand as well as the damn horse. He thought.

At least it took him a little longer than twenty minutes to fall, but not much longer.

The crowd was amazed, never having witnessed anything like it.

When Ree walked the horse over to the gate, the crowd erupted in applause.

Syn tensed and immediately, Ree try to calm him.

However, the horse tried to break away from her and started to rear up. Ree moved away from him and started the kissing noises.

After a moment, he calmed, put his head down and came back to her.

They both walked back to the barn, in triumph.

Chapter 24

Ree and Colin celebrated that night.

Colin was dying of curiosity but decided to wait until after dinner to ask her. They had a delicious dinner in his suite. He asked the chef to make her favorite, NY strip with baked potatoes and veggies.

As usual, she devoured her meal.

He would never get tired of watching her eat.

It was a sensual experience, something out of *Tom Jones*, his Uncle George's favorite book.

They decided to postpone dessert until later. They retired to the couch, with drinks in-hand.

"Ree, I have to ask you. You could have saddled and ridden that horse today if you wanted, right?"

Her grin was wicked.

"Absolutely, especially knowing his relationship with Najee, but I don't know if I could have done a simple dressage pattern with him. I don't know his history, so that will take me some time."

"How much time?"

"A few days maybe."

"Then, why so long? Why two weeks?"

Ree came so close to telling Colin about her deal with Jim, but at the last minute decided against it.

She knew he didn't like her putting herself in danger. How would he react if he thought she was spying?

No, he is better off not knowing, she finally concluded, though, she felt bad.

This was the first and, she hoped, the only time she would ever keep anything from him.

"Well, honestly, I miss riding, and that arena is beautiful. It gives me an opportunity to ride and use the arena. It's a win-win and I thought, maybe, Uday would let me come regularly to work the horse. If it appeared too easy, he might not see the worth in what I did."

Colin agreed.

"School doesn't start until next week. What are your plans this week with the horse and how can I help you?"

"Oh, Colin, I can't ask you for any more. You have been great. Honestly, without your moral support today, it would have been tough. I know you have a company to run, so don't worry, I'll be fine."

"I know you'll be fine, but I love watching you work with that horse. If I could be there, I would love to be."

"This is what I thought." She answered, after a moment of deliberation. "In the morning, from eight until eleven, I would work at the school. At four, I would head to the barn and work with the horse. Four seems to be a good time. Even though it's getting cooler, the heat of the day is always gone by four. I will probably work Syn for no more than forty minutes. This horse isn't used to work, so he needs to be built up slowly. Then, I'm done for the day."

"Sounds like a plan. What if, the days I can, I'll pick you up and bring you to the barn and from there, we can get dinner and spend some quality time together?"

"If you mean some quality bed time together, then I'm in!"

He hugged her close and kissed her.

They had their desserts and then later, in bed, started to spend that promised quality time together.

Chapter 25

After the excitement on Sunday, things calmed down and settled into a rather mundane routine.

School would not start for another week so Ree had the luxury of spending as much time as she wanted at the barn.

She worked at the school from about seven until noon.

The school was ready to open and everyone, including Ree, was chomping at the bit to meet their students and get started.

At noon, she went back up to her apartment and either continued to work on reports or tried to catch up on phone calls, emails or letters home. She was faithful in her reports home to Jim. Using the code he taught her, she told him about gaining access to the stables and also an added bonus of befriending some of the guards.

The guards, as well as the grooms, were very open when they spoke to her. One guard, in particular, was adamant that the US was wrong about Iraq. She tried to avoid politics, but if it came up, she was willing to listen and take mental notes.

She had to catch up with correspondence to her mom and Epee. They had written her numerous letters to her single response, but they both said they understood.

Like clockwork, every day at four, Colin would pick her up and bring her to the barn. She was lucky he was available every day except one.

Luck and coincidence were on her side, though. The handyman, John, that worked around the property, lived near the palace, so he took her.

John loved horses and heard about the work she was doing with Syn; he asked if he could watch. She was thrilled to say yes, but she missed Colin.

Syn's training was going very well, but she didn't need to or want to push him too fast.

It was obvious that the horse was traumatized. Thus, it would take some time to build up trust.

She was at the point, now, where she introduced him to the saddle and bridle.

He seemed to accept all with little reservation.

On Friday, on the way to the barn, Colin asked her when she was going to start riding. She gave a small laugh.

"I was just going to tell you. I'm going to put a saddle on him today. If all goes well, then I'll ride today. I'm so glad you will be there to see."

"I wouldn't miss it for the world."

"Great. I can use your muscles, also. I'm going to ride him in the round pen first, then I want to take him in the arena; if all goes well you can take down the round pen."

"Sounds good. Is there anything I should expect when you start riding?"

"I hope it's an anticlimax. He's been so good. I really expect little or no reaction. It will be interesting to see how much training he's had if he's had any at all."

"I've been meaning to ask you. How is everything going with the school? Are you ready for students?"

She smiled at him.

"Things are great. Yes! We're all ready. We can't wait for Monday, to meet the students."

They got to the barn and the suspicious looks they received in the past were replaced by small waves and even a shy greeting.

Although, Ree was a little concerned this day.

Usually, Najee was at the door to greet her, but today, he was nowhere to be found. Ree hoped everything was okay.

Colin told Ree he was going to find Shavo and tell him about the plan to take down the round pen on Saturday. When he was done, he would be in his usual place, the marble gazebo, overlooking the riding arena, if she needed him. She gave him a peck on the cheek and he went off.

Ree went over to Syn's stall; all seemed in good order.

The day she had him out for his first round-pen lesson, Shavo used the time to have the workers clean out his stall.

It was a mess, rarely being cleaned but now, it sparkled.

She got ready to take Syn out to groom and get him ready.

Where was Najee? Ree wondered, unable to shake the feeling something was not right.

She decided to leave the horse in the stall for now and search for the boy. She looked in all the usual spots Najee could usually be found and finally, she found him in the tack room, in a corner, crying.

Taking his hands in hers, she asked, "Najee, what's the matter? Do you want me to get your grandfather?"

The child looked up at Ree with the saddest look in his eyes as he shook his head.

"Can you tell me what is wrong?"

He shook his head, no again.

"Najee, if I'm going to help you, you have to talk to me."

He looked up again, with tears streaming down his face.

"Missy Ree, I'm dying and I don't know how to tell my grandfather."

"What do you mean, you're dying?"

"I'm bleeding to death," He said sadly, looking down at his hands.

Ree tried not to panic.

After all, he looked fine. His color was good and he was certainly aware of what was going on around him.

"Where? Show me where you are bleeding."

He shook his head again.

"I cannot, I promised my grandfather."

Taking her hand in his, Ree looked him in the eye.

"Najee, you are not making any sense. If you don't tell me right now I will bring your grandfather over here. Colin and I will tell him what you told me."

The child pleaded.

"No, please! You must not."

"Then, will you tell me?"

Finally, he shook his head yes.

"My grandfather made me promise not to tell anyone; you must swear not to tell my secret."

"I promise, Najee, cross my heart," She said solemnly, crossing her heart with two fingers.

He put his head down and spoke quietly.

"My name is not Najee; it is Nageena."

Curiously, she was not surprised.

She felt there was something feminine about the child from the beginning, but could not put her finger on it. A lot of things made sense about her behavior. She never played with the other boys. She kept herself separate from mostly everyone. Her grandfather dressed her the way he did, like a pile of rags, that no one would notice.

"Why did your grandfather do this Najee, I mean Nageena?"

"My mother died when I was very young. My father raised me, but he was in the army. Last year, he went out on patrol and never came back. My grandfather took me in to live with him, but he lives here and females are not allowed to live here. My grandfather had a choice: leave this job that he loved and that paid very well or turn me into a boy. So, I became a boy."

"How old are you?"

"I'm thirteen," She answered, shyly.

Things became clear. She had no women in her life to explain what happens to young girls when they mature.

She could understand Najeena's panic.

Yet, Ree was sure that Najee was not dying but had merely reached sexual maturity.

She sat her down and, as delicately as possible, explained the facts of life about becoming a woman.

Najee's eyes grew, almost as big as her head, when she heard what was happening to her body, but like the brave girl she was, she understood and accepted the facts.

As they finished up the conversation, Colin came in.

"Oh, here you are I thought something was wrong you are usually out there by this time." He saw Ree with her arms around Najee.

Good. Najeena finally told her.

He nodded to Ree and said he would be outside if she needed him. She smiled at him and gave Najeena a big hug.

"Do you think I could tell Colin what you told me Najee? I would like for him to know, so he could look after you also."

She thought for a minute.

"I guess it would be alright; Syn likes him, almost as much as he likes you, so if Syn trusts him, then I trust him. So yes, Missy Ree, it will be fine."

They hugged and left the room.

Ree and Najeena went over to Syn's stall and got him ready for the second big phase of the project. Ree was excited but knew to contain it so Syn didn't pick up on her heightened emotions.

Ree brought Syn into the round pen, while Najeena and one of the grooms carried the saddle pad, saddle and bridle.

They placed them in the center of the pen.

Ree worked with Syn for a short time in the pen. When he came to her she stroked him all over and cooed to him about what a good horse he was.

He was relaxed. Ree picked up his saddle pad and let him smell it.

When he was satisfied, she then proceeded to wipe the pad all over his body. If he tensed, she stopped and let him relax again.

Then, she would start again.

She repeated this with the saddle and bridle.

When Syn seemed relaxed, almost bored with the process, Ree took the pad and placed it on his back.

No reaction.

She put the saddle on, he tensed a little when she tightened the girth, but then relaxed.

She put the bridle on.

No reaction.

Ree was absolutely thrilled with Syn's calm acceptance of the tack.

She walked him around the pen and he kept his head down, relaxed.

She put him in the center of the pen and put a foot in the stirrup, adding weight; no reaction.

She added more weight; no reaction.

Finally, she swung herself up into the saddle.

He tensed but she talked to him softly. She told him how brave he was; slowly, he relaxed. With her legs straightened, ever so lightly, she encouraged him to go forward.

She walked him in one direction, then the other. She added a bit more pressure, asked for a trot and he floated atop the sand. His trot was exquisite.

She knew that he had to be touching the ground, but it didn't feel that way. He was a dream to ride.

Now, the question: Should she push him for the canter?

She leaned down to pat him on the neck.

"Syn, what about a canter?"

He seemed to read her mind; He effortlessly moved into a beautifully controlled canter.

Ree smiled from ear to ear; she was flying on this magnificent animal.

She did not want to tire him, so she ended the workout session after about fifteen minutes.

Syn was becoming better conditioned every day. It could be seen in his movements, as well as his coat and eyes; He shined.

She dismounted.

Colin, Shavo, Najeena and all the grooms, as well as some of the guards, clapped.

Smiling, Ree took a bow and then encouraged Syn to put his head down to also accept the praise.

Najeena took Syn to cool him out; that left Ree free to talk to Shavo and Colin.

As she approached, she realized they were talking about dismantling the round pen and grooming the arena for her to ride in tomorrow.

Ree thanked them both for planning the next phase when she was encased in a big bear hug.

Colin whispered in her ear as he encircled her in his arms.

"I am so proud of you Ree. You looked beautiful on that horse. You two were made for each other. It was like you moved as one."

Colin's praise brought tears to her eyes. She always appreciated the encouragement and praise from her parents, but coming from Colin, it was different somehow.

"Come on, sweetheart, it's been a long day. Let me take you home."

She nodded but didn't want to leave the warmth of his arms.

Chapter 26

Ree woke up with Colin wrapped around her.

It was a wonderful feeling; she felt safe and warm.

How, she wondered, *could I know someone only a short time and feel so connected?*

Maybe there was something to her mom's belief about souls finding each other, because when she was with him, she was complete.

She thought about yesterday.

She was so embarrassed.

She had just lost it; lost it big time.

She did very well, smiling and laughing in the beginning, but when Colin hugged her and told her how proud he was, the floodgates of every emotion she had harbored all week came to the top and fully erupted.

At least, she thought, she was able to wait until they got in the car before she started the really ugly cries.

Colin held her throughout the crying jag. He soothed her and told her all would be fine.

Later, he put her to bed and lay next to her. He held her until she fell asleep.

Sometime during the night, she reached for him and he was there.

They made love, slow and sweet.

God, he is an amazing man. She thought, knowing how lucky she was to have found him and how fortunate she was that he wanted be such a big part of her life.

Colin must have sensed she was awake because he stirred and pulled her close.

He whispered in her ear.

"How is my beauty this morning?"

She snuggled closer to him, without looking at him and answered contritely.

"Embarrassed."

He turned to face her.

"Ree, you have nothing to be embarrassed about. Damn what you've gone through this week, what you accomplished this week, the stress, well it would probably bring the biggest Navy SEAL to his knees."

"I know you're lying now, but thanks for cheering me up." She kissed him on the tip of his nose.

"I'm serious, Ree. It was fucking amazing what you did, how you got that horse to respond the way he did. I'm in awe; my hat is off to you. I have to admit, that maybe, I had the slightest doubt you could pull it off, but baby you did it."

She disentangled herself.

"Well, I did the first part; now we have the exhibition to look forward to."

"Are you concerned? Any doubts?"

She got out of bed and put her robe on.

"No, not at all. I'm confident we will do fine. In fact, we will do great, but I've learned from many years in competition not to count your chickens. And, that reminds me, where do you think Uday has been this week? I felt certain that he would have shown his face at least once. Maybe he's spying from one of the Palace's windows?"

Colin was distracted by Ree body as she put on her robe.

"I'm sorry sweetheart, what did you say?"

She laughed at him.

"Come on. Get you mind out of the gutter. I asked about Uday. Where do you think he's been all week?"

Colin sat up and positioned himself on the side of the bed.

"I was wondering that also, so I asked one of the guards, you know the one that is friendly, especially to you..."

Ree nodded.

"It's not what you think; He loves horses. He told me in his hometown, his father and older brother raise Arabians. He was heartsick about how Syn was treated. He is thrilled someone is able to work with him."

"Ree, Ree, Ree...For a woman who is so smart and so savvy, you can be very naïve. You take people at face value and believe everything they tell you; sometimes you have to look deeper."

"Maybe I am, but I like to believe the best in people first. I will tell you that if someone betrays that trust, THEY. ARE. DONE. Epee calls me a bridge burner. I admit, I'll do anything to keep the bridge up, but if someone betrays that trust, cut off." She made a slashing motion across her throat.

He got up from the bed, put his arms around her and kissed her neck.

"Remind me never to piss you off. You're brutal."

"Well, that would be easy. Always be honest with me and always love me."

"Can do, sweetheart. How does breakfast sound?"

"Great, I'm starved; Oh, you didn't finish about Uday."

He put on his sweat pants and shirt.

"That guard told me that Uday left on an assignment for Saddam the day after the party and is not expected back until late Saturday night."

"Do you think the exhibition will still be on for Sunday?"

"Yes, I'm sure. Shavo told me that Uday left instructions for the arena to be groomed in anticipation for Sunday."

"Good, because I don't think I could wait another week to do this. You are not going to believe this. Do you remember yesterday, when I was talking to Najee in the tack room?"

He did not want to steal her thunder, but he could not help himself.

"You mean Najeena, don't you?"

Ree's mouth flew open.

"How did you know? How long have you known? Why didn't you tell me?"

He shook his finger at her.

"Remember that conversation we just had about you taking people at face value, being too trusting? Well, I guess I'm a little more jaded than you are. As soon as I met her, I realized there wasn't something right about her; how she moved, how she dressed and more importantly, how all the other workers treated her. I realized that Najee was Najeena. I decided Shavo's reasons were good ones and didn't interfere."

"Wow, you're good. Honestly, I didn't know. Well, I did have a feeling that something wasn't quite right, but I guess I just ignored it. Do you think the grooms know?"

"Absolutely. I'm sure of it."

"Why don't they say anything?"

"My guess is their respect for Shavo. They know the situation; she lost her mother and father and she only has her grandfather. All the grooms like Shavo and don't want to see him leave, so they either ignore her altogether or treat her as a boy when they have to interact."

"Well, I hope it continues to work for them, but eventually, they are going to have to confront it."

"Why?"

Ree went on to tell Colin about her conversation with Najeena. His heart went out to both her and Shavo. He wished there was some way he could help them.

As they sat down to breakfast, Colin asked Ree what the plans were for the day.

She told him she planned on giving Syn the day off today.

Najee was going to brush him and of course give him carrots. She said the school was ready and she needed a day away to psyche herself for the big opening tomorrow.

She took a deep breath.

"I hope you don't mind but Sadira and I have decided to go shopping today. You know, shopping isn't really my thing, but Sadira begged me to go. She doesn't really know the city like I do, so I promised to go with her."

He tried to sound disappointed. Colin said he was, but he would get over it. He offered up a small prayer of thanks to Sid.

Now was his chance to really check out the school and that tunnel. He would call John and have him meet him there.

When they finished breakfast, Colin brought her back to the school, dropped her off and parked a little farther away from the school.

There, he waited for Ree and Sid to leave on their shopping expedition.

About ten minutes after he saw them leave, John pulled up and opened the front door. Colin joined him inside a few minutes later. They shook hands, John told Colin some of the latest intel.

Colin tried to have limited access to Jim Peterson for two reasons: one he didn't want Iraqi intelligence picking up any conversation between his company and the US state department and the second most important reason, he didn't want Jim to even suspect that Ree and his relationship had progressed as far as it had.

If Jim even had an inkling about how close they had become, he would have taken Colin off the assignment so fast, his head would've spun.

No, Jim could not know.

So, because of his limited access to Jim, Colin was pretty much in the dark about what was going on politically.

The news John told Colin was not good, and even John, a skeptic at first with looking for a fast way out, now saw it as a necessity. He was afraid to say that when it was time to get out, they would have to get out fast.

The news put a knot in Colin's stomach. He wanted to take Ree out now, but he knew she would never go no matter what he told her.

Unfortunately, it would just have to play out.

The first place they went was the basement. John told Colin that he checked with some of the older neighbors and they told him that many years ago, this building was a store and warehouse for meat and fresh produce. They uncovered the tunnel and guessed it was used for deliveries.

The original store owners did not want to bother the neighbors with early morning deliveries, so they dug the tunnel that came out onto a vacant lot behind the school. Deliveries could be made behind the store, through the tunnel. The underground passage kept the produce cool and it stopped the noise complaints from the neighbors.

It was a clever idea.

Colin was thrilled. He hoped he would never have to use it, but if he had to, it was there and it was good.

It provided everything that they would need: secrecy and cover.

John made note of everything and took the GPS location in case they had to send cars in to pick people up.

They made a general survey of the rest of the school and were satisfied that if they had to get people out safely, they could.

John left; Colin decided to use the school's phone to call Jim Peterson. He would keep the conversation light but informative.

Colin made the call. He hated keeping Jim in the dark but he knew it was for the best.

Colin knew he was the best and Ree needed the best to keep her safe.

Chapter 27

Where did the week go, she wondered; Ree could not believe it was Saturday already.

The week went by in a blur.

The first day of class on Monday was very successful.

She greeted teachers, students, and staff that morning, constantly being thrilled by the warm reception.

If she harbored any doubts about the success of the program, they were quickly laid to rest by the time the first class started.

Ree decided to teach one class; Women in Literature.

She picked one American author, one British author, and one Mideastern author. She chose books that centered on a strong woman as the central character. She was excited about the class but what meant more to her, was the opportunity to get to know her students.

She looked forward to lively debates about a woman's place in society and in the family.

Colin had been understanding and very supportive throughout her first week. When school was finished for the day, he was waiting for her outside to take her to the barn to work with Syn. As tired as she was most days, she became energized when she entered the barn. The work with Syn was improving every day. He was a joy to ride.

She usually rode big-boned, warmbloods; it was refreshing to ride a horse that was so light and responsive.

After her ride, Colin picked up dinner and they would either go to his hotel or her apartment to eat. On Monday, she was so tired she told him she wanted to lie on the couch for a minute. The next thing she knew, she was in bed and it was morning. As the week progressed, things became easier and the pace lessened a bit. The only hurdle left was the exhibition tomorrow, Sunday.

She had a great day with Syn today, perfecting the pattern that she would perform with him tomorrow.

Ree wanted to show his talents off to his best advantage and decided to use all three gaits: walk, trot, and canter.

She loved his canter; it was light and airy, almost like floating atop the sand.

As usual, Colin sat in the marble gazebo and watched her put Syn through his paces.

In dressage, when the rider starts or finishes a pattern, they go to the center of the arena, stop in the center, which is referred to as X. The horse is halted and the rider bows her head and salutes the judge.

When Ree saluted at the end of her ride, Colin and Najeena stood up, clapped and cheered. Colin had taught Najeena how to whistle, so she added that to mix.

Ree's heart warmed at the sight of Colin and Najeena; he had his arm on her shoulder.

She was beaming.

Ree was thrilled they had become such close friends in a short amount of time.

When Ree and Syn left the arena, Najeena caught up to them and took the reins from Ree; the girl loved cooling the horse out and spoiling him with carrots. Watching them both walk away, she sighed with contentment.

Life was perfect.

Colin reached for her hand and pulled her to his embrace.

"Well, Ms. Malloy, it looks like you are going to kick ass tomorrow. Any butterflies?"

She shook her head and fell into his embrace.

"Absolutely none; he is a wonderful horse; he is so responsive and so kind, I can't even imagine what was done to that horse to turn him into what he was."

He stroked her back but didn't answer. He was told some horrific stories from the grooms and some of the guards about Syn's treatment. He hoped Ree never found out.

Syn was put away for the night. Ree checked all the tack in anticipation of tomorrow. They said good night to Shavo, who promised her the footing in the arena would be groomed to perfection. She told them she was planning on getting there at seven, just to recheck everything. She would start grooming about eight and bring him out to warm up about eight-thirty.

Uday was expected to be there at nine, so she should be right on time.

"What do you want to do for dinner?" Colin asked as they got into the car.

"I hope you don't mind, but I'd really like to go my apartment tonight, eat a light meal and go to bed early. I'm sorry, but I really need to focus."

He grabbed her hand and kissed each finger.

"Ree you never have to apologize to me. I understand. Hell, I don't know how you kept up the schedule you did this week and then, to have the added pressure of this hanging over your head. I think it's smart; I'll drop you off if you promise to do what you said."

Smiling, she nodded yes.

"Good. I'll pick you up about six-thirty. Is anyone from the school coming?"

"I didn't ask if anyone else could come, but Sadira and John were so helpful throughout this whole process, do you think it's possible we could sneak them inside?"

"I already checked with Shavo; he said it would not be a problem, but it would be best if they stayed in the barn and watched from there."

"That's what I told them. I thought we could go out to celebrate when it was all done."

"Very sure of yourself, aren't you?"

"No, I am sure of the horse. He is such a good boy, he has such heart. I think he is the type of horse that would face lions for his master."

"Exaggerating a bit with that one, aren't you?"

"No, really. Did you know that many Bedouin tribes consider their horses, the Arabians, to be part of the family? The horse lived in the tents with the family. They even babysit the children. It was not an unusual story to hear of a horse putting himself between a lion and his owner. Some have been known to attack an adversary if their owner was attacked. There have been many stories of a horse running themselves to death in order to save their owner. So, no, absolutely no, I'm not exaggerating in the least. He is that type of horse; he has a big heart. I just know he would turn himself inside out for me as I would for him."

When they arrived at her apartment, Colin got out of the car, opened Ree's door and walked her to the door of her apartment.

"Do you want to come in for a bit?" She asked.

Colin put his arms around her and pulled her into his embrace. He took a deep breath, smelling the floral scent in her hair.

"You know, Ree, if I come in, it won't be for a bit, and you won't get the rest you need. No, go inside, eat dinner, and go to sleep. Tomorrow is going to be a big day. Ree, remember, I'm your Arabian. I would stare down that lion for you. Hell, I would try to kill it bare-handed if I had to. You know that, don't you?"

She looked up into his beautiful green eyes and sighed.

"Yes, I absolutely do and I'm yours. I love you. See you in the morning."

Colin made sure she locked the apartment before he got back in the car and returned to the barn.

Ree was too trusting, but he wasn't. He intended to sleep in front of that stall to make sure nothing happened. When he arrived at the barn, he approached Syn's stall and saw a bundle of rags in front.

Colin grinned.

He picked up some blankets, covered both of them and together, he an Najeena kept watch for the night.

Chapter 28

The alarm went off at five-thirty. Ree jumped out of bed. She had a great night's sleep and could not wait to get started.

She showered and put on her riding clothes.

The traditional show outfit for dressage was white breeches, black boots, a white shirt with a white stock tie and a black or blue jacket.

She did not have show clothes with her though, so she had to improvise.

She used her tan-colored breeches and black boots that she brought from home. She used a white shirt and a black suit jacket to round out the outfit.

During her shopping trip with Sadira, she bought a piece of white material that she used for a stock tie, the usual neckwear for a dressage rider and the outfit was complete.

She was ready by six-fifteen and used the time to clear her mind and meditate while she waited for Colin.

Colin, on the other hand, did not have a good a night.

The cement floor in the barn was cold and hard to sleep on.

When he woke, he found that Najeena had solved the uncomfortable floor problem by lying across him like he was a mattress.

He checked his watch; it was four in the morning; time to get up.

As he tried to disentangle Najeena, Shavo came over, picked her up and brought her to their room. He promised Colin he would take over the watch of Syn.

Colin had enough time to go back to the hotel, shower and change, before arriving to pick up Ree at six-thirty.

Always on time, she stood outside to wait for him, in her usual brown robe, covering her riding attire.

They decided not to stop for breakfast, but Colin did stop to pick up some much-needed coffee for him and some tea for Ree.

When they arrived at the barn, Ree was a little confused when she heard one of the grooms ask Colin if he slept good and then laughed.

Ree asked what that was all about, but he just ignored her.

She decided that it was some kind of inside, guy joke and didn't press the matter.

Najeena had Syn out in the aisle on cross ties and started to groom him.

Ree checked the arena and true to his word, it was perfection.

Ree picked up a brush and curry comb and went to work. A combination of exercise, fresh air and regular grooming had turned Syn into a spectacular-looking horse.

His coat shined, his eyes sparkled, and he had muscled up beautifully.

When she was done, Ree stood back to admire him. Black Beauty and the Black Stallion had nothing on him; he was truly God's perfect creation.

Ree had worked on his tack yesterday; everything was clean and shining. Colin also checked all the tack as he handed it to Ree. He told Ree he was checking for spots she missed, but in reality, Colin could not shake the feeling something wasn't quite right.

His Spidey Sense, his seal team would say, was tingling like crazy. He just felt things had gone too easy.

Would Uday give in this easy? Colin doubted it.

However, all the tack looked and felt good, so Ree saddled up and headed to the arena to warm up.

About ten minutes later, Ree noticed that Sadira and John had arrived.

Colin greeted them and led them to a shaded area outside the main barn.

At eight-forty-five, Ree heard a bit of commotion coming from the front of the barn. She looked over at Colin and saw him pointing to the walkway from the barn to the gazebo.

Walking along the path, she saw Uday and a small woman walking next to him. Behind him were two guards. They were seated in the gazebo; a guard broke away and walked towards Ree. Colin also started to walk towards Ree, curious to find out what was going on.

The guard reached Ree and requested that she meet with Uday before the start of the exhibition.

She looked at Colin and he nodded.

She got down, took the reins and walked towards the gazebo.

The guard stopped her and indicated that he would hold the horse and that they should proceed to Uday.

Colin's Spidey Sense was heightening by the second, but there was nothing he could do, other than follow Ree.

He would try to keep the horse in view at all times.

When she looked into the Gazebo, she spied Uday.

His picture should be in the dictionary under "fake smile" because that's what his smile was – fake.

As she approached, he extended his hand.

"Reanna, it is so good to see you again. From what I have heard, things have been going very well for you."

"Yes, thank you, Sir. They have and thank you for the honor to work with, train and ride such a magnificent animal."

He shook his head.

"I've heard you have some, shall we say, unusual training methods. Now, we will see if these methods prove to be fruitful. I have been reading up on your Dressage. It is an interesting discipline, maybe something I will invest in, in the future. I have also been familiarizing myself with some of its rules. I understand you will be doing a "test" for me, is that correct?"

"Yes, that's it, exactly. What will happen, is I will enter the arena at a trot from the other end of the arena, this is called centerline. I will stop about midway, I will bow my head. Traditionally, this is asking permission to begin the ride. If you agree for me to begin, you will nod, and then I will begin the pattern. I will go to the right in the arena first, or clockwise. In this direction, I will do a series of big and small circles at a trot and canter. I will then reverse direction, counter-clockwise and repeat the same pattern. I hope you do not expect too much. I have had only two weeks with this horse, so we will be doing only basic moves, nothing fancy. Although, if you continue his training he is capable of upper-level movements."

"Good, good," He said, "Let us get started. One more thing. I noticed that in your rules if you at any time become separated from the horse, either voluntarily, say you dismount, or you are thrown off, you are immediately disqualified, is this correct?"

"Yes, absolutely. That is the rule."

"Good, then we will go by your rules. If you become separated from the horse between the time of the two salutes, then you are disqualified and lose the bet. Agreed?"

Not sure where he was going with this, Ree nodded.

"Agreed."

She turned and walked away with Colin next to her.

"What do you think that was about?" She whispered.

"I don't know and I don't like it. Just be very careful, Ree, promise me. Remember, the school is great but it's not worth your safety."

Colin's Spidey Sense wasn't just tingling; it was

bashing him on the head. Yet, he still could not figure out what was wrong.

Ree entered the arena. She noticed the guard brought Syn down to the end where she would start her pattern. She thanked him and mounted.

Syn tensed a bit, so she leaned down and stroked his neck, cooing him about what a good, brave horse he was.

Ree started at a posting trot and went down the centerline. She stopped at X, in the middle of the arena. She sat up straight and put her full weight in the saddle and started to salute.

As soon as she sat down, Syn reared up and started bucking. If she was not such an experienced rider, she would have easily been thrown. She gained control and leaned a little forward and spoke to him; he calmed.

Yt, when she started to sit back down; she felt him tense. She lightened her seat. She asked him to walk forward testing the weight in her seat as she went. As long as she kept weight off the back of the saddle, he was fine. If she deepened her seat on the left he was fine, but if she put even the slightest on her right he tensed. Her only option was to ride with as much weight as possible in her stirrups and pray that Syn understood her signals using only the lower part of her leg.

She could not figure out what happened.

Everything seemed fine during the warm-up.

Perhaps, he has a sore spot that will work itself out. Ree thought.

Colin was ready to run into the arena and drag her off the horse when he saw that she got Syn under control.

He could not figure out what could have happened in the short time they were away from the horse.

Prior to that, he was perfect. He knew it could not be drugs; nothing would work that fast. As he mulled this over, he watched Ree. She appeared cool and calm, but he could tell she was tense and so was the horse. He watched the pattern she practiced many times; he knew it by heart.

Why was she doing something different?

Ree tried as hard has she could to keep the weight off her right seat bone, but she needed that weight to do a right lead canter.

This was so the horse could push off using his left hind leg allowing the right front to lead in a canter: if a horse was going in a counter clockwise direction he would lead with his left front; clockwise, right front. This helped the horse to balance himself, especially with a rider on his back.

Ree decided that Uday would not know a left lead canter from a right and hoped she made the correct decision. She did her pattern to the left counterclockwise; she walked, trotted and cantered.

She was able to keep her weight off the right seat bone.

When she had to reverse the pattern, going clockwise, she could walk and trot him without using her weight on the right, however when it came time to canter, she needed that weight.

She did not practice the counter-canter with him and she prayed he would understand; she asked him to counter-canter.

This is a difficult move for horses and only horses that were strong and very balanced were able to do it with a rider on their back.

The time came for the canter to the right; Syn tensed, but she didn't ask for a right lead canter.

Instead, she asked for a left lead canter or counter-canter.

He took it flawlessly.

They completed the pattern, moved up center line, stopped and saluted.

After Uday acknowledged her, she immediately jumped off, went to his head grabbed his face and gave him a big kiss on his soft, velvety nose.

A guard stopped her and escorted her over to Uday. Ree turned and noticed that Colin and Najeena took the horse and were walking him into the barn.

A look of pure fury was on Uday's face.

"Ms. Malloy, you did what you said you could do, so now, I must do what I said. Monday morning, my wife will be at your school. Do not ask for anything more." With that, he left; the young woman trailing closely behind him.

Ree ran back to barn, not knowing what to expect.

Why did the horse tense?

She did all the checks prior to her ride; his back was fine. He wasn't lame, it was a mystery.

When she entered the barn, she saw Syn on the cross ties. A group of people surrounded him.

Najeena held something and was crying. Colin looked like he was ready to kill someone. John held his arm and was talking to him.

Shavo was at the horse's head, petting him.

When she approached, they all looked at her but didn't say anything.

What was wrong? She wondered, as her fear heightened.

Finally, Najeena broke away and gave Ree the saddle pad.

"Missy Ree, look what they did to our Syn."

Ree held up the white saddle pad and looked.

Underneath, there was a big blood spot. She looked up at Syn's back and there, matching the spot on the pad was a dark spot, probably blood.

"I don't understand what happened," Ree said, confused. "I checked the tack myself. There was nothing on the pad or the saddle."

Colin broke away from John and put his hand out to Ree. She looked down as he opened his hand; there was a sharp metal burr.

"When Uday got you away from the horse, the guard must have slipped it under the saddle. We are lucky he could not get in further back, otherwise, there would have been more extensive damage." Colin gathered Ree in his arms and hugged her. "I am so sorry, Ree, I should have known. I thought something would happen but I just didn't know. I can't believe he would pull something like this."

The full weight of what happened to Syn hit her.

Ree had always been a calm person, seldom losing her temper.

This was the rare exception; she saw red.

Her Irish temper emerged. She pushed away from Colin and started to speak very quietly.

"I'll kill him. I'll kill him." She chanted, like a mantra and started to walk towards the palace.

Colin quickly realized where she was headed and grabbed her by the waist, picking her up.

If it was not so serious, it was almost comical.

Ree's feet were off the ground but still at a run with Colin trying to hold her back.

By the time he grabbed her, she was screaming at Uday.

They did not want to attract this type of attention, so Sadira went to the back of the barn and closed the doors. As she did this, she saw Uday enter the Palace, look back at the barn and smile.

It was a smile that sent chills down Sadira's spine.

Colin finally broke through Ree's haze of anger and little by little, she started to calm down.

What really did it was when Colin said, "Ree, don't you think you have someone to thank, big time?"

With tears running down her cheek, she nodded, went up to Syn and gave him a big hug as well as another kiss on the nose.

Shavo and Najeena tended to Syn's back.

Shavo assured Ree that it looked much worse than it was; it didn't need stitches. He patted her on the back and said he understood why she rode the way she did. If she did not, the damage could have been much more extensive.

Shavo shooed her off and told her that he and Najeena would take care of Syn. Now, she needed to take care of herself.

Colin led an emotionally drained Ree out of the barn and into a waiting car.

Ree appeared to be in shellshock when Colin sat down next to her.

"Ree, sweetheart, do you want to cancel the luncheon? Sadira and John will understand. It's up to you."

"No, I think what Syn did deserves a celebration. I didn't do it; he did."

"Okay, sweetheart. I'll tell them to meet us."

Sadira and John met them at the hotel restaurant where they enjoyed a wonderful lunch and good conversation. There were quite a few toasts to Syn, but when Colin tried to toast Ree, she could not keep the tears from falling.

"Ree, what's wrong? You did great, the horse did great, and you pissed Uday off big time. I don't think he will ever get over being bested, especially by a woman. Sweetheart, I don't understand why you are upset. The school is safe and now you have the Palace's endorsement. You can't ask for more."

"But at what price?"

"What do you mean? Everything worked out fine."

"I should have known something was wrong. I thought it was nerves, both his and mine. He probably never performed in front of that many people before and as much as I tried to be calm, I'm sure a little of my nerves came through. I thought it was that, but I should have known."

"What should you have known love?" They were sitting in a booth, so Colin put his arm around her shoulder and pulled her closer to him.

"That it was more than nerves; I should have known he was in pain. I should have known," She insisted quietly, with her head down.

Colin turned her so she was looking him in the eye.

"Ree, look at me. You could not have known. No one knew, only Uday, and the guard who put the burr under the saddle. Tell me this, if Syn continued to rear and buck, would you have dismounted?"

"Yes, absolutely. I would have known then and there that there was definitely something wrong."

"But he didn't continue to buck and rear, he calmed down. You figured he had a sore spot and worked around it."

She nodded.

"But, I still should have known."

"Ree, if you use that logic, it's my fault because I should have known. I was afraid Uday would try something and was on the lookout for anything strange; so were Shavo, John, and

Sadira. All of us, we all did not see anything unusual, so if you are going to attribute blame, then we all share in it."

Shaking her head, she was still not convinced.

"Look, Ree, I do understand how you feel, but let's give Syn some credit. Didn't you tell me yesterday what a big heart the horse had?"

She nodded.

"Then, allow him to do something brave for you. He knows you saved him. Allow him to be your hero. Allow him to save you from the lion."

Smiling, with tears in her eyes, she fell into his arms and had a good cry.

Chapter 29

Ree was outside, greeting all the students on Monday morning, when a black, government car pulled up. A guard got out, opened the back door and out came the woman from yesterday.

The guard and the woman approached Ree.

The guard asked if she was Ms. Malloy; Ree nodded yes.

With her identity confirmed, he introduced Uday's second wife, Tahira. The guard informed her that they would drop her off ten minutes before school started and would pick her up at exactly at 12:15.

He also informed Ree that she was solely responsible for Tahira. She was not to go out of the building or make any calls; she was to go to class and that was all.

Ree nodded her understanding.

Speaking in Farsi, Ree asked Tahira what classes would be of interest to her.

She smiled at Ree and in perfect English said, "I would like to look at your class list."

"Come to my office and I'll go over the courses that we offer."

They entered the office and Ree motioned for her to sit in one of the chairs in front of her desk. Ree grabbed the course listings and sat in the chair next to her.

"Would you like the course listings in English or Farsi?"

Tahira nodded.

"English would be fine."

It took her a few minutes to look over the courses; Tahira smiled up at Ree and asked: "If it is acceptable, I would like to take a class in business and the women in literature class."

"That's wonderful," Ree said, "There are openings in both classes, but Tahira, may I call you that?"

"Yes, please. I would like that very much and Miss Ree, please do not tell anyone who I am. I do not want to make anyone feel uncomfortable."

"No worries, Tahira, and you must call me Ree."

"Thank you so much, Ree, I cannot tell you how excited I am to be here and take these classes. It is wonderful to practice my English again."

"I hope you don't think I am being nosy, but you speak English perfectly. Where did you learn?"

"Thank you. My family lives in Tikrit. I lived there with my mother, father and older brother; my father is a doctor and my mother is an accountant. Both my parents went to college in England so they made sure we learned English. It was my dream to go to Harvard medical school, but my life did not work out that way."

Ree did not want to push the girl. She squeezed her hands and smiled at her.

"Come, let's get you settled in a classroom. I'll get you your books and supplies. If there is anything you need, you know where my office is, so come see me anytime."

At the end of the day, Tahira left the school carrying her books and smiling. She seemed like any other college student.

As the weeks went by, one week seemed to blend into the other. Ree was busy with school and thanks to Shavo, she continued to work with horses at the barn. She also sent reports to Jim Peterson and assured him that nothing unusual was happening inside the barn, nor stored in, or near the barn.

There was no strange or unusual military activity anywhere near the facility.

Things took on a comfortable rhythm with Colin as well. He worked at his office during the day and most afternoons, he took Ree to the barn.

He was particularly interested when she started to work with Secretariat's progeny.

Colin liked horses but did not have horse fever like she did. However, she saw how all that could change with Storm Dancer. He was a magnificent horse; a gray, standing at least eighteen hands.

He was a horse big enough for Colin. Colin always had a lump of sugar for him.

Casually, he mentioned to Ree one day what she thought the chances were that Uday would sell Storm?

Her response required no thought.

"Between slim and not a chance."

That was his feeling also.

When Colin could not take her to the barn, John did. John was a big guy like Colin, with blond hair, cut in a buzz cut and had the bluest eyes. He was a very handsome man with a great body, wide shoulders and a slim waist.

He looked like he was in the military, so she asked him one day. He told her he was from Texas, like Colin, and when he graduated high school he joined the Marines. He came from a long line of soldiers so he followed a family tradition.

He explained that he was deployed in many different areas and finally ended up as security for the embassy in Bagdad. He was there for three years when he met his wife, an Iraqi woman. She was a government worker, so their jobs often crossed paths.

Eventually, he gathered the courage to ask her out and the rest, so they say, is history. He lived in the nice area of Bagdad with their two small boys. John loved to show her pictures of his kids. Ree had to admit, they were cute. John retired from his military career and now did private security work, primarily for the state department. His current assignment was the school.

The weekends even took on a steady rhythm. Usually, she caught up on correspondence on Saturday morning and Saturday afternoon, Colin would pick her up and they would either go out to eat or stay in his suite at the hotel. He often got movies from home so they stayed in on Saturday nights and watched movies or just talked.

Ree never got tired of his stories, especially about his Uncles. She could not wait to meet them. She found out he was very close to his mother and sister in law. He felt responsible for their care and safety, but only because he loved them both very much. He adored his niece and nephew and loved to spoil them.

Sunday was the day she looked forward to, because on Sunday, they did something unexpected.

Colin loved to surprise her.

Many times, he would blindfold her and she would have to guess where they were going.

She was usually wrong, but she didn't care; she just loved spending time with him.

They would go to the museum, the open-air markets, or visit the little shops in downtown Bagdad.

Ree learned early on, not to admire anything though, because whatever she said she liked, Colin would insist on buying it for her. She felt so spoiled, so much like a princess; she loved every minute of it.

Chapter 30

September flowed into October and October into November. Then, in the blink of an eye, Ree found herself in the beginning of December.

The original plan was for Ree to stay with the school until the beginning of December, but because of the unmitigated success of the project, they asked her to stay longer.

After they got Uday's grudging support, they were able to advertise in the local paper and on the Bagdad TV station. The response was overwhelming.

They had so many students, Ree suggested that they open a satellite school in another area of Bagdad.

Ambassador Ryan was thrilled with the idea of another school and immediately threw his support behind the new project.

Thus, the idea was quickly given the go-ahead.

As much as Ree missed her family and friends, this was a great opportunity and it didn't take her long to say yes. It was decided that she would stay until May.

Colin was not thrilled with the idea of Ree's extended stay in Bagdad. He got constant updates from home about the deteriorating political situation between the two countries. Things were going to blow up soon, but he could not convince Ree.

Other than kidnapping her from her apartment and duct taping her to the seat on the plane, which he considered, there was not a whole lot he could do, other than support her.

Ree called her mom to tell her she would be staying in Iraq a few more months. She expressed how sorry she was she would not be home for Christmas. She promised her mom she would definitely be home by May.

Her mom did voice her concern about the situation between Iraq and the US, but Ree assured her that all would be okay.

She didn't tell her mom about her reports to Jim, but she believed that they had to make an impact on the decisions about war.

She reported there was nothing there; no gas, no bombs and no weapons of mass destruction (WMD).

When she told Epee, that was another story. Epee was ready to get on a plane and drag her friend back home. Epee didn't calm down until she told Epee about Colin.

When Ree said, "Epee, I found my Jamie," Ree was sure you could hear Epee's scream all the way to Bagdad.

She promised to keep Epee updated, send a picture of Colin and did the pinky swear to seal the promise to keep herself safe.

Chapter 31

Ree could not believe where the time had gone.

It seemed like she had just opened their doors and the next thing she knew, she was closing the doors as the semester drew to an end.

She was pleased that both students and teachers were sad to see the semester come to end and were looking forward to the next term.

All of the students signed up for the next semester.

Ree was especially gratified to see that Tahira signed up for an accounting class and the second part of Women in Literature. She was a joy to have in class and lit up when she entered the classroom.

Christmas was in two days.

Although only a small part of the teachers and students were Christian, she decided to end the semester with Christmas Eve and run the break through the New Year, setting the date to reopen for January third. The satellite school was ready to go and that school would open at the same time.

Colin had plans for Christmas but refused to tell her.

He wanted to surprise her. He didn't tell her too much other than to pack a bag for five days and to be sure to include the black dress she wore in London.

She also included some casual clothes and a bathing suit.

Ree was usually good at guessing his surprises but this time she was stumped.

Colin asked her to be ready that afternoon, about four. He knew her and how she got involved in a project, so he made sure Sadira hurried her along.

Sadira did her job well. She kicked Ree out of school at two and told her to get ready.

Right on time, Colin knocked on the door.

"Are you ready for the big surprise?"

"I'm ready !Do I get any hints?"

"Absolutely not. In fact, I'm even thinking about blindfolding you."

"Oh, sounds a bit kinky. What if I promise to keep my eyes closed?"

"I don't know. Somehow, I think there will be some cheating involved. Come on, let's go. I don't want to be late."

They got into his car and drove out of the city. When they got a few miles out of the city, she started seeing signs for the airport.

"Are we flying somewhere?"

"Patience, my love. All will be revealed soon."

They pulled into the airport where the private jets were located. Colin pulled up to one of the jets with the Thistle Oil logo on the side.

"We are we are flying somewhere. Come on, Colin. Where are we going? I'm dying of curiosity."

Colin turned his head and smiled, but said nothing. He got out of the car, opened her door and whispered in her ear.

"What happened to the curious cat, my love? Patience, I promise the surprise will be worth it."

They walked into the plane.

Ree was still blown away by the beauty and comfort of a private jet. She knew it would be hard to fly coach again. She sat down on one of the club chairs and tried to open the window shade.

It would not open.

"Colin, there's something wrong with the shade

I can't open it."

He walked over to her and took her hand away from the shade, before he placed his hands on either side of the club chair.

"Now, now, Ms. Malloy...There will be no peaking on this flight. We are flying in a blackout condition. There will be no guessing where we are going. Buckle in and get ready for takeoff."

Ree was dying of curiosity.

Where could they be going?

In a jet, the options were almost endless though, so she gave up guessing and grabbed the blanket from the back of her chair.

Time to take a nap.

It felt as though she had just closed her eyes, when she heard the pilot come over the loud speaker to get ready for landing. She checked her watch. They were in the air less than an hour.

With that information, she narrowed down the country; they were probably still in Iraq.

But where?

When the door opened, Colin took her arm, turned her toward him and kissed her gently on the lips.

While she was distracted with the kiss, he slipped a silk scarf over her eyes.

"Colin, no fair! Where are we?"

"Patience, my love. All in good time."

He led her down the stairway, into the back of a waiting car. He joined her in the back.

With the blindfold on, she seemed to lose all track of time.

Finally, the car came to a stop. She felt Colin get out and her car door opened. He reached for her and put his arm around her shoulder.

"Are you ready?"

"Colin, if you don't take this blindfold off, I won't speak to you, ever again."

"Well, we can't have that, now, can we? Especially, since I enjoy hearing your beautiful voice so much."

With that, he removed her blindfold. She was standing at the entrance to the International Hotel on Corniche Street, in Basra, the Venice of the East.

Stunned, she looked up at him, with her mouth agape.

"Oh my God, Colin, we're in Basra. How did you know? I've always wanted to visit here. It was the one place that my Dad and I didn't go to in Iraq."

Basra is located on the Shatt al-Arab River.

Historians say that it is the fateful location of Sumer, one of the ports from which Sinbad the Sailor journeyed. It is also a proposed location of the Garden of Eden because of its lush gardens and temperate climate.

"Ree, I honestly don't know how I knew. It couldn't be the countless times you mentioned that you wanted to come here?"

Ree gave him a playful slap on the arm.

"I didn't mention it countless times. Well, maybe once or twice."

Colin raised his eyebrows in mock disbelief.

"Once or twice?"

"Come, let's go get registered! I can't wait to start walking around."

They had a beautiful suite, overlooking the canals and the many parks in the area.

If you looked only in a certain area, it truly did look like Venice; one of her favorite cities.

They quickly put their things away and started to explore their wondrous surroundings.

They walked down the streets, filled with sights and sounds that seemed to be from another time, before turning a corner, only to return to the twenty-first century, with the eastern Times Square.

It was a beautiful contradiction; one that worked seamlessly.

Before they knew it, it was dinner time.

They decided to have dinner in the hotel and go to bed early to get a fresh start exploring the city in the morning.

The menu at the hotel restaurant was incredible.

Ree wanted to try one of everything.

Colin encouraged her to do that, but even she knew that was way too much food.

Ree was so excited, she didn't know how she was going to get any sleep tonight.

Although, the last thing she told Colin, was to make sure she was up by seven.

****

Colin gently kissed her nose, then her cheek and started to move down her neck. Ree tried to swat him away. He whispered in her ear.

"Get up sweet, you don't want to miss the day, do you?"

Colin's voice finally got through her sleepy haze.

As soon as she realized where she was, Ree sat up and stretched.

"My God, what time is it?"

"Eight o'clock. Thought you were going to sleep the day away. I've been up for hours."

"I can't believe I slept so soundly. I feel great but why didn't you wake me at seven?"

"I tried but you wanted nothing to do with getting up and you looked so peaceful. Ree, you had a busy, stressful few months. I think last night was the first time you went to sleep without a thousand things on your mind and concerns about how you were going to get everything done."

She got out of bed and put her arms around his waist.

"You are right...As always. Thanks for letting me sleep. I don't think that I've felt this rested in months. So, what's on the agenda for today?"

"Did you remember that today is Christmas Eve?"

"No. With all the excitement, I forgot. I have to call home."

"I know, I thought of that. I just ordered breakfast. After we eat, I thought we could make our calls to family and friends. When that's done, we can head out for the day."

"Sounds like a plan."

Ree talked to her mom and all was good at the barn.

Epee's mom was having Christmas dinner the next day, so the plan was for Margaret to go there for dinner.

Her Mom and some of her friends were going out to a local restaurant for Christmas Eve dinner too, so her schedule was full.

Ree was glad her mom was so independent but she still felt guilty that she wasn't here.

She vowed that next Christmas, she would be home to celebrate with her Mom, but the question was, would it be with or without Colin?

She and Colin never really talked about what would happen next, when either one or the other had to go back home.

Would they continue to see each other? Would they keep in touch?

Before too many of these negative thoughts filled her head, however, Ree focused on today and what a great time Colin had planned.

Colin came out from the bedroom after making his calls.

The first thing Ree noticed was that he looked upset.

"Colin, is everything alright?"

"No worries for you, just family stuff. I'll tell you later. Come on, let's go and start our Sinbad adventure."

Much to her surprise, Ree found out he wasn't kidding about a Sinbad adventure.

They walked down to the docks where Colin hired a boat to take them to Sinbad Island.

The place was amazing; parks, beautiful homes and even some casinos.

They stopped into one and tried their luck. No instant millionaires this day.

They had lunch in one of the many cafés that lined the river.

Ree tried the Sabzi and chopped spinach stew.

Colin took her word that it was good but to him, it didn't look appetizing.

He had the fish, cooked with Indian spices, that he gave a thumbs up sign to.

They spent the rest of the afternoon on Sinbad's Island, exploring little, out of way places that some friends of Colin's had told him about.

Before they knew it, it was getting dark and a little chilly. They were lucky the average temperature in December was in the sixties, but they were having an unusually warm spell and the temperature was in the seventies all day.

As soon as the sun set, though, the temperature dropped right down.

They both decided to opt out of getting dressed for dinner and just order something in the room.

Colin suggested Ree shower first, since he had some calls to make.

All showered and dressed, Ree came back into the sitting room and heard Colin on the phone again.

This time, he sounded angry. He was yelling at someone that he wanted the results of the tests ASAP. With phone in-hand, he came into the sitting room and saw Ree.

"Colin, I'm a big girl is everything alright?" She went over to him and put her arms around his waist.

He rested his head on the top of her head and sighed.

"Ree, just trust me. Right now, I just want to enjoy a beautiful Christmas Eve with my beautiful woman and forget the outside world exists."

"Yes, my love, that sounds wonderful. Are you going to take a shower?"

"Why, Ms. Malloy, are trying to tell me I smell?"

"Actually, you smell yummy. But, I'm hungry and the sooner you shower, the sooner we eat."

He kissed her on the forehead and headed for the shower.

They were sitting on the couch watching Die Hard II, laughing, when their dinner arrived.

For some reason, Bruce Willis looked hysterical speaking Farsi.

Although neither one of them were practicing Catholics, there were some things that were ingrained in them and one of those traditions was having fish on Christmas Eve.

Colin ordered up a variety of different fish choices. Ree thought one was better than the next.

After overeating, typical of holiday meals, they went back to the couch.

Colin sat on the end of the sofa and put Ree on his lap.

"Have you been a good little girl this year, Reanna Malloy?"

"Yes, Santa. Sometimes, I was a very good girl but sometimes I was a very bad, bad girl."

Colin started to tickle her until she almost fell off his lap.

At the last moment, he grabbed her and pulled her tighter.

"That's just the way Santa likes his girls and because of that," He sat up and pulled a bag from underneath the couch, "Santa brought you coal, like all bad little girls."

Ree was stunned.

"You bought me a present? But, I thought this trip was the present?"

"Ree, this trip is just the wrapping. It is just one part of your present. Here is another one."

She took the bag looked inside and saw two small wrapped boxes inside. She pulled them both out.

"Should I open any one first?"

"Makes no difference."

She decided to open the long one first.

Inside, was the most beautiful, platinum, braided necklace.

"Oh Colin, I love it! This is beautiful. Thank you so much."

"I'm glad you like it. Now, open the next one."

She opened the smaller one next and inside, was a pair of exquisite, diamond earrings, the perfect size.

"Oh my God, Colin, these are beautiful, but it's too much."

"Stop it, Ree. It's not too much. Please, just accept my gift graciously, but they come with one condition."

"And that is?"

"Tonight, you come to bed wearing only the earrings and the necklace."

She laughed.

"Done."

She stood up in front of him and slowly took off her clothes. She put on her jewelry, took his hand and led him off to the bedroom, where Ree proved to Santa that she could be a very, very bad girl; much to Colin's delight...

Chapter 32

Ree woke up to the feeling of falling.

Although, it was a common dream, hers was caused by literally falling out of bed.

She loved Colin with all her heart, but he was a bed hog.

She told him about it a few times but all he did was shrug sheepishly and remind her that he was a big guy. That was true, but she looked at the bed.

He was sprawled out, taking up eighty-five percent of the available real estate, leaving her with only a tiny corner and he even tried to hog that!

As she looked at him now, though, she wondered how she could possibly be angry at this wonderful caring man. She rarely got the opportunity to watch him sleep and decided to make use of the time.

He was always up before her.

She decided that he could fully operate with only a few hours' sleep, whereas she was cranky if she didn't get a whole eight hours.

Ree could not believe his stamina. Thinking of that stamina made her blush as her body heated up again.

The sun was just coming in the windows and some rays landed on him, giving Colin a golden glow. His deep, chestnut hair was now shining red. It was also long and curled up a little on the bottom. With hair like that, he certainly did not look like the conservative CEO of a major oil company, but more of a bad boy from the other side of the tracks.

Somehow, she thought, he would be more comfortable with that image.

Her eyes traveled down to his face. She noticed that his eyebrows were thick and the same color as his hair. She never noticed his eyelashes before, but now, she could not take her eyes off them. They were black, lush and long; they even curled up little on the end. If women had eyelashes like this, she thought, it would bankrupt the mascara industry.

She knew underneath those eyelashes were green eyes. She also knew the color seemed to change with his mood. When angry, they were a deep, deep green, almost black and when he was happy, they were a sparkling green, like the tops of the waves when the sun hit them.

She noticed that his beard had started to grow.

He had that sexy five o'clock shadow, which only accented his chiseled jawline. He had a straight nose, with one little bump on it, indicating that he broke it at one time.

He was lying on his stomach so her eyes traveled down his back. She had noticed that he had scars on his back before, but never got a chance to examine them. He had two scars that looked like his skin puckered up; one was on his right shoulder and the other on the back of his left arm. She wondered if maybe this was from a bullet and shuddered at the thought.

No, it must be something else. She decided, hastily.

The biggest, ugliest scar was one that ran about eight-inches long and about one-inch wide. It ran along his left side, from his front to his back. It must have hurt when it happened, and there must be an interesting story to go along with it.

His shoulders were wide, and his back looked strong; in fact, everything about Colin screamed strong. A sheet covered his ass, but without having to look, she knew it was perfectly formed. In looking at the whole picture again, she thought David had nothing on Colin; he was a perfect example of masculinity.

Lost in her musing about how perfect Colin was, she did not notice that he opened his eyes and was watching her. She sighed deeply, remembering how this strong body felt wrapped around her, when she heard him laughing. She blushed.

Can he read my lustful thoughts? She wondered.

Colin rolled on his side and his arm reached out for her and he pulled her into his embrace.

He whispered in her ear, "Merry Christmas, Ms. Malloy."

She smiled up at him.

"Merry Christmas, Mr. McLeod. Now, the question is, have you been a good boy this year, or do you get coal in your stocking?"

He bit the tip of her ear.

"Well, you tell me. Was I a good boy last night?"

She blushed but enjoyed the repartee.

"Yes, more than once, you were an especially good boy and because of that, Santa left presents for you."

He sat up like a little boy.

"Well, then Santa's helper better bring those presents before Santa changes his mind."

Ree had shopped for people who were tough before, like her dad and her aunts, but Colin brought tough to a whole new level. What do you buy a gazillionaire who actually has anything he wants and if he doesn't, he could go out and buy it? She took a deep breath, reached under the bed, pulled out four packages and placed them on his lap.

"I hope you like them. You know, you are impossible to buy for."

He sat up in bed with his back to the headboard. He reached over for Ree and pulled her to him so she was sitting next to him.

"Sweetheart, you did not have to give me anything. Whether you realize it or not, you have already given me the best gift I've ever received."

"I don't understand."

He hugged her close and kissed the top of her head.

"You gave me love and you gave me hope, hope for the future...though, presents don't hurt either."

He opened the big one first and inside were two shirts; one white and one green, made of the finest Egyptian cotton.

"Wow, Ree, these are beautiful."

She grinned proudly.

"John told me about a tailor near him that does custom shirts so I "borrowed" one of your shirts and brought it to him and he made these. I thought the white one would be good for work and I had to get one in green to show off your eyes." Excited now she urged, "Open the next one!"

He picked the next one up. The first thing Colin noticed was that it was heavy.

"I don't have a guess."

"Good. Then, you will be surprised."

He opened the present. He saw three frames, face down. He picked one up and there was a great picture of him and Storm. He remembered the day when it was taken. Ree had just gotten finished working him and she asked him to hold the horse for a minute. He noticed Shavo taking a picture, but he didn't think much of it at the time. The next picture was Syn with Shavo, Najeena, him and Ree.

"Wow Ree this is great! This was taken right after the exhibition."

She nodded.

The last picture was of Ree and Syn working in the arena. It was an exquisite shot of Syn extending the trot, with all four feet off the ground. It really did appear as if he floated on top of the sand.

Feeling a bit choked up, he hugged Ree closer.

"Love, thank you so much. I will treasure these and the memories that go with them."

"You have one more. Come on, open it."

He took the smallest of the gifts and ripped the paper, exposing a small box. He opened the box and there were two beautiful silver cufflinks of horses' heads, but he noticed an interesting braid of 'something' framing the horse heads. He looked at her, confused.

"Oh, I so glad you noticed. The one cufflink has the braided tail hair of Syn wrapped around. It and other has the braided tail hair of Storm around it. Do you like it?"

Colin was rarely speechless, but this was one of those times.

"How did you do this?"

"Believe it or not, in one of the markets Sadira and I visited, I found an artist that does beautiful weavings and he even uses horse hair for some. In that same marketplace, I found the silver cufflinks. So, it was just a matter of putting the two merchants together and coming up with this design. I think I might have given them a new idea for a joint business venture."

"Ree, you are too much; I love them and I will wear them with pride." He thought for a moment, before he aded, "Come on, Ree, let's get going. We have a full day today."

"Any hints; Is it still a surprise?"

"Well, one thing we are going to do today is a gondola ride."

Squealing with delight, she got out of bed and joined him on the other side. She put her arms around his neck and whispered in his ear.

"Will you sing to me and feed me dates?"

Colin disentangled himself from her arms, turned her towards the bathroom and gave her a playful slap on the ass.

"No, I think you should sing to me and feed me dates."

"Come on, let's shower and I'll show you how grateful I am."

Chapter 33

They got out of the shower.

Ree was towel-drying Colin's back when she was reminded of the scars.

She lightly traced the one on his side, he flinched.

"I'm sorry, did I hurt you?"

"No, just a little sensitive there."

"I can see why. That must have been a nasty injury."

"Yes, it hurt physically, but I think it injured my pride more."

"How did it happen?"

"Ree, out of all my scars I can't believe you want to know about that one; My biggest humiliation."

"Now you have my curiosity up. Come on, Colin, spill."

Colin twirled the towel and was getting ready to snap it at her.

"Remember what happened to the curious cat?"

Ree put her arms around him from behind, bent down and kissed the scar.

"Please."

"Okay, okay, I'll tell you over breakfast, but no laughing."

"Cross my heart and hope to die. I promise, not even a snicker."

Colin told her to dress tourist casual, so that meant comfortable clothes and shoes. She checked the weather; it was going to be another beautiful day, high in the upper sixties.

When she entered the sitting room, breakfast had already arrived.

Colin was reading the London Times and drinking a cup of coffee. She poured herself a cup of tea and dug into the eggs and bacon.

After a few minutes of quiet, Ree said, "Okay Colin, no hiding behind the paper. It's time to entertain me with your story."

He let out a sigh and put down the paper.

"You are just like a dog with a bone, you won't let it go?"

"Nope," She said smugly.

"Remember I told you about the uncles?"

She nodded yes.

"I think I told you how they were interested in battles, setting up battle scenes and even getting involved in reenactments."

Ree nodded yes, again.

"They were also interested in weaponry, especially medieval weaponry. In fact, outside of the British Museum, they had the most extensive collection of medieval weapons, primarily Scottish, in the world. Historians from all over would request permission to come and study the weapons. My uncles were only too willing to show them off."

"Yes, I remember you telling me this at the British Museum. You told me that the uncles would take you there and they would study one weapon for an hour."

"Yes, but sometimes I don't think they were studying it so much, as trying to figure out how to steal it and add it to their collection. They were especially angry about an English museum having Scottish weapons. I guess they knew how the British got most of those weapons."

"Okay, now focus on the scar."

"Right. Well, my uncles were not just caretakers of these weapons, they were also experts in their use. They could wield a Claymore, a broadsword, a dirk or an epee as well as any Highlander during any era. They would practice, hours on end, against each other, or with fellow Scots from the village and beyond. They still take part in the highland games and show off their skills."

"Now, let me guess? From what I know of you, and I gather you were not that much different as a teenager, you could not wait to get your hands on those weapons."

He reached across the table, grabbed her hand and squeezed it.

"My story to tell, love, but you do know me very well." He flashed an amused grin before he went on. "But, you were only half right in what you said. The uncles could not wait to teach me to use these weapons, but they were very serious about safety, so I was only allowed to use the weapons under their supervision and only when I had been properly trained. We started with the dirk, moved up to the epee, then sword and finally the broadsword. I had mastered the skills without much effort; after all, I had all those months of chopping and delivering wood to most of Scotland, so I filled out and got really strong in a relatively short period of time."

"Did you mind their rules?"

"I did, until the devil got the better of me. The one weapon they would not let me use was the Claymore. The claymore is a large heavy, two-handed weapon that is both difficult to use and extremely deadly. And of course, being a teenager, when an adult tells you, you can't do something, it's the only thing you want to do."

"Oh God, I see where this is going."

"You're right. One day, after school, while the uncles were in another part of the castle, me and Liam McKenna, my best friend at the time, snuck into the weapons room and got the Claymore down. We took it out to the practice field. I raised it up over my head and because of the weight, I immediately lost control and it sliced me across the back."

"Oh my God, Colin! You could have been killed."

"At the time, I thought that might have been preferable to what the uncles were going to do to me. Thank God, Liam was there, because I probably would have bled to death otherwise. He went running for the uncles. They packed me up and took me to the hospital, where I got eighty-seven stitches. It hurt like hell."

"What did the uncles do?"

"You know, that's the funny thing. They are two of the bravest men I've ever known. They would run into a burning building to help someone. I've seen them do it; one of the tenant's cottages. They would go into a field of competition with determination, never fear, but on the way to the hospital, I saw fear on their faces. When I was declared fit to go home, they both hugged me and Uncle George said, 'Laddie have you learned your lesson?' With tears coming down my cheek I hugged them back and promised I would never do anything like that again and I would never disappoint them again. I never did."

Chapter 34

They finished up breakfast and made their way out of the hotel.

As promised, the weather was beautiful.

Before they stepped outside, Colin asked her to wait and she saw him talking to the hotel manager. The man was smiling at Colin and looked over at Ree. He gave her a little wave, so she waved back.

When Colin came back to her, she asked what that was all about; he just grinned.

"All in good time, sweetheart; All in good time."

One of the biggest open-air markets or bazaars, as they were known in Iraq, was Hanna-Sheikh.

Customers were told that if a buyer could not find what you were looking for there, both legal and illegal, then it did not exist.

Ree thought they were exaggerating when she was told this, but she had to agree that everything a person could imagine was sold here: from beautiful fabrics to fine jewelry, colorful carpets, all types of food and even furniture and appliances.

She dubbed it the Harrods of the East.

Colin checked his watch and said it was nearly time for their Gondola ride.

They made their way over to the canals and there was a beautiful one waiting for them.

The Gondolier was very friendly and knowledgeable about the city.

As they passed places of interest, he would give them a short history of each place.

About a half hour into the trip, Ree noticed they entered a park area. He told them they were going into Akhera Park, one of the parks in Basra, which he personally felt was the most beautiful in all of Iraq, maybe even the world.

She marveled at the beauty and just when she was going to ask Colin if they could walk around the park, the gondolier pulled the boat up to the bank and told them they were here.

They both thanked him for a marvelous ride and she saw Colin give him a generous tip. They made their way up the embankment to a beautiful, scenic, park.

Ree grabbed Colin's arm.

"Colin, this place is breathtaking. Beautiful doesn't even begin to describe this place. I totally get why people think this park was the original Garden of Eden. I completely understand now why Adam and Eve where so upset when they were sent out of here. It truly is a paradise."

"Come," He said, "I have something to show you."

They made their way, following a path with the water on their right, until they came upon a big tree, with long, overshadowing branches.

Underneath, Ree saw their picnic hamper, with a blanket laid out with plates, glasses and a bottle of champagne, on ice.

Looking up at Colin she whispered, "Is this for us?"

"No," He said, "It's for you, Ree; All for you."

"Is that our picnic hamper from London?"

He nodded.

She threw herself at him, arms around his neck and legs around his waist, kissing him deeply.

Chuckling, he walked them over to blanket, disentangled Ree and they both sat down.

The view was spectacular, with the water on one side and the most magnificent garden on the other side.

Many flowers were still in bloom, so the fragrance in the air was sweet and spicy at the same time.

Ree sighed. Looking around, she felt like pinching herself, because, she quickly decided this could not be real.

She said a short prayer.

Thank you, God. Whatever good I did to deserve this, to deserve this man, thank you.

Colin reached for the champagne and popped the top; he poured them each a glass. Ree looked up into his eyes.

"Do we make a toast?"

"Yes, absolutely. To our future."

Colin sat next to Ree with their backs up against the tree. He took her hand and brought it up to his lips and kissed it.

She looked over at him.

"I cannot begin to tell you how happy I am, how happy you have made me. I love you so very much."

Still holding her hand, he looked into her eyes.

"Ree, I have to ask you or tell you something." Feeling tongue tied for the first time in his life, he continued. "I mean, I have news. The news is good and bad and depending on how you feel, it will depend on what you think is good news and what you think is bad."

Ree squeezed his hand with reassurance.

"Colin, you are scaring me. What's wrong?"

"Oh hell, here goes."

Getting into a kneeling position, he asked Ree to stand. He changed his position to one knee and took a small, black box out of his pocket and placed it on the ground, next to him.

"Oh my God, Colin." Ree's heart felt like it was going to jump out of her chest. She was breathless.

Colin took both of her hands in his and looked up into her beautiful, blue eyes.

"Ms. Reanna Catherine Malloy, will you do me the honor of becoming my wife?"

Ree fell to her knees and put her arms around him.

"Yes." She spoke quietly at first, then louder, "Yes," And finally, she was yelling, "Yes! I will marry you."

Tumbling together on the ground, they sealed the deal with a kiss.

Colin sat up and reached for the box by his side, opened it, took the ring out and placed it on her finger.

Ree took a good look at it and was in awe; it was perfect.

It was a platinum setting, with a flawless three-carat, square diamond in the center, with smaller diamonds surrounding it.

"Colin, it's perfect! I will be so honored to become your wife."

Colin reached for her hand and kissed the finger with the ring on it.

"And I am honored you agreed to be my wife. Ree, I hate to say this now, but when we get back to Bagdad, I think its best we keep this secret until we get back home. Do you agree?"

"Yes, I agree it would complicate things too much. I think most people know something is going on with you and me, but I think it best if we don't make it official just yet. Can I tell my mom and Epee?"

"Ree, I'm a little old fashioned. I would like to ask your mom's permission first; have her meet me, at least, but if you want to, that's fine with me. Be sure to tell her I wanted to wait."

Colin gently touched the platinum around her neck.

"This is one of the reasons I gave you the chain. I had hoped that you would be willing to wear the ring on the chain next to your heart."

"Absolutely, but today I want to wear it on my finger." She beamed for a moment, but then, with another thought, her glimmer of joy lost some of its luster. She stared at Colin seriously. "You said there was good news and bad news; this could not possibly be bad news. This is the best news."

"Well, sweetheart, I'm glad you think so because if you didn't want to marry me, then it would have been bad news, at least for me."

"Then, what would the good news be?"

Colin sat up with his back up against the tree and pulled Ree on his lap. He stroked her hair.

"Remember the other day I was on the phone and you said I looked upset? I told you I would tell you about it later."

She nodded.

"Unfortunately, I got a call from my sister-in-law. It seems, my mom has a blockage in two valves in her heart and requires surgery. They are hoping to be able to do an angioplasty, but if that doesn't work they will have to do open-heart surgery."

"Oh, Colin, I'm so sorry. You have to go to be with her."

"You know this is one of the reasons why I love you so much: your compassion and your understanding. So, yes, I do have to leave."

"When?"

"The surgery is scheduled for Monday, January third, in Houston. We will have to cut our trip short and leave tomorrow. I'll drop you off in Bagdad. I already had my aide pack my things from the hotel, so I will continue to London. From there, I'll catch a commercial airline back to Texas."

"Tomorrow. So soon..."

Colin hugged her tighter. Ree rested her head on his chest.

"I'm sorry, sweetheart. You know, if it was any other situation, I'd stay here with you but..."

"I absolutely understand, Colin. If it were my mom, I would do the same thing. Do you want me to go with you? It would be tough to arrange, because we are just opening the new school, but I could manage something."

"No, Ree. You stay here. There's nothing you could do anyway. Get that new school opened and I will be back before you know it."

"How in the world could you possibly think that would be good news for me?"

"Well, if you didn't want me around, this was your chance to get rid of me."

Ree looked up into his eyes.

"I never, never, ever want to be rid of you. I will be miserable until you come back to me."

"And I will miss you as well. Before I forget, is there anything you want me to bring back from the States?"

It didn't take Ree long to answer.

"Yes. Snickers bars. A whole box, if you can and I need some more microwave popcorn, with extra butter; we ate it all."

"We?"

"Well, you did help and if you can fit it, a package of Oreo cookies?"

"Okay, no problem and I know you bought some things for your mom and Epee here. If you want, I will send the gifts to them when I get home. Our Postal Service is much more reliable than international. Make sure you give me the addresses before I leave. And, if you think of anything else, call me. You know, we probably won't be able to talk very often with the poor state of international calling. So, if you really need to reach me have the state department get in touch with me."

415

"I'm going to miss you so much. Any idea when you will be back?"

"We are hoping that it's going to be a simple surgery and if that's the case, I'll just stay a week, but if it's more involved, then I will need to stay longer." He grinned, trying to lighten the mood, "Besides, it will give me more time to stock up on condoms. I didn't realize that I would meet a sex-crazed girlfriend on this trip and go through a case of condoms."

"Well, maybe if that girl's boyfriend wasn't so hot, she wouldn't be so sex-crazed."

"Thanks, Ree, but seriously...We have been playing Russian Roulette the last couple of weeks, not using condoms. What if you got pregnant? What if you are pregnant?"

Ree unconsciously moved her hand down her stomach.

"Would that be such a bad thing? Don't you want children?"

He thought for a moment.

"You know, Ree, I never thought I did want children. I had my niece and nephew to carry on the McLeod legacy, but with you, yes. I definitely want children, but not in Iraq. The situation here is way too volatile. Maybe when we get home and get settled, we can talk about it."

Ree looked away and started to tear up.

Colin brushed a tear away.

"Ree, did I say something wrong? Why are you upset?"

"Colin, do you remember the conversation we had when you first ran out of condoms? I told you the doctor told me that because I get my period so infrequently, that it would be very difficult to become pregnant? He said that in the future, if I decided I wanted children, I would have to go for fertility treatments."

"Yes, I remember the conversation and lucky me about your period."

Ree gave him a pretend slap on the arm.

"You perv."

Colin looked in her eyes and kissed her sweetly.

"Honey, I'm marrying you because I love you, not because I want a baby-making machine. I'm a lucky man. I have my niece and nephew, whom I love dearly. I don't want anything that would put your health or your life in danger. If we decide we want to try for kids in the future then we will look into the options, but until then, no more chances. I'm bringing a suitcase full of condoms back with me."

"You mean, I'm out of luck tonight?"

Colin rolled her over so she was on her back and he was on top of her resting his weight on his forearms.

"Well, maybe later tonight we'll take one more chance," Kiss, "Or two," Kiss, "Or three," Kiss.

Colin sat up and pulled Ree into a sitting position.

"Okay, enough of this, before we get arrested for public indecency. Let's dig into this food and enjoy this day, in our own little Garden of Eden"

Colin opened up another bottle of Champaign.

"Let's pretend we're Adam and Eve, the only two people in world and just forget everything else."

And they did just that!

Chapter 35

Could you miss someone so much that it actually hurt physically, Ree wondered?

Sadira and John had been great in taking her mind off Colin, but it seemed wherever she looked, she would see him there.

Heck, there were even a few times she swore she heard him calling her name.

She thought she would spend New Year's alone but John invited her and Sadira over to his house to celebrate an American New Years. He asked them to bring an American dish.

Ree did her best with wings; they turned out better than she thought.

Sadira made pizza; it was delicious.

John's wife made the Iraqi version of hamburgers and hot dogs.

They stayed up until midnight and they toasted the new year with a bottle of Champaign that Ree brought. She stepped outside a few minutes after midnight, looked up at the stars, and said a little prayer out loud.

"Whatever you are doing now, my love, know I'm thinking of you and missing you. Happy New Year, sweetheart." She toasted Colin.

The next school term started the following week and all the students, plus more signed up for the next semester.

The satellite school opened on the same day and was a rousing success.

They were filled to capacity.

Ree was thrilled that Tihara came back.

She was surprised that Uday allowed it, but from what she had been hearing, he was a little busy.

Tihara took another accounting class and also took the second part of the Women in Literature, that Ree taught.

After class, while waiting for her ride, she and Ree talked in Ree's office, usually with a cup of tea. They talked about things going on in the school or incidents happening in or around Bagdad, but on this particular day, they continued the discussion they were having in class.

One of Ree's favorite authors was Khaled Hosseini who wrote, *The Kite Runner*. Ree decided to incorporate his second book, *A Thousand Splendid Suns,* into the curriculum.

The book was about two women who were brought together by war, by loss and by fate.

These women then formed a bond that made them sisters and even mother-daughter to each other.

In class, they were discussing the depth of love a woman has for her family and what will she sacrifice for her family.

Tihara asked Ree the question, "Do you think love requires sacrifice? Can you have love without sacrifice?"

Ree thought about the questions and didn't really have a good answer, so after class Ree brought her question up again.

"You know, Tahira, your question about love and sacrifice was very interesting. I would like to know what you think. Do you think you can have love with sacrifice?

"Honestly, I don't know. I can only speak from my experience and that is that family is all important to me. The people I love are all important to me and I would do anything to help them and to protect them. If a person does not have people to love, then who are you? Aren't they the reason for our survival, as is indicated in the book? I also think it doesn't just have to be our family, but any person who is important in your life and whom you love."

"What made you so wise for one so young?"

"I had no choice. I love my family and I would do anything for them. I have done everything for them." Tahira wiped a tear from her eye.

"Do you want to tell me about it?"

"I told you about living with my parents and their occupations."

Ree nodded.

"I remember."

"I wanted to become a doctor like my father," She continued, "Sometimes, he would take me on calls and he would explain what he was doing. When I got older, I assisted him in simple cases, like stitches or helping him to set a fracture. One day, he was called to the government building. A soldier was injured. This was not unusual; in fact, we were called there frequently. This day, though, it wasn't just a soldier; it was one of Uday's personal guards. By the time my father realized, it was too late and Uday had seen me. Uday asked my father about me and our family."

Tihira voice wavered a bit as she continued.

"My father told me it is his biggest regret in life, that he didn't think quicker and tell Uday I was engaged, but my father didn't think of it. I was only fifteen. Uday told my father he was doing our family a great honor and that he would make me his second wife. We were then told to go home and to prepare me. They would come in an hour to pick me up. My father was livid; I was in shock. We got home and only my brother was there. He wanted to take me away to England or America, but we all knew it wouldn't work. Before we knew it, the government car was outside our home and I was taken away from my family."

"I don't understand, why couldn't you father refuse Uday?"

Tihira shook her head back and forth.

"You do not refuse the Hussein family in anything. If my father refused, they would have killed him and my brother. They would have tracked down my mother and either killed her or put her in prison and the result would have been the same. Either way, I would have ended up in that government car."

"So, you truly do identify with these women. You sacrificed everything for your family."

"Would you not do the same? What would you sacrifice for Colin?"

"Everything," She whispered.

"But in some ways, I don't see it as a sacrifice," Tihara continued. "I see it, just as something any person would do, because they love. That's why I wondered if all love requires sacrifice?"

Ree nodded her understanding.

"I think, if you love, then, as you said, you will always be required to sacrifice; whether it be your time, giving the last piece of food, or putting your own wants and desires aside for someone else, but I think if you truly love, then, I don't think people see it as a sacrifice. I think it is something I would gladly do if it helped someone I loved."

"Yes, I agree. I certainly did not want to go with Uday, but I wanted to protect my family, so I was honored to do so."

"Is life so bad in the Palace?"

"Not now. Now, everyone leaves me alone, but when I first got there, it was terrible. The first night, he raped me. I fought and fought and it seemed the more I fought, the better he liked it. Each night, he would come and each night I would fight him. Finally, one night, I was so tired I didn't fight any more. I just lay there. I remembered a technique I read about in one of my father's journals called meditation. I tried some of the techniques and thought it was very useful, especially for people who were in chronic pain. So, I started to meditate. My spirit or my soul left my body and I felt nothing.

I sent my spirit to a happy place. When I stopped fighting, he lost interest and has not bothered me since. That was over two years ago."

"Where is the happy place you go to?"

For the first time, Ree saw Tihara smile.

"A variety of places, but usually, a small lake by our home. My brother's friend, Omar and I would meet there often. He wanted to become a doctor also. He was two years older than I, so we made plans. He would go to medical school in America first and set everything up for me. I would then come two years later and join him. He was going to become a surgeon and I wanted to become a gynecologist. We would sit by the water and talk about opening our combined practice and helping the people of our community. We would talk about a child." She suddenly stopped short, realizing what she just said.

"So, you loved Omar."

Tihara looked up at Ree with the saddest eyes.

"With all my heart. I think of him and pray for him every day. Ree, I don't want this to just be my life. I want to make a difference."

Ree held the girl tight.

"Don't you think you have already made a difference by protecting your family? And as Uday's second wife, you must have some power at the Palace, power to change some things?"

A tear appeared on her cheek; she looked away from Ree.

"He never married me; I am simply his whore."

They both heard the dreaded knock on the door, indicating Tihara's ride was here. They both got up and Ree put her arms around the girl.

"Somehow, I don't think your story is over; you will make a difference."

They hugged and Tihara walked out.

Chapter 36

Ree could not believe that it had been over a month since Colin had left. She missed him every minute, every second. The last she heard, his mom had done well with the surgery but then developed serious complications.

She was in the hospital for over a week; then Colin had to arrange for health care at home. Due to her fragile state, he didn't want to leave right away.

Ree completely understood and would have done the same thing for her mom, but that genuine understanding didn't stop her from missing him.

The last message she got from him, through the State Department a few days ago, said he would try to be back to Bagdad in about ten days.

Ree wanted to mark the days on her calendar but was afraid of being very disappointed if he wasn't back by then.

John and Sadira had been great.

John and his wife had her over for dinner at least once a week. She enjoyed their company, especially the little boys. They were the combination of John and his wife.

Sadira kept her busy with shopping and going out to eat.

Even the Ambassador had her over to the embassy for dinner a few times.

Time really was moving quickly, but when she thought about Colin, she realized it was never quick enough.

Still, there were many bright spots in her day.

The school was a smashing success and the horses she was working with were all doing fantastic.

Syn, was especially doing well. She had started upper-level dressage work with him.

He was so willing to learn and was so athletic, that all the movements came easily to him.

She wondered if Uday would ever consider selling him.

Laughing to herself, she could hear Colin say the chances were between very slim to no way.

She agreed.

The brightest spot in her day, though, was her afternoon conversation with Tihara. Her guards were coming later and later to pick her up, so Ree got in the habit of having tea with her in the office.

Tihara would steal some cookies or sometimes scones from the palace's kitchen, so they would have an official afternoon tea.

The more Ree spoke to the girl, the more amazed she was by her intellect, her strength, and her quiet dignity.

Given the same situation, Ree doubted that she could have come out of it as strong.

One day, Tihara mentioned how she would love to tell her family she was doing fine and that they should not worry.

Ree was shocked that she was not allowed to communicate with them and offered her to get letters to her parents.

Tihara was so grateful she threw her arms around Ree and sobbed.

They arranged for Tihara to write the letters in class; then Ree would take them and send them to the addresses Tihara gave her. She smiled as she remembered Tihara's concern.

"Ree, I worry that they will find out what you did and it will get you in trouble."

"If it makes you feel any better," Ree said, "When Colin gets back, I will have him send them from his business. If you think about it, he could probably have an employee send it from anywhere in the world. It should not cause any suspicion."

Tihara noticed the sadness in Ree's eyes when she spoke of Colin.

"You miss him very much, don't you?"

"Miss who?"

"Now, now, Ree, you know who I am talking about: the man who lights up your face when he is near you, the man you are pining for because he is gone."

"Am I that transparent?"

"No, not to most people, but to one who has felt like that, you cannot hide it. When is he expected back?"

Rees shrugged her shoulders and sighed.

"I don't know. His last message said maybe ten days, but I don't want to get my hopes up. I know he is needed by his family. It's one of the reasons I love him, is his dedication to those he loves, but it doesn't stop me missing him. I will just be surprised when he gets here. And, that reminds me, I want to give you this paper; it has all the numbers where you can reach me and all the numbers you can reach Colin."

Pointing to a number she continued. "This is Colin's personal cell number. Almost all of the time, you can reach him at that number when he is here in Bagdad. The other number is my cell. Unless I'm riding a horse or teaching a class, you can always reach me."

"I thank you so much, Ree, but why would I need the numbers? I know my life and no one can alter it," She said sadly.

"I know, Tihara, I know we can't get you out of the palace. Believe me, I wish we could, but with the current situation, we don't know what's going to happen. If you feel like you are in danger, please believe that Colin and I would do anything to protect you and help you get to safety."

Tihara hugged her.

"Thank you, truly, Ree. I will keep you in my prayers every night."

That conversation seemed to have brought them closer together.

The next day, Tihara gave Ree some addresses and each of the following days after class she gave Ree a letter, with instructions on whom to send it to.

Until Colin got back, she gave the letters to John and he mailed them from his neighborhood. They agreed that if her parents responded, they would mail the letters to John; he would give them to Ree, and finally to Tihara.

One night, about the middle of February, Ree's cell rang. Her heart started beating loudly hoping that maybe it was Colin.

Although initially disappointed when she first heard her friend's voice, she rebounded and was thrilled.

"Epee, what in the world are you calling me for? Do you have any idea how expensive this call is going be?"

A very angry Epona was on the other end.

"I don't give a damn how much it costs; Kevin encouraged me, no, told me to call you. Ree, you have to listen to reason. You have to get your ass out of there and come home. All they are talking about here is war. The talk has changed from if to when. Ree I'm really, really scared for you. Your mother is beside herself with worry. Please, Ree, I know you. You read my emails and then say to yourself that I'm over reacting, but not this time, Ree."

Ree tried to get a word in edgewise but it was impossible.

Finally, Epee came up for air.

"Epee, nice to talk to you, too."

"Don't be a wiseass, Ree. I'm serious. You have to take this seriously. Where is that fiancé of yours? He should be dragging your ass on his private jet and bringing you home. I don't care if he has to duct tape you. In fact, give me his address over there and I'll send him the duct tape. I'll make sure it's blue, your favorite color."

"Are you done?"

"No, I'm just beginning, but I promised Kevin that we would not have to mortgage the house to pay for the bill. Please, Ree, I know what you are like when you dig your heels in, but it's getting crazy here. You should hear the talk on TV. Please, come home."

"Epee, I really do appreciate your concern and I love you too, but really, I'm safe here. I don't think there's going to be a war; there's no reason for it. I think it's just men having a pissing contest. Knowing the Husseins, they will posture and bellow, but eventually, like any bully, they will back down. Honestly, the people here are not worried. If it was getting bad, don't you think the State Department would insist that I go home? I promise, when this term is up in May, I will come home. And no, you can't have Colin's address. Knowing you, you would tell him all types of embarrassing stories about me."

"God, Ree, you are stubborn. Okay, I can't make you come home and Kevin won't let me go over there and kidnap you, to bring you home. So, at least, promise me that you will be careful and do what the experts tell you to do...No heroics."

"Epee, you know me. I'm not a hero and may I remind you, I'm one of the experts. Look, I promise to take care. I promise not to put myself in any dangerous situations." Ree crossed her fingers as she said this. "Besides, Colin should be back any day, so I promise to do whatever he says."

"Okay, I believe you, but understand that we're scared. I don't want anything to happen to you. This is my chance to be a matron of honor."

"I promise. Now, get off the phone before Kevin has a coronary, and please give my mom a big hug and kiss from me and tell her not to worry. I love you, Epee."

"I love you too." Ree hung up the phone and cried. She missed her best friend, she missed her Mom, but most of all, she missed Colin.

In the middle of the night, Ree was awakened by the oddest sensation of something tickling her nose. Every time she would shoo it away, it came back.

Finally, she made a grab for it and felt her hand make contact with skin.

She opened her eyes, tried to sit up in bed, ready to let out a scream, when the light came on and she heard what she was longing to hear for seven weeks.

"Ree, it's okay. It's me, Colin. I'm home, sweetheart."

She looked up into his very tired, very ragged face and sighed.

"I missed you so much. I am so glad you're home."

"I missed you too, mo duinne (my heart)."

That night, they put an impressive dent into the supply of condoms Colin brought back from the US.

Chapter 37

When Ree woke up, the world seemed brighter, sharper and more vivid.

She sat up in bed and stretched. She was a little sore, but a wonderful sore, because the man of her dreams had finally come home.

She heard the shower turn off and a few minutes later Colin came into the bedroom, with a towel wrapped around his waist.

Her lustful eyes drank him in. He was even more perfect than she remembered. She sighed and blushed a little, thinking of the night before.

"Ree, what did I tell you about looking at me like that? You have classes in an hour and I have to get to my suite, unpack and check in with the office."

"You mean, you came here straight from the airport?"

"Hell, yes. I couldn't wait to try out the new condoms."

She got out of bed, walked over to him and put her arms around his waist.

"And, how did you like them? Did they disappoint?"

He kissed her on the top of her head.

"Not at all. In fact, they exceeded expectation. Now, go shower and get dressed, because if you keep holding me like that with no clothes on, I can guarantee that you will be late for class. What do you think that old ugly school marm that's in charge of the school will say to you?"

Not letting go, she looked up at him.

"I happen to know for a fact that she would tell me to be late because we are very close, but you are right, as usual. I have an early morning meeting with some of the people from the satellite school for new equipment. What are your plans today?"

"The first thing I have to do is get settled back into the suite, then I have to go to the office, see what needs attention there and finally, I have a meeting with Ambassador Ryan."

"Ryan. Why?"

"Ree, we really didn't have time to talk about it last night, but the situation here has gone from worse to disastrous. I'll talk to you about it tonight. Come to the hotel for dinner and I'll get you up to date with the home situation, but Ree, it isn't good."

"Epee called me last night and she tried to tell me how bad things were getting but I thought she was overreacting, as she usually does."

"Whatever she told you, multiply it by a thousand and it's still worse. You have to face the very real possibility of having to evacuate, sooner rather than later."

"Colin, I don't think that will be necessary. We both know that there are no WMD's here. We know it and Ambassador Ryan knows it. They can't just invade a country with no evidence."

"Ree, I'll talk to you about it tonight. I'll have more information for you after I talk with Ryan. In the meantime, I want you to pack a bag to be ready to take if we have to leave in a hurry. Will you promise me you will do that?"

She nodded yes.

"Great, sweetheart. I don't want to scare you, but we need to be prepared. Okay, you get ready and I'll send a car for you about five."

He kissed her and left for the day.

Ree went through her day, but something felt off. Maybe it was the warnings from Epee and Colin, or maybe it was just her imagination. She was thrilled Colin was back, but somehow, his mood was foreshadowing darkness.

All she knew, was that in a few hours she would be in his arms again.

Colin left Ree's apartment and headed to his suite.

Once there, he packed up the few remaining things that he had left and following his own advice, had a bag packed with things he would need if he had to bug out.

He had his black pants, shirt, cap and bulletproof vest out and ready to put on, if needed.

Somehow, he couldn't shake the feeling, his Spidey Sense he guessed, that he was going to need it sooner, rather than later. He still could not believe how things seemed to go out of control so quickly at home. It seemed when he left in September, Iraq was casually mentioned. A few months later, the powers that be were talking all-out war.

Colin brought his bag of his last remaining things with him to the office. He would have an aide send it home on the next flight out. He put out a few business fires both here and at home, shot off some emails, made some calls, and he was done for the day. Somehow, it felt like he was closing things down; not a good feeling.

After leaving the office, he headed over to the embassy for his meeting with Ambassador Ryan.

As soon as he entered the compound, he could tell things had changed. Extra security was everywhere and everyone was fully armed. He had to go through two checkpoints before he even got close to the embassy.

Finally, getting inside, there was a little delay when he had to show his weapon, before going through security. After showing his military ID and clearance, he was waved through. He checked his watch; he was ten minutes late.

Oh well, Ryan would just have to understand.

Colin went into the Ambassador's office where a secretary showed him to the dining room, where lunch was set.

Seeing Colin enter the room, Ryan stood up and extended his hand.

"Good to see you, Colin. I hope you bring me good news, because all the news I have here is bad."

"I'm sorry, Ryan. The only news I have is bad and I'm afraid what's coming will be even worse. I spoke to Jim Peterson when I was in Washington and the news he told me isn't good. It seems the administration is focused on finding evidence of WMD's and going to war. All of Jim's contacts in Iraq dispute this, but the powers that be don't want to hear it. I spoke to some of my SEAL contacts and this is where the news gets worse. They are in full preparation for invasion."

"Yes, unfortunately, I'm hearing the same thing. I'm just waiting for the order from the

President to evacuate American personnel and close the Embassy."

"That's my main question. Why haven't you closed down operations? Why is the school still operating? When are we going to get those people out? Damn, if I didn't have to come back here, I wouldn't have. The place is going to blow up in a very short period of time."

"All good questions and I'm sure you are not going to like some of the answers. The administration doesn't want to closedown anything, including programs like the school, or especially the embassy, because they don't want to show their hand. The government doesn't want the Iraqi's to get the jump on our plans and have the time to hide things, like WMD's, so the feeling is to keep everything running as normal. As soon as a decision is made, we will evacuate and shut everything down and that includes the school. And by the way, I'm glad you came back. We can use you."

"Thanks for your support, but I don't like playing politics with people's lives," He said firmly.

"Again, I agree, but the best we can do is be prepared. I'm sure you have your people ready to evacuate the school and get the civilians to the airport."

"Yes, absolutely. We've practiced different scenarios so we are ready. We will keep everyone safe."

"Yes, I'm sure you will; especially a very pretty director of the school. Is she the reason you came back?"

Taken a little off guard, Colin didn't quite know how to respond.

"It's okay, Colin. No one told me. No one had to; Just seeing the way you two look at each other spoke volumes. I know she has become more to you than just an assignment. Besides, you should have seen how lonely she was when you were gone. Christ, I was ready to go back home and bring you back myself."

"You are absolutely right. She has become so much more than an assignment. She has become my whole life."

"Well then, congratulations. Maybe something good will come out of this damn mess. Be sure to invite me to the wedding."

They shook hands.

"You got it, and I promise, I'll be ready."

"So will we."

Chapter 38

Colin had dinner all set up when Ree walked into the room.

"Yum, something smells great. What's for dinner?"

He hugged her and kissed the top of her head.

"Your favorite, steak mashed potatoes and broccoli, with strawberry shortcake for desert."

"Wow. What's the occasion?"

He grabbed her by the waist and swung her around.

"The occasion is, I'm finally home with my favorite fiancée."

"I better be your only fiancée."

Colin hugged her closer.

"Of course. Come on, let's eat."

They kept the conversation to small talk, with both of them wanting to avoid the elephant in the room for as long as possible. They needed to enjoy each other's company and forget about the rest of the world.

Ree related all the latest news from the barn and in the school. She told him Tihara's story and that she gave Tahira his cell number. She hoped he didn't mind.

He was not shocked to hear about Tihara's story. He heard similar stories about Uday and his perversions. He said, of course, he didn't mind and only voiced regret that there wasn't more he could do to help her.

One of the first things Ree asked Colin was about his Mom.

It was probably the only good news he had. He told her she was doing great, had finished rehab, and had made a full recovery. He didn't tell Ree that his mom didn't want him to go back to Iraq, but knew it was necessary.

The last thing she said to him was, "Colin, you go bring that girl back home. I want to dance at my son's wedding and then, I want to hold a new batch of grandbabies. It's about time this family had some good news."

He promised her he would.

They talked a little about business and then not being able to avoid it any longer, Colin put his napkin down and leaned back in his chair.

"I met with Ambassador Ryan today."

"Oh, I forgot. How did that go? Did he tell you how well the satellite school is doing?" Ree tried to sound unconcerned but she could tell from Colin's face this conversation was not going to go the way she wanted.

"Ree, honey," He reached across the table for her hands, "The situation here is not good. I'm not sure when, but soon, we have to start to think about getting out of here. Did you pack the bag like I asked?"

She nodded yes.

"But don't you think things could turn around and life could get back to normal?"

He thought for a minute and took a deep breath.

"Anything is possible, but in this case it's not probable. We have to plan for the worst-case scenario. So," He got from the chair, "I know it's a school night. I want to get you back to the apartment. Pack all your important things. Tomorrow, I'll swing by and pick them up and take them to my office. They will be safe there. If nothing happens, I'll return them and we'll laugh about it. But if something does happen, your things will be safe. Agreed?"

Ree nodded yes.

Colin drove her back to the apartment and made sure she was safely inside. She told him she was exhausted and was going right to bed. He kissed her goodnight and asked her to dream of him.

Colin got in his car and headed back to his suite. He could not shake the feeling something wasn't right. He got back to the hotel and made some calls.

He looked out the window; all seemed quiet in Bagdad.

He checked his bag to be sure it was ready to go, if needed.

He was about ready to go to bed when his cell rang.

He thought it was Ree wishing him goodnight.

He checked the number and didn't recognize it, but answered it anyway.

He heard a quiet voice, almost a whisper, on the other end.

"Hello, is this Mister Colin?"

"Yes," He said, "Who is this?"

"My name is Tihara. I am a student of Miss Ree. Please, you must listen to me. I heard the men talking and in a little while, they are leaving to pick up Americans and put them in prison. One of the people they are getting is Miss Ree. Uday said if the Americans bomb us, he will use them as human shields around the palace. He laughed when he said Miss Ree would be chained to the barn and could die with her horses. Please..."

At this point, he heard a man's voice in the background, speaking in Farsi.

Colin was only able to pick out a couple of words: *traitor* and *bitch*.

He heard her quietly say something to him. It sounded like the word *love*.

The next thing he heard was a gunshot.

The phone went dead.

Colin dressed in his black clothes and donned his bulletproof vest. While he was dressing, he called Sadira and told her what was happening. He asked her to call John and be prepared to pick them up at the designated spot at the school.

He got in his car.

Thankfully, he told them not to valet park it out front. The trip to the apartment was ten minutes.

The trip from the palace was about twenty minutes, so he had time but not a lot.

While he drove to the apartment, he called Ryan and apprised him of the situation.

Ryan told him he would have everything ready at the airport. He would begin rounding up US citizens and getting them out.

Ryan's next phone call was to the President.

Colin got to Ree's apartment in record time. He let himself in and made his way to her bedroom.

Ree was fast asleep. He grabbed a pair of jeans, a sweater and a pair of sneakers. He laid them on the bed.

He sat down next to her, shaking her gently.

"Ree, honey, it's time to get up. Something happened. Come on, love, you have to get up and get dressed."

She moaned it was too early.

Shaking her a little harder, she finally came awake.

"What's wrong? Why are you here and why are you dressed like that?"

"Ree, we have no time. Your friend. Tihara called me. Uday is coming to take you prisoner. We have to get out of here NOW. Get dressed."

Ree could not process what Colin just said but she got dressed.

"Colin, I don't understand. I didn't do anything wrong. Why would Uday arrest me?"

As she was getting dressed he looked around the room and saw she packed up most everything, but left two pictures.

One was Ree and Colin with Syn and the other a picture of her Dad. He grabbed them and put them into his bag.

She was taking too long getting dressed so he started helping her. When she was finished, he grabbed her arm and pulled her out of the room.

She stood her ground.

"Colin, I'm not going anywhere until you tell me what's going on."

"Honey, I'm sorry there is no time. We have to go, now."

Ree planted herself and would not move.

He knew Ree and how long explanations could take.

He looked out the window and saw headlights of two cars coming down the street. He did the only thing he could think of...

He put the two bags down, walked over to Ree, picked her up and threw her over his shoulder. He picked up the bags and walked out of the room.

"I'm sorry, Ree, there is no time. Uday's men are already at the front door. Be quiet and maybe, just maybe, we will get out of here without becoming human targets."

When they got to the door of the basement, he heard the guards breaking down the door to her apartment.

Ree wiggled on his shoulder.

"What was that?"

"Honey, that was the guards breaking down your front door. It is just a matter of time before they came downstairs into the basement. Can you be very quiet?"

Colin felt her nod her head and he patted her ass in reassurance. He set Ree down to move the wardrobe.

Once he moved the piece of furniture, he took her hand, turned the flashlight on and entered the tunnel. The tunnel smelled terrible. They talked about cleaning it, out but he didn't want to bring any unwanted attention to the area.

Thus, he had decided to leave it alone.

He heard Ree trying not to gag.

He squeezed her hand and whispered, "Try not to breathe too deeply."

He felt the ground start to rise; he knew they were coming to the end of the tunnel. He turned the flashlight off and waited at the entrance. He set Ree down and hugged her in front of him to give her the greatest amount of protection.

Ree whispered to him, "It's really happening, isn't it? I'm not dreaming, am I?"

He kissed the side of her head and whispered quietly in her ear, "No, love, I'm sorry, it's not a dream. Trust me, we'll get out of this. Everything will be okay, I promise."

They waited for what seemed like hours.

Colin checked his watch; it was less than ten minutes.

From their practice, he knew it would take John and Sadira about fifteen minutes to bring the car to the designated spot.

Thank god, that it was a moonless night so they had the advantage of darkness. As he was watching for the car he felt Ree tug on his sleeve.

Colin whispered to her.

"Ree, we are in danger, please be very quiet, nod if you understand me."

She nodded yes.

Colin continued.

"In a little while, we are going to run for a car that's going to pull up there." He pointed to a spot on the street. "Do you understand?"

Again, she nodded yes.

"Good," He gave her a little squeeze, "Do you think you can run? If not, I'll carry you, but it would be faster if you ran."

She nodded again yes.

"Good girl. As soon as I tell you, we are going to run for it."

At this point, Colin heard voices in the back of the school. His luck held.

They obviously checked the basement but didn't look behind the wardrobe.

He saw a flashlight beam scan the area where the tunnel was located. They did not see anything and started looking to the other side.

Colin saw the car advance down the street, lights off, blending into the night.

If a person didn't know what to look for it would have been missed.

He prayed the guards missed it.

"Are you ready love?" He whispered to Ree.

She nodded and he set her on her feet.

She staggered a little but then stood upright.

"Ree, are you sure you can make it?" He felt her stagger.

"I'll be fine. Just, tell me when," She somehow croaked out.

Colin saw the car was in position, so it was now or never. He grabbed her arm and made a run for it.

They were halfway to the car, when Ree's foot got trapped in a hole.

She let out a small yell and went down.

Colin stopped and picked her up.

There was enough movement and sound to alert the guards and send the flashlight beams over their way.

One of the guards spotted them and yelled to the others.

They started to fire.

The back door of the car was open. Colin was sure he could get Ree inside, when he felt like someone hit him with a baseball bat in the middle of his back.

He went down, with Ree under him.

John came out of the car, grabbed Ree and put her in the back of the car.

She heard Colin tell John to take off without him.

"No!" She cried and jumped out of the car to help Colin.

That was her last conscious memory.

****

Colin tried to get up.

He realized he was hit, but thanks to his vest, the worst that would happen would be some bruised ribs.

At least, he knew Ree was safe when he gave John the order to take off.

He could deal with the few guards, without having to worry about Ree.

However, before he could make another move, he heard Ree yell and leap from the car, towards him.

He watched her take a bullet in her right shoulder, stagger back and hit her head with a sickly sounding whack, on the door of the car.

"Fuck."

Colin managed to get up.

He picked Ree up and jumped into the back of the car.

"Go, go, go! Get the fuck out of here."

He cradled Ree in his arms, trying to assess the damage. He could feel blood on her shoulder. He felt around her head, no blood.

Thank God, he thought, but still, he could feel the beginning of a goose egg on the side of her head; probably a concussion.

He felt all around; it appeared she didn't sustain any other damage. He rooted around his bag, found his towel and pressed it on her shoulder wound.

Sadira turned around.

"Commander, how is she? Is it serious?"

"Can't really tell, but it looks like the bullet went right through; the bleeding seems to be slowing. I'm more concerned about her head injury. She really hit the back of her head hard. I'm sure she has a concussion. What's our ETA to the airfield?"

John checked his watch.

"About fifteen minutes. I'm taking the long route trying to avoid major streets. The guards should be trying to find us about now, but with the backtracking, I think we lost them."

"Good, just what I would have done. I think she's stable, but Sid, gave a call to the flight crew and tell them we have any injury."

He kissed Ree lightly on the forehead.

"Yes, Commander, I'll give them our ETA."

He held Ree close and suddenly, he felt her giggling.

"Ree, are you awake? Are you okay? Where do you hurt?"

She sounded like she was drunk, slurring her words a bit and whispering loudly.

"Colin, they are calling you Colonel. They are messing up your name don't you think that's funny..." She started to giggle again.

He tried to sound lighthearted.

"Yes, love, it's funny but tell me where you hurt."

"I'm afraid." She closed her eyes.

"Why, love? You have been very brave." He shook her lightly to keep her awake.

"I hurt all over and if I start thinking about it, I'm afraid I'll start crying."

"It's okay. Love, you can cry if you want. I've got you and I promise, nothing more will happen to you. We're about ten minutes from the hospital. You will get something for the pain very soon. Ree, you have to tell me...Why did you jump out of the car? You were safe."

"Why do you think? You weren't safe. Would you leave me there?"

"Of course not, but I would have been fine. Remember, love, I'm trained to handle a situation like this."

"I don't care. I would hurt a thousand times more to keep you with me...and besides, it worked; you're here."

Colin smiled down at the concern in her eyes.

"I can't dispute that logic, love. Thank you. Now. start telling me where it hurts."

"Okay, well when I fall from a horse, I stay still for a minute and I take a mental inventory of my body to see what works and what doesn't. I'll do that now."

Ree closed her eyes.

"My left ankle is sore; I think it's sprained. My right hip hurts; probably bruised. My chest hurts; can't take a deep breath. My right shoulder is on fire; can't think about it. My head really hurts. It feels like I'm drunk. It's hard to say things." Ree started to slur her words.

He stroked her hair.

"You did good, love. Now rest. We will be there in a few minutes. I love you, Ree."

"I love you too, Colin. I'm glad we didn't leave you behind."

Ree fell into a deep sleep, which considering her injuries, was a good thing.

They pulled onto the airfield and up to a waiting cargo carrier.

The first thing Colin noticed was a stretcher waiting with two medics.

Thank God, he thought.

They pulled up and he carried Ree out of the car, to the waiting stretcher.

The one medic looked down at Ree.

"What's her condition, Sir?"

Colin went through everything Ree told him and added his own concern about her head injury.

He told the medic about her slurred speech and feeling like she was drunk.

They brought her into the body of the plane with Colin, John, and Sadira following.

Sadira grabbed one of the medics and told him about Colin taking a bullet in his vest, possibly resulting in broken or bruised ribs.

The medic approached Colin and asked to examine him. Colin thanked him politely but told him he was fine.

Colin went up to talk to the pilot to find out when they would be leaving. The pilot told him they were waiting for about sixteen more people; Ambassador Ryan was among them.

Their ETA was about five minutes.

By the time Colin got back to Ree, he saw more cars coming onto the airstrip.

He checked Ree. She seemed to be resting comfortably, so he checked with the medic.

The medic told Colin he was sure she had a concussion, but the shoulder wound was not bad; it was a clean shot.

She didn't lose a lot of blood, thanks to Colin's quick action.

All in all, he felt she would make a full recovery with only a small scar.

With a big sigh of relief, Colin thanked him and went to talk to Ambassador Ryan.

Colin met him at the car. He apprised him of the situation; getting him up to date with his phone call from Tihara, the escape through the tunnel, the guards and Ree's injury.

Ryan could see the blame written all over Colin's face.

"Colin, it's not your fault; she was trying to save you. She didn't know you could take care of yourself. Besides, she'll be fine."

"I know, Ryan, I know, but Christ, when I saw her go down my heart stopped...But you're right, she will be fine. I just wanted to let you know, I'm staying. I have some things to finish up here. I'll take either a military transport out or find my own way out. Tell Jim Peterson I should only be eight to ten hours behind you."

Shaking hands, Colin walked away from Ryan and headed for the car.

"Commander, wait up. Where are you going?"

Colin turned to see John and Sadira walking towards him.

Colin told them he had to finish up some last-minute details and he wanted to see if there was anything he could do for Tihara.

He said he would take another plane out.

"Commander, we talked about it, and Sadira and I would like to stay...to help you. We both have things here that need to be taken care of," John told him adamantly.

"John, I thought you got your family out?"

"I did, Sir, about a week ago, but there are still some things I have to do. Please, allow me to stay and guard your back."

Colin patted John on the back.

"I would be honored but Sadira, I have a big favor. You know how important Reanna is to me. I would really appreciate it if you would stay with her and make sure she gets the best care until I can be with her again."

John and Sadira smiled at each other.

"We knew you wouldn't let both of us stay, so we're prepared," Sadira said, "I would be happy to stay with Ree."

They shook hands and went their separate ways.

Sadira went to watch over Ree, while John and Colin concentrated on doing everything they could to disrupt Uday's plans and if they were lucky, neutralize him entirely.

Chapter 39

Ree didn't remember too much of what had happened throughout the past twenty-four hours, but she did remember Colin telling her she was injured and he was taking her to the hospital.

She had a funny dream about people calling him commander instead of Colin.

Every time she thought of it, she started giggling but she had no idea why.

What she could not understand, was why some guy kept waking her up all the time. It seemed she just got to sleep and he was shaking her shoulder awake again and for some reason shining a light in her eyes. He told her she hit her head, but she didn't remember that. She did remember falling and twisting her ankle.

She felt all this attention was overkill for a sprained ankle.

Colin told her he was taking her to a hospital, but this did not look like or sound like a hospital. She heard this constant buzzing noise, like she was on a plane, but she knew that wasn't possible.

Why would he put her on a plane when there were perfectly good hospitals in Bagdad?

Oh, well... She thought. *The more I think about it the more my head hurts.*

So, she fell asleep again.

The next thing she remembered, she woke up in a real hospital. She decided that everything else must have been some very weird dream. Sadira was sitting in the chair next to the bed, reading the paper. When she moved to sit up, a pain shot through her shoulder and she cried out.

"Ree, you're awake. Thank god. I was so worried. You've been out for a long time," Sidara said, concerned.

"Can I have a little water? My throat is parched."

"Let me check with the nurse. I'll be right back."

True to her word Sadira was right back with a glass and pitcher of water.

"The nurse said you can have it, but drink it slowly."

The water tasted wonderful.

"Thanks so much, Sadira. What hospital are we in? I don't recognize it."

"Now, don't get upset, Ree. A lot has happened since you got shot."

"What? I got shot? Where? When? How? Where is Colin?"

"I'm so glad the Ree I know is back. One thing at a time. What's the last thing you remember?"

Ree closed her eyes and thought hard. She lifted her left arm to rub her head.

"I think I hurt my head."

"Good. What else?"

"I remember Colin trying to wake me up. He told me some ridiculous story about Uday wanting to arrest me and chain me to the barn, but that can't be real, can it?"

"I'm sorry, Ree. It's very real. Colin got word from your friend Tihara that Uday was planning on taking you prisoner, as well as other Americans and British, to use them as human shields if the Americans start bombing."

"Oh my God! I thought I imagined that. I think I remember Colin telling me that. I remember getting dressed and Colin looked really angry at me. Next thing I know, he flung me over his shoulder and we went into the basement. But it wasn't the basement, it was a tunnel."

"What else do you remember?"

"I remember going into the tunnel and I couldn't breathe...The smell was awful. I started to gag and then I heard Colin. The next thing was, we were running. Then, he picked me up and then he fell. I think, somehow, he put me in the back of a car and said to leave him. I couldn't let them leave him. Somehow, I think I was to blame. I don't remember how...And the next thing was, I got up from the car and stood up to get to him and then...and then... nothing. Does any of this make sense? Did I dream it?"

"No, you did not dream it. You remember a lot more than I thought. I'll try to fill in the blanks for you.

"I do remember you being in the car. Was that possible? And you and John, yes John, was there, you were calling Colin...Commander? I don't know why but I thought that was so funny and started giggling.   That's when Colin promised me he would take me to a hospital."

Sadira then spent the next hour filling in the blanks for Ree, patiently answering all of her questions.

Sadira knew the question of Tihara would come up and she answered it as gently as possible.

Ree's reaction was predictable.

"What do you mean, he killed her?"

"Ree, we don't know for sure but from what Colin heard, he's pretty sure that the guard shot her. I'm so sorry. I know she was your friend, but she saved your life. In reality, she saved a lot of lives. She is truly a hero. Not many people are brave enough to stand up to Uday and betray him."

Ree was trying not to cry.

"You have no idea how brave my friend was. She worried that her life would have no meaning and in reality, her life was all about others and saving them."

Ree went on to tell Sidara all about her brave, heroic friend, Tahira.

After a while, she started yawning and fell asleep. Sadira left the room and went to the cafeteria for lunch.

Finding a table near the door, she sat down to enjoy a burger, fries and a coke, food she sorely missed in Iraq. She was halfway through her meal when she felt someone give her a big bear hug her from behind.

"Sid, it is so good to see you."

"John! Oh my God. It's good to see you. How did everything go? I expected you way before this. Colin said you would be eight to ten hours behind. It's been two days."

John took a deep breath and ran his hand through his hair.

"I know. I'll tell you, Sid, it was a real cluster fuck. It was one of those missions, if it could go wrong, it did. Thank God for a little luck, otherwise, we would have been guests of Uday. All of Bagdad is in a heightened state of alert and if you even remotely look western, you're taken, prisoner. All the journalists, those brave enough to stay, are holed up in the Bagdad Hilton. So far, the government hasn't gone after them."

"Colin had a couple of targets in mind. We wanted to check two areas where they claim the WMDs are hidden. We got to one; we couldn't find anything. We were so close to the palace at this point. Colin wanted to get to the barn and warn everyone there. Evidently, he had some kind of plan that he talked to Shavo about and told him to get ready. Colin wanted me to leave him at that point, because he wanted to check the Palace, to see if that friend of Ree's, the one that saved all of our hides, was still alive. I told him no way. She saved all of our lives. I owed her too. Best decision I ever made. Anyway, we did some recognisance in and around the palace. We found one of the guards that was very friendly to us. Unfortunately, he told us he saw some of Uday's guards carrying out a body that looked like a woman."

"It went to hell after that. We were on our way out of the Palace when we tripped some type of alarm and Security was ready for us. Colin was hit pretty bad, up by his hip. It just missed his femoral artery. Anyway, I was able to get him back to the barn where Shavo hid us. You'll never guess where?"

Sid smiled.

"No, don't tell me. Syn's stall?"

John had a big grin on his face.

"Yup. Shavo brought some medical supplies so Shavo and I were able to do some field medicine on Colin's leg and stop the bleeding. Then, it got crazy. We heard guards coming into the bar. Shavo left us to try to steer them in the other direction. We were up against the near wall of the stall, so if you just glanced in, you would not see us. Syn, on the other hand, was thrilled we were in his stall. All he wanted to do is sniff us and push us around. We heard a guard approaching so we tried to push as far into the wall as possible. I heard him outside the stall and looked up into the eyes of a guard. My heart stopped. I thought we were done for. Then, the unbelievable happened, he tapped his gun on the bars of the stall door and, as if on cue, Syn charged the door. He smiled at us and I realized it was the guard who liked Ree. The other guards were coming near us when Syn was kicking at the door. I heard one of them say that that horse was still crazy and that all was clear. I swear, I think I held my breath so long, I turned blue."

"Oh my God, John, that story is unbelievable. How did you get out?"

"We stayed in the stall until morning when Shavo hid us in the hay truck. By this time, Colin was in pretty bad shape. Shavo was able to get us to the oil fields and to Colin's business. When we got there, we realized there were still some Iraqi employees there, who arranged for a Saudi plane to get us out of there."

"Wow! Really, wow! That is quite a story. How is Colin now?"

"He's in surgery. They said he was very lucky.

He's not going to lose the leg, but he's looking forward to some intensive physical therapy; Otherwise, he'll have a limp for the rest of his life. I see you are still here, so that must mean Ree is still here. Colin will be happy to hear that. I know he's worried about her. How is she doing?"

"She just really woke up today and remembers more than I thought she would. The doctors are pleased with her progress. She's even getting her sense of humor back."

"Did you tell Ree about Tihara?"

"I did. She was very sad but she did handle it better than I thought. Now, how about you? You look like hell. Does your wife know you're here? I saw her. She and the boys are getting settled in at base housing. She's excited about being in Germany."

John scratched his three-day-old beard.

"No, I just got here. You are the first person I talked to. I'm planning on heading out to the base, take a shower, shave and put on some clean clothes. If I came home looking like this, my wife would throw me out."

"I know your wife, John, and somehow, I doubt that but probably a good plan anyway."

"What are you planning? Are you going back to see Ree?"

"No, she was really tired. With the concussion, they kept waking her up so she really hasn't gotten a lot of rest. I'm just going to let her sleep. A shower and change of clothes sounds good, so if you don't mind, I'll catch a ride back to base with you."

They agreed to meet back at Colin's room around four. John figured Colin should be out of recovery by that time and reasonably coherent.

Chapter 40

Ree was having the best dream.

She was home, in Princeton, riding one of her horses and Colin was there; He was riding Storm.

It was a beautiful day and then all of a sudden, a bad storm came up and she got very cold. It started to thunder and lightning. Her horse spooked. She fell and was in pain.

The pain woke her up.

Oh no! She thought, feeling a stickiness between her legs. *I can't believe I'm getting my period.*

She got her period infrequently but when she did the cramps were unbearable. It's been a few months.

Why couldn't it wait another few weeks or even a few days?

She didn't need any more pain.

As another bad cramp hit, she tried to curl into a ball to ease the pain. From experience, nothing but Advil worked. She had cramps before but these were the worst.

The nurse at the station noticed the low blood pressure alarm for Ree, so she grabbed her chart and went to check on her.

Looking down at the chart, she entered the room.

"Well, Reanna, I heard you were awake. Now, what's with this low blood pressure?"

Looking up, she stopped herself from gasping, laid the chart down and went over to Ree.

"How do you feel, dear. Any pain?"

"Yes, can you believe it? I'm getting my period, on top of all this other pain? I'm having the worst cramps of my life." She was hit with another round of bad cramps and wrapped herself into a tighter ball.

The nurse went to the doorway and called out some orders that Ree didn't understand.

A few seconds later, more people came into the room.

She tried to sit up but was very dizzy and nauseous.

She saw they were removing her bedding.

She tried to tell them no; she was so cold, but when she looked over at the blanket and saw it was covered in blood.

That can't be my blood, she thought, *I don't bleed that much when I get my period.*

She started shivering and was hit with another round of cramps.

When she tried to move again, her shoulder started to hurt. Her head felt funny. She heard a doctor come in the room.

The last thing she heard was, "Prep her..."

It was about three-thirty when Sadira got back to Ree's room and was surprised to find it empty.

She went to the nurses' station and inquired about her, but due to privacy laws, the nurse wasn't able to tell Sadira anything.

As Sadira walked away, the nurse came up behind her.

She knew Sadira was with her the whole time.

"Look, off the record, I'll tell you this. There was a complication, a serious complication. She was taken into surgery and it's my understanding that as soon as she is stable, they will send her to Walter Reed."

"Can you tell me the complication?"

Shaking her head no, the nurse walked away.

All Sadira could think of was; *What am I going to tell Colin?*

It was four-fifteen by the time she made it to Colin's room. She went inside.

When John saw her he said, "Here she is, better late than never. What's wrong?"

She looked down at Colin in bed and had to admit, for a guy who just came out of surgery, he didn't look bad. She bent down and gave him a hug.

"It's good to see you, Commander. John caught me up on everything that happened. You were lucky you had John with you."

"Damn straight. He saved my life. I'll never forget it. How's Ree? Did you just come from her room?"

She looked down, not sure what to tell him.

"Sid, tell me before I get out of this bed and find her myself." He tried to sit up but had little luck.

"Colin, she was fine this morning. We had a long talk. She has remembered more and more. I think eventually, she will remember everything...I told her about her friend, Tihara."

"I know John told me; she took it well?"

"Yes, very well. She was sad, obviously, but she agreed her friend was a true hero. After the conversation, she got very tired and wanted to sleep. She told me to go home and get some rest. That's when I met John."

"Yes, what happened next?"

"I don't know. I went back to her room at three thirty and it was empty. I went to talk to the nurses, but they told me because of privacy laws they could not tell me anything. I was walking away when one nurse took pity on me and told me she was in surgery. There was a complication. As soon as she was stable, they were sending her directly to Walter Reed."

He tried to sit up and get out of bed.

"Where is she now?" He demanded.

"Colin, stop it. I don't know and they won't tell me. Lay back down before you hurt yourself." She looked over at John; He read her thoughts and left the room to get a nurse.

"God, damn it to hell, Sid, get me the fuck out of here! That's an order."

She just stood there.

"Do you hear me? That's a goddamn, fucking order! Help me up." He tried to stand but Sid was there to hold him in place.

The door opened. John and a nurse came in.

The nurse looked concerned.

"What's all the shouting about, Commander?"

"I have to get out of here. My fiancée is here and they just took her for surgery. I have to see her."

Both Sadira and John tried not to appear shocked at the announcement of their engagement.

The nurse spoke as calmly as possible.

"Commander, if she's in surgery, there's nothing you can do now. You have to rest. The injury to your hip is serious. Remember what the doctor said. You have to keep it immobile for at least a week," While she was talking to him, she put a needle into his IV. "Now, I'm giving you some more antibiotics..." And added as she watched him fall asleep, "As well as a strong sedative. There. That should keep him quiet for a while."

Sadira and John thanked her.

Colin slept for a full day.

Chapter 41

When Ree woke up, the first thing she realized was there was no pain.

Had she died?

No, she didn't think heaven smelled like a hospital.

She opened her eyes and looked around the room. There, sitting in the chair next to the bed, was her mom. She tried to reach for her hand but was so weak, she could barely raise her arm.

"Mom," She said quietly.

Must have been mother's instinct because Margaret Malloy woke up immediately and looked into her daughter's eyes.

"Oh, my dear girl! My baby, you're awake. I'm so happy, I'm so glad, oh honey you had me so scared, you had everyone so scared. You're going to be okay, now. I just know it; I just feel it."

Trying to hug her but not knowing how with all the tubes, she grabbed her head and kissed her.

"I missed you too, Mom, and I'll be fine. Where am I?"

"You're at Walter Reed. After the surgery, they transported you here as soon as they could. Do you remember anything?"

"To tell you the truth, Mom, I don't know how long it's been, but I seem to have lost a lot of time. I remember bits and pieces of stuff but nothing whole yet."

"The doctor told me that that's normal and although you hit your head pretty hard, he doesn't think your memory will be affected permanently. He said the concussion was bad, but no brain damage. He assured me you should remember everything."

She closed her eyes and almost willed herself to remember.

Her Mom held her hand.

"Ree, don't try too hard. The doctor said it will all come back in time; relax. Now, how do you feel? Any pain?"

"No, for the first time in a while, no pain, but I'm so weak. I can't even lift my arm."

"I know, dear, that's from the blood loss."

"I don't understand, Mom. The shoulder was all closed up. Why did I lose more blood?"

Her mom was just about ready to tell her what happened, when the doctor came in and asked to speak to Ree. Margaret left the room and waited outside.

The doctor sat down on the bed next to Ree.

"How do you feel today, Reanna?"

She smiled at him.

"Good, I was just telling my mom, I have no pain but I just feel very weak."

"Well after everything you've been through, I'm not surprised. I don't know how much you remember but I'll go through everything. Do you remember twisting your ankle while running from the guards?"

She nodded yes.

"Then, you were shot in your right shoulder."

Again, yes.

"When you were shot, you fell back and hit your head with some impact on the door of the car."

"Oh. Is that what happened to my head? The medics kept telling me I had a concussion, but I could not remember how it happened."

"Good. Now, we got you to the hospital in Germany and we were able to take care of that, but then, you started having very bad cramps. Do you remember?"

"Yes, I thought this was a terrible time to get my period," She replied, a little embarrassed.

He took her hand.

"Reanna, it wasn't your period. I'm so sorry, but you were pregnant. You had a miscarriage. You lost the baby."

"I was pregnant?"

"You didn't know?"

She shook her head vehemently.

"No, my doctor told me I would have a hard time getting pregnant. My period was always late. Sometimes, I wouldn't get it for months, so it wasn't unusual."

"When was the last time you had your period?"

"In September. I remember it was right before I left for Iraq."

It looks like you were just about two months gone. There was some tearing, so you had to have emergency surgery. They fixed everything, but you lost a lot of blood.

That's why they shipped you here so fast. They didn't have enough of your blood type on hand so they gave you enough to stabilize you and sent you home. We've been giving you blood, so by this time tomorrow, you should be much stronger."

She thanked the doctor.

He left and her mom came back in.

Margaret looked at her daughter's face and could tell the doctor had told her about the baby.

The only thing she could do was hold her while she cried herself to sleep.

The doctor came to see her the next day and announced she was doing really well. He asked her if she wanted to do physical therapy here or at home.

Ree opted for home.

All she wanted was to get home, but more than anything else, she wanted to hear from Colin.

Everyone she asked didn't know anything. She tried his cell phone but there was no answer.

Her Mom told her Jim Peterson was coming to visit today though, so maybe he knew something about him.

Colin did mention, more than once, that they knew each other.

Around ten o'clock, there was a knock on her door and in popped Jim Peterson, carrying a bouquet of flowers.

Jim looked at her and was obviously choked up.

"Ree, I am so sorry. I am so, very, very sorry this happened. If I thought for a minute that you would be in that type of danger, I never would have sent you. I sent the best team to surround you. They are top-notch. I don't know how they allowed it to happen."

"I know I hit my head but what are you talking about? Team? What team? What are you talking about, Jim?"

"Well, Colin, of course, and he brought Sadira and John on board, the best in the business. Colin said he would not work with anyone else. God, Ree, I don't know how it happened, but when I see Colin, I'm going to ream his ass. I told him how important this assignment was, how important you were. I told him it was personal; that's why I asked for the best."

Letting this information sink in, she was devastated.

"I was his assignment? Nothing more? He pretended to love me. They pretended to be my friends because I was their assignment?"

This was going on in Ree's mind like a continuous loop; *I was his assignment...*

Meanwhile, Jim continued to rant and rave about how they should have taken better care of her.

"Jim, stop it; It's not their fault." Ree finally said, firmly. "I disobeyed Colin's orders. I thought he needed help and I left the car to help him when I got shot. Colin shielded me with his body. He got shot because of me. I fell and he came back to get me and carried me. The guard shot him. I didn't know he had a vest on. It wasn't his fault; he did a great job. In fact, they all did. They are all very, very good at what they do. Now please, I'm very tired. I need to rest."

When Ree's mom came into the room, she found her daughter staring into space.

Ree was finally able to tell her mom what Jim told her. Margaret tried to convince Ree maybe she didn't really understand the situation and maybe she needed to wait to talk to Colin. Ree was adamant. She never wanted to hear from Colin again.

Margaret did the only thing she could think of to help her daughter through this.

She called Ree's best friend, Epona.

Chapter 42

Colin was so frustrated.

He was ready to get off the hospital bed and start throwing furniture around the room; that is if he could get off the bed. He felt so helpless and that was one feeling he detested. He had to get to Walter Reed to be with Ree. He could not imagine what was wrong. He knew the gunshot was clean and they had stopped the bleeding.

Sid told him the concussion was bad, but not life threatening.

Therefore, he could not fathom what the problem could be.

His mind kept conjuring up different scenarios; one was worse than the next.

Just lying there, thinking, was making him crazy.

He tried pulling rank. He tried being nice. He tried bullying the nurses and the doctors. He even tried cursing at them, but nothing worked. They were bound and determined to keep him here. They told him it was for his own good.

Fuck my own good! He thought. *I want out!*

Just when it seemed he was ready to explode, yet again, his door opened and the doctor came in looking very serious.

"All right, Commander, you got your way. I don't know who you called, but I'm going to release you, but not before you sign some papers."

"I'll sign anything. Just get me the hell out of here and off to Walter Reed."

"Commander, you have to understand that these forms are releasing everyone and, I mean everyone, including nurses, doctors, the hospital, the military, the President, even God, from any responsibility for this decision. You are also signing that you are wholly responsible for this decision and if anything goes wrong, you cannot blame anyone except yourself. Do you still agree to sign these papers?"

He grabbed the papers and signed. He nodded yes that he understood.

When he was done, the doctor handed him copies and shook his head.

"Your friends are outside. They tell us that normally, you are a very nice, patient guy and not to judge you, but I have to tell you, Commander, you made it hard."

He felt a lot like a scolded child.

"Doctor, I'm sorry for my behavior, but if someone you loved needed you, wouldn't you move heaven and earth to be there for them?"

He put his hands up in surrender.

"Yes, I would, and I guess that's the main reason I'm releasing you, but Commander, Colin, please be careful. You could not only lose your leg but your life. Now, I did one more thing for you, not that you deserve it, but I arranged for a military transport to fly you back to the States. An ambulance will take you to Walter Reed. There will be a medic onboard the plane, so he can monitor the pressure in your leg and check for blood clots."

With much effort, Colin sat up in bed and shook the doctor's hand.

"I don't know how to thank you, doctor. Please, thank everyone for me and tell them I apologize for my behavior."

"The biggest thank you can give us all, Commander, is, you can never get injured again and if you do, DO NOT and I repeat DO NOT come back to this hospital. Oh, and you can invite me to the wedding."

He gave the doctor a big grin.

"I promise."

In a short, while Colin was on his way back home and, he prayed, back to Ree.

Colin arrived at Walter Reed about eleven at night. He was put in a room on the third floor. It took some fast talking, but he found out Ree was still there and was on the floor above him.

It took all his self-control not to hobble up to her room, crawl if he had to, but at this point, the pain was pretty bad.

The nurse convinced him that Ree would be there in the morning and he needed rest.

Besides, she told him, he looked like hell and a good night's sleep would remedy that.

He reluctantly agreed.

He was asleep before his head hit the pillow.

Colin was in the middle of breakfast when he had his first visitor. Jim Peterson came in looking somber and ready to chew someone out.

Colin knew who that someone was.

"Hi, Jim. Good to see you on this fine, sunny day. How's everything?"

He shook his head at Colin.

"Don't you give me that. First, it's raining out and that's just fine. It fits my mood. Why the hell did you get yourself shot? I feel guilty about wanting to ream your ass out."

"When did pity ever stop you? Besides, I'll be fine. The doctor told me."

"Is that the same doctor you threatened to court martial? When that didn't work was it the one whose car...and house, you threatened to blow up? That same doctor?"

Colin looked a little embarrassed.

"Could be. Maybe I was a little harsh."

"A little harsh? Let's just say the entire floor of workers had a party after you left. No, that's not why I'm angry. I'm angry because you had a simple assignment, protect Reanna Malloy. Keep her from harm. And what happens? She comes home shot, with a concussion and almost bled to death. How is that protecting someone? Jesus, Colin, I don't know how she made it out alive."

"There are explanations for everything."

"I know. She told me." Jim grabbed a piece of toast off Colin's plate.

"You spoke to Ree? How is she?"

"Well, in spite of your best efforts, she is going to be fine. And she had nothing but the highest praise for the work you, Sid and John did. She told me how professional you all were and how it was all her fault, that she didn't follow orders. In fact, she's taking all the blame, even for you getting shot. She said that you all took the assignment very seriously, especially you, Colin. She said you went above and beyond what was expected."

Colin's face turned white.

"What did you say to her?"

He sat down next to the bed.

"I told her I thought I sent the best team to watch over her. I told her that they take their assignments very seriously and I believed she was in the best possible hands. And that reminds me, just how closely were you NOT watching her. She must have been seeing someone over there because she got pregnant and miscarried. That's what almost killed her."

"What did you just say?" Colin demanded, feeling as though all of the air was sucked out of him.

"About what? Her getting pregnant? Do you know who it was? Do you think I should tell him? Or should I let Ree decide?"

"You already told him."

"What? I don't understand. Told who, what?"

"I'm the father. I was having an affair with her."

Jim got up from the chair and threw his hands in the air.

"Damn, Colin. Are you serious? You know better than to get involved with the assignment. It clouds your judgment. Is that why you didn't tell me?"

Colin shook his head yes.

"I know I should have told you, but I was afraid you would replace me and I still believed I was the best to protect her."

"Do you still believe that?"

"I don't know anymore. Does she know?"

"Know what?"

"That I was assigned to her; it was my job to protect her."

"Yes, I told her yesterday."

"How did she take it?"

He sat down again.

"I guess, okay. I didn't notice any change in her. She didn't get upset. She didn't yell at me. In fact, she became adamant that you did an exemplary job. She strongly defended all of you."

He pushed his food away and tried to sit up.

"Help me up. I have to talk to her. I have to explain."

Jim tried to help Colin.

"What are you going to explain? That you had a little fling and it's over. Don't you think you did enough damage?"

Colin broke out in a sweat from the pain of sitting up.

"It wasn't a fucking fling, Jim. I love her. I asked her to marry me. I'm devastated she miscarried, and you're right, it was my fault. I was selfish. I have to go see her and beg her forgiveness and see if I can salvage anything from our relationship."

He held onto Colin.

"I'm sorry. If you told me, I never would have said anything. What can I tell you? Ree is a warm, forgiving person, so I think you have a shot. Do you want me to get someone to help you up to her room? Do you want a wheelchair?"

Colin braced himself for the most important meeting of his life. He grabbed the crutch, stood up, winced, and hobbled down the hallway.

Chapter 43

Margaret contacted Epee after Ree's meeting with Jim Peterson and subsequent breakdown.

She knew when a girl needed her best friend and this was the time.

Epee and her husband took the train to Walter Reed Friday night. Margaret got them a room at her hotel. Ree was scheduled to be released Monday morning so the plan was Epee's husband, Kevin would drive them all home, using Catherine's car.

Margaret met Epee and her husband, Kevin for breakfast and then left for the hospital.

During breakfast, she filled Epee in on all that happened to Ree.

Her heart broke for her friend, but something just didn't seem right.

Before she kicked some Navy SEAL ass she had to talk to him first.

She wondered how she was going to accomplish that, though.

After all, the last Margaret knew, he was still in Iraq.

Kevin dropped Margaret and Epee off at the entrance to the hospital. He told them he would park the car and meet them later.

He wanted to give Epee some private time with her friend.

They went into the room just as Ree was finishing breakfast.

When she saw her best friend, they both let out a squeal, like they were five years old.

Epee went over to the bed and gingerly hugged her friend, trying not to hurt her.

Margaret sat on the other side, each holding Ree's hand.

They sat and talked quietly for a while, when they heard a knock on the door.

Assuming it was Kevin, Epee called out, "Come in."

Ree looked up with a smile on her face, expecting to see Kevin.

Standing there bathed in a halo of light, looking like an avenging angel, was the subject of all her dreams and, lately, her nightmares.

Taking a step into the room, he said, "Hi, Ree. May I come in?"

In shock, unable to speak, she nodded.

It was obvious to Epee and Margaret who this man in the doorway was.

So, they quietly excused themselves, left the room and shut the door.

Before Ree could respond, she was left alone with this man, the man she loved more than life itself.

But to him, she was nothing more than an assignment.

She had been fighting with herself, tossing and turning, castigating herself ever since she found out.

How in the world could she have believed that a man as talented and handsome as Colin could ever be interested in a mousy little school teacher?

She knew she should not blame him. She was the one who was delusional.

Colin leaned on his crutches and looked at this beautiful woman in the bed, lying there because he didn't do his job. He was not able to save her from the bullet. His lack of self-control almost caused her death.

He wanted to tell her so much but the only thing he could choke out was, "Ree, I'm so sorry."

Ree assumed he apologized for misleading her.

"Colin, or should I say, Commander, its' okay. I understand. I didn't make the job easy. It's not your fault. You did a great job protecting me. I guess I don't take orders very well. But, I do have one question. It only requires a one-word answer, yes or no, and I beg you to please be honest with me."

"Anything."

"Was I just an assignment?"

He wanted so much to say no, to tell her how much he loved her, but he realized that his love almost killed her, not once but twice. Colin did the hardest thing he had ever done.

"Yes."

Ree closed her eyes and tried not to burst into tears. She took a deep breath to stabilize her emotions. She reached under her hospital gown and took the chain with the ring off her neck. She threw it at him.

"Here, you might need this for your next assignment! Now, get out."

Colin looked at her; he wanted to say more, but just clumsily turned opened the door and walked out.

Epee and Margaret were sitting on the bench outside Ree's room when the door opened and Colin hobbled out.

Epee was struck by the fact that a hopeful man walked into the room and a broken man walked out. He didn't look at them, just hobbled down the hall, to the elevators.

They heard Ree crying so they both went into the room. Margaret reached her daughter first and comforted her. Epee started for the bed when she looked down at something sparkly. She picked it up and recognized it as the ring Ree described to her that was from Colin; her engagement ring.

513

She put it in her pocket.

Epee saw Ree was well taken care of by her mom, so she left the room and ran down the hall to catch up to Colin.

She found him waiting for an elevator. She tugged at his sleeve.

"You're Colin, aren't you?"

He didn't look at her.

"Yes, who wants to know"

"A friend of Ree's."

He turned around slowly pivoting on his crutch. He looked down at this woman, whom he recognized immediately.

"You must be the famous, or infamous, Epee."

She put her hand out.

"Yes. Do you have a minute to talk?"

He shrugged his shoulders.

"I don't know. What is there is to say?"

"Humor me." She pointed to the chairs that sat a little way down the hall.

They sat down. Epee really looked at him, not pulling any punches.

"The truth. Was Ree just an assignment to you?"

He signed and rubbed his face with his hands.

"Does it matter now? Does anything matter now?"

"Yes, it does because if she was just an assignment, crutches or no I'm going to kick your Navy SEAL ass all the way down the hallway and then Ree's mom is going to kick it all the way back and you're going to be a SEAL soccer ball until we think you had enough...and that might take days."

For the first time in days, he actually smiled.

"For some reason, I believe you would do that."

"Bet your sweet ass I would. Now, spill."

Colin smiled again. He remembered this as one of Ree's favorite expressions; he wondered did she pick it up from Epee or the other way around.

"Come on, Colin, no stalling. Answer my question." Epee was holding one hand in the other trying not to hit him.

For the second time in less than an hour he was asked the same question, but this time he knew he had to give a different answer; the truth.

"No, she was more than an assignment. She stopped being an assignment by the second day. I started falling in love with her in London and haven't stopped. I love her more every day. That's why I told her she was an assignment. I'm no good for her. Hell, I almost got her killed, not once but twice."

"Well, I must say that is really fucked up logic, but no more fucked up then Ree believing she was never good enough for you; she wasn't pretty enough, smart enough, you know all that bullshit. She's actually blaming herself for falling in love with you because she knew it could never be reciprocated. You two have some shit to work out and maybe it's best you both take some time and work on it."

He raised his eyebrows.

"And, how much time are you giving us?"

Epee's answer was dead serious.

"Only a few months. If you two don't get your shit together by then, well I'm going to somehow kidnap you both, lock you two in a room, and not let you out until you work your shit out."

Colin shook his head back and forth.

"I believe you would do that too. Epee, how did you know?"

"Know what?"

"Know that she meant more to me than an assignment. How did you know that I truly love her?"

She thought for a moment deciding whether to tell him.

"I didn't at first. I was going to kick your ass down the hall, but then I picked this up."

Fishing around in her pocket, she pulled out the chain and ring, holding it up, in front of Colin.

"I don't understand. How could the ring make any difference?"

"It isn't a 'canardly.'" Epee answered smugly.

"What the hell is a canardly?"

God this woman doesn't make any sense, he thought.

"You men don't know anything. You know the diamonds that are so small you 'can hardly' see 'em? If you got her one of those, then that was just a prop. This ring, this ring screams I love you. It has it written all over it, so I thought you deserved a chance to explain."

He smiled at her again; it felt good.

"You know, Epee, you are seriously strange, but I really like you. Let me tell you, girls in Texas have nothing on you. You are tough."

"I'm a Jersey girl and we are tough. Don't forget, Ree is a Jersey girl too. She is tough but this, this is asking a lot. Her Mom and I will help her get through this but Colin, eventually she is going to need you. You cannot stay away forever. Besides, if you stay away too long I'll find you and it won't be pretty."

 He let out a big belly laugh, the first in a long time.

"Epee, you are one of a kind. Somehow, you're giving me some hope for the future." And in that the first seed of hope, Colin began to form a plan; a plan of forgiveness for himself and for Ree.

"Now, you big lug, do you want some help getting back to your room?" She stood up and offered her arm for assistance.

"Much appreciated, mame." He draped his arm over her shoulder and walked towards the elevator.

"Don't you ever, ever call me mame. I'm not old. Now be quiet, I'm going to tell you some really embarrassing stories about Ree when she was a kid."

For the first time, in a long time, Colin believed in the future.

Chapter 44

September 2004:

Seven months into the war

Jim Peterson was scared. He was not comfortable with this feeling. In fact, the thought of being scared terrified him. He was a man that stared down Presidents, Prime Ministers and Dictators.

Why was it that a meeting with one tiny woman had him quaking in his boots?

He was driving for over an hour and still could not find the words to say to her, to convince her. Was he even doing the right thing by asking her?

One of the things he hated about his job was putting people in harm's way for the greater good. He already put Ree in danger the first time he asked her to go to Iraq. Could he ask her again? Both he and her Mom agreed that she lost that spark of life that made her so unique, over there. It was that spark that was so vivid in her when anyone was around her they could almost feel it. Could she find it again? Was it even right of him to ask her? Was it worth the cost?

He saw the sign for Second Chance Farm, put his blinker on and turned into the driveway. About halfway down the drive, he stopped the car.

I can do this, he thought.

After all, two people's lives depended on it.

He pulled the car into the parking spot by the house, got out of the car, and walked up the redbrick walkway, to the front door.

He prayed Margaret Malloy was home for some moral support.

He knocked.

No answer.

He was about to walk towards the barn when a big brindle mix breed dog came running right for him. Jim had a fleeting thought that getting mauled by this dog was preferable to this meeting with Reanna.

The dog reached him and ran around his legs wagging his tail.

Jim grinned. He hoped this was a sign of things to come.

One of the farm workers came up the path and told him Ree was in the barn and to follow him.

As he entered the barn, he saw Ree, grooming a big, black horse.

He stood in the doorway for a moment, watching her.

She looked the same, but he knew from Margaret, that she wasn't.

Jim took a deep breath.

"Hi Ree, it's good to see you. Did your Mom tell you I called a few times, asking about you?"

Jim noticed that the horse tensed as soon as he spoke. Ree immediately put her hand on the horse's neck to calm him. It worked. Ree turned around and looked at Jim.

After what seemed an eternity, Jim cleared his throat.

"I didn't see your Mom up at the house. Is she home?"

Ree turned away from him and concentrated on the horse.

"Mom went to Florida with a client to look at some new horses. She'll be home Sunday."

Well, Jim thought, *at least she's talking to me.*

"How is she doing?" Jim walked a little closer to Ree.

"Mom's doing great. She certainly keeps me busy here at the farm. She's always coming up with a new project. It's good, though. How's Sarah and the kids?"

Jim's shoulder relaxed and he took another step closer to her.

"The girls are doing great. In fact, that's why I'm in the area. We took Jim Jr. for a tour of Princeton. He loves the school. I think it will be his top choice. He would be our last one, going off to college. I don't think Sarah is ready for the empty nest yet. Are you still teaching there?"

Jim knew the answer. He had talked to Dean Tomes a few times about Ree and each time, the Dean agreed to back Ree up in whatever decision she decided to make about going back to teaching.

However, Jim wanted to know Ree's take on the situation.

"No, Dean Tomes gave me an indefinite leave of absence. The administration has been very understanding. My therapist told me I would know when I was ready and I'm not there yet."

"Your Mom told me about the counseling. How's it going?"

"I love my therapist, Dr. Brown; she's great. At first, my doctor wanted to give me medication, but I couldn't take it. It made me feel...blah. When I first started the counseling the dreams stopped altogether. Lately, though, I guess because the news of the Iraq war is everywhere, they started up again."

Jim was about to ask more about her therapy when Ree turned to him looked him right in the eye.

"Why are you here?" She demanded.

Jim looked down at the ground, trying to gain some time and courage.

"Ree, I'm sorry. I'm here because I have to ask you something, something that's very important to the State Department, but I also think it's important for you."

"I don't understand."

"Have you been watching the news coming out of Iraq?"

"How can I avoid it; it's everywhere. I try but..." Ree whispered and sat down on the closest storage box.

Jim shook his head in understanding.

"I get it, Ree, but there have been some positive changes with the surge. The military has doubled its efforts and things are finally quieting down. Order is being restored."

"Maybe if you listened to me, there wouldn't be any need for a surge because there would not be any need for a war."

Jim moved closer to her and placed his hand on her shoulder.

She winced.

Damn, he thought, *I forgot about the injury to her shoulder.*

"I appreciate your feeling, but you have to understand, it was out of my hands. What happened, happened and now we have to make the best of it."

Ree got up and started to pace.

Finally, she threw her hands in the air.

"Make the best of it? Tell me, Jim, just how are we doing to do that? Most of Baghdad has been bombed to Kingdom Come. People I loved are probably dead. The horses, oh God, the horses!" She took a deep breath and sat down again. "You asked if I watched the news. The last time I watched, they were showing people looting the Palace and the stables. They were leading the horses, those beautiful,innocent horses, out into the street. Do you know what the newscaster said?"

Jim shook his head no.

"He said that these horses were some of the most valuable in the world and would probably be butchered and end up on an Iraqi dinner plate."

Jim put his arms around her.

At least, he thought, *she is showing some emotion.*

According to Margaret, she had been walking around like a zombie. Maybe he was seeing a break through.

"It's okay. I understand. You have to believe things are not as bad as they show on TV. Look, the surge is working; law and order is being restored in Baghdad. We want to show the people that life can return to normal."

"How are you going to do that? Turn back time?"

Jim could not help but smile at the last comment.

The fire is still there! He thought.

"The government wants to restore successful programs that we had before the war."

Ree's eyes flew open wide.

"No, no, no! You cannot ask me to start up the school again."

"I'm sorry, but your school was very successful. The State Department wants to reopen it. We need you. It can work again and this time it will continue. We have Iraqi and Iraqi-American women willing to teach the classes. The people love you; if they see you there, we hope they will have more trust in the program. Besides, we will only need you there for a short time, maybe two weeks."

"But how? Most of Baghdad was bombed. I'm sure there is nothing left."

"Believe it or not, that neighborhood was hardly touched by the bombs. I've had my people check it out. The school and your apartment are still standing. Here's the best part, the neighbors loved the program so much, that when the war started, they went to the school and took all the computers, books, and supplies, and hid them. They are waiting for you to come back."

"Are you kidding me? Really?"

"Yes, really. I was told the effort was led by a Mrs. Hadine, the next-door neighbor. She told everyone you would be back. What do you say, Ree? Are you willing to give it another try?"

Ree sat down on one of the storage boxes. She put her head down and put her hand over her face. She was quiet for a long time.

Eventually, she looked up at Jim.

"I am willing to give it some thought."

Jim hugged her.

"I'm thrilled. I'll leave you a packet of information of what to bring. Also, I'll send you directions on where to meet and time of the flight. Sorry, this time its military transport."

Ree put up her hands.

"I haven't said yes yet, but if I do, I have one condition."

"Name it."

"I don't need a handler this time; I don't want to be anyone's assignment. I can take care of myself."

"Don't worry, Ree. I'll be going with you, so more than likely, you'll have to take care of me."

After Jim left, Ree retreated to her office, put her head down on her desk and cried.

She cried for all she lost. She cried for what could have been. She cried because she felt so broken.

Maybe this was just what she needed to make her life whole again.

How did everything go so wrong?

Jim left the farm and for the first time since this whole project blew up, he was optimistic. He was sure that Margaret could convince Ree to go back to Iraq.

Once he got her there, though, then the ball would be in her court.

Chapter 45

After Jim's visit, Ree was not able to sleep.

The reality was, she hadn't been able to sleep since she came back from Iraq.

Jim's visit just exacerbated the problem. She tossed and turned all night, with all types of images going through her head: people, places, horses.

Sometimes, they would all blend together into one nightmare.

Sometimes, it was a sweet dream of a wonderful memory.

Ree decided she was her psychologist's ideal patient, with all her dreams. Her shoulder hurt every time she had the recurring dream.

Lately, her shoulder hurt continuously. Her Mom noticed her constantly rubbing her shoulder and recommended she go back to psychical therapy, but Ree knew it was psychological.

Ever since she came home, her mom and Epee tried to shield her from what was happening in Iraq.

Papers were never left around and her mom always had some back station on the TV, never news. This was working fine, until one day, she was in the doctor's office for a follow-up exam.

CNN was on in the waiting room.

It was the day that the bombing stopped and they were showing Iraqis looting many government buildings including the palaces.

She tried not to watch, but then, the newscaster said, "Even the royal stables were not spared. More than likely, these majestic horses will end up on an Iraqi dinner plate tonight. Sad."

She looked up and saw Iraqis leading horses out of the stables and into the street. She thought she recognized someone leading one of the horses, but she knew it was wishful thinking.

She was so upset, she had to leave the doctor's office and was unable to focus for weeks.

The only thought she kept having, was that someone killed and then butchered her Syn.

The thought made her nauseous.

Most people who dealt with Ree thought she made a full recovery. She went through her day, seemingly happy and content.

Princeton called her and asked her back for the fall semester, but she told them no.

They understood and agreed to hold her position for one more year.

She told them she wasn't ready to answer questions about the war because she had no answers. They were very understanding.

Dean Tomes did ask her to write about her experiences in Iraq, pre-war.

Ree was thrilled to do that; in fact, she found it cathartic.

The only people whom Ree could not fool were her Mom and Epee.

They knew she was a woman who was just going through the motions of life. There was no joy left.

Epee was just about ready to put her plan of kidnapping her and Colin into action, when Ree called her and told her about Jim's proposal to go back to Iraq and restart the school.

Ree was shocked when Epee actually encouraged her to go.

Epee told her she did not want her to go back to Iraq, but understood she had to; Ree left part of herself there and needed to find it to make herself whole.

Ree hated when Epee tried to be deep, but maybe there was something to what she said.

Ree would be interested in her mom's reaction to Jim's proposal.

Ree did not sleep well Saturday night, between the dreams, the nightmares, and sometimes, not being able to tell the difference between the two.

It was not a good night.

She got up her usual time, feeling out of sorts, wondering if she made the right decision about going back. If she changed her mind, she needed to tell Jim by Monday morning; otherwise, they would be leaving on the first military transport out, either Wednesday or Thursday.

She needed to talk to her Mom.

Her mother's plane was due in, from Florida, at 2:30 in the afternoon, arriving at the Trenton airport.

After feeding the horses, she was able to work two horses and teach a lesson.

Before Ree knew it, it was time to go to the airport. She left early, fearing Sunday traffic, so she was relieved when she got there in plenty of time.

Ree stopped at a WaWa, picked up a chai tea and the latest scandal sheet to read while she waited for the plane.

Entering the airport, she checked the board.

Her Mom's plane was on time. Ree sat down and drank her latte while reading the paper.

There was an article about a benefit for wounded soldiers with pictures of the celebrities that backed the program. Ree was half looking at the pictures when her eye caught a familiar face.

There, in all his full-color glory, was Colin, and sidled up next to him, was a very beautiful redhead.

The caption read, "Texas' most eligible bachelor, Colin McLeod and friend, enjoying a benefit for wounded soldiers of the Iraq war."

Her heart was beating so loud she thought the person next to her could hear it.

She could not sit; she had to get up and walk around and calm down before her mother saw her.

How could he still affect me like this? Why does he still have so much control over me?

The only answer she could come up with was; *I guess I still love him and I probably will never stop.*

Her second thought was; *Well, that sucks.*

She got herself under control by the time her mom got off the plane.

They got the car and headed back home.

Ree asked her about the buying trip in Florida. Margaret told her it went really well. The woman bought both horses; one for each daughter. She said that the new owners would be shipping the horses up to their barn in two weeks, after the vet check.

Ree was quiet. Her mom sensed something was on her daughter's mind.

"Do you want to talk about it, honey?"

"You can read me like a book, Mom." She told her about Jim's visit. Ree wasn't sure if she should tell her about the picture so she decided not to mention it.

"Honey, I'm not going to tell you to go or not to go. You have to make that decision on your own, but I will tell you this; Something's not finished there and until it is, you are just walking around like an empty shell. Now, I don't want you going back to that dangerous place, but if it's going to make you whole again, then I think you should go."

There you have it, thought Ree; *Your mom thinks you should go; Epee thinks you should go...*

Was seeing the second picture of Colin a sign? He really did get back to his life. What was she waiting for?

****

For someone who only flew first class, Colin could not believe he was actually looking forward to the military transport to take him back to Iraq.

He had been away for a few weeks and hoped all was going according to plan. He received the latest request from Shavo and had the container packed, ready to go.

If all went well, he would fly out of Texas on Friday. When he spoke to Jim last week, he promised Colin he would arrange for some help with the horses.

Jim told him that maybe in the next week or two he could find someone.

Colin was frustrated but understood that the wheels of bureaucracy moved slowly.

Colin was thankful to his Mom and sister-in-law for helping with the business.

Mary McLeod knew where her son's heart was and that this was something he had to do to heal. She would do anything for her son, even run the business, if she had to.

His Mom did get a second in command, to relieve her of a lot of responsibilities and besides, Colin hoped it would only be for a few months before he would be back, fulltime.

Colin did make an appearance every now and then, and while he was home, he could gather the supplies that they needed back in Iraq.

Due to his military and government connections, it made cutting through red tape easier to get what he needed, transported.

When he was home, he caught up on business. He also attended the important charity events. He hated them, even in the best of times.

Colin made a deal with his Mom. He would go, but he would pick the ones he wanted to attend.

Colin delayed his departure for the Wounded Soldier Program, one that he was particularly proud to sponsor. This program gave financial and medical aid to Iraqi war veterans.

The only drawback was that he had to escort the latest debutante or starlet.

Well, he thought, *at least it's for a good cause.*

He could not get over how his life had changed.

A year ago, he would not have thought twice about escorting beautiful women to different events; now, all he did was compare them to Ree.

They all came up short.

Chapter 46

Ree could not remember ever being so tired and so sore.

This was obviously a very different trip to Bagdad from her first trip a year ago.

Military transports were definitely bare-bones.

So, if she thought a coach seat was uncomfortable ever again, she made a mental note to remember this experience.

As she was trying to stretch out the knots from travel, she still could not get over that it had been a year since her life had changed.

It seemed unbelievable; it was like she lived a lifetime in only a few short months.

Was it a dream? Even if she thought or even hoped it was a dream, driving through Bagdad from the airport to the embassy proved to be more of a nightmare than a dream.

Beautiful homes and buildings that she remembered were either gone or so badly damaged there was no saving them.

Her heart broke when they went past the Bagdad Museum and she saw the devastation there, caused by both bombs and looters. She could not imagine that the priceless artifacts that were not only the heritage of the Iraqi people but the heritage of the world, were now likely lost forever.

Thankfully, they did not go by the Palace.

She honestly didn't think she could handle the emotional tug of war that would cause.

She was an Iraqi expert, so she, more than anyone, knew of the horrendous things Saddam and his regime had done to Iraq and the Iraqi people, but she also knew he was a stabilizing force in the region.

She feared the results of destabilizing the area and the effects it would have on the rest of the Middle East.

Only time will tell, she thought.

The good news she saw, while driving from the airport, was that the surge seemed to be working.

Electricity was on; there seemed to be signs of trade, stores were open, and she even saw some children coming home from school.

She could only pray that it worked and Iraq returned to some type of normalcy soon.

She showered with tepid water.

At least it's tepid and not freezing cold, she thought as got dressed.

Jim told her to dress for a long hike, so she made sure she wore her boots, jeans, a t-shirt and jacket.

Checking the time, she decided to send off an e-mail to her Mom and let her know she arrived safely.

When she entered the dining room, she saw Jim with some other State Department Representatives.

She got her breakfast from the buffet and joined them.

The talk centered on the surge and what else needed to be done to get Bagdad up and running. A few of them asked her advice.

Great, she thought. *When I sent them my advice, they didn't follow it. If they had, we would not be in this mess!*

However, in place of being bitter, she was gracious and answered their questions, offering some good suggestions, mainly on trying to win back the hearts and minds of the Iraqi people.

Getting up from the table, Jim looked at Ree.

"Well, are you ready?"

"Yes, I'm ready, but I really wish you would tell me where we were going and why it's a big secret."

"You'll see; you'll see."

There was the typical black military SUV waiting for them out front, driven by military personnel.

Ree and Jim took the back seat and headed out. While they were traveling, Jim get her up to date on all that was happening in Bagdad since the surge started.

He had his people inspect various areas in and around Bagdad and the very good news was that the school, her apartment, and most of the neighborhood remained relatively untouched.

Jim assured her, again, that they checked the inside of the school and found that all the books and equipment were safely stored in a neighbors' basement.

An elderly lady from next door came by when she saw his agents checking out the school and she told them her son took everything from the school and stored it at his home to keep it safe.

Ree could not help breaking into a big grin.

It had to have been Mrs. Hadine. She wondered if she made them cookies.

Jim went on to say that the woman inquired about Ree and hoped the school would open soon. Her granddaughter could not wait to go back.

Ree looked outside and noticed that they were going outside the city.

"Jim, where in world are we going? I never had any dealings outside the city."

"You'll see. You must have patience."

Ree crossed her arms over her chest.

"You know, you are getting very annoying."

"Just getting annoying?" He wiggled his eyebrows. "Like I said, patience, Ree. All will be revealed soon."

They seemed to be driving forever, but a check of her watch indicated that they were only about ten minutes outside the city. They turned off the main road and took a dirt road.

The SUV stopped at the end of the road, at the bottom of an embankment.

"Come on, let's get out," Jim said.

Ree heard him tell the two soldiers to stay in the vehicle; they might not be that long.

Ree got out and gave Jim a puzzled look.

"Alright, Jim, let it be revealed."

"Ree, you know I love you like a daughter and I had nothing but love and respect for your Dad."

She nodded.

"I don't think I will ever forgive myself for sending you to Iraq. You could have died."

"Jim, you apologized already and I told you there is nothing to apologize for. Knowing what I know now, I would do it all over again. In fact, knowing what I know now, I would have been pissed if you didn't send me. I would have done anything to get you to change your mind. Jim, there were some tough times, but the overall experience was wonderful. I'm just so sad for my friends and my adopted country."

"I know, Ree, but I also know that you left something of yourself here; Something you have to find again."

"Obviously, you have been talking to my Mom. I'm fine, or I will be. I just need time."

He shrugged his shoulders and pointed up the embankment.

"Up there is something, I think, that is going to help you find yourself and, most importantly, forgive yourself. If you are brave enough, and I know you are, take a walk up to the top."

Still confused but more curious, she started the climb up the embankment.

It took a few minutes but finally, she reached the top. She looked down and saw a valley with small buildings. She looked closer and noticed corrals with horses inside.

There was something familiar about some of the horses, but she just could not place them.

She saw a tall man, dressed in traditional dress, coming out of one of the buildings.

The first thing she noticed about him was he was tall, much taller than average Iraqis and he walked with a limp.

There was something familiar about him too but again, it couldn't be...Could it?

There was a sign near the door that the man came out of.

She tried to read it but refused to believe what she thought she made out: "Second Chance Farm 2."

That was the name of her farm in New Jersey.

She started to make her way down the other side of the embankment, her mind in turmoil. About half way down, she heard a voice yelling. She looked around.

No, it could not be. She saw them lead the horses out of the Palace. *The newscaster said they would be slaughtered, but it looked like her horses!*

Not able to control herself anymore, she started running towards the horse, yelling his name: "Syn! Syn!"

The person on the horse turned around and stood completely still until recognition dawned.

"Missy Ree, Missy Ree!" She yelled as she galloped toward her.

Najeena jumped off Syn when they reached Ree, right into her arms.

"Missy Ree, I knew you would come back. I told Colin you would come back, but he said no. He said he let you down, but I knew you would come back."

Ree hugged Najeena, crying and laughing at the same time. All of what Najee said did not register with Ree.

She was overwhelmed.

How did this happen? Who made this happen? She wondered.

Syn was pushing her back with his nose until finally, she let Najeena go. She turned and put her arms around Syn's neck and kissed him.

"Oh, my beautiful boy. I thought you were lost. I prayed for you all, every day."

Ree felt someone watching her. She turned and there was the tall man with the limp. He removed his headscarf.

Ree was shocked. She would recognize those green eyes anywhere. Her brain was in a tizzy.

It could not be Colin.

He was in Texas, dating supermodels and starlets. He limped toward her, finally putting his hand out.

"Hello, Ree. When Jim told me he was bringing me help, I didn't expect the best horse trainer in all of Iraq."

"But how, how did you do all this? Why did you do all this?"

Colin looked in those beautiful, blue eyes, that had haunted him for months.

"For you, all for you. I would do anything to gain your forgiveness."

Tears streamed down her face. She could not move.

Finally, Syn nudged her with his nose, towards Colin.

It was the push she needed and she ran into his arms.

He held her, finally feeling at peace.

Ree was where she belonged, next to him. He stroked her hair and soothed her while she cried her eyes out.

It seemed like a long time, but she finally gained her composure. She pushed away from Colin.

"How did you do all this? I saw a news report that the horses were looted and probably slaughtered."

Colin put his arm around her shoulders. He started to lead her into one of the buildings.

"Come on. Let's get out of the sun and I promise to tell you the whole story. Did Jim bring you here?"

"Yes," She nodded, "Wait until I see him. He didn't tell me anything about this."

He turned her to look at him.

"If he told you, would you have believed him?"

"I don't know, maybe...I don't know."

Najeena was standing next to Ree, so Colin asked her to go tell Jim that Ree was staying and he would take her back into Bagdad.

Second guessing himself, he looked at Ree.

"If that's okay with you?"

She nodded her head, unable to speak, overwhelmed with emotion.

"Come over here. I'll get you some water. I think you need to sit down."

Colin opened the door to one of the buildings and they both entered the dining hall. There were tables and benches all around with a small cooking area in the back. They sat down on the nearest bench.

After a while, her heart stopped beating like it was coming out of her chest and she was finally able to put some coherent thoughts together.

"How did all of this happen? I thought my friends, the horses, were all dead. I worried about Najeena and Shavo and everyone else. You saved them."

Colin sat down next to her. e reached over for her and put her on his lap.

"I missed you. I will never let you go again."

Ree snuggled in Colin's arms and rested her head on his shoulder. She never felt so warm, so loved.

Was she wrong about everything?

"You remember when I came back to Iraq?"

Ree nodded.

"I knew then that the political situation was getting critical. I tried to tell you. Your mom and Epee tried to tell you. In case you didn't know it, you are one stubborn woman. You absolutely refused to believe anything bad was going to happen. So, I had to plan for the worst. You were my main concern, getting you out safely, and then protecting our friends and horses."

Colin tried to lighten the situation.

"Okay, I know you want me to 'spill' the whole story so here goes: In case the war started we, Shavo, a few of the grooms and I, had a plan about what to do with the horses. I arranged for this place to be built, knowing it was far enough away from Bagdad and had no military significance.

As soon as Saddam got out and the looting started, we put our plan into action.

Shavo, the grooms and I led the horses out into transport trucks. We then brought them here. Shavo, Najeena and the grooms have been caring for them ever since. I'm sorry, Ree we did have one fatality. One of the older mares got hit with a stray bullet and didn't make it. And Storm..."

"Oh my God, Colin, what happened to Storm?"

"He bowed his tendon pretty bad; We think it was from climbing into one of the trucks. Shavo knows his stuff. He put poultices on it and wrapped it faithfully for weeks. He's almost one hundred per cent. I ride him, but he'll never race."

"I still don't get why you didn't tell me. I could have helped."

"Believe me, sweetheart, it was a difficult choice but in the end, I decided not to tell you."

"Why?"

"Ree, what would you have done the night they came to get you and I told you about the horses? Would you have gone home?"

"No, absolutely not. I would have stayed and helped you."

"And your presence would have jeopardized the operation. Uday was after you. YOU. He wanted to make sure that you paid for besting him. He was planning on chaining you to the barn and using you as a human shield. His guards were looking for you right up until they fled Baghdad. If wasn't for Tihara, who knows what would have happened? She saved many lives by her sacrifice."

"I know, Sadira told me what happened. Do you think that somehow, she might have survived?"

Colin held her hand and kissed it.

"No, honey. I'm sorry. I think she knew when she made that call what would happen and she was willing. We will always honor her memory."

Ree looked up into his beautiful face, she noticed some lines that were not there before. As she put her fingers through his hair, she noticed some gray hairs that were not there before, but he was still gorgeous; Her Scottish warrior.

Tears started rolling down her face again.

"I've missed you so much," She sobbed.

Hugging her to him, he thought they were the sweetest words he'd ever heard.

"I've missed you too, more than you will ever know. Sweetheart, you have to believe me. You might have started out as an assignment, but you quickly became my life, my love. I would do anything for you and I am so, so sorry that I let you down."

She wiped her tears with her shirtsleeve.

"Colin, how in the world did you let me down? I gave you a chance to explain about the 'assignment thing' and you just apologized. I thought you meant you were sorry that I was only an assignment."

"Honey, you were never an assignment. Well, maybe the first day, but you quickly became so much more than that. I think I fell in love with you that day in Hyde Park. I know I fell into a deep lust, but you have weaved yourself into every part of my life. I love you, Ree and I never want to let you go. I was saying I was sorry because I let you down. Fuck, Ree. You almost died, twice, because of me."

"How do you figure?"

"I wasn't able to protect you getting you out of the apartment; you got shot."

She rolled her eyes.

"I seem to remember disobeying orders and leaving the car to help you. Do you really think I would allow them to leave you there? If I had to do it again, a thousand times, I would not change a thing. And what was the second?"

Looking into her eyes she was able to see the pain there.

"When you lost the baby. Jim told me you could have died. Why? Because I could not control my desire for you."

"Well, I didn't die and you know what? What about my desire for you? Do you think you made the decision to have sex without a condom all by yourself? It seems to me that I assured you I would not get pregnant. No one was more surprised than I, when they told me what happened."

Colin picked up her hand and put it close to his heart.

"I'm so, so sorry we lost the baby. I'm so sorry I wasn't able to be there for you."

"And I'm sorry I wasn't able to be there for you."

Colin kissed the top of her head.

"I guess we're a pair. Your friend, Epee was right. She told me we both needed to and I quote, 'Get our shit straight' before we could move on. I guess we did that."

She snuggled closer to him.

"I guess we did."

Colin reached his arm around her and pulled a chain from under his shirt and gave it to her.

"I never stopped hoping, believing, that I could give this back to you and you would accept it. Will you marry me Reanna Malloy and wear my ring?"

"Yes, I will! With all my heart. I love you."

They kissed and the kiss quickly became serious. Colin was just about ready to pick her up and bring her to his room when there was a knock on the door, followed by a familiar voice.

"My granddaughter told me that Miss Ree is here. Could it be true?"

Ree squealed with delight and leaped up from Colin's lap and ran to the door, opened it and there stood Shavo, with the biggest smile on his face.

Ree fell into his arms.

He embraced her.

"My dear, I have missed you. The horses have missed you. My Najeena has missed you. But the one that missed you the most, is that big guy, sitting over there. He wasn't the same when you were gone. You took the light with you. I am so glad you are with us again."

Ree tried not to cry again.

"You have no idea how much I missed all of you. Thank you so much for doing what you did to save the horses. I was so worried about them."

He sat down next to Colin, with Ree between them.

"It was all Colin. It was his idea and he had the resources to carry out the plan. We were just there to help."

Colin was a bit choked up with the praise.

"Thank you, but it was a group effort. We all did it because we cared about the horses and wanted to do something for Ree. It was a way for me to find redemption in her eyes."

Ree leaned on his shoulder.

"You never needed redemption. I never stopped loving you." Ree leaned up to kiss him, but before things got hot and heavy again, Najeena and the other grooms came in to greet Ree.

Dinner was prepared and while the group ate, they caught up on the missing time.

That night, Colin brought Ree to his room, where he showed her just how much he missed her.

Chapter 47

The following morning, Ree got up early and helped everyone feed the horses.

It felt great, renewing friendships and seeing for herself that all her horses were safe and sound.

When they were just about finished, she heard Colin, frantically calling her name. She ran over to him, thinking something was wrong.

Yet, when he saw her, he instantly relaxed.

As she neared he reached for her hand and pulled her into his embrace.

"Don't do that to me, honey. I woke up and you were gone. I thought it was all a dream." He hugged her tighter.

"I'm not a dream and if I am, I want to stay in it always because that's where you are." She pushed out of his embrace, "Come on, let's eat! I haven't been this hungry in a long time."

During breakfast, they discussed the plans for the day.

Colin would take Ree to the school, where the people assigned to the school were working.

Ree thought that was a great idea. She would be able to see how much they accomplished and what more needed to be done.

Colin was going to the Embassy to see Jim and try to arrange for the supplies Colin had shipped to Iraq to be delivered to the compound.

With the plan in mind, they jumped into the armored Humvee and set off.

As they drove through the neighborhood where the school was, Ree was amazed to see little or no destruction.

Colin explained that the US and allies tried to keep the bombing to essential targets and avoid regular neighborhoods.

Mistakes were made, but this area was lucky.

When Colin dropped her off, Ree knew her first stop was to see Mrs. Hadine and thank her for everything she did to save the school.

Colin continued to the Embassy where he had a meeting with Jim at ten o'clock. He arrived at the embassy and noticed that security was tighter than normal. The only reason he could think of for the cause was the increased number of State Department people here with Jim.

After showing his ID, he was waved through.

Colin made his way up to Jim's office and when he got there, the door was closed. He could hear yelling coming from behind the door. Whatever this was about, Jim was definitely not happy.

Colin didn't wait long, when the door opened and out came six very unhappy State Department workers.

Jim saw Collin standing outside and invited him in.

Jim extended his hand; Colin took it and pulled Jim into a bear hug.

"I don't know if I want to get down on my knees and thank you for bringing her back to me, or strangle you for bringing her back here."

Jim broke away from Colin and smiled.

"You know, after what I just heard, I feel the same way. She was miserable at home. Her mother, her friends, everyone knew it. I knew she had to see what you did. She had to understand how much she means to you and the lengths you would go for her. "

"Damn straight; she is my life. But what's the problem? Everything worked out fine. We talked. We realized what we said was in the heat of the moment. She agreed to marry me again. After she finishes work at the school, she will help with the horses until I can arrange something permanent for them."

"The problem is that this so-called surge as they are calling it, isn't a surge at all, it's a trickle. They are only sending a fraction of the troops they promised. All the experts on the ground here say the place will blow up again in a short amount of time. You both have no time. You have to get out ASAP."

Colin sat down and let out a breath.

"Fuck, Jim. What am I going to do? I mean, if it was just the school, I could talk her into leaving, but she's seen the horses. I know her. She will not leave without them."

"Then, get them out."

"How am I supposed to do that? It would take a miracle."

"I don't know, Colin, but with your contacts and your resources, you will think of something. Now, I have more meetings to attend and, I think, more yelling to do, so why don't you work on a plan? You know, if I can help, in any way, I will."

"How long are you staying?"

"About a week. I'm going to oversee some of the projects we started. I'm hoping the school will remain open with the local teachers we hired. That should make Ree happy. I don't know about some of the other programs. Their continuation will depend on how safe we can make them. If you want a target date, then get everyone out within two weeks, maximum."

Colin ran his hand through his hair.

"That gives me more time than I thought. I have some supplies to pick up, then I'm going to pick Ree up from the school. I'll do my best to convince her, but you know Ree. I'm going to have to come up with a better plan."

"Good luck. Keep in touch."

They shook hands.

Colin picked up the needed supplies and headed over to the school. When he got there, he went inside and was hit with the memories of that night.

The door that Uday's guards broke was fixed. He noticed that a lot of the equipment was returned and people were setting up classrooms.

He heard Ree's voice from her office.

As he entered, he saw Ree talking to an Iraqi woman. When she saw him, she broke out into a beautiful smile. She introduced Colin to the woman, who was the new director of the school. They exchanged pleasantries and left the building.

On the trip back to the compound, Colin was quiet. Ree wasn't sure the reason and hoped it was nothing she did or didn't do.

Finally, she could not take the silence any longer.

"Any reason why you are so quiet?"

Colin reached over for her hand and gave it a squeeze.

"Honey, I have something to tell you and I'm trying to gather my thoughts to discuss this with you."

Ree smiled at him and teased.

"Are you trying to tell me that I really am just an assignment?"

"Someone hasn't lost her sense of humor. But, yes, actually. I am thinking about an assignment and you are part of it."

Colin went on to tell her what Jim said.

They both sat in silence the rest of the trip back to the compound.

When they arrived, Colin immediately noticed two extra Humvees parked near the dining area.

They got out of the vehicle.

Colin took Ree's hand and walked towards the voices coming from the building.

He heard a lot of male voices, with American accents, talking loudly to each other.

Colin heard one voice in particular and smiled.

As they got to the door, Colin pushed Ree behind him and they walked in.

"What the hell are you bunch of reprobates doing on my ranch?"

His miracle had arrived.

Chapter 48

Six men stopped their conversation immediately when they heard Colin's voice.

Ree peeked out from behind Colin's back and noticed one man stand and shout, "Attention."

All six men stood up and saluted Colin.

Ree could feel Colin tense as he stood straight and proud, returning the salute.

He smiled at them.

"At ease, men."

The men pulled away from the table and approached Colin with arms outstretched. They did a combination of handshakes, arm holds, and man-hugs. They all were talking at once.

Ree, still behind Colin, tugged at his shirt to get his attention.

He looked down at her and smiled.

"Okay, okay you bunch of losers, calm down. I have someone I want you to meet. Ree, I would like you to meet SEAL squad two, some of the finest, bravest men I've ever had the honor of serving with. Men, I'd like you to meet Reanna Malloy, soon to be McCleod, my fiancée."

There were whistles and big smiles from the crew. As each man approached Ree, Colin introduced them.

"This is Lieutenant Cade Cassidy or CC, he took over my position and from what I hear, he is doing a damn good job."

Ree noticed he was a big guy like the rest, with blond hair and hazel eyes. He was very handsome and when he smiled at Ree, he had two of the cutest dimples. When he took Ree's hand, she could not help but giggle like a school girl.

Colin scowled.

Colin introduced the rest. Will Martin, Jose Rodriquez, John Johnson, Tim Cheney and finally, Jake Souza.

Ree was amazed they were all so big and so handsome.

Her first thought was of Epee, who would have had a field day in this room, with these men.

They all sat down at the table, Colin making sure Ree was securely tucked next to him.

"I know you didn't come here to eat all my food, so what brings you all to my humble compound?"

They grinned at Colin.

CC was the first to speak up.

"We had some R and R and we heard you were running some kind of dude ranch here, so we decided to visit. Jake told us his grandmother owns horses and he knows how to ride, so he volunteered to give us all riding lesson."

Jake smiled at Colin and nodded his head in agreement.

They continued to banter back and forth for a while until Ree realized they wanted to talk to Colin alone; she excused herself.

"Colin, if you don't mind, I'm going to check on the horses and maybe take Syn out for a ride. You talk to your friends. I'll catch up with you later. It was nice meeting you all, gentlemen."

Colin gave her hand a squeeze as if to say thank you and gave her a kiss on the cheek.

This, of course, led to whistles and catcalls from the crew.

Colin watched her walk out of the room and closed the door before he turned to the men.

"So, what really brings you to my compound?"

This time there were no smiles.

CC looked serious.

"Commander, we heard about what you were doing out here and we think it's great but I don't know if you have the latest intelligence. Things are about to blow up, big time. We don't even think you are safe out here. You have to get your woman out. She's beautiful by the way, much too good for you. What is she doing here to begin with?"

"It's a long story, about Ree. She was working with the State Department on a project here in Iraq before the war. That's how I met her. She was led to believe that things were safe, so she came back to start up her school again. As for intelligence, yes, I just came from a meeting with Jim Peterson from the State Department. He apprised me of the situation. I'll tell you guys, I'm between a rock and a hard place on this one. I'm glad Ree's here, but I want her out.

I know her and I'm positive that she will not leave without those horses. How the hell am I going to get her, the grooms and the horses to safety?"

They all started talking at once throwing ideas around.

Finally, Tim banged on the table to get everyone's attention.

When he had quiet he said, "Okay, I know this might seem crazy, but I think I might have an idea."

Jake snorted.

"It'll be the first time."

The Lieutenant put his hands up.

"Alright, let's hear what he has to say."

Tim stood up and took a bow.

"We know we need big vehicles to transport the horses and if they are armored, that would be even better. We know we need a large transport plane. And last we knew, we need security to get down Route Irish. Do you all agree?"

They all nodded.

"They problem is, we can't do it alone. We need help. Specifically, we need the Army's help."

They all groaned but agreed.

Tim grinned at the group.

"Are any of you familiar with the Disney movie, *Miracle of the White Stallions*?"

Cade nodded his head and smiled. "Yes, I know the movie. It was my little sister's favorite movie. She was horse crazy and every time I had to babysit her, she made me watch the movie. I didn't mind it too much; it was about WWII."

Colin was intrigued. What could a movie have to do with their situation?

"What's the movie about?"

"It's based on a true story that took place during the WWII." Cade continued. "Are any of you familiar with the Lipizzaner horses?"

Jose spoke up.

"Yea, I saw them in Brooklyn once. They put on a show for us poor kids at the Brooklyn Academy of the Arts. They're dancing horses. They are all white and the riders wore these really cool uniforms. They told us that the horses were taught these moves to help their riders in a time of battle. Some of the stuff they could do was...Wow."

Colin's eyes lit up with recognition.

"I know the story; I read about it. The horses were in Austria. The Allies were moving east and the Russians were moving west. The owner of the horses feared the Russians would get there first and kill the horses for the men to eat, so he appealed to the Americans to evacuate the horses. But how does that help us?"

Tim smirked at Colin.

"Do you remember the General that ordered and supported the evacuation?"

The light bulb dawned on Cade.

"Patton."

"Exactly. Patton." Tim took another bow.

All the men clapped, except Colin.

"I still don't get it."

Cade patted Colin on the back.

"You've been out too long. Are you familiar with General Carter?"

"Yes, he's regular army. I had to deal with him a few times. Good guy, but by the book. How can he help us, or more important, why would he help us?"

Cade just shook his head at Colin.

"When you were in his office, did you notice anything different, unique?"

Colin sat back in his chair trying to recall his meeting with the General.

"Pictures of Presidents, some family pictures; wait he had a big picture of General Patton hanging right in the middle of his office."

Time smiled.

"Bingo."

Colin looked over at his men.

God had sent him a miracle.

It would be the miracle of Saddam's Horses.

"You gentlemen, help yourselves to more food and set up your gear in one of the buildings. I have an appointment to make with a General."

Chapter 49

Ree, Colin and the team, all met for dinner later in the day, where the men tried to outdo each other with telling embarrassing stories about each other.

Ree could not stop laughing, especially when the team told stories about Colin and his candy addiction.

Later, Colin got the men settled in one of the supply buildings and headed back to Ree and his room.

He could not decide how much to tell her and finally decided to tell her everything and beg her to leave early.

Ree was already in bed when Colin came into the room.

She noticed that even during dinner, he seemed happier than he was after the meeting with Jim. Maybe it was seeing his men again.

As Colin was taking off his clothes, he turned to Ree.

"I know we talked about what Jim said regarding the situation here, but we didn't talk about what we are going to do?"

"What do you mean? I'm staying here with you."

"Sweetheart, we can't stay here. That's one of the reasons the guys came here, to tell us how bad things are going to get. They don't think we'll be safe here. You have to leave."

Ree got out of bed.

Colin smiled.

She had his Navy t-shirt on.

"Colin, we've been through this before and the only way we are separating is if one of us is forcibly taken away and we know that will not happen. Right?"

"Honey..."

"Don't honey me, sweetheart me, dear me. I'm staying with you and that is final." She sat back down on the bed with her hands crossed over her chest and lips pouted.

"You are not going to make it easy on me, are you?"

"You're wrong. With me here, it will make it easier on you. That's, if you let me. I can help. Please, Colin, don't make me leave."

He sat down next to her and gathered her in his arms.

"Okay sweetheart, here's the plan so far."

Colin proceeded to tell Ree everything that he discussed with his team and the plan to meet with General Carter.

"What time is your appointment with the General?"

"It's at ten, tomorrow. Do you want to go to the school tomorrow or stay here?"

"I'm really not needed at the school. The woman in charge is fantastic. She's doing a great job. Do you think they will close the school again?"

"According to Jim, they are going to try to keep it open. It's in a safe area of Baghdad, so he's very confident it will continue."

"I'm so glad. The neighbors really love it. It was great seeing Mrs. Hadine again. I still can't believe what she and her son did for the school. They saved everything. I promised to write her and told her when it was time, to contact me when her granddaughter was ready for college. I would do anything I could to help."

"That's great, sweetheart, but everything *we* can do. I'll help too."

Ree hugged him closer.

"You are such a great guy. Now, what is my assignment in Operation Saddam's Horses?"

"God, I missed you. Obviously, I'll need you to coordinate the logistics with getting the horses on the trucks and onto the planes. You will also have to gather any medical equipment we'll need, food for the horses and any other equipment that we'll need. You will also need to talk to the grooms about their role. I've already discussed the plan with them and told them that any of them that wants to come to the US with us was welcomed."

"What about Shavo and Najeena?"

"Shavo wants us to take Najeena with us, but he does not want to go. You know, we can't take all of the horses, right?"

Ree sadly shook her head.

"I know. The two mares are almost ready to foal and I'm afraid the three older ones won't make it. That makes eleven horses that we are evacuating and five that are staying."

"Yes, that's what I figured. Shavo insists on staying with those horses. Three of the grooms are staying with him; the rest are coming with us."

"Good, that gives me four extra sets of hands. Do you think I can change Shavo's mind?"

"If anyone can, it would be you but don't get your hopes up. He's very determined to stay. I'll do everything I can to make sure he's safe. He will definitely be safer with the Americans gone."

"Well, Commander, are there any other orders?"

Colin pushed Ree down on the bed and covered her with his body. His hand started caressing her leg, moving up her body.

Ree groaned.

"Yes, I have one final order."

"Yes, Commander?"

"I love this compliant Ree. Maybe I'll enlist you in the Navy and make you part of my team, then you'll have to follow my orders all the time."

"Yes, Commader."

"I have two direct orders that you are to follow exactly."

"Yes, Commander."

"One, you will stay safe, at all costs. You will not, ever, put yourself in danger. Are we clear?"

"Yes, Sir...And the second?"

"Take the damn t-shirt off. I want you naked."

Chapter 50

They all met at breakfast the following morning to discuss the assignment. The team was going to do reconnaissance.

They were going to look for suitable trucks to transport the horses.

Lieutenant Cade was also going to check outgoing flights and try to find a big transport plane that was bringing a lot of equipment in and leaving empty, one that would accommodate the horses.

Ree, Shavo and the grooms were going to get the supplies ready and do what they could to keep the horses comfortable.

Colin had the most important meeting of his life, with General Carter.

By the time all the groups went their separate ways, Colin was still trying to figure out how he was going to approach the General.

He decided the direct approach was the best.

His ride into Baghdad went by in a flash and he still had no real inspiration. He found his way into Army headquarters and was directed to the General's office. He knocked on the door and a familiar voice told him to come in.

There, on the wall, in a place of honor, was a picture of General Patton.

They shook hands and sat down.

"So, Commander, what brings you to Army headquarters?"

"Well, General, I have a favor. It's a rather large favor and you are the only one that can help."

"Navy asking Army for a favor; this is going to be good."

"Are you familiar with the Disney movie, *Miracle of the White Stallions*?"

The General looked annoyed and stared right at Colin.

"Is this some type of joke? You want to discuss Disney movies?"

Colin smiled.

"No, General, just humor me. Are you familiar with the movie?"

"No, not the movie, but I know the history. If it wasn't for Patton, those beautiful horses would have been lost to mankind. He was a by-the-book kind of guy, but in this case, he did the right thing. Sometimes, you have to look at the greater good than rules and regs."

Colin let out his breath.

For the first time, he actually believed that this scheme could work.

"But tell me, Commander, what does that little-known part of history have to do with you and your favor?"

"I don't know, General, if you heard of the fate of Saddam's horses?" Colin went on to tell the general in an abridged form the history of his and Ree's involvement with the horses.

"Wow, that's quite a story. Are the horses still at your compound?"

Colin nodded yes.

"So, what exactly are you asking?"

"General, I need the Army's help. I need two, but three would be great, armored transport vehicles; two for the horses and one for supplies. I also need an empty or near-empty transport plane to fly the horses out of here. I would eventually like to get them back to the States."

"What about security?"

Colin wanted to raise his hands in the air in happiness. He was actually considering this.

"General, I can't ask you to put your men in harm's way so my team, a few grooms and myself will be the security."

"I'll tell you what, Colin. I'll ask for volunteers. I'll tell the men about the mission and if any want to help, I'll let them. I know you'll need more security than a few men, but I can't promise you."

Colin was floored by the generosity of this man.

"General, I can't tell you how much I appreciate anything you can do."

"I don't think there will be a problem with the trucks. It will take a little coordinating with the plane, but I think it's doable. And, as I said, I'll check with the men." The General stood up.

Colin knew the meeting was over.

As they walked to the door, the General put his hand on Colin's shoulder.

"You know, I read reports about the looting of the museums and the Palace...and the horses. I didn't care about the things, but I was heartsick about those horses. I never knew what happened to them and honestly, I thought the worst. It's a good thing, what you did and I promise, I'll do everything I can to make this happen. I know, if Patton was here, he would also do everything in his power."

They shook hands and Colin left the office. He could not help himself. When he got outside, he let out a big holler and fist pump.

On his way back to the compound, he stopped at a black-market place where he paid an outrageous amount of money for two cases of beer and a bottle of wine. It was time to celebrate!

Chapter 51

Ree opened her eyes and realized that today was the day, Ree could not believe it.

The vehicles were supposed to be at the compound at nine.

The trip to the airport should take about an hour.

The transport plane was scheduled to leave at noon.

Colin was already up and dressed.

She talked to Jim Peterson yesterday.

He was on his way back home but he reassured her; the school was up and running and so far, it was very successful.

Colin told Jim about the plan to evacuate the horses and he wished them luck with the operation.

Jim also was able to fast-track some paperwork which allowed the horses, grooms and Najeena to enter the US.

Ree got dressed, grabbed her packed bag and went outside.

Colin was there with the team, watching three armored trucks coming towards them.

Ree stood next to Colin and put her hand in his.

He squeezed her hand reassuringly.

"Colin, I can't believe that they are here, that we are really doing this."

He put his hand around her shoulder.

"I know, Ree. Everything just fell into place. I know we didn't settle this last night but I still want you in one of the armored Humvees with the team. You will be safer there. The cab of the truck is not secure. If there was an attack, you would be too vulnerable."

"Where are you going to be?"

"I told you last night. I'm going to be driving the lead truck with six of the horses, followed by Cade, with five horses in his truck. One of the grooms, Ori, will be driving the supply truck. The rest of the team will be driving the three Humvees, surrounding us for protection."

"And I told you last night, I would be where you are. This is not open for discussion, Colin. I've made my mind up. I'm going with you, end of story. The only way I'm going without you is if you knock me out and tie me to one of the other vehicles."

"Don't tempt me, sweetheart."

"And if you do that, I will never and I mean never, speak to you again. I will never let you touch me again. Are we clear?"

"Ree, honey, it's just that if anything happened to you, it would kill me. I can't lose you."

"And how do you think I feel? God, Colin. Those months without you were the worst of my life. I can't image life without you. This is how it's going to go down. We die together; we survive together. There is no other option."

Colin put both hands through his hair and started to walk away from her, but turned at the last minute.

"You know, you can be the most frustrating woman in the world. Okay, you are with me, but you have to promise me that you will do everything I tell you."

Ree nodded.

"Not good enough, sweetheart. Promise me."

Ree gave him the girl scout salute.

"I promise, I will do everything you tell me." Very quietly she added, "As long as I agree with it."

"Ree, you're killing me. I'm not kidding, here. You agree or You. Are. Not. Going."

"Okay, okay, I promise. What are all those other vehicles doing here?"

Colin looked up and saw about twenty vehicles following the three transport vehicles.

"I don't know, but we'll find out soon."

The three transport trucks pulled over to the side, where the horses were and the rest of the vehicles stopped in front of Colin and the men.

General Carter got out of the lead vehicle. Colin went up and shook his hand.

"Great to see you, General. I'd like you to meet Reanna Malloy."

"Very pleased to meet you, Miss Malloy. Colin told me about your role in all of this. It was quite a story. You are a very brave woman."

Ree blushed.

"Thank you, General Carter, but I think I did what anyone in my position would have done."

Colin went on to introduce the team.

General Carter looked around the compound.

"Quite a place you have here, Colin. If I knew about it, I would have come and visited. As you can see, I brought a few volunteers."

Colin was shocked by the number of vehicles.

"How many?"

"How many here or how many volunteers?"

"I don't understand."

"When I told the men about the mission and what was needed, I had over three hundred volunteers. I picked fifty, because that's all the vehicles we had available. The rest were very disappointed."

"Why? This is a dangerous mission."

"They gave me two reasons. One, they felt this was one mission where they were doing something positive, something good."

"And the second?"

The General laughed.

"They didn't want Navy getting all the credit."

Colin laughed.

Ree called to him.

"Colin, who else is coming?"

Colin looked at the General.

The General shrugged.

"I have no idea."

Ten vehicles parked behind the American vehicles.

The lead vehicle's door opened and out stepped the unmistakable uniform of the British Armed Forces.

A gentleman approached General Carter and Colin, saluting.

"Captain Stewart, at your service, gentlemen."

The General and Colin returned the salute then introduced each other.

"Right, good. I'm in the correct place."

"Captain, I don't mean to be rude but what are you doing here?"

"Isn't this where you are transporting the horses to the airport?"

Colin pointed over to the corrals where the horses were and nodded.

"Yes, it is."

"Good, then I am at your service, Commander. We are here to help. I brought about forty men and ten vehicles for security. I also have some men with extensive knowledge of horses that can help with the loading. Just tell us what to do."

Colin was speechless.

"How did you hear of the mission?"

The Captain smiled.

"You know how things get around in the service. When we heard what you Yanks were up to, well, we wanted to help. After all, you Americans can't get all the credit when they write about this someday."

The Captain looked over at the road.

"Oh, bloody hell, I knew the Aussies would try to get in on this."

Sure enough, six more vehicles pulled up behind the rest and the Aussie contingent got out.

Colin got the officers together and they met in the dining room to discuss a plan of action and placement of vehicles.

Colin could not believe what was happening. This was more than a miracle; this was direct divine intervention.

He appreciated the help but was worried for everyone's safety.

The airport road they were going to be traveling on to get to the airport was considered the most dangerous seven miles in the world.

Some people referred to it as the Highway of Death or I.E.D. Alley, because explosive devices, suicide bombers and snipers were a regular occurrence on this road.

The military called it Route Irish, because it was the main link between supplies and the green zone in Baghdad where the Americans and allies set up command.

Why Irish? Because Ireland is synonymous with the color green.

Colin knew the more protection surrounding the transport vehicles, the better the chance of success they would have and the less chance for attack, meant the less chance for injury.

They were ready.

It was decided that Ree would lead Syn into the truck first.

Colin knew he would go through fire for her, so going into a truck would be easy.

He would lead Storm into the other truck while the grooms and the horse-knowledgeable English soldiers would lead the rest of the horses.

It went without a hitch.

Shavo hugged Ree goodbye.

"You remind me so much of my daughter. She had your inner-light. I know you will take good care of my Najeena. It is a better life than pretending to be a boy. Go with God, child."

Ree tried not to cry.

After the goodbyes, Najeena was placed in one of the Humvees with the SEALS.

By that point, the horses were getting restless, so they were off.

It was decided that Colin would take the lead until they hit the airport road, then the caravan was divided up between British, American and Aussie vehicles, surrounding the three supply vehicles.

When they got to the ramp for Route Irish, Colin pulled over and the smaller armored Humvees took up position.

Once they were settled, they started the most dangerous leg of the trip.

It took the vehicles about twenty minutes to cover the seven miles. The trucks could not go too fast, fearing for the safety of the horses.

Therefore, it was the longest twenty minutes of Colin's life but they made it without incident.

No bombs, no snipers and most importantly, no injuries.

The trucks pulled up next to the plane that would take them out of the country. The convoy surrounded them and helped get the horses and supplies off the trucks. When they were almost ready to leave, Colin and Ree went up to each man, shook their hand, and thanked them for their help.

The convoy left with every man smiling, believing they all did a good thing today.

Cade could not wait to ask Colin.

"Why do you think there were no attacks? I mean, it was like we were waving a red flag, with the amount of security we had."

"I don't know, but I have my suspicions. Wait here."

Cade saw Colin go up to the groom named Ori.

When Ori saw Colin coming towards him, he didn't know what to do.

He tried, for months, to stay off the radar.

Whenever Colin or Ree came near him, he always had his head down and never spoke.

Should he run? No, it was time to face the music.

"Ori, can I speak to you for a moment?"

Ori looked down and approached Colin.

He nodded.

"You know, I have been negligent in not thanking you for helping me in the past and I think I owe you a big thank you for today. Isn't that right?"

"I don't understand."

"Ori, look...Let's not play games. I've known from the beginning that you are the guard from

Saddam's Palace that was friendly with Ree. I know you were the one that told me about Tihara and I know that you were the one that didn't give John and me away in the stable. You saved our lives that night. What I want to know now is, do I thank you for such an uneventful ride to the airport?"

Ori smiled up at him.

"I might have put in a few words with some people I know. But Mister Colin, what will you do with me now? Can I still go to America with you?"

"There was never any doubt. You will be an honored guest and, if you wish, I will do everything I can to make sure you stay. You will have a job working with horses, or whatever you wish. But, I have one favor."

"Anything."

"Could you put the word out to those friends, to leave Shavo and the compound alone?"

Ori gave Colin a big smile.

"Already done."

Colin patted him on the shoulder and they entered the belly of the plane together.

After a brief stop in Germany, they arrived at Fort Dix, in New Jersey, four days later.

Everyone was tired, but safe and happy.

Epilogue
Two years later:

Ree looked over at the time and smiled. She put her hands over her belly and caressed it.

"Well, my babies, it's been you and me for the past nine months and in a little, while I'm going to have to share you with the rest of the world."

That's okay, she thought.

She could not wait for Colin to hold his son and daughter. These babies were going to meet some of the most incredibly loving people in the world.

When they discussed names for the babies, she jokingly wanted to call them Miracle I and Miracle II.

Even though they were miracles, Colin convinced her they needed more traditional names, so their son would be Colin John and their daughter would be Tihara Margaret.

After she and Colin were married a year and she did not get pregnant, not for lack of trying, she finally convinced Colin to allow her to consider fertility treatments.

It wasn't that Colin was against them, he just worried about Ree's health.

After much pleading, he agreed. They went to a clinic that Ree researched in Dallas that had a wonderful reputation for success.

It really was a miracle because, after four treatments, she was pregnant with twins.

She got up, felt another pain and looked at the clock.

Not too bad, she thought.

The contractions were about fifteen minutes apart. She still had some time. She got dressed and looked over at the bag she had packed.

It reminded her of another bag that she had to have packed in case she had to leave fast.

That seemed like a lifetime ago.

She made her way downstairs.

When another pain hit, she sat down.

After the pain let up, she picked up her wedding album that was on the table next to her.

She opened the book and smiled at the first picture. It was a picture of her and Colin, taken right after they exchanged vows.

They had a wonderful wedding. They both decided that it was to be small; a family and close friends' affair only.

They held it on the grounds of the ranch at sunset.

Ree remembered it like it was yesterday.

Mary, Colin's mother, and Connie, Colin's sister-in-law, loved planning the wedding.

Ree was only too happy to hand the reins over to them.

She laughed to herself when Colin approached her with a favor for the wedding. He was almost nervous, very unlike him. He knew the planning of weddings was, in his words, a woman's only job, but he had one request.

As he stuttered and stammered through the request, Ree was speechless.

Finally, she blurted out, "You want to wear a kilt?"

He looked embarrassed and crestfallen.

Ree immediately got up, hugged him and whispered in his ear, "Why is it you always seem to know exactly what it takes to make my every dream come true? I can't think of anything I would love more."

Colin picked her up and spun her around.

On the day of the wedding, she knew the groom was supposed to be speechless when he saw his bride for the first time, but when she saw Colin, standing at the front of the gazebo, adorned in full, Highland dress, her knees went weak.

To honor him, she had her dress redesigned to include a belt with the family plaid.

As something old, Colin's mom gave her an ancient gold pin in the shape of a thistle with amethyst stones. She wore it proudly on the front of her dress.

The next picture her mother called 'the royal family' because of how they were all posed.

Ree and Colin were standing in the center. In front of them, sitting down, were Colin's niece and nephew, whom Ree adored.

Next to them, stood hers and Colin's adopted daughter, Najeena or Jeanie, as she now liked to be called.

Ree was amazed how well she had adjusted to life in America. She was a teenager now, much to Colin's chagrin.

He jokingly told Jeanie if she brought a boy home, he would be cleaning his gun...At least, Ree hoped he was joking.

Next to Jeanie were Epee's two kids, Ree's godchildren.

The next picture was Colin; his Uncle Colin, Colin's best man; and Colin's Uncle George. They all looked so handsome in their kilts. Colin was touched that the Uncles agreed to come to the wedding. The last time they left Scotland to come to the US was when their sister got married. Ree was thrilled to meet them.

They were just as wonderful and eccentric as Colin told her.

Ree smiled at the next picture.

It was of her matron of honor, Epee.

Epee was beaming in the picture, so happy for her friend who found her 'Jamie'. Colin told Ree about the conversation he had with Epee in the hospital and after laughing at her friend's antics, her love for her grew.

Epee, her husband, and kids still lived in New Jersey.

Ree missed her terribly.

The last time they visited, she heard Colin talking to Kevin about all the coaching opportunities in Texas and how big football was in Texas. Maybe she was putting too much into it, but she hoped he looked interested.

She loved all of the pictures, but she was especially fond of the one of her and her Mom, Margaret.

Margaret understood Ree moving to Texas, but she still missed her daughter. Colin tried to lure her to Texas by telling her how he would expand the barn and put up an indoor arena but Margaret was adamant. She was staying on the family farm.

That reminded Ree, she needed to call her. The last few times she called the house, Margaret wasn't home and Amy, the new trainer at the barn, was very elusive with her answers as to where Margaret was.

Hmmm, a mystery that needed to be solved. Ree thought, deciding that she would put Colin on the case.

Next to the picture of her and her mom was one of Colin, his mom, Mary, and the uncles, Mary's brothers. The family resemblance was amazing; they were all very handsome people. Mary was doing wonderfully since her heart surgery. She made a full recovery and she was absolutely thrilled about being a grandmother again.

Ree smiled at the next picture; it was Colin's sister- in- law, Connie, with her date for the wedding.

According to Colin, when he was away in Iraq, Connie had to fill in at the business and became very friendly with their new CFO, who recently lost his wife to breast cancer. Colin knew him and liked him. He was happy for both of them.

The next picture, Colin called the Iraqi contingent.

His entire SEAL team came to the wedding. None brought a date except Cade and, surprise, he brought Sadira.

Ree would really like to hear the story of how that came about. The rest of the SEAL team stood next to Cade.

As soon as they helped with the horses, the team was sent back on a mission, this time to Afghanistan.

Unfortunately, Will was badly injured on that mission and the early prognosis was he would not walk again, but when Colin went to visit him at Walter Reed, he told Colin he would dance with Ree at the wedding.

True to his word and with the help of a walker, Will walked into the wedding and danced a slow dance with Ree.

The whole crowd gave them a standing ovation. It still brought tears to her eyes, just thinking about it.

John, his wife and kids were also in the picture.

Both Sadira and John resigned their jobs at the State Department and were currently working for Colin, heading the security team for Thistle Oil.

John loved being able to raise their sons in the US.

Although, his wife was having a hard time adjusting to life in Texas.

Ree and Sadira did all they could to help her adjust.

Jim Peterson looked dashing in the next picture. He was standing next to General Carter and, unbelievably, the doctor Colin had harassed mercilessly in the hospital in Germany.

Dr. Kardos came with his wife.

He brought the well-wishes of the hospital staff and wanted a promise that Colin would never get injured again.

As Ree paged through the book, she started getting choked up, looking at all the people who had come to mean so much to her and Colin.

When Ree and Colin came back to the US, they stopped first at Second Chance Farm in Princeton, where Colin asked Ree's mom's permission to marry her daughter.

Margaret, needless to say, was thrilled for both of them.

When Ree returned from Iraq she had her spark back and the broken man Margaret saw leaving Ree's hospital room was now whole.

After their visit, they left New Jersey and headed to Texas.

When they got to Texas, Ree was welcomed with open arms by Colin's mom Mary, sister-in- law, Connie, as well as his niece and nephew.

Mary was thrilled her son was home, so she could hand over the running of the company to him.

After much discussion, they decided to live in Texas, mainly because of the company.

Ree loved and respected everyone in the pictures, but when she came to the magnificent animal next to Ori, her heart burst with love.

Her Syn, her wonderful, beautiful Syn. She thought she lost him.

Colin gave her many gifts, but Syn was the greatest.

The trip from the compound to the airport was the most frightening experience of her life. She wasn't afraid for herself, but for the people who so courageously put their life on the line for these horses. They would remain in her prayers for the rest of her life.

She could not forget the people who were at the wedding in spirit. It was her mom's idea to have a remembrance table with pictures of loved ones who had passed. Ree was a little hesitant to ask Mary and Connie about it, but when she asked they both got tears in their eyes and thought it was a wonderful idea. Connie asked if she could design it.

Ree, of course, agreed. Ree didn't see it until the day of the wedding and it was stirring.

There were pictures of Colin's dad and brother,

Ree's dad and a picture of Tihara.

Ree had no idea where Colin got the picture but it was a beautiful picture, taken in happier times.

The picture that brought tears to her eyes, though was Shavo's.

Colin received word about three months after Ree and Colin got home that Shavo passed peacefully in his sleep.

Colin told Ree that Shavo confided in him in Iraq that he was not well.

Shavo told Colin he prayed to God every night to keep him alive one more day to care for his Najeena.

Both Ree and Colin knew he died at peace, because he knew Najeena was in good hands.

As she got to the last page, some travel brochures fell out.

She laughed.

Before the wedding, Colin came to her with a handful of travel brochures to all types of exotic locations: Bali, Tahiti, Greece, and Rio. He told her to pick one and they would spend a month away from it all on their honeymoon. She looked them over, but there weren't any places she wanted to go. They all looked great, but a vacation like this wasn't for her.

After a few days, Colin asked again where she wanted to go; she just shrugged her shoulders.

Colin looked her in the eye and said, "Ree, remember, always be honest."

She told him all the places looked great and if wanted to go to one, then he should pick.

Finally, Colin said, "Ree, where do you really want to go?"

She looked at him and smiled.

"Scotland."

So, right after the wedding, while Jeanie stayed with Mary, Ree and Colin traveled to Scotland with the Uncles to spend their honeymoon at the seat of the McKenna clan.

Ree was thrilled beyond belief to be staying in an authentic castle, drafts, ghosts and all.

In preparation for Ree's visit, the Uncles renovated the stable and hired four horses for their use.

Many times, the four of them would ride out and visit local villages or just explore the countryside.

Her favorite memories were when Colin would tell her stories of his time growing up there.

One day, they were riding to an abandoned castle. When they got there, Uncle George took the bag he was carrying off the saddle, opened it and gave everyone a wooden sword.

Ree looked up at Colin confused.

"Ah, my lassie, we're going to storm a castle."

With that, Colin and the Uncles let out a loud battle cry and ran to the castle like banshees.

Ree, of course, joined them.

Sometimes just Ree and Colin rode out. On those occasions, they would stop in a secluded glen and fully explore each other.

When Ree and Colin left, the Uncles told them they forgot how much they enjoyed having horses on the property and asked if at their next visit, Ree or maybe her mom would pick out some horses for them to purchase.

Although Ree was honored, she suspected this was the uncles' way to get her and Colin to visit more often.

Like she and Colin needed an excuse!

Ree didn't really put it together before, but Uncle Colin mentioned Ree's mom a lot during their visit.

Though, Ree had noticed that the pair seemed to get on very well the days before, during and after the wedding.

In fact, she never saw her mom so happy and so relaxed as when she was around Uncle Colin. She acted like a carefree young girl again. She knew that her mom drank too much whiskey during the wedding, which she never ever did and Uncle Colin volunteered to bring her back to the hotel.

I wonder...She thought.

Just then, she was hit with another pain.

Smiling to herself and caressing her stomach she said to her babies, "Well, I guess it's time for you to meet the world!"

TO THE READER

Thank you for reading my first book. This story has haunted me since I saw the news report about Saddam's horses. Yes, the incident that I write about in the book is true. I was watching the nightly news about the war in Iraq. The reporter was showing Iraqis looting the Palace and museums; the camera zoomed in on men leading horses out of the Palace. What the newscaster said was forever etched in my mind.

"These horses belonged to Saddam. They are probably some of the most valuable horses in the world and will probably end up on the dinner plate tonight."

As a horse owner, trainer, rider, and lover, I was absolutely devastated. I do not know what really happened to the horses.

Honestly, I don't want to know. I would prefer to think of them, happy and healthy living in Texas with Ree and Colin.

Most of the book is fiction, but there was a war between the US and Iraq in 2003. There were a few mini surges that didn't work. It wasn't until 2007, four years after the war started, that the US sent a large number of troops and equipment into Iraq to stem the violence. This large surge worked for a while but Baghdad still remains in turmoil.

General Patton, during World War II, did save the Lipizzaner stallions from the Russian army. Disney does have a movie called Miracle of the White Stallions, based on that event. It is still one of my favorite movies.

There is a Route Irish and it was considered to be the most dangerous seven miles of road in the world. It was so named because the Allied position in Baghdad was known as the green zone. Green is associated with Ireland so the soldiers called the road from the airport into the green zone Route Irish.

The only real historical figure in this book is Uday Hussein. Uday was the eldest son of Saddam Hussein by his first wife, Sajida Talfah. He was a nasty individual. His actions included allegations of rape, murder, and torture. He reportedly tortured members of Iraq's' Olympic athletes and the National football team when they did not perform up to his expectations.

Even by Saddam's standards, Uday was considered unhinged and was imprisoned several times, exiled and received a death sentence by his father's government. He was killed during the US invasion in 2003, after a three-hour gunfight.

To all the dressage riders out there who read the book, please don't judge me too harshly in my descriptions of riding, canter leads, and round pen work. I had to adapt my descriptions for people who know little or nothing about riding, so please pardon any mistakes.

I honestly believed this would be my first and last book, but as I was writing other characters, stories started to emerge.

Some of my friends requested a love story about an older couple, so the story between Margaret, Ree's Mom and Colin's Uncle Colin is in the works. What was going to be one book is turning into a series called The Second Chance series.

So, stay tuned for the next book about Margaret and Colin, tentatively entitled *The Faerie Glen*.

Excerpt
THE FAIRY GLEN

Margaret opened one eye then the other. She groaned. She tried to sit up but the pain in her head made her lie back down.

She lifted the sheet and realized she was naked.

Memories of the night before flooded her mind. She blushed.

Startled by a soft snore, she looked at the man lying next to her. He was on his back with the sheet barely covering his muscular body.

Oh, my God! What have I done? She thought. I slept with my son-in-law's Uncle Colin!

Ignoring the pain in her head she got up and went in search of her clothes.

Both her clothes and Colin's were strewn all over the hotel room bedroom and the sitting room. As she picked up the clothes, flashes of what happened the night before came to mind.

She was talking to Colin at the bar when he challenged her to try a real drink; Whiskey.

For some unknown reason, she took him up on his challenge. He was an arrogant, opinionated, maddening man, but he was also very handsome and very fit.

She could not deny her attraction to him. It had been a long time since she was attracted to anyone. She had honestly believed that part of her was dead.

He made her feel like a young girl again.

Margaret was not a drinker, especially hard liquor.

She enjoyed a glass or two of wine at dinner, but that was it. She knew she was a lightweight when it came to alcohol.

Why did she drink whiskey? She wanted to blame Colin but knew he certainly did not pour it down her throat.

She somehow got her dress on. It was a little askew because she could not pull the zipper all the way up.

At least it was covering the important parts.

She looked over at Colin and sighed, knowing that she had to accept the fact that geography was her enemy.

Margaret's first husband, John, had a job that was heavily based in Iraq and Colin lived in Scotland.

Her home was at her farm in New Jersey and she had no intention of leaving…ever.

If she was going to move for anyone it would be for her daughter who just moved to Texas and even she could not tempt her to pull up roots.

She sighed again, took one last look at what could have been and tip-toed out the door.

As Margaret walked down the hallway, she groaned.

I can't believe I'm fifty-two years old and for the first time in my life I'm doing the walk of shame. She thought, praying she didn't meet anyone she knew from her daughter's wedding on the way to her room.

She made her way to the elevator, the doors opened and there stood one of her daughter's husband SEAL team, Cade.

He looked at her, with scx-messed hair, dress askew, swollen lips and shoes in hand.

He grinned.

All she could think was: BUSTED!

Patricia A. Chenoweth lives in Barnegat, New Jersey, where she currently owns and operates Hidden Creek Farm, living out her passion as an equestrian by training, boarding and breeding horses.

Before starting this endeavor ten years ago, Patricia was a high school social studies teacher for thirty-two years, during which time, she engaged in the hobbies that would eventually lead her to write her debut book; Saddam's Horses.

Patricia started writing three years ago, having been inspired to write Saddam's Horses years earlier, after watching a news broadcast in late

2004, that showed Iraqi men leading horses out of the Palace stable.

When the newscaster reported that the horses, some of the most valuable in the world, would probably end up on the dinner plate that night, Patricia was horrified.

So, after mourning the fate of those poor, beautiful horses for the rest of the evening, that night, Patricia dreamt of a different ending for the horses; a happy ending.

Saddam's Horses is carefully constructed to tell that story. When Patricia isn't writing, or tending to the horse inhabitants on her ranch, Patricia enjoys riding her horses, one of which, Xeena, is featured on the cover of Saddam's Horses, reading, traveling, spending time with friends and cooking.

Made in the USA
Middletown, DE
02 January 2017